the orphans

book one: The lost race trilogy

Deborah Riley-Magnus

The Orphans

Book One: The Lost Race Trilogy

This book is a work of fiction. Names, characters, businesses, organizations, places, events, and incidents either are the product of the author's imagination or are used fictictiously. Any resemblance to actual persons, living or dead, events, or locales is entirely coincidental.

Published in the United States by Little Pen Press

ISBN: 978-0-9980273-1-9

Book and Cover design by Natalie Preston

For my mother Genevieve, the brightest angel in my life.

YESTERDAY

"To hell with that shit! Three *Penthouses* for six packs. Regular, Tony. None of those faggie menthols either!"

It was a hissing negotiation, typical for Monday afternoon between sixth period and study hall. Tony Ibanescu had connections in Clarksburg, a pretty girl with tits that tasted like cherry candy, or so he said. Whether the other boys believed him or not was another thing all together. Cherry Tits provided Tony with cartons of cigarettes (no one could quite figure out what she got in return) and Tony made whatever deal he felt like. He didn't smoke, but porn? He did love porn.

Ibanescu was a big kid, already almost six feet tall. He played football as brutally as the pros, struggled with his lessons, and could have shaved if he was permitted. His hair was dark and insistently spiky, imitating a style some pay good money for. His eyes were inky black but his cheeks, pink as a girl's. If he wasn't in the middle of a scuffle, he was at least at the edge of it. His voice crackled to the point of being a man's, but Tony was only fifteen. His buyers were older, sixteen and seventeen. Wally Dean was almost eighteen.

Tony shook his head solemnly. "So sorry, Master Dean." He liked to address his fellow inmates at the orphanage as "Master." It pissed them off so he loved it. "Three for three. Think of what you went through to steal those magazines, buddy. Isn't it safer to take my deal and get them out of your room before the old biddy house mom finds them? Can you imagine what she'll do to you? Shit, I don't even wanna think about it."

Tony waited. Patient. Silent. The four other boys, all jonesing for a drag on whatever cigarettes Wally could make the trade for, held their breath. Finally, a head nodded and product exchanged hands.

As the others raced back, Tony flipped through the magazine and gazed at the inviting centerfold with a grin. He tucked the porn into his belt, hidden under his gold-crested blue jacket, put his head down and made his way through the chilled autumn afternoon to study hall.

He never made it.

Wally Dean and his friends had no answers when they were asked where Mr. Ibanescu was last seen. Yes, their supplier was missing. Yes, it was frightening, especially since there was blood discovered in the grass less than a mile from the courtyard gates and near the stream where they'd met. But there were other things to consider. Did they want to lose their privileges for confessing that they traded stolen *Penthouse* back issues for most likely stolen cigarettes? And what about Tony? How would he be punished if they snitched about his sexual escapades, real or imagined? There was too much at stake.

Young Anthony Ibanescu's mutilated body was found twenty-four hours later.

They weren't supposed to be where they were. Weren't supposed to be doing what they did. And Tony wasn't supposed to be dead.

"Childhood is the kingdom where nobody dies.
Nobody that matters, that is."

~ Edna St. Vincent Millay, 1892–1950

1

was five when my mother brought me here. It's how I know I really don't belong in this place. Ariel's Gate is an orphanage but I'm not an orphan. At least at five, I wasn't. Until I turned twelve I believed I'd get sprung, that my mom would show up at the door and demand her daughter. I know, pretty lame, just like this place—a boarding school for orphans, far from anything remotely normal. Yeah, that's the way to prepare us for the world.

Seven forty-five in the morning. I grabbed my journal, tossed a few books over it, and slammed my locker door closed just in time to get a prime-time view of Jenny Perkins letting Ryan Sutcliff slip his fat fingers up her plaid wool skirt. She had that look of rapture on her face, like she knows what ecstasy feels like. He gave me a stupid glare. Jenny's my roommate. I could reveal that the supermodel pretty girl in his arms looks like a deranged woodland creature in the mornings, but it's not worth it. He probably likes that kinda thing. I pushed past.

I was almost late for class but that wasn't my destination. I'm a pro at finding the best ways to cut algebra and disappear into nothingness. It's easy here. There are angels, and probably a whole mess of devils, watching over me wherever I go. Ariel's Gate is not a state-run home, not a welfare facility, not sad or dilapidated. This place is eerily spic and span and as modern as possible for such an old building. It has a big staff of instructors, cooks, cleaning people, and maintenance men. I guess it could have been worse.

I once saw a document on the headmaster's desk. He was standing outside his office door talking with his secretary, so I read it. I read pretty fast. Remember everything I see and hear, too. The paper said that Ariel's Gate's financial support comes from unnamed patrons. Well, actually it was a bank document stating that funding to the tune of a million dollars had been anonymously deposited into the orphanage's account less than a week earlier. Anonymous? I'm guessing that means people who don't want to be connected to the place. I asked Headmaster Allerton why none of us ever got a shot at living with foster parents. All he said was that we were better off here. I know two hundred student residents who wouldn't agree.

This orphanage has been standing for more than a century and a half, but the most ancient thing about this place is the name, Ariel's Gate. Ariel is an Archangel, the patron angel of wild animals. I think the name was chosen because someone thought Ariel was female, motherly, and nurturing. From everything I read in the library and on the internet, high-level Archangels were warriors. Life was great for celestial beings back then, before humans came along and made a mess of everything. Those fancy-named soldiers of God don't do battle anymore. I'm pretty sure they hold down desk jobs these days.

There are angels all over this place. They peek over the railings and gaze down from the pillars in the main quad. We have granite gargoyle angels and brass relief angels. There are work rooms, lecture halls, and chapels named after archangels. They're part of the architecture and carved into the landscape. Their stories are etched into the marble walls. They are stony watchers the instructors teach us about, but most of us pay little attention to that stuff. Especially those of us so close to leaving.

The magic number is eighteen. Survive the boredom and limitations that long and we're free. Yeah, there are Acclimation courses, but those don't even happen here, so bring it on. No more worrying about earning good-kid points for computer privileges, dealing with limited cable and internet access, or keeping our grades high enough to compete in or attend inter-league football or basketball games with normal parented kids. The nearest town is ten miles away and we always lose anyway. A little over a month, thirty-five days, and I'm free. I'm actually crossing off the days on a stupid calendar.

I zigged and zagged, cut through the cafeteria dedicated to Zadkial, and past Jophiel's Hall, named for the patron angel of the arts. None of the kids in my class can draw or paint, but some really cool art gets created. A monster black and silver dragon made of chicken wire and papier mâché lives there. Its massive belly is covered with a billion folded foil liners from sticks of gum and cigarette packs. The thing is twice as tall as me and cool as hell. It was actually shown at the tri-state art show last year. Won second prize. Now it graces the art hall to mock us. Nobody wins first prize at Ariel's Gate.

Staring at the dragon, I almost tripped turning a corner too tightly. I'm a little creeped out. The police have been in the Gate all morning. I never liked Tony Ibanescu but I am sorry he's dead. Granted, there aren't a lot of people around here I do like, but he was, well, just an oversized, obnoxious kid. The cops found him on a nearby farmer's property. I heard one of the cafeteria workers whisper that the body was chewed up and slashed to ribbons. It made me sick enough to pass on breakfast.

We do have a few wild animals here in the wild hills of West Virginia, but nothing I know of that could slash a big kid to shreds. Maybe a black bear but when unthreatened, most times they just walk away. Leave it to Tony Ibanescu to tick off a bear, or maybe the bear was rabid. We all wander too far sometimes. I really wanted to take a walk along the stream later, just to think alone and maybe see what I could see. Doesn't look like that's in the cards. This time I'll be following the lockdown rules. I like my skin the way it is.

My head swung left and right. I took a quick glance behind then slipped into the Makha'el Lecture Hall. The place is humungous, seldom used and except for special occasions, off limits to students. It's reserved for big lectures when people from all over the world come to hear powerful guest speakers. The minute I discovered it, I knew it would be my safe place, my silent place to think and write in my journal. Almost there, the second bell hadn't rung yet. I'd make it all the way to the pillars lining the back of the enormous amphitheater just in time. No one would find me. The pillars are pink carved marble, at least thirty feet high and wider than my outstretched arms. I felt like a cat weaving through a heavenly forest of sequoias, but my favorite pillar was just ahead.

Sweat made the hair at the back of my neck stick to my skin but this was no time to seek comfort. I was in the danger zone. Discovery would dump me right where I didn't want to be, sitting next to smelly Lenny and doing algebraic polynomial equations.

"Gracious Caine?"

Headmaster Allerton. Busted. No point in making up a lie to get out of this one. There was no justifiable reason on the planet for me to be there. "Uh… I…I just needed…"

The headmaster's a big man, usually stern, his face as hard as the statues all around me. He stepped forward, not like he was pissed off or anything, but like someone had broken something inside him. His steady gray eyes were rimmed red and he reached out his hand. Patting me lightly on the shoulder, he sighed. "I know, I know. We're all seeking a little peaceful solace today. Don't miss any more classes, though, Gracie. Lord knows you need no help with algebra, but your phys-ed skills leave a lot to be desired."

I hate gym class. Cutting gym is the only reason I ever end up in Headmaster's office.

He turned and left, his broad shoulders shifting with his determined steps. He looked like a man on a mission.

Letting out a long breath, I ran a hand across my sweaty face and stepped behind the pillar. Sliding to sit on the cool floor, I blinked and swallowed hard. Something was really different, and my gut sensed it was bigger than poor Tony's death. The second bell rang loud, echoing and bouncing along the pillars around me. Eight o'clock. First period had officially begun.

~*~

SOUTH SIOUX CITY IOWA DRUNK TANK, EIGHT A.M.

"Cole Masters," called the officer. "Masters. Cole Masters."

The reeking tattooed beast on the metal bench next to him shoved an elbow into tender, bruised ribs. That woke Cole faster than the shouting cop.

"What?" He groaned, looked up and shuffled to his feet. Nearly twenty-four hours and still the police couldn't sort things out. A bar brawl, nothing more, nothing less. Normal for these parts, seeing as that very year Sioux City held the dubious honor for the highest crime rate in the country. Second time in jail in as many days and it actually scared him a little, wondering what was coming next. For the hundredth time, Cole tried not to compare his current situation with a reality he either wouldn't acknowledge or refused to believe. He wasn't the intellectual type. He wasn't about to figure it all out. Knowing was bad enough. Believing was another thing altogether. Best to ignore it all when things suited well enough as they were. He knew his own kind, ran with a gang that, noticeably, was nowhere in the communal cell with him. So much for loyalty among thieves. He knew a gun, no matter how complex the thing was. He'd mastered survival on the fringes of felony and ambiguity. Cole was becoming comfortable with it. Sort of.

He was like an old-time cowboy, except his saddle was mounted on a rumbling engine. He didn't mind, it got places faster. Cole wanted to get places faster. Ride harder. Run away. He was fearless and that made him dangerous. Being fearless is easy when you know things you shouldn't. He could outsmart anyone he met and steal anything he wanted. Over the past year he'd proven it, and was just slippery enough to get away with it. So far.

Was this the end of the line? Had this backward, mid-west police station put together the pieces no one else could? And what of it? He'd had a few laughs, enjoyed a lot of women, got to see most of the country, and some of the world. What a journey it turned out to be. Nothing like he could have imagined as a kid back at Ariel's Gate, even if he had the imagination.

"Masters. Cole Masters." The cop grunted and scowled.

His gut shuddered but Cole sauntered to the bars and eyed the officer. Waited.

"You can go after your hearing and fine, Masters." And the door swung open.

Relief washed over him, but not in a way the cop would ever read. It looked more like defiance, and that usually got him into even more trouble. Cole lowered his eyes behind a curtain of dirty hair and followed the man. He sat in the courtroom, awaited his hearing, then stood quietly before the magistrate and held his breath.

"Masters," the judge said with a snort. "Get up here."

Oh, oh. At first his feet wouldn't move. So much for being fearless. He cleared his throat and tried again, making the six long strides to the high bench. He looked up at the magistrate, trying his hardest to appear at least a little contrite, hoping he didn't look as afraid as he was. Maybe he should stay in jail? Maybe it would be the best place for him? Maybe? But, man, he hoped that decision wasn't coming out of the guy's mouth.

"What's wrong with you?" the judge whispered with an angry hiss. "Look at you. Barely twenty-one, your whole life ahead of you and here you are… sitting two nights in a row in a stinking jail cell. You're a decorated former marine, son! Get your goddamn act together."

Cole gulped, squared his shoulders. He'd heard this lecture before, he could take it.

"I see you anywhere near my jurisdiction again, causing any more trouble, and I swear!" His hiss had become a shout. "I'll find some reason to lock your sorry ass up for a year! Do you hear me?"

"Yes, yeah, I hear you. I hear you." Cole figured most of Sioux City could hear him.

"Get yourself a little pride and dignity, Mr. Masters. Now, today you're lucky, no one's pressed charges, but it's going to cost you two-hundred-forty bucks to get your Harley out of the pound."

Cole blinked. Did this guy really let him off the hook?

"If you don't have the money—"

"I got it," he croaked.

"Good, go over there to that nice lady and pay the fine. And listen…"

Cole held his breath. Now what?

"Clean yourself up, Marine."

He nodded and shuffled off to pay his fine, digging the last of his cash from his wallet. He didn't take a deep breath until he left the courtroom.

The Harley was worse for the wear, sporting several gouging scrapes along the side, like someone had laid her down at seventy-five. Did he do that? Was that how he hurt his ribs? No matter, he had bigger troubles to think about, things far more pressing than bikes, and fights, or threats from a magistrate. Cole was late.

Could he catch up with the guys? They'd have sped through Valentine hours earlier, so he bypassed Nebraska altogether and raced north along Rt. 29. The sun was rising over flat nothingness, making the landscape look like Mars, all red and glowing.

Iowa into South Dakota on Interstate 90, he was making a beeline west for Rapid City, then Sturgis, and finally Spearfish and the big take. Cole wasn't about to miss out on that. His not-so-loyal buddies might think he was out of the equation but he sure as hell wasn't.

Somewhere near White Lake, he pulled off the highway. Stepping away Cole stretched his arms high and twisted. Yeah, the ribs were going to hurt for a while. He tied a filthy red bandana over his wild hair and straddled the bike. At the first gas station, Cole filled the tank and sped off without paying. He stopped at the next road stop restaurant, ordered a burger and did the same, driving off and never thinking twice about it. Sin and survival were his personal shadows. Part and parcel of who he'd become. It was áll he knew and in his inexplicable situation, all he cared about.

He chuckled, an internal rumble to match the growl of his engine. Sin. It was his escape from everything he learned in Acclimation. Sin had a sharp flavor, vivid color. It had heat and power and vitality Cole had never been able to control. He wasn't following, he wasn't trying to rise above, and he sure as hell wasn't trying to understand. He was just living. Just sinning. There was no indignity in it if he admitted it.

Sin hurt. It was the only thing he allowed himself to feel. It defined his strange reality and gave him the comfort of familiarity. The thing he feared most was being called into account. He'd made a vow during Acclimation and been faithfully ignoring that fact since his honorable discharge from the Corps. The Marines gave him structure and integrity, sin gave him pleasure. Neither felt right, but sin felt a whole lot better.

Speed fed his need. He ran like a rat away from responsibility, toward the gang and a well-planned take. So much money, all in one place. It made Cole drool. It made him twitch in his seat, and it made his mind wander. Cole didn't care where the money came from or where it was supposed to go. He just wanted his share.

But why? What did money matter? He lived simply, rode all day, slept most nights on the side of the highway. He spent his cash on gas, food, whiskey, women, and bail. There was a time it mattered. A time when he had dreams and plans. A time just before leaving Ariel's Gate. Before Acclimation.

No. No, he couldn't let his mind drift there. Not there.

He shook himself back into control and watched the badlands fly past. He was fighting more than reflections and images that tore pitifully at his guts. Cole was fighting exhaustion, having slept little the past two nights, sitting up in the crowded cell. His body ached and struggled against a tremor that rippled up his spine, threatening a full loss of control at eighty miles an hour. He swerved off the highway at the Murdo exit and revved the engine to intimidate an old couple in a shiny Buick waiting at the light.

Less than five miles south, Cole pulled over and bumped slowly along the prairie grass until he found a mesquite low and wide enough to shelter him and the bike from the growing heat. A stream trickled nearby and he dipped his aching head into it, flipping his sloppy wet mop of hair in a spray. Cool water ran down his neck, mixing with sweat and sandy grit. He wrung out the bandana and settled under the tree for a nap. If he didn't rest, he'd never make it to Spearfish in one piece.

He spread the cool, wet bandana over his face and sighed. He breathed deeper and felt his muscles melt into restfulness. A sound, the skitter of a prairie rabbit, insects in the dry grasses, the distant cry of an eagle. His eyes flickered opened. The red cotton fabric was warming in the hot breeze. With a sudden jolt, Cole snapped the bandana away, panting to catch his breath. Something didn't feel right, and when something didn't feel right his first instinct was to get the hell away from it. He kicked a billow of dust and leapt onto the bike. Another rev and Cole was back on the road. He'd sleep after he hooked up with the guys. He was only six hours from Spearfish. He could make it.

He went south a bit further toward Mission, figuring he'd finger a cup of coffee at a gas station. He might just be able to charm a pretty Sioux girl into giving it to him. Karma. Whatever karma was, Cole suddenly wanted to be on its good side for a change. He neared a gas station, lowered his chest, and sped recklessly.

He didn't see the old rusted car pull out. His reactions were slack, even his abrupt escape from gravity seemed slow to Cole. There was no time during his timeless flight to shout or swear or even cry out like a scared little girl. No time to think about much of anything. He felt weightless, then heavy as hell as his hip and back slammed against the hood of the car. The air shot out of his lungs then everything went black.

Blue light flashed inside his eyes, thrumming a rhythm that quickened his heart and terrified him. That's when he heard the voice and received his marching orders. "Now," it said, rumbling low and vibrating like his racing heartbeat. His eyes popped open, swiveled right then left then squeezed tight.

"Damn," he groaned. There would be no take in Spearfish. Three years ago, he'd made a vow and he'd just received his call to action. "Damn, damn, damn it!" he hissed, waving off the scared teenagers in the car that hit him. "Damn it all to hell." He hauled the bike up, climbed on and headed for Route 90 east. Did he really think he'd never see Ariel's Gate again?

2

here was no gym class in the cards for me after all. The news blasted over the speakers and vibrated against the marble walls, making me cringe and cover my ears. Headmaster Allerton announced a full assembly right there in Makha'el's Lecture Hall. I slipped into one of the back seats near my pillar and leafed through my journal. "Hey!" His arm reached right over my shoulder, snatched the book away then quickly pushed it down the front of his pants. "You want it, come get it." Ben Wheeler always smiles like he thinks something is secretly funny.

It's a shame that I like that smile so much it makes me want to smile back. Ben's a good friend, my best friend… and I'd so like it to be more. He's different from the other idiot boys at the Gate, not all macho and demanding. He's caring and kind.. Well, most of the time.

I opened my algebra book and ignored him while he climbed over to sit beside me. He laughed when I moved a seat away. I like his laugh. "Give me my journal."

"Nah, I need some good reading material late at night. Maybe tomorrow."

My heart skipped a few beats but instead of grabbing for it, I gripped my hands together tight enough to feel fingernails cut into my skin. There's so much in that journal to hide, but I know this game. Pretend it's unimportant and he'll lose interest. I didn't think he'd bother reading the thing anyway. With guys, it's all about the threat. I grinned. "Suit yourself," I said and slouched deeper in my seat while kids and teachers noisily filed into the hall "Where did you come from anyway?" I never saw him in Makha'el's Hall. I guess my secret quiet place wasn't so secret after all.

"Meet me here tomorrow and I'll show you something you've never seen before."

"Doubt it."

"Get here before breakfast, like at six. I'll give your journal back."

I looked at him and twisted my mouth. "The lights aren't even on in this part of the building at six."

"Trust me… it's worth skulking around in the dark to see what I want to show you."

"First of all," I turned to face him, having to talk louder as the noisy crowd around us grew. "You have nothing I want to see. And second, I'm not Jenny Perkins. Try to get your hands up my skirt and you'll be crying in the nurse's office while she splints broken fingers." I didn't really mean that but I said it, so I had to follow through. I put on my meanest face.

"It's not what's under your skirt I want, Gracie. I think you're the only student here who might be able to make heads or tails out of what I found."

I can never tell if someone's lying or telling me the truth, but looking directly into their eyes makes them think I can. Yeah, pretty green eyes but that's beside the point. He was dead serious. In a split second, I knew I wanted to see whatever secret he had found. "Fine, six o'clock. If you're not here—"

"I'll be here."

Wally Dean climbed over my knees like the klutz he is and dropped like a log onto the seat between us. I glared… he didn't glare back. In fact, Wally looked like he'd been crying. Tony was his friend I suppose, but crying had never been a part of Wally's repertoire. Nor had associating with the likes of me or Ben. Wally normally hung around students with low GPAs and future criminal records.

"You okay, man?" Ben asked.

Wally shook his head.

I reached out, touched his shoulder, and felt him tremble under my fingers. I glanced at Ben, then we both focused on the stage where Allerton, housemother Drummond, and several of the instructors huddled, a few waving their arms around, others just listening. I noticed that the cops were nowhere in sight. My heart thudded and I decided that I didn't really care what anyone thought. I needed comfort and so did poor Wally. I took his hand in mine and held it. Ben did the same thing. Wally didn't pull away from either of us. That scared me even more.

On the stage, the headmaster stood his full height, which seemed like ten-feet-ten to me. His arms spread wide and that action alone silenced everyone in the massive lecture hall. There was no preamble or easing into anything. I was prepared to hear a comforting sermon about the loss of a student and a lecture on the dangers of roaming too far from the front gates, but he made a statement no one was prepared for.

"Ariel's Gate will be closed and dismantled… within days."

Shouts, yells, and cheers from students rose and bounced from the ceiling. The teachers' desperate attempts to quiet the crowd added to the racket. I stood and watched Allerton. I expected a tremendous bellow, one that would get everyone's attention. His arms slowly opened again, his head fell back, and his eyes closed. He allowed it all and in a few minutes, everyone, like me, stood and watched him in silence. My knees wobbled. I dropped into my seat and found myself laughing silently, unsure if joy, or excitement, or terror had taken over. Maybe I'd just lost my mind. Close Ariel's Gate? How was such a thing possible?

Wally and Ben stared at the stage then sat, too. "Is he serious?" Ben whispered.

The headmaster cleared his throat and spoke. "In light of recent developments, this facility will be closed. Mrs. Drummond will explain the schedule and preparations to be made over the next few days. By Friday, you will all be on a journey to your new homes… infants, teachers, students, workers. All safe. Safe." Allerton's voice cracked. He turned on a heel and left the stunned lecture hall.

"We can just leave… I bet we can just walk out of here." Wally trembled and looked to us both, eyes wild with tentative hope.

Ben shrugged. "He's right, you know. Wally, you're ten days from Acclimation. I'm what… two weeks?"

Wally nodded more enthusiastically.

"I've got a whole thirty-five days," I whispered, realizing that suddenly it meant nothing. Acclimation, in all our minds, was graduation and commencement into the real world. We could just leave. Walk through the front gates. Be free. But there was that word, *safe*. Why did Allerton say it like that? Like we weren't safe already? A wild animal attack is scary, but not everyone dies from something like that. "You have a gun?" I looked to Ben and he laughed.

"Hell no."

"Can you get one?"

"Where would he find a gun in this place?" Wally started shaking even harder.

I wanted to form a practical strategy of escape, but the housemother stood at the podium and laid out the plan I'd be stuck with. Thirty-five days. Maybe the risk of getting ripped to shreds by a wild animal wasn't the smartest option. Maybe I could wait. Maybe.

"Preparation has already begun for infants and children under the age of five. The nursery is closed. The little ones will be gone before dawn tomorrow," she announced, like she was reading the week's cafeteria menu.

By dawn? I'd spent a few hours every day helping in the nursery. I wouldn't even get a chance to say goodbye to the caregivers and babies. I gripped my books to my chest and my feet shuffled like they wanted to run.

"Grades one through five," housemother continued, "teachers and students are to be packed and on the road by noon tomorrow, no later. Buses will be provided and ready at eleven. Your itineraries and destinations will be distributed once you're all on those buses. No stragglers, please. Please," she repeated quietly.

"Ah man, Mary Elaina. Sorry, Gracie." Ben reached over and squeezed my hand.

Mary Elaina is in the fifth grade. She sits with me during lunch. She's a math and technology whiz, really funny, and always made me feel special. I never feel special. How could I lose Mary Elaina? My hand shot up and waved for attention. I had to ask. There had to be another way. Maybe I could go with the fifth graders and help out. Mrs. Drummond's focus settled on me for a moment then she continued.

"Grades six through eleven… students, teachers, and all staff, you are to pack and meet in the courtyard Thursday morning at three A.M. You'll be split into groups and taken to your specific destinations by various transport. Again, all pertinent information will be distributed at that time.

"Seniors are to be packed and meet Thursday morning in the cafeteria at eight. You will be shuttled to Yeager Airport. Tickets and itineraries will be given to each of you when you arrive at your specific charter flight departure area. No more than one suitcase and one carry-on, please."

Wally gripped my arm. "What the hell are we running from?"

"There are a few exceptions," Mrs. Drummond shouted over the growing noise and nervous activity. "Sit tight for one more moment, please. Quiet everyone. There are a few exceptions. The following students are to meet in headmaster Allerton's office on Thursday morning at seven." The hushed room held its breath. "Mister Ryan Sutcliff and Mister Wallace Dean."

Wally gasped and choked for a moment.

"Also, Miss Jennifer Perkins, Mister Benjamin Wheeler, and…"

The housemother who practically raised us all paused and drew in a long breath. I looked around. I was about to lose everyone I cared about.

"And finally, Miss Gracious Caine. The five of you will be leaving at ten Thursday morning. You *must* be prepared and waiting in the headmaster's office on time. Pack your belongings tonight to assure there are no delays. There are several very important things for you to take care of tomorrow." She paused, then her sad eyes scanned the entire lecture hall. "It's most critical that each and every one of you follow these orders to the letter… God bless you all." And she walked away from the podium.

We weren't dismissed, so most students turned to their teachers for guidance. There was no guidance. People trickled out of Makha'el Lecture Hall like abused dogs, silent, afraid, shaken. Did none of them know that the Archangel Makha'el is all about battle? Were we already beaten?

Ben leaned close and whispered in my ear, "Don't forget, six tomorrow morning."

"Why? What does it matter now?"

"I have a feeling it matters a lot."

~*~

Sleeping was out of the question. Writing in my journal was impossible because Ben had it. I was reduced to watching the alarm clock and trying hard not to think. Could I just leave? Right now? I'd packed my bag already so that was done. Just toss on my uniform, grab my backpack and duffel, and walk out the front gate. I could do it, right? I could. I wanted to.

I stood, dressed, and huffed a deep breath that made sleeping Jenny snort like a disturbed princess. Blazer on, bags in hand, I stepped toward the door and reached for the knob. Instead I turned and opened the closet then dropped inside and slid to my butt. Pulling the door closed with my foot, I stifled a sob. Was I really that scared of a wild animal trying to kill kids like me? No. Was I afraid of the truth, whatever that truth was? Absolutely. I didn't know why, but I clearly sensed I was in danger. We were all in danger. Not danger like getting detention kind of danger. Danger like you see on television. On the news. In terrible parts of the world.

I sniffled quietly, folded myself neatly on the floor of the empty closet, and sighed. Maybe I could sleep there. I felt a tiny bit safer. At least I thought I felt safer, then my fingers trailed along the wall. Someone or something had really scratched up the plaster. I never saw the inside of that closet before Jenny filled it up with her clothes, shoes, hats, and purses. She never wore the same thing twice for any non-uniform occasion. Me, I had a few tee-shirts, a few pairs of jeans, underwear, socks, a coat, and an extra pair of tennis shoes. Most of the time we all wore our uniforms, but even with Jenny's uniform, there was always something fashionable added—a bracelet, a pin, textured stockings, a scarf. None of it was expensive or had any value. Jenny bought it with her allowance, all online at very low prices. It was her taste that made them look so cool and special. I knew girls who envied Jenny, thinking she had a stash of cash so she could wear Dior and Hilfiger. None of them knew it was all cheap knock-offs. Just me. I knew a lot about Jenny that no one else knew.

The empty closet left a lot of space for me and my bags. I shuffled out of my jacket and laid my palms against the back wall, sliding them carefully until I found the scratches again, my finger carefully following the lines. The words. Breathless, I dug into a backpack pocket and found my tiny flashlight. Aiming it at the wall I blinked, gasped, then almost cried out.

IS GOD HERE FOR ME, OR AM I HERE FOR GOD?

Blinking again and again I had to run my hand across the words to make sure they were really there. I had been writing those exact words in my journal since I first started keeping one at the age of nine. I'd never seen them in the closet before. I felt suffocated and escaped the tight space as fast as humanly possible.

"Okay. That was weird," I whispered. The alarm clock glowed 3:00 A.M. I couldn't sleep, but I knew what I could do.

Slipping from the room, I tiptoed down the hall, past numerous stone angels who should be watching over me better, and across the vestibule. I could see lights on in the nursery. I knew it was supposed to be closed, but maybe I could help. There were thirty babies under the age of five in there. I opened the door to exactly what I expected. Mayhem. Crying infants, giggling toddlers, terrorizing two year olds. The poor nurses, teachers, and housemother Drummond raced around like headless chickens. I reached out and caught an escaping crawler then settled in the playroom with a call to the toddlers. They loved story time, maybe I could help them and myself to get our minds off what was happening.

The head nurse smiled and led a line of creeping ducklings into my circle. While I read *Snow White*—using special voices for every one of the seven dwarfs—the kids drifted off to sleep. Like magic, the nursery was packed up, duffels loaded and labeled and all lined up at the door. At exactly four o'clock I was politely asked to leave.

"Why? I can help get them on the bus. The minute you start moving them you know they'll all be awake and spinning like tops. You need me," I said, starting to sound desperate.

"Get some sleep, Gracie," Housemother said gently, closing the door between me and the babies.

Sleep? Was she nuts? I thought to watch from the stairwell window as the little ones left Ariel's Gate, but I didn't have the heart. Digging my tiny flashlight from my pocket, I wound my way to Makha'el Lecture Hall. Ben said he'd be there at six. I planned to beat him.

My hand caressed the carved door handle leading to the hall, my fingers pausing on the elegant curved feathered wings. "I hate this place. I'm so glad to be getting out of here," I whispered as tears slid down my face.

Sliding my feet silently along the carpeted floor, I edged my way deeper and deeper into the dense darkness. My flashlight was useless beyond a foot ahead, so I turned it off and reached out my hands. Following the outer wall would be a much longer trek to my destination, but a far safer one.

I listened to the silence and the thumping of my own heart. My breath was shallow and controlled, my footsteps light and careful. Within my ridiculous photographic memory, I knew exactly where everything was around me. The podium and stage adorned with elegant ceiling-to-floor blue velvet curtains behind, hundreds of amphitheater seats filling the center of the space, and the elegant frescos above—a panoramic painting of raging battle between angels with white wings and angels with dark wings.

At the top of each wide, tall, sturdy marble column reached out a carved body of Makha'el, each one holding a different weapon or shield, each face with a different, frightful expression, all twenty-eight of them. I'd studied them, imagined the orders being shouted from those mouths, and wondered at the reason for the fight. They were comforting and terrifying at the same time. I was almost happy that it was so dark and I didn't have to face Makha'el's anger as I inched my way to the back of his battlefield. As always, I pondered. Who were the good guys? Who were the bad?

Then my foot touched something. It grunted softly and I jumped at least a mile. For what felt like forever, I held my chest to keep my freaked-out heart from splitting right out. At my favorite pillar, I discovered that I hadn't beat Ben after all. He was curled on the floor, sleeping soundly. I slouched in a seat and awaited my own drop into unconsciousness.

~*~

Cole was dreaming a dream he'd never had before. He knew it because he only had one dream. A dark dream. The kind that drove him to do anything that might keep him from dreaming at all. Whiskey was the best solution, but drinking was out of the question on his speeding race to Ariel's Gate, especially if he planned to make it there alive. Thus, the new dream. The flash of brilliant sunlight on a polished blade. The fleeting hope of death. The desperate need to survive. *"Now,"* said the voice. *"Now!"*

A sudden sharp pain in his ribs brought him awake and he looked up at the million West Virginia stars speckling around Headmaster Allerton's head. The face was lit by headlights from a nearby yellow school bus. That face didn't look happy.

"Hey man," Cole grunted up on his elbows. "S'up?"

"Get your sorry ass to my office, Cole. I'll be there shortly."

"Least you could do is tell me why I'm here. Not like I don't have a life somewhere else, ya know." He climbed to his feet, fighting bone rattling fatigue. He couldn't have slept more than twenty minutes over the past forty-eight hours. Someone should be thankful for his sacrifice.

Allerton turned away and focused on more important things happening all around him.

Dog-tired when he arrived, Cole had dropped just outside the gates and slept in the soft damp grass. His bike was carefully leaned against the solid brick wall. It had been running on fumes until it sputtered and died three miles away. He shook his head and rolled the Harley inside the gate, skirting the mad activity in the courtyard. It looked like organized pandemonium, with adults headed to the buses burdened with struggling, screeching babies, and heavy luggage.

"Don't want to know," he whispered to himself. Kick-standing the battered Harley safely out of the way, he moved as if on autopilot, walking through the building like he was just there yesterday. Memories slammed and tangled as the smells, sounds, and energy of the place mocked him all the way to the headmaster's office. He stood at the window and watched the courtyard below. Whatever shit had hit the fan, it had sure done it with flair. No one leaves Ariel's Gate until they're eighteen. They never move the babies. On a brighter side, Cole imagined that those little ones might be raised by parents like normal kids. Would that be a good option or not? He suddenly stepped away from the window. The buses were pulling out and Allerton was heading into the building. Cole looked around the office.

Not that seat. That's where he'd sat the day the headmaster removed him from the football team. Not that seat either. He'd sat there when Allerton assigned detention for an entire month. Something about smoking in the boy's room. "Seriously?" Cole grunted. The third and last guest chair in the office was the one he'd chosen right before his Acclimation. "Ain't sitting there either," he whispered.

That left the headmaster's big leather chair, but before he could skirt the massive desk and belligerently drop into it, Allerton entered. Cole leaned back against a bookshelf, locked his hands, and tilted his head.

So much attitude and none of it made him feel any better. Time for a reality check. Headmaster Michael Allerton scared the living crap out of him. He was the boss, the final decision, the taskmaster during his entire eighteen years at Ariel's Gate. Allerton was witness to Cole's Acclimation. He knew things about Cole that no other living being knew. In Cole's mind, Allerton was more than headmaster of the place. He was leadership personified. He never made a wrong or even slightly incorrect decision. Never wavered. Never questioned himself. What a great dad Allerton could have been to someone, Cole mused. A son could really look up to a man like that. Follow in those footsteps without question or doubt. Instead Allerton, easily in his fifties, had chosen to run a stupid orphanage with an iron hand. And Cole wondered for the first time, had the man ever left Ariel's Gate? Had he grown up there, too?

"You were almost too late," Headmaster said as he sat and checked his watch. "Sit down, will you?"

"Nope, I'll stand. Just what the hell am I doing here, Michael?" Yeah, it was big time disrespectful but Cole didn't care. He was no longer under Ariel's Gate control, so why the hell couldn't he call the man by his Christian name? Then something strange happened.

Allerton rubbed his tired eyes and ran a hand down his chin. There were grey sprouts among the dark stubble growing there. With a deep, aching sigh, he looked up. "Sit down."

Cole sat. He had no choice. The crack in Allerton's armor was enough to knock him to his ass. What the man said after that made him want to throw up. Was he serious? Shut down Ariel's Gate? Was that even possible? Even bigger than that, was it smart?

"Why close this place? It's the safest place anywhere."

"Not anymore."

"Michael… why am I here?"

No answer.

"Seriously, I'm the biggest fuck-up ever acclimated out of this place. Why was I called back?"

Allerton pulled open a desk drawer and drew out two glasses and a bottle of scotch. Good scotch. The mere sight of the label made Cole's mouth water. At first, he refused the offered glass but Allerton looked into his eyes.

"Trust me, you need it. We both need it."

Cole gulped, savored the burn and slid the glass for a refill.

Two drinks later, the man leaned back in the leather chair and eyed him. "You are going to acclimate five kids… all within the next thirty-odd days." He opened a file folder and took a breath, preparing to say more.

As long as he'd known Allerton, the man never once prepared a person for what was about to come out of his mouth. Cole's hand shot up. "Hold on! You're out of your mind."

"No. The first is in ten days. Wallace Dean. He's a pro at detention, so you two have something in common." Allerton actually grinned.

"I can't acclimate anyone. Hell, I haven't accepted my own—"

"The next is just two days later… Ryan Sutcliff, the Ariel Warriors quarterback. You two have something in common, too… so…"

Cole stood. "No. I can't do this, man."

"You can. Sit. The third is Benjamin Wheeler. Good kid. Take it easy on him. After that you have two girls."

"I said, no!"

"Jennifer Perkins on October third… and finally Gracious Caine… Gracie… on October eighteenth."

He had to get out of there. Cole charged for the door but amazingly, the older man beat him to it.

"Sit down!" bellowed Allerton.

Cole wanted to cry. He felt suffocated. "Don't make me do this, please."

Did he really say those words? Like that? Like a scared kid?

"Sit down, Cole."

"I cannot acclimate anyone, much less five unsuspecting kids. I just can't do that!"

Allerton gripped Cole's upper arm and led him to a chair. "You can and you will. You're a former Marine, Cole. You've seen what the world is… and you've seen what you're capable of."

"No." It was followed by an embarrassing sob.

"You took a vow." Allerton poured another drink and gulped it. Sitting, he leaned back and eyed Cole. "Didn't you take that vow? Right in front of me? Right after your Acclimation?"

Cole closed his eyes and tried to think of anything else, anything to give his flailing mind something to grip onto. Something he could understand and deal with. The smell of burning tires on the highway, the feel of a stack of cash in his hands. The sensation of skulking silently with other men in a faraway desert, armed to the teeth and ready to kill anything wearing pajamas.

"You took that vow, Cole."

"I took it because I never thought I'd have to follow through!" He stood again, pacing the room like a caged animal in front of the man he respected and feared more than God. "This place is safe! Impenetrable! Protected! What in the world would make me think that would ever change? I didn't intend to follow through on any damn vow I made to you."

"You have no choice."

"But—"

"No choice. Pull yourself together… you take those kids Thursday morning."

Cole's mouth opened but nothing came out.

"You're tired. I've had a faculty suite prepared for you… put together some clean clothes… I see your inner-city hood fashion sense hasn't improved."

Did Allerton actually grin? Was he mad?

"Take the files with you. Acquaint yourself with these kids over the next twenty-four hours. We'll talk more later. For now, get some sleep. I'll send breakfast for you."

Defeated, he took the folders and turned to the door.

"Oh, and Cole. I'll give you ten grand for the Harley."

"What? Why? How the hell am I going to get—"

"Away?" Allerton gave a snort. "You'll be driving a van full of teenagers. The bike won't help you protect them. I'll sell it back after this is over."

"Over? How are you even going to find me? And how the hell am I going to get ten grand to buy it back? I'll need to use that money for this stupid mission."

Allerton's face became familiarly stern. "I'll be holding the money for you."

"And how do I feed five teenagers? Fill the tank?" *Get a few more guns, ammo, maps*, he thought silently.

"God will provide. Take a shower, you smell like hell."

3

Something tickled my nose and light burned through my closed eyelids. "Wake up, we overslept. Come on."

"What time is it?" I scrambled to my feet in the glow of Ben's big flashlight.

"A little after seven. Follow me."

From behind, Ben looked goofy. His hair was sticking up, he'd gotten down on his hands and knees, and it sounded like he was snorting. "Is there a reason you're pretending to be Raffie?"

Raffie's the school mascot, an English bulldog of unknown age. He hung out with us in the dorms, the lunch room where he got most of his nourishment, and in study hall. The mere scratch of his paw or bouncing "Uff" gained him access to any room in the entire place. I've seen teachers stop a lecture to give Raffie entrance and verbal permission to monitor their class. He was with us when we cried, snuggled close for comfort, and he ran like a champ when we played basketball, skidding on his big thumping paws across the gym floor and knocking players over with joy and abandon. Everyone loved Raffie. He had the biggest heart of us all. Most likely he'd left with the babies. My heart sank at the thought but then Ben turned and smiled at me.

"Actually, that slobbering dog showed me this place." There was a scratching sound then he grunted and pulled hard at a piece of marble that lifted with a whoosh. "Look!" He shined the flashlight inside. All I saw were steep steps going down into the darkness. "Come on."

"Wait! How do we get out?"

"Same way we get in. Hurry up and go down. Do you want someone to catch us?"

I honestly battled with myself but nosiness won and I turned to step down the ladder stairs. When I met Ben's grinning face, all I wanted to do was kiss it, but instead I sneered and stepped deeper into the darkness. Turning, I watched Ben's bulk move down, then the room was suddenly fully lit.

"Aaackk!" I gasped and covered my eyes. "How did it get so bright in here?"

"Light switch, dummy. This way."

Following him, I couldn't help but laugh at myself. I was so sure we'd find dead bodies down there, like in the catacombs. The hallway was clean and bright with fluorescent lights along the center of the ceiling. The grey linoleum floor seemed to lead to the end of the world, but Ben stopped about twenty yards down the hall and reached into a small alcove. With the push of a few fingers, another hidden door opened and we walked in as he switched on the light. Now this room fulfilled my fearful imaginings in a different way. It was dark and dingy and lined with row upon row of dusty ancient looking books. Who knew all this was right under my feet all these years?

Ben rushed to the far end of one of the aisle and carefully tugged a tome from the shelf. On a worn and scratched up reading table, he opened the book to the first page. "There," he said.

I coughed, waving away the puff of dust, and looked around. "What is this place?"

"I'm thinking it's where they keep the secrets. I found this book the first time I found this room. It's usually right here, open to a page somebody was reading. But seriously, how could anybody read this? It's no language I can find anywhere on the internet."

He was right. The writing was the oddest I'd ever seen. It had the feel of ancient Hebrew or possibly some obscure Sanskrit script. Maybe ancient Japanese symbols. Maybe older than most people had ever seen. The pages were yellowed and delicate, but the lettering looked like a stylized inking of some kind, like it was written with a special pen nib. "This is so strange."

"Stranger yet," Ben added, smearing dust across his forehead, "for the past few weeks this book has been right here, opened to different pages… every single day. Now today, after Allerton announced that this place is to close down, it's back on the shelf. Gracie, can you figure this writing out?"

"I doubt it, at least not before we leave. It could take a lifetime… if I even could. Do you think it's important?"

"The timing alone makes me feel like it has big meaning for us."

"What about all these other books?" I turned full circle, amazed at how many of them there were.

"Every other book I looked at is in plain old English. They're all like legal dockets, you know, listing each resident's name, the date they came to the Gate, who brought them, how old—"

"Who brought them?" Again, my heart jumped. "Can we find my information?"

"I already found it." Ben smiled and scurried off like a mad librarian. Thumping a book on top of the mysterious writing, he flipped the pages. "We're all in here… all of us acclimating this year. They must have entered the information into books based on our eighteenth birthdate rather than our arrival." His finger slid down the tight handwritten columns. "Here you are. Gracious Caine, born October 18, 1998. Accepted into Ariel's Gate care, February 3, 2003… um… age five years and four months… brought in by… um, here it is, Natalia Rooker."

"No, that's wrong. My mother brought me here."

Ben looked at me and shrugged. "Maybe they made a mistake? Sorry. I thought you'd be impressed."

"No, no, I am. Real impressed. You found this place, all this information, even that weird book. It's just that, well I remember everything, and the woman who brought me here was my mom."

"What was her name? Maybe they wrote it next to another kid's name."

I closed my eyes and shifted from foot to foot.

"Gracie? What was your mother's name?"

I turned away to hide a surprise tear. "Mom… Caine. Her name was Mom. Can we get out of here?" I was only five. Of all the things I remember, I could not remember my own mother's name. I remembered tasting my first smashed banana, having my diaper changed. Birth. Yes, birth. Not my favorite memory but it's there. Why isn't Mom's name there?

Ben's arms wrapped around me and we stood that way for a few minutes. He finally closed the docket, then opened it again and pulled a pen from his jacket pocket. Scratching out the name Natalia Rooker, he scribbled really large, MOM. "There, fixed. And…" He brought my journal from his pants and handing it to me, dropped it opened to the last page I'd written. "Oh man, sorry." He bent to pick it up, disappearing under the table. "Uh… Gracie? You might want to see this."

I lowered to my knees, a little thrilled, figuring it was just his way to get me close to him again, then I looked where he pointed. There, on the panel beneath the reading table, were scratched the words, the same words from my closet, the exact same words on my opened journal page.

IS GOD HERE FOR ME, OR AM I HERE FOR GOD?

I slapped the journal closed, stood, and held it close to my chest. "I'm leaving."

"Yeah," he said from behind. "Me too. That was way too creepy. But hey, I'm taking this weird book with me."

I swung around and slammed right into him. "No, leave it."

"Nope. If anyone can figure this out, it's you. Gracie. You're the smartest person I know." The book disappeared into my journal's previous hiding place. With the snap of a few light switches, a climb up the steep ladder, and the whispered closure of the secret door, we stood again in Makha'el Lecture Hall just as the automatic 8:00 A.M. lights came on.

I jumped with a squeak.

Ben gave a nervous chuckle as we rushed out of the hall and off for breakfast.

~*~

He'd never seen the teachers' quarters. Yeah, he'd dreamt about them as a horny teenager. Ah, Miss Milcroy. Shapely, pretty, wearing that tight dark blue skirt with the little slit up the side. He hadn't thought about her in a while. Cole looked around. The suite was a lot like Allerton's office, well furnished, squeaky clean, polished, and appropriate. He leaned to peek into the bedroom. Did Miss Milcroy sleep in there? In that bed?

On the dresser lay the clean clothes Allerton promised, next to them a bottle of aspirin and a glass of water. The hangover from forty-plus hours earlier still trembled in his brain, piercing at every nerve ending and thought. A few pills and a gulp of water, then he stripped and headed for the bathroom.

The shower was steamy hot and satisfying but the clean clothes felt even better. His life since Acclimation had been a series of events, speed, racing away then running toward. He couldn't remember the last time his clothes smelled so good or clean hair floated loose around his face.

Daylight had arrived and Ariel's Gate should have been a mass of noisy running students heading for breakfast. In the eerie quiet, panic began to set in. Cole had to get out of this situation. There was no question he'd fail, and when he did, people would die. There had to be an escape. A tiny light glowed at the end of his dark tunnel. A solution. It was so simple he couldn't believe he hadn't thought of it already. It was also painful and the absolute truth.

He was unworthy of such a monumental task and he could prove it. Cole was suffering from PTSD complicated by severe criminal tendencies. That should shock the grin right off Allerton's face. Knowing the truth, there was no way they'd place five impressionable teenagers in his care. Someone else would have to do the job. He pushed the folders off the bed and dropped like a rock. Before his second bounce on the mattress came a knock at the door.

"Go away."

"It's Housemother Drummond. I have your breakfast, Cole."

"Damn," he groaned. He loved nothing about his life at Ariel's Gate, except Mrs. Drummond. He stood, tucked in his tee-shirt, pushed his hair back from his face, and opened the door.

She bustled in with a tray, set it on the table then stood, drew in a deep breath, and took a good long look at him. Her eyes roamed his frame. Her lips tightened then she sighed and gestured toward the chair. "When was the last time you ate, young man?"

Cole sat, but didn't lift the fork or even glance at the plate in front of him. "Mrs. Drummond, what the hell is going on here?"

She settled across from him and fingered his napkin. "Things have changed and we need you, my boy. You look so tired and thin. Please, eat."

Oh, he wanted to. With all his heart, he wanted to devour everything he smelled. Eggs fried in butter, the tangy scent of bacon, and the aroma of coffee called to him but he felt suddenly sick. There was only one real way out of his dilemma. Allerton would dismiss anything Cole told him, but if he made his confession to Mrs. Drummond, if he bared his soul to the woman who'd raised him from diapers, if he exposed himself to the only person he cared about, it might just turn the tide and get him and his Harley back on the road. Her deep-seated instinct to protect those kids would prevail and Allerton would have to release him from his vow. Whatever was happening to Ariel's Gate didn't matter. All that mattered was avoiding the assignment. Acclimate six kids? They were insane to imagine he could do such a thing.

"Are you all right, Cole?"

Her eyes showed concern but he couldn't melt to it, couldn't allow himself the satisfaction of sweet comfort and assurances that he was capable of anything. It was her M.O. and he wasn't the only inmate to fall prey. A few kind words from Housemother Drummond and a person believed they could do anything—pass a history exam, win the game, fly, survive… survive even Acclimation. He dropped his eyes to the plate and cleared his throat.

"Are you ill?"

"No. Listen… I can't do what he wants, you know."

"Yes, you can, Cole. I have faith—"

"I cannot do this."

"My dear boy, you can. You have accomplished amazing things!" She shifted closer in her chair and reached to lay her hands over his. "I know what you did in Afghanistan. All those men you saved. Cole, it was—"

"Stop!" he pulled his hands away and slammed them hard on the tabletop. The sound made her blink but nothing more, so he shouted as loud as he could. "You don't know anything!"

Her voice was steady and calm. "I know it's hard. I know a lot of soldiers who came home… different."

"Soldiers like me? Soldiers who started out… different?" He stood and glared down at her.

She sat, wordless.

He had no choice, he had to finish what he started. "I'm not what you think. Not who you think."

She blinked a silent *go on.*

"I've killed men." He held his breath.

"It was a war, Cole."

"Damn it." He started to pace. "You don't get it! I've been in so many jails I can't count them. I've robbed old ladies, stores, anything I wanted. Been a drunk, done drugs. I've had sex… crazy, raw, terrible sex… with married women… with old women, young women… women so young I can't imagine they're old enough to drive. I've run from everything. I've broken laws, I've—"

"Enough."

He took a breath, stopped pacing and looked at her. Was it finished? Could he get the hell away from the Gate forever this time?

"What does any of this have to do with our needs, Cole?"

"Huh?" He thumped down onto his chair. "I just told you. There's no way you should give me all this responsibility."

"Do you plan to rape the girls in your care?"

He gulped, bile burning up his throat. "Of course not!"

"Do you intend to go on a crime spree in the next thirty days? Dragging five innocent teenagers with you?"

"No."

"Then what are you telling me?"

Not a word could be formed.

"Cole Masters, you are what you are. You're dealing with your own existence. Everyone has a capacity for good and evil. You've done a lot of bad things, and that *greatly* disappoints me, but listen to yourself. Would you be so deeply aware of those things if you didn't already know they were wrong? Listing them only shines a light on the goodness in you."

"Oh man… stop, please. It doesn't matter. I can't do this. I don't want to do this."

"So," she stood and squared her shoulders. "Don't."

He stood too, wondering what new trick she had up her sleeve.

"Just… just… fucking leave." She turned and headed for the door.

Housemother Drummond said the 'F' word. He was seriously confused now. "Wait. I don't think I can just leave." He reached the door and gripped her arm. "I don't even know for sure if I want to."

"Then stop crying over it. You made a vow, young man. People are counting on you. Keep your precious indiscretions to yourself. Others won't see through that shit the way I do. No one, Cole… no one is more qualified for this responsibility than you. Accept that. Eat your breakfast and get some damn sleep." She huffed, turned away, then back to face him. "And forgive my colorful language. Few people have ever made me quite this… irritated." Her heels thudded all the way down the hall and around the bend before he closed the door.

"That went well," he groaned.

~*~

"I don't know whether to laugh or cry," Jenny said, looking around the library table at the rest of us. Her expression was wild and jittery, like a person who'd just won the lottery and couldn't believe it.

We had kind of won the lottery. Headmaster just left, but not before explaining a ton of things and handing out a mess of stuff none of us ever imagined we'd own. I fingered the newest model iPhone, a shiny laptop in its brightly colored pristine box, and best of all, the bank card with my own name on it.

"Let's review our great fortune, ladies and gents." Ryan gripped Jenny's fingers in one hand and the list Allerton left for us in the other. "Each of us has a full scholarship to the college of our choice. UCLA for me and Jen, no questions there. Sunshine, beaches, and I'm going to win the Heisman. Where are you going, Gracie? After all, you're the only other one here with the brains to get into a college."

Everyone laughed but I bit my lip. Of course, I had a college in mind. My whole life I imagined going to Radcliff, but that was like my dreams of a big beautiful wedding to a handsome groom. Neither was ever going to happen so why seriously think about it? Dreams are one thing. Plans are something else altogether. They were all still looking at me so I shrugged. "Radcliff."

"Lovely choice. What will be your major? Childcare?" Jenny had that mean edge in her voice, the one she used when she felt inferior.

"Maybe Special Ed. I don't know."

"Leave her be." Ben came to my aid with the wave of a hand. "She's got a little more time than the rest of us to decide. How cool is all this?"

Wally scratched his head so hard his hair crackled and rose. "Okay, so none of you think this is a little weird? Do you think every kid acclimating out of this place gets all this? Or maybe something's trying to kill us all and the old headmaster feels guilty 'cause he has to close the place down?"

"You're such a dumbass, Wally." Ryan leaned back and gave his best quarterback glare. "Just because your idiot buddy got himself dead doesn't mean we're all gonna die. The world can be good for the rest of us."

They talked on and on but I focused on the paper in my hand. It was strange that they'd make us live such limited lives then send us off with so much abundance. The bank card would be activated the day after my eighteenth birthday with a five-figure account ready and waiting to buy whatever I wanted. So odd. But the bank card wasn't the only card with my name on it. There was a gas card for a car I didn't own yet and had no license to drive, an American Express card, and another for medical coverage. And there was that super weird card we were only to use in a dire emergency. That was just a business card with a phone number. No name. No address.

"Bullshit!" Ryan shouted. The argument had escalated and Ben was on his feet. I looked around. There was no one else in the library, not even a librarian to tell us to be quiet. We were already on our own in some ways. No classes, no teachers, no homework. Just the scary future.

"We should really think this through," I mumbled.

"What? Quiet, the fair Gracie speaks."

"Shut up," I said with a hiss. Ryan was always doing that, making me feel like, well, what I am, plain as a green apple, boring, and a little less sweet than the other pretty apples in the orchard.

"Seriously, what were you saying?" Again, Ben to the rescue. It irritated and flattered me when he did that.

"I'm saying we should think this through. Ryan's right, but so is Wally.

Ariel's Gate is being closed down because of what happened to Tony Ibanescu. We don't know exactly what happened to him, but he's dead and now the Gate is closing after something like a million years. Those are things to think about. And," I raised my hand to stop the shouting, "Ryan is right, too. This is great stuff we just got… money, phones, computers, scholarships. And since we're all out of here so soon, what happens to this place really isn't our concern anymore." Now they were all cheering, so I raised my hand again. "But… I know I'm not the only one who feels like something bad is happening." I looked around the table. Joyous expressions went blank, eyes lowered, Ryan stopped fondling Jenny, and she stopped looking at him like he was God's gift.

Wally finally spoke. "I'm freaked out, big time."

"Well, yeah." Ryan shuffled in his seat and pushed back his hair. "Your friend got killed. That would freak anyone out."

"No, man. It's more than that. I feel like something super bad is out there. That's why they're sending us all away so quickly."

Ben and I shared a glance. There was something out there. I could feel it, too.

"Maybe we can get the headmaster to let us stay in the building, at least until we're acclimated?" That brilliant suggestion came from Jenny.

"Don't you get it?" Wally rubbed his eyes. "Whatever's out there," he pointed to the window, "wants to get us. How would sticking around in this empty building protect us? UCLA? Like that's gonna happen. All you're smart enough to be is the jock's convenient fuck buddy and—"

"Hey!" several of us shouted.

"Okay, sorry… sorry, Jen." He opened his hands in apology. "But hiding in here is not the answer."

We were quiet for a while, fingering the dubious treasures on the table.

"You know," Ben finally said, "Allerton's no idiot. If we're leaving, he won't be sending us off alone. Maybe he's going with us."

"Well, *that's* not a fun prospect." Jenny flipped her hair, embarrassment still painting her expression. She'd actually slid a few inches away from Ryan after Wally's remark. "I'm tired of being watched like a prison inmate."

"Someone will be going with us." I gathered up my new toys and packed them all in my backpack. "We go, we do as we're told, we get acclimated and… well… then we start our lives." I looked down at the skeptical faces. "At least that's what I'm going to do."

I left the library. All the way down the hall, down the steps, out of the building and to the football field. When I reached the huge tree just inside the high brick walls—the tree where the Archangel Gabriel's name was carved decades ago—I threw the backpack down and crumbled into a heap. I'd never been so afraid in my life, but I did stop crying long enough to check that the phone and computer weren't damaged. They were way too valuable to drag around in a back-pack and wouldn't even be activated for another month. Still, they were beautiful and mine. The coolest things I ever owned.

The leaves above me had begun to turn gold and red, flashing and danc-ing when a warm breeze rushed by. Soon it would be winter. Where would I be when the first snow fell? I couldn't help but shiver at the thought that something wanted to kill me. Me? Why? Nobody should die before they even get a chance to live, right? I wanted to pray but only a few words came to me. Is God here for me… or am I here for God?

What did those words mean, and why had other students and teachers at Ariel's Gate pondered them? Carved them in closets and secret rooms? Some-times the words felt so cryptic I believed it was a riddle with no answer. Other times it made perfect sense. Was the universe a symbiotic relationship? A matter of equilibrium and disparity in the search for clarity? What clarity? My brain, usu-ally running on all cylinders, seemed to screech to a halt every time I tried to think it through. Besides, it didn't matter right now. All that mattered was to get away from whatever bad thing was coming to get me. I glanced up at the Gabriel carv-ing. "Any suggestions?" He was silent as usual, like all his cohorts at Ariel's Gate.

The fourth period bell rang. Odd, there were no students there but us.

I hiked the heavy backpack onto my shoulder, looked toward the gym and wondered. What kind of training would I learn that was going to help if my life was really in danger? The ancient Samurai learned how to die well. Was I about to become one of those?

4

A few hours of sleep had altered his attitude so Cole's point of view was a little less dark and volatile. The time had come to see what was what, so that he could explore the possibilities of succeeding with this fiasco. He'd never had real responsibilities, never been a leader in the Marines. He only waited for orders and did what he was told, just like living at the Gate, except for once, just once.

It was a long hike to the gym from the teacher's quarters all the way to the other side of the massive building, but he did his best to focus on the twists and turns of Ariel's Gate rather than what lay ahead. How did his simple life get so complicated? One damn choice. A vow. If he followed through adequately and safely acclimated five kids, if he got them through it all without death or damage, he could be proud. If it went badly, he could always fall back on the truth. The judge was right. At just twenty-one he was a failure, pure and simple. Men his age were earning degrees, playing professional baseball, working at jobs, saving for a future, maybe even starting families. How had he missed the boat by such a wide margin? Oh right, Acclimation. That's how.

His brain felt like the television screen at a sports bar, split, one side showing Team Acclimate, and the other screen showing Team Cole robbing a storage cubicle in Spearfish, South Dakota. The reality was confusing but clear as a bell. He was neither, he was both. Reaching for the gym door, he stopped, rushed outside and puked into the bushes. "Yeah, that's better," he grumbled and wiped his mouth, then a thought washed over him with a shivering chill.

Those kids had to be totally freaked out, and that could present scenarios even his Marine training might not be able to overcome. There's unpredictability with scared teenagers. He knew that for a fact because he still lived it every day. The kids waiting for him in the gym had an extra few layers of anxiety. Two days ago, a student was murdered. He and Allerton knew exactly what killed him, and it definitely wasn't an animal. If a dead fellow student wasn't terrifying enough, everything those kids believed to be solid was about to vanish. Ariel's Gate was just an orphanage, but it was the only home they'd ever known. For it to simply stop existing was kind of like their past disappearing, too. He felt a deep kinship with them, but that also made him uneasy. He couldn't show weakness. He was only a few years older, and they had to trust and respect him because the next thirty-odd days were critical to both his and their survival.

One more gag, a clearing of his throat, and he reached for the door, hoping he could tap into the Team Acclimate side of his reality and hold the line for the duration. It was only a month. He could do that. He'd survived Camp Pendleton, survived boot camp, survived Afghanistan, survived everything that came after. Granted he wasn't trying to survive. Truth be told, he kind of hoped he wouldn't. All in all, he knew he could do whatever was necessary, and getting oneself dead is nowhere near as easy as people think. He ran a hand through his hair, over his clean-shaven face, down his thumping chest, and he drew in a long cleansing breath. Strong. He wanted them to think he was strong. Beyond that, they'd all have to play it by ear.

The gym smelled the same, looked the same, too, except for the banner hanging on the west wall. *Go Warriors*, it boasted in bright yellow paint. No more Warriors, no more Ariel's Gate basketball or football. Too bad. He walked toward the visitor bleachers where Allerton stood speaking to the five facing Acclimation. There he was, all official in his shirt and tie, jacket opened, looking like a Wall Street executive. Cole waited several paces behind, listening to the speech he recalled, almost verbatim.

"This is what you've been waiting for… what we've all been waiting for… your opportunity to fly from the nest and live the lives you deserve." Allerton paced, taking a moment to look into each kid's eyes. "Now, as you know, we don't have graduation or commencement ceremonies here at Ariel's Gate. The focus is reaching your eighteenth year. You have all passed every state and national high school requirement. Officially, you have already graduated from high school… however… we have a responsibility to also acclimate you before letting you loose on the world. Ariel's Gate is a closed environment, we recognize that, and there are things you need to understand before you leave." Allerton cleared his throat and paced slowly in front of the quiet, attentive kids.

Cole observed. Maybe it wouldn't be so bad. If they were that well behaved, they might just do as they're told and things might go fine and dandy. It would sure be a bonus. That's where the remembered speech changed.

"Usually," the headmaster continued, "I do this differently… one on one. I'd take each of you to my office a few days before your eighteenth birthday and together we would explore your future. Talk about your quality and your value. We have no time for such pleasures… such farewells. Forgive me for this lapse in tradition… and know that each of you is held in my heart with deep love and respect. You all have potential… every one of you. You will step from your Acclimation and into a world you have the power to change, to improve, to expand beyond your dreams."

Allerton suddenly turned away, pressed thumb and fingers against his eyes and took a deep breath. Before returning his attention to the kids, he noticed Cole and nodded.

"There is another lapse in our grand old traditions," he continued. "Until now, each student approaching their eighteenth birthday was handed into the care of a guide, hand chosen specifically for them. Together they would leave Ariel's

Gate for Acclimation training. Today… with all that's happening… we cannot do that. I do have for you an exceptional guide who will train each and every one of you before sending you on your way."

He reached out his hand and Cole stepped forward. "This is Mr. Masters… acclimated out of Ariel's Gate, and a former U.S. Marine. He is your guide, your protector, your advisor, and your direct superior until you are acclimated and free to leave his care. Is that understood?"

Several but not all heads nodded acceptance. The others just stared at Cole. He took the folder Allerton handed over and flipped it open. "When I call your name," he said without looking up, "step forward along this foul line. Ryan Sutcliff."

The boy was so like himself at eighteen. Football team hero, well built, strong. He could do well.

"Wallace Dean," he called.

Slowly and with practiced belligerence the kid stood, tilted his head, and glared. "Marine, huh? I don't believe in that shit."

Cole's eyes swiveled to Allerton who coughed to hide his grin. This one too was like Cole, so much so, he could be looking in a mirror. Was he really that much of a dichotomy? Hero and villain? Something to ponder at another time, thirty-some days in the future, but not now.

"Quiet, Mr. Dean. You'll find yourself believing in a lot of new shit." Eyeing the list again he looked up. "Benjamin Wheeler."

A little wimpy, but he seemed sure and steady enough. Wheeler didn't glow with self-importance or fevered contempt and rebellion. He might be a good ally if needed. So far so good.

Cole made the mistake of checking out the girls before calling their names. Which was the beauty contestant and which was the pretty bookworm? "Jennifer Perkins."

The princess stood and she was stunning, a lovely chocolate-skinned girl with delicate black ringlets circling her face and tumbling down over one shoulder.

Her eyes sparkled then one actually winked. This gal could prove to be a handful.

"Glad to meet you, Mr. Masters," she said with a voice that could melt butter. She sidled close to Sutcliff and made her silent declaration. Either she was telling Cole she belonged to the quarterback, or that she would only follow one leader. "Stand where you were, Perkins. Beside Wheeler."

She blinked but followed his order, a little girl lost expression on that pretty face. Damn Ariel's Gate for that. Those poor kids believed that the actors on television reflected real human behavior. Each one of them was a caricature. He still hadn't fully figured out how to maneuver in the real world himself. Maybe he could help with that during their time with him. He put it on his growing mental agenda.

"Gracious Caine," he called, as though she wasn't the only kid still sitting on the bleachers. Her eyes were a lovely golden green, her hair, rich auburn, simple and flowing to her shoulders. That face could catch anyone's heart. Maybe even his if he wasn't careful. He swallowed hard, cleared his throat, and pointed to the foul line. "Up here, Miss Caine." She stood and hobbled into line. His eyes couldn't return to her lovely face. He couldn't think about how he'd help this ragamuffin fit into life outside the Gate. All he could see was her mangled foot, twisted inward but holding her still and sturdy.

He turned on a heel and grunted as he passed the headmaster. "Allerton, your office. Now."

"Hey, Mister Marine! What are we supposed to do?" shouted rebellious Wally.

Cole turned a glare. "Don't care. Be here at four, sharp. Bring everything you plan to take with you. If you're late you will be—"

"Mr. Masters," warned Allerton.

Cole charged out of the gym, ready to uproot a tree or flatten the headmaster into the ground, whichever opportunity presented itself first. Swinging around with fisted hands he growled like a dog before forming words. "What the hell is wrong with you?"

"Follow me." Un-rattled, Allerton led him around the building to the garages.

~*~

"What the… that's the guy who's going to acclimate us? He acclimated, what, fifteen minutes ago? I'm outta here." Wally hissed, grabbed his backpack with the swing of his arm, and headed for the door. Ryan tackled him to the floor with a loud thump. "Ow! What the hell?"

"Use your head. It's the only safe way out of this place! Masters was a Marine, he can protect us."

"Don't care." Wally grunted and pushed at Ryan's superior weight and strength. "I don't like that guy. I don't trust him!"

I sat on the bleacher and looked at my foot. I never think about it. No one at the Gate ever even looked at it anymore. It's just my foot. I realized for the first time that Mr. Masters' reaction was going to be everyone's reaction to me. For the first time I grasped the fact that outside of Ariel's Gate, I am handicapped, and different, and suddenly not so happy about it.

Ben sat close and hugged me. "Ignore them. I'm with you. Let's just do what we're told and get on with life when they set us free."

His eyes were sincere. Too bad he had no idea what I was thinking. We were going to be free out in the big world. Free? Free to do what? Be looked at like a twisted monster? Who was ever going to love me? Who wants to hang out with a gimp? A cripple? I tucked my foot under the bleacher and looked away.

"Nobody cares, Gracie," he whispered.

"Everyone will care. Masters cares. What if he won't take me? What if…"

Ryan and Wally rolled on the gym floor and Jenny checked her manicure.

"What if he leaves me behind?"

"I won't let him!" Ben shouted and all eyes turned to us. He glared at the wrestlers. "Did you see how that guy reacted to Gracie? Are we going to let him do that?"

Wally scrambled out from under his attacker and stood. At first, he seemed confused then his expression changed and he nodded. "That guy doesn't know anything. You're fine. We'll straighten him out." He glanced toward Ryan, visibly relaxing when he received the nod of agreement.

"Don't worry about him." Ryan brushed off his leg.

"What if he won't take me?" I almost gasped. "If we're really in danger… what if he thinks I can't keep up? What if I *can't* keep up?" I looked around at them. Except for Ben, I'd never had a serious conversation with these people, yet there we were, contemplating our survival together. The silence was heavy and I figured I was going to be on my own, wondering if there were any weapons at all—with instruction manuals—somewhere in Ariel's Gate that I could take with me when I left. Alone.

"Hey," Ryan said with the assuring grunt of a leader. "We're a team, we stick together. We don't go without Gracie."

Jenny's mouth opened but she didn't protest.

"Say it," demanded the quarterback. "Say it!"

"We don't go without Gracie," they shouted to the ceiling and Ryan pulled me into the huddle, all hands in the middle. "Survival on three! One… two… three! Survival!"

The shout rumbled in my chest but it didn't really register until Jenny reached across and squeezed my arm. "We don't go without you."

It was a nice moment but felt like a scene from a slasher movie. I would end up alone, sure as the leaves outside would fall off the trees. I was the last to be acclimated. They'd all be gone and I'd be alone. I'd always been sort of alone. No big news there. It felt daunting, especially since I was now faced with the handicap I'd imagined wasn't there for so long. On the bright side, at least Ben was with me.

~*~

He followed Allerton to the garages outside the entry gate. Cole was so agitated that he wasn't sure he heard them at first.

Masters. It sounded like rattling chains. *Cole Masters. You know where you belong. Bring the old one with you and come join us.*

He stopped dead and glared into the trees lining the long drive. His knees softened and fists tightened, ready to attack before he could take his next breath.

"Yes, they're out there. Ignore them. We've got a lot to go over before you leave in the morning." Allerton opened the garage door and waved Cole inside.

The space was huge and empty except for a large van, the kind that carries travelers to and from airport terminals. Gun metal grey, darkened windows, nicely discreet, and polished to a sparkling shine. It had more than enough comfortable space for five passengers, a driver, and some luggage. As his heart rate lowered to normal, it wasn't the van but the emptiness of the garage that sparked his curiosity. "Where are all the mowers? All the stuff the groundskeepers use?"

"Sold. Everything will be sold and gone in the next twenty-four hours. Now, about this vehicle—"

"Na-uh. Don't go changing the subject. Listen to me, Allerton. I can't take the Caine girl. You're going to have to handle her yourself."

Allerton rolled his neck, visibly controlling his frustration, but the tension in his jaw didn't intimidate Cole. He squared his shoulders, stood his ground, and waited. When the man didn't respond, he huffed and repeated. "I'm not taking her."

"You have to."

"Why not you? You've got that whole *promise and value* speech going for you. Use it on her and acclimate her. I can't deal with a gimp, man. This is way too dangerous. I cannot protect five kids if one of them is—"

"You protected fifteen Marines, six already severely wounded."

Cole nearly choked back a bitter laugh. "Trust me, the enemy was nothing like what we're facing out there!" He swung a hand toward the door. He swallowed back the next words, the ones admitting that he was terrified of failing, that the handicapped girl added too much risk.

Allerton walked to the back of the van and opened the storage door. "I've stocked you as well as possible. Two rifles, a few pistols. Ammunition. An old friend—also a Marine—shipped them… they just arrived this morning. He says, according to your records, you're prolific with these weapons… including the Glock hidden in your room. This should be enough."

Cole nodded, wordless.

Slamming the door closed, Allerton cleared his throat and avoided making eye contact. "Deeper in the storage compartment are the soul swords."

Oh hell. The last thing Cole cared to address were soul swords. Was his blade in the van, too? He'd sent it to Ariel's Gate for safe keeping after Afghanistan. Of course, it was there. He could feel its presence, but that wasn't the biggest concern. "Yeah this is good, now about the Caine girl."

"Cole, there's no time to fuck around here. You need to protect and acclimate Gracie Caine. She's very precious… very important. This isn't open for negotiation."

"If she's so important, you deal with her."

"She's extremely important. Cole, she's the reason I brought you back. She represents the vow you need to fulfill."

"Huh?" Cole's mind came to a screeching halt. "So why the others?"

"You may need their help."

"Like they'd want to." He snorted and kicked at the tire. "Those kids are going to run so far after—"

"Maybe, maybe not. I'm banking on a few good souls in the bunch."

"And you're banking on my life and theirs."

"Yes."

"What's so special about her?"

"You'll know when you witness her Acclimation… it will all be revealed."

Cole paced in a circle, fists tight, breathing hard. "I do not want to do this."

"And?"

Cole faced Allerton, tears burning his eyes. "I don't want to do this, but you damn well know I will. You're a real bastard, you know that?"

"I can live with that."

"Why can't you help me with this one? Just with Gracie? Can't you do this whole thing with me? Just to make sure I don't completely fuck it up?"

Allerton laid a hand on Cole's shoulder. "I wish I could. This place must be completely dismantled. I have reports to make and people to answer to. And… there's a new development…"

"What?"

"Something's missing. Something I'm hoping is in the hands of one of your five kids. That's either a good thing, or close to the end of everything."

"What is it? I'll find it when I inspect their kits."

Allerton chuckled. "You know how resourceful teenagers can be. Don't expect to find it in your inspection, but watch for it to turn up. It's a book."

"Okay, what kind of book?"

"The kind that should have never been in Ariel's Gate. The kind that warned me of this whole shit storm. Keep an eye out. If it shows up, let me know and I'll explain how to destroy it." The man huffed away his bottled anger, then unfolded a large map onto the empty worktable. "For now, we need to locate a safe place for you to take them."

They examined a vast area beyond Ariel's Gate, south to Florida, west as far as the Mississippi, north to the Canadian border, and east to the Atlantic coast. Allerton's finger circled then stopped at specific points on the map. "Ley lines," he explained. "Locations infused with magnetic, mystical, and spiritual activity… some from Colonial Euro-Christian activities, most from Native American aboriginal practices. Anywhere circled with these ley lines will be the safest… sucking the energy from the enemy so that you can be stronger."

Cole eyed the map, examining the complex lacework of powerful ley lines across the entire area displayed. "Ariel's Gate is completely circled by these lines, man. What are they doing just outside the courtyard wall? And how did they get to that kid… the one who died?"

"Tonight, I'll share what I know about their proximity. As for the murder, I have a few theories. Tony Ibanescu might have wandered too far from the center of Ariel's Gate where his soul sword is held… he could have been carrying no protection—"

"Protection?"

"Amber. Like the amber you carry in your pocket."

Cole felt his face heat. Carrying a tiny chip of amber was the singular superstitious habit he'd held on to after Acclimation. A lucky charm. Allerton huffed and dug into his own pocket, displaying a similar golden chunk of fossilized tree resin in his palm, along with a few coins.

"We all carry it. It helps. Young Ibanescu might have lost or tossed it out." Unrolling another, more detailed map, Allerton added, "Then there's my other theory."

Cole's attention focused on Allerton's eyes, so intense they could have burned a hole into the map. "You waiting for me to guess?"

"Ibanescu might have flat out refused to follow the enemy, leading to his death. Or… he might have blindly agreed, not knowing what he was joining. Changing his mind would have brought the same result."

Cole gulped and tried to shrug off the chill that ran up his spine. "Why the hell would he do that?"

"You remember well enough. The hunger to get out of here. They're reaching for what they think is freedom." He slowly shook his head. "Listen, Cole. They're kids. They don't know what you know. Be prepared for anything. Be gentle… it'll go a lot further than shouting at them."

Every word locked tight in Cole's mind, but he grinned anyway. "Holy hell, have you gone soft?"

"Here," Allerton pointed. "This may be the best location."

Cole leaned in. The Blue Ridge Mountains. Minimal population, remote, webbed with ley lines, and speckled with hunting and fishing cabins.

"There's a small inn, closed for the season. No high-tech security. Easy to get in through the kitchen door." He handed Cole a silly brochure.

"You're sure?"

Allerton nodded. "We often use it for fall and winter Acclimations."

Cole drew in a long deep breath. He was really doing this, really taking on responsibility for the crippled girl, and really going to acclimate five unsuspecting kids. If he had to do it, the comfort of a nice fancy inn seemed only fair. "Fine, the Goodwin Summer Inn it is."

5

reat. We had two whole hours to kill. Ryan and Wally collected their duffels then came back to the gym to play basketball. Typical guys. One minute they're killing each other, the next, dribbling and shooting baskets.

Without Ryan glued to her side, Jenny seemed lost. I found her at Gabriel's tree, sitting with her too many bags and riffling through them, tucking things tighter in an attempt to make it all fit. Did she really think she could take all that stuff? Mr. Masters didn't seem the type to find mascara, sixteen pairs of stilettos, and mass quantities of colorful trinkets important.

Usually I'd just go somewhere else, but I sat in the grass across from her and fingered the costume jewelry in a plastic bag. Expecting her to snag it from my hands, I set it exactly where it was.

"Take something if you like it, Gracie."

I blinked. There was nothing I liked in the bag, but I felt compelled to open it and look closer. There was a thin silver chain with a small honey colored translucent heart pendant. I could wear it and hide it under my tee-shirt, that way she'd think I loved it, and I could keep my Plain Jane persona. "This one?" I asked and she nodded without even looking.

Tears glazed her eyes and she gave a sad sigh. She'd rolled all her fabric pretties—silky scarves, textured tights, short nighties, and panties so tiny they looked like sling shots. She was desperate to fit everything into her duffel but it was impossible. She pushed back her hair and tried again. Her eyes finally met mine. "Can you fit some of this into your bag for me?"

"Ah… I don't know. But hey, don't worry if you can't take it all. You can always buy new stuff after—"

"After?" she snapped. "I know I can buy stuff… *after*. I'm worried about between now and then. Ryan only knows me like this." Her hands swept down her body. "He likes me pretty. I need this stuff or…"

I leaned back on outstretched arms and blinked. "Are you saying he wouldn't like you if you didn't decorate yourself for a few weeks?" The minute the words came out of my mouth I knew it was the wrong thing to say. I actually scooted back in case she lashed out with her polished nails.

Instead she just gathered her things and stood with a glare. "How could I think you'd understand?" She grunted under the weight of her cherished possessions and stomped off.

I fingered the little heart dangling around my neck. When I'd first arrived at the Gate, I slept in a bed next to Jenny in the nursery. We have always been either in close proximity or roommates. We had nothing in common at all. I'm tall and skinny, while Jenny developed just like a Barbie Doll. Hips, boobs, curvy calves. She looked great in her gym uniform or wearing jeans and cowboy boots. Then there's me. A girl who never really got the robust girl parts to show off. Was that why I liked being plain and in the background? Did Housemother Drummond put me and Jenny together hoping I'd learn a little style and a few makeup skills? The idea angered me way more than it should have, and for a moment I felt rage that made me tremble.

I was mad about everything, so why not target the housemother? I wanted to know if it was true. I wanted to confront Mrs. Drummond face to face and demand an answer to why I'm not good enough as I am. I stood and gripped the silly chain around my neck with full intentions of tearing it free and tossing it as far over the wall as I could, then I realized I just couldn't do it. Jenny owned the silly necklace. She loved everything she owned so much that she was trying to make sure she could take it all with her. I couldn't treat it like a piece of trash. It was a gift—granted a gift given without much enthusiasm, but a gift all the same. No one had ever given me a gift before.

Is God here for you or are you here for God?

I blinked and turned to the high stone wall, so shaken by the strange voice and the words that I had to reach out to balance myself against Gabriel's tree. "What?" I said.

Nothing.

"Did someone say something?" I actually looked at the carving in the stripped bark near my fingertips.

Nothing.

"That's it!" I slapped my thighs in frustration. "I'm totally losing it!" All the speculation and fear, missed sleep and confusion was getting to me. "I'm way too young for this kind of crap." I stomped toward the gym, maybe because I felt there was safety in numbers, or maybe because I was tired of being inside my own head. Either way, it was time to be a person of action and not just a worry wart, imagining the worst.

Sitting on the bleacher bench, my mind followed my intentions like a charm. Just maybe the housemother wanted me to rub off on self-focused Jenny. Maybe Jenny and I were roommates because our Acclimation dates were so close. Ben said that's how they recorded our entrance into the Gate in the catacomb record books. They might have lumped us together so they wouldn't forget who was leaving when. It's a big, crowded place—well, at least it used to be.

I thought about all the things that had been freaking me out and making me so mad. There was no way Masters wasn't going to take me with the others. It was his job. I wasn't going to be left behind. And finally, I was going to be acclimated in thirty-one days, and I was going to be damn happy about it. I opened my journal and started a list of things I'd need for college.

~*~

Just as the warm afternoon clouded and became cooler, Cole inspected his troops. They were his troops, not his future buddies, not just a bunch of teenagers. They were all in this together, and even though he couldn't explain the specific dangers that threatened, he could at least protect them by making them ready. He'd abandoned the original acclimate-and-run strategy. A new sharpness vibrated in Cole's soul. It demanded the best of himself, with respect for his checkered past, and focus for the outcome he needed. There had been a terrible lapse in honor and effort since Afghanistan, but he'd re-grown enough backbone to do this thing. He could feel it tensing and tightening in his shoulders and along the back of his ribs. The strength he'd need would not fail him. At least he knew, really knew, he would do his best.

The kids had settled in different areas of the gym, their duffels emptied and displayed for him to inspect. Surprisingly the princess had positioned herself all the way across the basketball court from her quarterback. She looked a little sad, too, and Cole wondered what emotional dynamics might be coming on the journey with them. He went directly to Sutcliff and crouched in front of him.

"What's going on? Problems in the love department?"

Sutcliff blinked, glanced toward his girl then shrugged. "Maybe girl stuff. But hey, we all want to make sure we're taking Gracie with us."

"Why the hell wouldn't she be going with us?" Cole's eyes dropped and he fingered the stack of pure white tee-shirts and socks on the floor. "This looks good, but it's a little much. We'll be traveling light." He counted three tee-shirts, three pairs of boxers, two pairs of jeans, a pair of tennis shoes, a pair of leather hiking boots, and six pairs of socks. Tossing the extra items into a pile behind him, he then turned to the boy's personal items. A small shaving bag, deodorant, toothbrush, as expected. He lifted a copy of *Penthouse*, gave a glare that sufficiently embarrassed the boy, then playfully tucked the magazine into his own back pock-et. "Any books?"

"Uh, no. Just this stuff Headmaster gave us." He nudged his chin toward the stack of items.

Cole nodded. Still, he knew there were things not displayed. "No drugs?"

"Fuck no."

"Alcohol?"

"Nope."

"Weapons of any kind?"

Sutcliff snorted. "Just these." He raised his fists with a menacing expres-sion.

"Don't go postal on me, man. I have to ask. Anything else you plan to take that isn't here in front of me?"

"Just this," he said in a hush, pulling out and opening his wallet to display a nice stash of condoms.

Cole didn't respond. Where the hell did he get condoms in Ariel's Gate?

"Hey," Sutcliff leaned in and spoke quietly, making Cole stiffen like a board.

"What?"

"You're… Cole Masters? *Cole* Masters? Right?"

Cole swallowed and blinked. "So?"

"Man!" The kid grinned, still whispering like this was a big secret or some-thing. "You're a damn football legend around here! I almost broke your record last year. Thirty-one complete touchdown passes!" Sutcliff was damn near giddy.

"So?" Cole glowered. What did it matter? But he had to admit, his gut roiled a little at almost losing that record.

The kid shrugged. "Just wanted you to know I recognize you. These other nerds and incorrigibles might not know who you are, but I do."

"You know nothing." Time to move on.

His next stop was Gracie Caine—best to get this one done quickly to eliminate fears of leaving her behind. She was perfectly packed, but short on tee-shirts, which he pulled from Sutcliff's overage pile for her. She also had way too many books. He examined each one closely, flipping through the pages and shaking them upside down. Allerton wasn't clear about what his missing book looked like, but Cole would have bet money it wasn't on the girl. These were all school books.

"Caine, you don't need these and there's no reason to take them." He pushed them aside and looked into her golden green eyes, deep and thoughtful but laced with a little fear and anger. Naturally, she had reason to fear. She was physically limited, but he wasn't about to acknowledge a handicap. She needed to believe that he expected the same from her as he did from the others.

"Do you have any drugs on you?"

"What? No."

"Alcohol?"

"Nope."

"Anything else not right here in front of me?"

"This." She tugged a delicate chain around her neck to display an amber heart, giving him a sense of relief. The more amber on this girl, the better.

"Any other personal items?"

"Just my journal." She carefully repacked the duffel.

"Give it here," he held out his hand. Her eyes glowed but she handed it over. It was a small book. A quick flip through showed tight handwriting, most likely the kind of girl stuff he really didn't want to read anyway. He gave it back and leaned closer, understanding that a journal was a pretty private thing. "No problem. It's pretty small. Is that it?"

"Yes, that's it."

He wanted so much to be kind to Gracie Caine, considering his narrow understanding of her physical limitations and what the future held for her. But kindness was likely to breed dependency and he needed each of them strong and secure. He'd rather them fight with him, than run and hide behind him. "You can bring a few personal things, Caine." The words came out rough and a bit critical.

She blinked. "I don't have any other personal things."

"Okay," he mumbled, thrilled to move on to the remaining two boys. He reshuffled the overage and shortage of clothing, asked the questions, and strongly suspected the Dean boy of taking Allerton's book. He'd need to keep a close eye on that one.

When he crouched in front of Jennifer Perkins' massive pile of crap, his heart shook a little. He finally sat and fingered through it all, pushing everything peripheral aside. "Perkins, you can take something from one of these piles… one thing, no more."

"But—"

"There are no exceptions. This is temporary. You can buy anything you want after your Acclimation. Or maybe Allerton can put it all in storage somewhere for you to get later. You just can't take it all."

Tears rolled down her pretty face, making him way more uncomfortable than expected.

"Sorry. Pick."

He watched her struggle between plastic bags of cheap jewelry, a pile of pretty blouses, and a small cosmetic bag. Her hand hovered over one, then another, then back. This was difficult for her but it would make her stronger. He wanted the beauty queen tough, not primped and pampered for a photo shoot.

"Today, Perkins."

She snapped up the jewelry and glared. Just as he was about to tell her to pack up, the Caine girl reached over his shoulder and took the cosmetics bag.

"There," she said with a growl. "Now I have something personal." Her expression dared him to refuse her and he almost laughed.

"Okay, everyone, 7:00 A.M. in Allerton's office tomorrow morning. Get some sleep and be well rested. We drive out of here at eight."

He loaded all the extra stuff into a big brown garbage bag and walked out, dragging it behind like a dead body.

~*~

"Man, I really, *really*, hate that guy," Wally said, leaning back against the bleachers and staring up at the ceiling. "What do you say we all get outta here? Go to town and maybe get some pizza?"

"How? Allerton's already sold or sent away all the school buses, and there are no cars around to hotwire." Ryan looked directly at Wally. "I assume you can hotwire a car, right?"

"Shut up."

I was so tired of listening to people fight. With a huff—something I seemed to do a lot lately—I handed Jenny the cosmetics bag. "Maybe you want to trade? I'll carry the bobbles and you carry this?"

Jenny's eyes were all glassy like she was going to cry.

"Hey, it's no big deal. I had room, that's all. You can carry both if you want, I'm just afraid the General's going to have more inspections."

"The General?" Ben laughed. "Perfect."

"Maybe we can call him General Ass Hole," Wally added.

"At your own risk. Doesn't matter." Ryan stood, gathered his duffel and Jenny, then turned for the door. "It's all temporary. We'll all be done with him the minute we acclimate."

Wally ran to follow. "So, what about pizza?"

"No one's getting a pizza tonight," I said with authority I sure as hell didn't have. "We're eating whatever they give us in the cafeteria."

"You're no fun, Gracie Caine." Wally grinned then rushed out the door, leaving Ben and me alone.

The gym was creepy quiet, so much like a church that Ben actually whispered. "He knows the book's missing."

"Masters?" I'd forgotten about the book. Dropping my duffel, I paced in front of him then stopped, realizing that my pace didn't look like anyone else's. It was more like a hobble. Like the Hunchback of Notre Dame bumbling back and forth. "Put the book back."

"No. I know it's important. I just *know*."

"Maybe it's only making things more dangerous? Have you ever thought of that? That stupid book might be bringing bad stuff to us."

"It's not." His hand took mine and squeezed. "It's important, and you're going to help me figure out what that writing means."

I gave another huff. Holding his hand made my mind mix and mash everything together. "Okay… for now. If things get hairy, I'm telling Masters—"

"You mean General Ass Hole."

"No screwing around!" I pulled my hand free. "Am I the only one who sees how bad this might all be?"

"Maybe… but Gracie, we need all the help we can get. Yeah, I know Masters is here to help us, but we only need him until we acclimate. After that, the book might give us a way to see what's ahead. Or maybe it'll give us some insight into the past, why the Gate's like this, why it's closing down. Either way, it was important enough for someone to hide in that secret room. It's significant, I'm sure of it."

"I'm leaving." I walked away but he easily caught up before I reached the door.

"You go nowhere without me, girl. We've been friends for way too long. Let's just sit tight about the book. See how things go, okay?"

I shrugged then held my duffel over my head. It was pouring icy cold rain and we had a long run to the main building. We splashed through muddy puddles, slithered along the structure where the roof overhang protected us, then made a run for the courtyard. As we skirted the big shrubs near the entry steps, I heard something that stopped me in my tracks—something like a screaming animal, something in terror, something in pain. Ben and I stood still as stone, stared out at the opened courtyard gates and listened with all our might. The sound was so terrifying I swear I almost peed my pants.

There it was again, and I could sense Ben poising to run out there to see what was going on. Heart pounding, I reached to grip his arm but before he made a move, Masters raced past us like a speeding train. The rain in my eyes made him seem almost translucent, moving faster than I could focus.

I screamed. Ben gasped. And Masters charged back into the courtyard with Wally over his shoulder. Blood ran down Wally's arm into the splattering puddles.

"Put me down, damn it!"

"He's alive," Ben joked with a shaking voice.

I ran behind them all the way to the nurse's office.

"Go to your rooms!" Masters shouted as Housemother closed the door on us. But I saw it, deep gashes along Wally's arm and side, gushing blood while he gasped and cried out.

I turned to Ben. Rain dripped down our soaked clothes, making the floor at our feet slippery. For a moment I was determined to stay right there, rooted to the spot. Then I had a better plan. I turned and ran as fast as I could.

"Where are we going?" Ben was breathless, too.

"We need to tell Ryan and Jenny."

"Tell them what? About Wally?"

I slipped and thumped onto the hardwood floor at a tight turn in the hallway. Scrambling to my feet I kept moving like the troops of Armageddon were pounding on the door. "About Wally... *and* about the book."

Ben gripped my arm so tight I slammed back against him just outside Ryan's dorm room door. "I'm thinking that's not such a good idea."

"They need to know what happened!"

He leaned against the door, blocking the doorknob.

"They have to know about the book!" I was trying to shout but my throat was raw from screaming so much.

"This is not a good idea, Gracie."

I'm not super strong, but I'm not the weakest girl at the Gate. I was so mad I pushed as hard as I could, and when Ben hit the floor I wanted to laugh. Instead I turned the knob, gasped, slammed the door shut and covered my mouth, trying to blink away the vast amount of nakedness I'd just witnessed. "Uh—"

"Yeah," Ben climbed to his feet. "Like I said… not a good idea."

"What the…" The door opened. Ryan was thankfully covered with a towel. "Damn it! Don't you know not to just—"

"Wally's been attacked," I said, determined to hide my embarrassment. "He's in the nurse's office… bleeding!"

Ryan looked to Ben who nodded dumbly.

"Okay, okay. You had to let us know. Good. Give me a minute and we'll meet you at the nurse's office."

"They won't let us in," I explained, still unable to look into his face. "Is he…"

"He's alive," Ben pushed a hand through his wet hair and looked around. "Listen, why don't we meet in Makha'el's Hall?"

"Why there?" Jenny called, rushing around behind Ryan.

"No one will expect us to be there. It'll be a good place to talk," I answered.

"And," Ben added then cleared his throat, "there's something you guys have to see in there."

~*~

We waited less than ten minutes for them. Ryan looked like he was about to quarterback the Super Bowl and Jenny looked just plain terrified. The lights would be on for only another half hour, and if we wanted dinner, we had to be at the cafeteria in forty-five minutes. Nothing like trying to solve the problems of the whole world in the blink of an eye.

"Okay," Ben started. "I talk, you guys listen, okay?"

Heads nodded.

"Wally was outside the courtyard gates and screaming bloody murder when we got to the main building."

"What on earth was he doing out there?" Jenny's voice squeaked.

"No clue, don't care. Probably smoking. When we heard him screaming, Masters came out like Superman and carried him in. Wally has big cuts down his arm and ribs, lots of blood. This could be what killed Tony."

Ryan nodded. "So, are we still leaving in the morning?"

"No idea."

Ben led us to the back of the hall and I took a moment to look up and say a little prayer, asking Makha'el to protect us. The answer came in the form of a warning. The lights actually flickered and we all looked at each other.

"Wait here a minute." Ben pushed on the secret panel and lowered into the darkness, a darkness that didn't brighten when he clicked the light switch. "Damn." He grumbled and we noticed his flashlight brighten and finally sway around the dimness.

"You okay?" I called.

"Yeah, yeah. Just wait there."

"What's down there?" Jenny asked, leaning close to see down the steep steps.

"You'll never believe it."

Suddenly the flashlight was back and Ben emerged from the entry. He looked at me in disbelief. "It's all gone, Gracie! Not a single book left in that room."

"But there were thousands of books in there. How did they get them all out?"

He stood and pushed the marble panel back in place. "There must be another way in. Maybe out in the woods or something."

"Or," Ryan said with a snort. "Maybe there was nothing down there in the first place?"

"I have no interest in screwing around with you, man." Ben sat on the floor and tugged the strange book from his pants. "There were books down there recording all of our names, when we arrived, and who brought us here. Those books went back hundreds of years. Shelves and shelves of orphans, staff, management, carefully recorded all the way back to the 1840s. There were even records from colonial times that belonged to some other orphanage in Philadelphia. And," he set the book on the floor and flipped it open, "this was down there. It's different from all the others."

All heads leaned closer as the lights flickered and actually went out. Ben turned on the flashlight and Ryan lifted the book to get a better look.

"What the hell is this writing?"

"We don't know," I explained. "Ben thinks it might be important and… he seems to think I can figure it out."

Ryan and Jenny both shrugged like that was a given.

I needed to clarify. "I don't have a clue how to figure this out. I may never figure it out. This book might be trouble or worse yet, it could be really valuable and we're in a mess for taking it."

"No." Ryan tucked Jenny under his arm. "It's a secret room. They don't expect any of us to find it and they don't know you have it. You can figure this out, Gracie, but we'll all need to help keep it from the General to give you enough time, that's all."

Jenny sat straight. "Maybe we should all take responsibility for it, shift it around between us so he won't find it when he checks our stuff."

"That's actually a good idea." Ben closed the book and held it up. "Who wants it first?"

"I'll take it. I don't think he'll suspect the gimp." I tucked it into the back of my jeans and under my wet jacket. "Then tomorrow, Jenny. After that you guys can take turns."

"Now all we gotta do is find out what happened to Wally," Ryan said as we followed Ben's flashlight beam through the silent lecture hall.

~*~

Dinner with Headmaster. As a kid, it meant bucking up and taking it like a man. All his life, whatever reason Cole sat across from the headmaster deserved whatever he got. Reaching Allerton's private apartment, he had to shake off his boyhood terror. He wasn't that bad of a kid. Yes, he'd broken a few rules back then, but he hadn't learned how to break serious rules until after Acclimation. He had good reason. He'd been deceived, tricked into believing that he was just an average kid, facing a normal life and future outside a normal orphanage. He'd been lied to and that was unforgivable, or maybe not so much. Maybe Allerton was doing the best he could. After all, if Cole had known what lay ahead, how could he have ever enjoyed the simple, ordinary childhood he remembered? Maybe it was a gift. Either way Allerton had caused resentment Cole couldn't shake. An anger embedded deep in his being.

Inside, the table was set nicely with a white linen tablecloth and napkins, nice white china and polished silverware. Intimidating. Cole was in jeans and a black tee-shirt. It was, after all, the only clothes provided to him. Blessedly, Allerton was dressed the same. Was he mocking the younger man or seeking common ground?

"Wine?" Allerton held up a bottle of Bordeaux.

"Rather have a beer."

"Beer it is," and the headmaster left for the kitchen.

Cole sniffed at the food displayed on platters, enough to feed six people. Did the old man eat like that every day, or was he trying to impress? Too many questions, and all on the wrong topics. Cole couldn't let himself get sidetracked. There were vital pieces of the puzzle to be divulged before the morning's exodus. But the food smelled so good his mouth watered.

Allerton handed over a frosty beer bottle and sat, then reached out to fill Cole's plate. "No, I don't get roasted lamb every day. Mrs. Drummond likes you. Let's eat, then we can get down to business."

"Likes me? She's so pissed at me she's breathing fire."

"Yeah, I heard about your confessions. Nothing we didn't already know, buddy. Eat."

Cole lifted his fork then set it down. "No. Now. Tell me now."

"Tell you what?"

"Start with the Caine girl." Allerton was silent so he continued. "This place has the resources. That issue with her foot should have been corrected. Why is she… handicapped?"

"Actually, she's not." Allerton leaned back in his chair thoughtfully. "She arrived, five years old with a club foot. Severe. Unfortunately, something like that requires several surgeries that must be done early, much earlier than her arrival. Under our care she's had three operations and this is as good as it'll get for her. She's physically capable, Cole. She can run. It's not pretty, but she works hard at keeping up." He sipped wine. "She's important so it's a moot point. She must be acclimated—"

"Why is she important?"

"I can't explain that. You'll see when you witness—"

"Yeah, yeah… why don't you just tell me… ah…" Cole leaned forward and eyed Allerton. "You don't exactly know, do you?"

"I know she's important. I called you to fulfill your vow because I trust you. You will be the first to know the full truth about her. It's an… honor."

Cole laughed aloud. "Right. So, I'm walking into this even more in the dark than I originally thought. Nice. Real nice." He speared a slice of lamb with his fork. "Now tell me about the others. Everything you do know would be helpful."

The headmaster cleared his throat, and Cole prepared for a lecture. It was how their relationship had gone for eighteen years under the Gate's roof. No lecture came, just valuable information.

"Ryan Sutcliff, arrived at the Gate at three months old. True orphan and, as you can see, has overcome any insecurities he might have had about it. Strong, athletic, well suited for what lies ahead. I'd strongly advise that you get and keep him on your side."

"You think he can emotionally handle what's lurking outside the front gates?"

"I do. Same with Wallace, although I can only hope that he sticks close, for his own good… especially after Acclimation. He's not high on the emotionally tough gauge. Be prepared for rebellion, but it's all fear, Cole. Be compassionate.

"Jennifer Perkins. She comes from big power and big money. Not an orphan, but placed here for her protection. God only knows what her folks will do to me if she gets herself killed, or worse yet, pregnant." Allerton snorted. "Perkins' parents are some of my direct superiors. Do me a favor and take good care of her."

Cole shrugged. The way he saw it, it was none of his business. Perkins was just part of the job.

Allerton continued. "Gracie's not an orphan either. Not at the time of her arrival but she is now and has been for most of her stay at the Gate. Again, she was brought for her protection."

"You skipped the Wheeler kid."

"Yes, I did."

"And?"

Allerton rubbed his eyes and groaned a sigh. "Cole, Ben's my son. Mine. Do you understand?"

"Sure." He focused on loading his fork again, trying to avoid the man's face. "You ashamed of that?"

"Hell no. He's mine. Don't you get it? I'm trusting you with my own son."

Their eyes met and locked for a moment. "Does he know?"

Allerton shook his head. "And I don't want him to know."

The conversation ended. What Cole imagined to be a collection of misfits turned out to be quite the opposite. Should he be proud or scared to death?

"And," Cole said with a sigh as he set down his fork. "Tell me about your theory… about why the enemy is at your gates?"

"It's about balance, Cole. Balance. Right now, the balance is way off… and dangerously in their favor."

~*~

At seven on the dot we sat, crowded and bleary-eyed, in the headmaster's office. Sitting up all night, trying to figure everything out and getting more confused hadn't helped. Jenny looked like she never even washed her face, and the guys just glared at each other. Ben insisted he should hold the book, sure that Jenny or I would blab about it if things got intense, and I kinda think he was right. I was tired, hardly ate any breakfast, and felt like I was going to be sick.

Minutes ticked by and Allerton wasn't there yet. It's not like him to be late for anything, especially a meeting in his own office. Worse than that, Wally was MIA and our fearless leader was nowhere in sight.

Ryan's knee bounced so hard I could feel the floor moving under my feet. I sighed and looked at Ben. "What are we going to do if Wally's—"

"He's not dead," Ben said with an angry hiss.

"Don't be mad at me. I didn't take a stroll outside the front gate."

Wow, my voice was shaking, but before I could get an apology out, the door opened and Allerton walked in, smiling like it was any day of the week and he had great news.

"Is Wally—"

"Yes, yes, Master Wally's just dandy. He's on his way. Sorry you couldn't have a better day for your journey, children, but Mother Nature makes these decisions."

The statement was accented with a rumble of thunder as rain spattered harder against the windows.

"What the hell happened to him?" Ryan demanded.

We never talked to Headmaster like that and I slunk back in my chair. The heavy mood broke with a grunt and a crash of the opening door as Wally pushed his way in and thumped on the chair beside me. He didn't look at any of us. I wanted to scream, but instead I just glared at him.

He glared back. "What're you pissed about? I'm the one with fifteen stitches."

"What happened out there?" I'm pretty sure I wasn't the only one asking.

"He passed out and scraped himself against the gate," Allerton explained as Masters joined us.

I looked at Wally who gave a barely visible shake of his head. I swallowed hard and tuned in to Headmaster's explanation. His voice was calm, but the subtle grin on his face gave me the willies.

"Our boy Wallace here has been trying to quit smoking. Two whole weeks, right?"

Wally nodded with a scowl.

"Yes well, lighting up and taking that first drag made him lightheaded and he just… swooned." Allerton actually chuckled.

Ryan leaned across me. "You okay, man?"

"He's been stitched, received a tetanus shot, and is carrying a course of antibiotics. He's fine." Allerton leaned back and smiled.

"No," Masters said and the energy in the room ramped up along with the volume of approaching thunder. He stared at Allerton for a moment, ignoring the man's irritated expression. "No. We're not doing this. These people are in my hands and they're going to know what's what, or all deals are off."

"Cole—" Allerton hissed.

"No! I'm doing this my way." He turned to us and I almost gagged back bile burning up my throat. "Wally was attacked. There is something out there and it's out there to hurt or kill you—"

"Cole! For Christ's sake, they're kids —"

"They need to know." Masters shot a lethal glare at Allerton. "You want me to do this, we're doing it my way, and they need to know." His attention turned to us. "You are all in danger. When I say stay in my sight, I mean it. No one… for any reason… leaves my sight. You don't take a piss without me in the room. You don't go off for a smoke or a…" he pointed at Ryan and Jenny and bobbed his brows, "well… anything at all. Not unless you want to die before you reach Acclimation. Do you understand?"

We all blinked. Holy crap, we really were in serious trouble and if I'd had the book, I would have handed it over right that minute. Ben was right, we needed custody of it. Even if I could form words I wouldn't have snitched on him. Allerton lied to us. He lied by not telling us the truth. I felt a growing sense of respect for the General. At least he was preparing us. How could Allerton have kept us in the dark so long? What kind of a person does that?

"Hey, Masters," Wally piped up. "What about after Acclimation?"

"The danger's pretty much over then… after Acclimation, nothing wants to kill you, unless you get yourself dead all by yourself." With those words his eyes drifted away, carefully not looking at any of us. What wasn't he saying?

"What?" I croaked. "What *thing* wants to kill us now?"

Masters ran a hand down his face and groaned. "I know you want explanations, but some things just can't be explained right now. Trust me, Gracie… all of you… I'm going to protect you and get you through Acclimation. I swear."

My face was wet. I didn't even know I was crying. All I could hear was his promise. All I could do was trust him. Lord knew I didn't trust the headmaster anymore.

My mind spun with thoughts, images, voices I'd heard that had no explanation, the words in the closet, in my journal. Without realizing it, we were up on our feet and being herded toward the courtyard. Everyone that mattered was walking with me, like sheep to the slaughter, out into the pouring rain.

A cool van was waiting for us, already loaded with our duffels, boxes, and coolers full of food. A teary-eyed housemother hugged each of us, whispering about the special treats she'd packed. Chocolate for Jenny, chips for Ryan, extra bandages and peppermint for Wally, and beef jerky for Ben. I was dragging my feet, looking at the van like it was some kind of monster about to swallow me and take me to the depths of hell. I wasn't afraid of the world outside The Gate, but I discovered I was terrified of actually going there. All my life I thought there was nothing more exciting than getting away from the orphanage. Turns out, my bravery was more fiction than Allerton's omissions of the truth.

Housemother hugged me close for a long time, whispering encouragement. She looked into my eyes and smiled kindly. "You will be amazing, Gracie. Your good heart will carry you through this. And…"

"Uff!" I turned, shocked and thrilled to see Raffie in all his uncoordinated English bulldog glory, racing from the building to join us. He jumped at my feet, barked and pawed my leg until I rubbed his ears then he leapt into the van.

"He can go with us?" I squealed with the first real happiness I'd felt in days.

"Of course," Housemother said. "He's been waiting to travel with you all."

Masters shook his head. "I can't believe that smelly dog's still alive. Will he stick close?"

"He will. He knows where his kibble comes from. I packed dog food. He's not going to be a problem." She leaned closer to Masters and tugged on the collar of his tee-shirt. "In fact, he's going to be a lot of help."

Even with Raffie along, and my friends cheering and playing with him, it seemed almost impossible to step up into the van. I closed my eyes for a moment and all I could see was that strange writing in that weird book. It was all connected, I could feel it—the danger, the book, the journey, the past, and the future. Someone tenderly gripped my elbow and I opened my eyes to see the General himself.

"Come on, girly. We gotta hit the road."

I pulled my arm free. "I can do this myself."

6

*JEFFERSON NATIONAL FOREST
FIVE MILES EAST OF TAZEWELL, VIRGINIA*

arta opened her eyes to the pale growing dawn while the night's tree frost melted into dewy drops. They plopped with noisy cracks onto the ground and the bright blue tarp above her head, waking her in harmony with the brittle chill in the air. She'd have much rather slept inside the camper, but she didn't want to disturb her patient. Pain and Tobias never made for good company. Blessedly this time his wounds were minor, easy to pray and magic away. Rest was all he needed to heal. The recovery of his focus was another issue altogether. There were no potions or spells for that. Her nose twitched to the scent of brewing coffee. At least the cantina was alive and well after the night's scuffle.

Tightening her frayed blanket like a royal robe, she sauntered along the silent midway and past the creaking Ferris wheel, its seats rocking in the breeze. Autumn whispered on the air and soon the show would need to head south. She walked under the sign proclaiming the Emmaus Magic Show to be the eighth wonder of the world, and it was. Her nose led her along the strengthening scent of beckoning caffeine and pancake batter. Getting there so early meant offering to help Cookie prepare breakfast, but no problem there. Garta had learned long ago that the healing energy from her fingertips seeped into the food she touched and helped cure any ails among her fellow travelers. It would be a good way to start the day.

"Tobias okay?" called a voice from the vans and campers just beyond the cantina tent. She raised her hand in acknowledgment and confirmation, grinning at the "Thank fucking God," response. Yes, thank God indeed. Where would they all be without Tobias?

The communal cantina tent was warm and inviting. She pushed inside the canvas flaps, walked past the long tables and folding chairs then rose on her toes to look into the battered food truck window. The kitchen was Cookie's sacred place.

"Cookie, can you use some help?"

He gave a grunt. "Yeah. Gotta peel and dice potatoes, crack a couple hundred eggs, fry the sausage, and griddle the pancakes. Which ap-*peels* to you, Doc?" His eyes twinkled.

She started on the potatoes. Cookie was a large, middle-aged man. He took up the majority of the food truck space, but Garta was small so it didn't bother her. They worked well together, at times in silence, but Cookie wanted to talk that morning.

"Think we'll be moving on today?"

Garta shrugged and reached for another potato. "Tobias is feeling well enough, but there are strange blocks in his aura. His clarity is tangled like grapevines. He says something's coming and we're supposed to stay put for a while… or at least slow down our travel. Meet it head on… whatever it is." She rinsed the naked potato, sipped from her coffee mug, and took up another spud. "He may take another day. We can do one more show… posters can go up in Bastian this morning. We're only five miles outside of the town limits. Not too far. We won't even have to move."

"Yeah, one more show. One more day. Then he'll have his crap in order?" Cookie stopped working and eyed Garta suspiciously.

"It wasn't a bad wound. He's going to be fine. If his head's screwed on straight, we'll most likely hit the road real soon."

"Where to, do ya think?"

"Only God and Tobias know that. Shall I chop onions for the potatoes?"

"Sure. Then do what you can to get his damn head working right, okay? We gotta start moving south. This weather's killing my joints."

"Let me help." Garta reached over and tenderly laid her hand on Cookie's gnarled arthritic knuckles. He sighed with instant relief and she smiled. "After breakfast, come to my camper. I'll finish the job. Have you as good as new in no time."

"Good as new?" His laugh was boisterous and heartfelt, and Garta enjoyed the warmth as his growing energy wafted around her.

Thirty minutes later, the tent was filled to overflow with workers, performers, and the all-important leadership committee. Clanking forks tapped tin plates, clinking spoons stirred sugar into strong coffee, and the music of multiple conversation circles accompanied the hot meal. For a crew that had faced the enemy only hours earlier, they played hard at being in good humor. Did they think they'd won? If so, Garta was glad for it. She had treated far fewer wounds than usual, but the treacherous encounters were rising more and more often.

Tobias managed the walk to his seat in the center of the long table and gulped down his fair share of turkey sausage and buckwheat pancakes. Putting on a brave and proud expression, he chatted easily with anyone who wanted to talk. Tobias was a real showman.

Garta took a precious moment to look around and take in her extraordinary world. The Emmaus Magic Show was the perfect place for misfits to share and celebrate their commonality. The gypsy life wasn't for everyone, but Tobias had his ways of making it as palatable as possible. There were educated and uneducated people in their ranks, racially different people and spiritually different people, people who naturally belonged and people one might never imagine would choose the carnie lifestyle. Ah, but they all did it for a reason. The one and only reason. The reason was the same, but each man and woman followed that reason in line with their own motives. How else could this work?

Across the tent, Billio and Frank Pincer—the show's Snake Man and road mechanic, respectively—shot off their mouths and entertained the troops. Distraction was the name of the game, and those two knew that the funny bone was most in need of a good twang when it was painfully raw. The mere possibility of losing Tobias ran a low level electric current beneath all their bones. The comedy performance put the clowns to shame, but the extended dwarf family cared little. They didn't even chuckle, just stared at Tobias, determined to hold their leader tight to reality, lest he disappear in a puff of smoke.

Roars of laughter and snorts rang through the cantina as the forced, tense smiles altered and became genuine. There was a war going on and only the clear of heart could fight well. A good chuckle washed clean all fear and trepidation. Garta was pleased.

Tobias was not bothered by the noise. He smiled with fatherly pleasure. He was paler than Garta liked, but eating well. There was no scent of infection and the wound had long since ceased seeping. It was the alteration in his center that revealed itself to her knowing eyes. This was far more painful than an injury of muscle and bone. This was a battle within the battle. What would come of it? Did she even want to know?

She pushed food around her plate, stabbing eggs or potatoes with her fork, tasting nothing. Beside her the show's cleaner, Jack Beacher, shoveled food into his large mouth, swallowing without hardly chewing, his eyes determined and dark. He'd had a very long night. Many of the enemy had died, but only two of their own. All needed to be disposed of efficiently and cleanly. Jack had his own way of healing the tribe.

Beauty Low ate daintily across the table. Her beard was neatly trimmed, her dark eyes sparkling and adorned with tattooed lines. Her yellow and red striped dress was massive, hanging in folds from her shoulders. Beauty was losing weight, having decided that her health was more important than the bearded fat lady illusion she used in her ring mistress act. She sipped coffee and eyed Tobias suspiciously. Noticing Garta's attention, she lowered her eyes and grinned. There were no potatoes on Beauty's plate, only a spoonful of scrambled eggs, and one lean turkey sausage. She was committed. Too bad the strict diet made her a little irritable. Her body was getting healthier, but Garta worried for the woman's soul.

The lovely Dawn Elizabeth St. Mary sat at Tobias' side. It was her right as his woman. She advised and consulted Tobias in all matters, and Garta expected that whatever decision would be announced at the table that morning began with a gentle nudge from his lover. Dawn was one of the privileged, acclimated out of Ariel's Gate. The young woman was all the colors of a coming dawn—blue eyes that darkened or lightened with her mood, brilliant glistening hair that billowed deep red and gold, and when kissed by the sun, orange and even fuchsia. She was a warning morning sky, yet they all sailed into the coming storm, thanks to her unique abilities. It was the power and knowledge behind those remarkable eyes that the troops—and Tobias—needed. She was the show's strategist with remarkable extrasensory abilities. Dawn could see the future far better than the gypsy fortune teller she pretended for the crowds. Great respect was given to the girl from Ariel's Gate who was graced with skills, education, and a safe Acclimation. That day even Dawn ate little. As with most of them, post-battle nourishment came from other sources, no matter how hard Cookie worked.

Ballister Green arrived at the table late, still wearing grease paint and his brilliant blue wig from last night's performance. The acrobat and recruiter had other things on his mind. He'd disappeared after the skirmish, following his standing orders to track the enemy and gain intelligence. He hadn't made his report to Tobias yet, Garta was sure. Her heart tightened so she lowered her fork to the plate with a sigh. Whatever Green revealed would guide their lives. Things had escalated. Something was coming. A gypsy's life was never easy.

Outside the sun rose higher, glowing like a growing fire through the yellow cantina tent walls. A decision had to be made. All eyes landed on Tobias, who stood achingly then grinned.

"Nothing to worry about, just a bruise or two. Now," he looked around the tent, strength and determination pronounced in the creases of his sun-worn face. "Pack us up. We move out in two hours." Cheers mixed with the clacking sound of folding chairs closing and tables being disassembled. Within moments the tent was empty, the kitchen closed up tight, and all activity moved outside.

The tactical committee meeting could begin.

Tobias smoothed crumbs from his wrinkled grey linen shirt and cleared his throat. All eyes focused on him and he gave an uncomfortable shrug. "No, I have no specific, defined plan."

"You always have a plan," Beauty said with a snort.

"Not this time. We need to circle the wagons, self-protect... and wait."

Jack shook his head. "Wait for what?"

"Not a good idea, Tobias," added Green. "Not based on what I've learned. They're amassing across three states. Worse yet, they seem to have some kind of agenda, something far more calculated than usual. We can't just try to hold the fort against the onslaught charging our way."

"They're not coming at us, Green. We just happen to be in their path. There's a responsibility ahead, I just need time to identify and define it." Tobias glared around the table, challenging anyone to argue. Sliding his focus from one to the next, he finally drew in a breath and continued. "We can do this." His eyes glittered. "We've done it before."

Green leaned across the table, pushing Beauty aside in the process. "We're not all ancients, dude. And frankly, I'm not so sure this is the place to take a stand."

"We're not taking a stand, my friend. We're to do that in another place, in a time not too far in the future. Our duty right now is to blend with the energies, back off... be silent. Let the war go on without us for a bit."

"How long?" Green wasn't alone, several voices, including Garta's, harmonized the all-important question.

"Exactly thirty days."

"Exactly?" Jack snorted then laughed aloud. "Exactly?

"Yes."

"Tobias," Garta said with great gentleness. "I am concerned—"

"Not for my physical health, Healer. The real concern is that you don't understand my reasoning. Something is coming and we must be prepared for it. We break camp this morning, travel the day and all of tomorrow, then reset under the veil tomorrow night. We will be fine."

Garta's heart thudded. In truth, there were only two ancients among them capable of constructing and maintaining a protective veil, and one of them, Tobias, was still recovering from a wound. Garta was unsure of her abilities for such things these days. Could she summon such power? Would it not drain strength from her healing capacity?

"Not at all." Tobias tenderly patted her shoulder showing his uncanny and long honed skill to read her mind. "Together we can do this. We must reach our destination first, then wait… thirty days… for whatever is coming."

Green slumped deep in his chair. "Great. Tell me, Tobias, is what's coming a good or a bad thing for us?"

Tobias smiled and looked down at his hands.

He doesn't know! Garta held her breath. *He truly doesn't know.*

"Jack." Tobias cleared his throat and proceeded in a most determined voice. "Prepare the troops to move out. We head south, then east into the ley lines. I'll know where to stop and set up the veil. Keep our destination quiet. The enemy has their telepathic spies, too, so talk among the crew about Florida. It might push our foes off track. Make sure everyone's ready to hit the road soon, then hold the final ceremonies." Jack stood, actually gave a sharp salute, and left the table.

"Green, I want a full report this afternoon. Schedule weapons retraining… we only have a month to become sharp as a tack." Green nodded and walked out of the cantina.

"Beauty, Garta and I will need all of your illusion powers to assist with the veil."

"You got it, boss." The large woman beamed and went off to pack, holding her skirts high to protect from tripping.

"Dawn, my dear," he said in a whisper. "Meet me at the camper. We'll get packed up as soon as I'm finished here." With a blank expression, his lover did as she was told.

Tobias turned to Garta. They were alone in the silent tent, a place designated for meals and important communal events among his unusual show folk. They prayed in that tent. Weddings and passing-on ceremonies were held in the tent. Strategy sessions were developed in there, and arguments were settled under that canvas. Before it was lowered that day, they would say farewell to their lost comrades. Now, due to the coming inclement autumn weather, weapon and battle training would take place in the tent, too. He took Garta's hand in his.

His face and body seemed diminished somehow, smaller, wrinkled, not the robust leader she knew. Could the wound have been much deeper, or of some magic she couldn't repair?

"Tobias, are you sure? Are you absolutely—"

"You're right, I am not sure… but it is the directive. The first in many, many years. I will follow. Something is coming. Good or bad, we will be prepared."

~*~

"Red team, haul!"

Grunts and groans followed as the seven-member crew of the red team slowly lowered their six-foot-wide strip of dyed canvas from the big top loop holding it in place. Teams were broken into colors, but also for skill and practical reasons. Tobias smiled as he watched the first, the best, his red team do their job without damage to the canvas or complications from tangled ropes and fabric. Each team was responsible for keeping their two swaths of canvas dyed brilliant colors, clean, mended and ready for a show at a moment's notice. The red team also represented the primary camp warriors. These people, men and women, worked under Ballister Green. They were all extremely athletic, acrobats and high wire performers, but also the first line of defense when battle reared its ugly head. Some of them, like Green, were recruiters and responsible for growing the crew's numbers.

Tobias rubbed his eyes and returned his vision to the high steel ring holding the colored fabric. Each strip was attached to the roof bars of various campers and vans, trucks and wagons, all the same height and parked in a perfect circle. It was Tobias's idea of the perfect big top, filtering air and drops of rain, sunlight and moon glow between strips of bright canvas. Red, blue, yellow, white, and green. The center post was forty feet high and the finished big top had a circumference of over one hundred feet. The bleachers had already been dismantled and packed away along with the old Ferris wheel. The dissolving big top was as satisfying to him as a developing big top. The path of the journey. The moving on. But this time it meant so much more.

"Yellow team, haul!" he shouted only moments later as the mechanics, ride builders, and carnie workers took over. This was another well-coordinated and skilled group of laborers, and the big top continued to dissipate before his eyes.

The blue team was the illusionists among them. It was never pretty, but the bright blue canvas always came down unscathed. The Emmaus Magic Show was all illusion, so their important talents lay elsewhere, and were needed to keep the show going. White and green teams were new travelers, cooks, teachers, healers, and novice warriors. He always stayed to encourage them in their efforts and often stepped in to assist. That would not happen today. His body felt like it was on fire, and his hands longed to touch something far softer than canvas.

"Tobias, Jack says Dawn's asking for you. What do you want me to tell her?"

"I'll go to her. You help the bumbling ones get the last of the canvas down and folded."

The midway was gone and loaded vehicles were lining up for the move. A few last-minute elements remained, the cantina tent and a dozen or so campers had yet to be lowered, tightened, and shut down. Garta's was among them and he considered stopping there before heading to his own packing. A line stood, shuffling their feet and waiting at her door. Perhaps another time would be better.

He turned a slow circle. Trash had been packed away, except for the small package of antacids he picked up with a groan. Tobias smiled. Dawn did not enjoy the healthy food Cookie served. She was always happier with greasy carnie food. He smiled. He could feel Dawn's touch on the torn paper. Another glance at the disappearing camp and he was pleased. No one would ever know they had been there. He respected the earth and treated the land as a brother, with care and affection.

"Tobias!" came a call that shivered along his spine. Something was wrong. Dawn ran toward him and before his hands reached out to her, he could feel the enemy's touch all around her being. With a jerk he pulled back, but thankfully not in a way she noticed. She ran into his arms and he held her close. Dawn wasn't a small woman, but then again, he was a large man, nearly six and a half feet tall. The smell on her tickled his throat, threatening to turn his stomach.

"Too close," he whispered with a gasp. "You got too close, my dear. You can never get so close."

"I heard something… followed it. I knew it could have helped us, but I couldn't understand. It was garbled at first." She sniffled and ran a hand under her nose. Her tears had made dark marks on his shirt. Her palms tenderly slid over his heart.

He clasped her closer. His first instinct was to reprimand her, but the situation demanded his attention. Holding her at arm's length he looked deep into her troubled eyes. "What? Exactly what did you hear?"

She gulped, blinked then squared her shoulders. "They said… 'off,' again and again. And something about blood not winning. They also said 'she's coming'. Who's coming, Tobias? Should we be running the other way?"

Garta and several of those awaiting her attention had circled Tobias and Dawn. The action served to hear better, but also to block the enemy spies' ability to eavesdrop. Dawn visibly shrunk into herself, embarrassed by her own fear, but also grateful for the crew's protection. They had all turned their eyes away respectfully, so she continued quietly, watching every muscle in their leader's face. "Seriously, maybe we need to step away from this one, not fight, or wait, or whatever your plan is."

Garta spoke soothingly. "Perhaps she's right, Tobias. We have a long drive ahead. I'm sure a clearer plan will come to light. Please be calm, my dear. You are safe."

"No one's safe!" Dawn shouted, rubbing hands down her arms as though a thousand flies had landed there. "Tobias, you need a better plan."

He stepped back, widening the circle around him. His mind spun. This was not a plan; it was a directive delivered in a dream. It was the first directive he'd received in so many years he couldn't count. A clear directive. "I have no choice," he whispered as pain ripped along his back. "I must do this. It's not a plan and it's nothing we can plan for. We must wait. It's not something I can ignore." More and more of the crew circled him and he turned, realizing the worst, hoping for the best. "I understand all of you may not want to do this… *ahh!*" Pain shot through his feet, almost dropping him to his knees. Hands reached out but he glared. "You are free to walk away. Free to leave. All of you. *AHH!*" his fists clamped tight and Dawn cried out, pointing to the blood dripping from those desperate fists.

Tobias opened his hands to see the welling of red in each palm. He glanced down at his blood-soaked shoes, then placed a hand on his side, also gushing blood. Looking up with fear, he sought Garta who was the only one willing to step closer.

"What wounds are these?"

"It's not my blood, Healer. It's… not… my… blood." With a deep sigh, he raised his bloody hands and turned for all to see. "This is my directive, my friends. You are all free to walk away, but I must follow the directive."

Each head shook slow and firm. The stigmata. No one was leaving that day. Garta placed bandages on the amazing wounds and before long the bleeding stopped, the openings closed and clean. Something else had started and Tobias understood the first part of the puzzle. They had all battled the enemy for years, but this was the real beginning of the war. He stared out at the woods, feeling the enemy's eyes upon him. Holding out his arms he thought, clear and loud, *Go ahead, give it all you have. You will not win.*

~*~

Thirty-eight hours later, Tobias sat in the high cab of the lead eighteen-wheeler, chatting pleasantly with Green and watching the headlights sweep a turn, dancing off the trees and expanses of muddled darkness ahead. Behind him followed seventeen vehicles. Another trailer truck, nine large campers, several small pop-up campers, and flatbed trucks loaded with canvas and camping gear. The weather had cooperated and the night was warmer than the day they left, heading further south.

He was still shaken by the mysterious stigmata that had solidified his soldiers at his side. Those around him had become a little distant, so he'd made efforts to ride in each of the caravan vehicles, talk with each of his troops, and comfort them in any way he could. It had begun with the final ceremonies for the lost ones and continued to that moment. What could have been an exhausting effort, only served to energize him. The directive would be followed, and whatever was asked next of him, he knew he had the army to help him accomplish the goal.

"Trail mix?" Green held out an open bag of homemade goodies.

Tobias munched on a handful, grateful for Cookie who seemed to think of everything. Not once did the caravan require a stop for fast food. Bathroom breaks and major shopping for supplies was all time allowed so the crew was efficient. The second eighteen-wheel trailer was already loaded with food, additional supplies, various weapons, and comforts for the month of waiting. But waiting wasn't all they'd be doing.

Soul swords hummed from the pit of every vehicle, creating a long snake-like line of mystical power they'd need when the time was right. Everyone would face a stringent schedule resembling basic training boot camp. Even the weakest would learn how to fight and protect. Even Dawn.

Tobias scratched his head. Poor Dawn had no real clue what was going on. None of them did. Even he felt deep in the dark, but well aware of the importance of their obedience. She was special to him, the first true love he'd held in centuries. He'd need to make efforts to keep her close and satisfied. He'd need to—

"Stop!" His voice rang loud in the cabin and the driver did his best to make a slow stop, protecting against fender benders behind. The vision Tobias had seen lay before him. A wide green opening surrounded by trees, fairly level and big enough for the camp he was to build. "This is it." He opened the door and gingerly lowered himself to the ground. With arms wide and guiding, each vehicle streamed past him, into the space, maneuvered, settled, and awaited further instruction.

Unlike a normal show camp, where everything spread out from the big top and midway, Tobias arranged this camp as he'd seen in his vision. The nose of each vehicle was tight against the tail of the next, forming a firm protective circle. Each of the four huge tractor trailers were positioned in the east, north, west, and south. Guards would be posted atop them night and day. Finally, campers and the cantina tent occupied the center of the safe space. Soul swords were in hand and all listened patiently for Tobias and Garta's instructions.

"Hold them high, soldiers. They will add to the power of the veil, they will solidify the illusion and form our protection."

Moonlight glinted silver and blue off the raised metal, lighting the magical way as Tobias, Garta, and Beauty Low with her powerful mystic illusion abilities left the army and slipped outside the circle. With slow steps, quiet chants, the stinging scent of burning sage, and words whose meaning even Tobias couldn't remember, he led the way around and around the growing veil. Like a shimmering mist, the ethereal veil dropped from the heavens and rose from the earth. Stepping carefully, the three walked around the camp four times, summoning the help of the spirit, the heavens, and the earth to assist. Finally, with little fanfare, they re-entered the circle and looked into the concerned eyes of the loyal soldiers in their care.

Tobias smiled as Dawn scurried, nervous as a field mouse, to his side. "No one leaves this circle," he announced. "No one without my direct orders… until the time has come for us to move on. Green, you stand guard at the east gate. Billio, you're on the north gate. Jake, take care of the west gate. And… uh…" he searched for the face he wanted. "Haitham, you'll stand guard tonight in the south." Expecting and receiving nods of acceptance, he turned to the rest of his people. "We're safe here. Everyone, get yourself some rest. I'll have more instructions tomorrow. Oh, and Cookie, can you please make sure one of the carnie vendor trucks are open and serving? Poor Dawn will starve if we keep them locked up." He chuckled, dropped an arm affectionately over her shoulders, and left for his own welcoming bed. But before reaching his private heaven, Garta tapped on his arm and looked up into his eyes.

"Tobias, are you sure I should leave the veil tomorrow?"

Pressing his reluctant lover ahead, he leaned down to whisper to the healer. "Garta, Beauty Low is far more powerful than even she knows. She'll be able to hold the fort while you search for your healing herbs. I'm made to believe that everything you need to replenish your stock is within a quarter mile of this spot. I can send someone with you if you'll feel safer."

"Lord no! You'd just be putting them in danger! I'll be fine, as long as the veil is fine… and you're fine…"

"I'll be fine after a good night's sleep. So will you. Off with you, old woman."

Watching her leave in the darkness of their quiet domed protection, he took in everything. He'd done all that had been asked of him, yet still he worried.

What if they were preparing to take on more than they could handle? What if they were unable to prepare enough for what lay ahead? What if, what if, what if?

They had reached their destination. They would hone their battle skills, pray, and wait with all the patience they could muster. It was all they could do.

T-minus twenty-nine days.

7

ole Masters was used to speed, two wide wheels beneath him and the wind in his face. It mystified him how long it took to drive a bulky van filled with kids, food, soul swords, and a smelly dog from point A to point B. There were gas and repeated bathroom stops, because of course, his passengers couldn't possibly synchronize their needs because hey, that would make things easier. Granted, the weather was uncooperative and at least once he felt it safest to pull over and wait out the downpour and high mountain winds. The van stank of unwashed teenagers and Doritos. That wasn't the worst of it. He was hopelessly lost.

He was supposed to be running this show but they were a full day past their estimated arrival at the elusive Goodwin Summer Inn. He was desperate to locate not only the inn, but the all-powerful ley lines protecting it. He'd been hearing enemy voices for miles, threatening, taunting, enticing, terrifying. His guts knotted and he hadn't been able to eat all day. Darkness had risen all around them for a second time, and solid walls would have given him some sense of safety. Again, he drove a fifty-five-mile circle and the kids behind him groaned.

"Hoh, man! I recognize that sign. Do you even know where you're going?"

"Sit down and shut up!" he shouted over his shoulder. The soul swords raised the intensity of their ever-persistent hum as he turned down yet another unmarked country road. Was that a good sign or a bad one? The dog barked and Cole tensed. There was no way he'd stop and let that dog out for a piss in this stormy darkness. On the other hand, maybe he'd just let the thing out and drive away. Raffie raced to the front of the van and nuzzled with urgency at his ankle. Cole thought to kick the soft face away, but instead he looked down and growled like a wolf.

"UFF! UFF!" Raffie shouted back at him and Cole glanced up to the windshield, gasped and slammed on the breaks. The wheels locked then slid on mud and gravel before coming to a complete stop. Teenagers, duffels, bags of snacks, and plastic bottles of water and soda tumbled and rushed forward, slamming into the back of his seat but Cole was transfixed.

"Damn!" he said in a hush, disbelieving his continued shitty luck. The sign was there, pristine as could be, but just beyond the well-groomed trees and shrubs, the elegant Goodwin Summer Inn was blackened to charcoal and burned to the scorched ground. "Damn it! Damn, damn, damn…"

"What the hell, General?" Ben and Ryan said in unison.

"Shut up."

"Hell, no," Ryan blustered. "You don't know what the hell you're doing! Is this where we were supposed to stay? I'll be damned if I'm going to sleep in this van again tonight! Take us back to—"

"I said… shut…up!" His passengers went silent, even the stupid dog sat and looked up at him with a tilted head. "That's better. We're going to have to sleep in the van again tonight, so no more crap about it. In the morning I'll need to locate someplace else for us. We've got time." His mind spun. Some time, not a lot. The first Acclimation was in six days. He'd find something by then. Something inside the ley lines. Something safe. Wouldn't he?

"Why don't you call Headmaster Allerton?" not-so-on-the ball Jenny asked. "I'm sure he has a plan B. I know he wouldn't want us cooped up in this stinky van for another night. Call him."

Cole turned, determined to control his expression and failing. He'd rather she feared him than what really threatened them all, so he permitted his unwavering scowl. "Missy, do you think I haven't tried to reach Allerton? Twenty times? Thirty? He's not available to help us. He's got a lot of… shit… on his plate!" *Like we don't?* he thought, realizing for the first time that he was on his own to solve this mess. "Now, all of you… get to your seats and be quiet while I figure this out."

Even the boys shuffled back. Having no idea how much trouble they were in, he understood that they felt safer falling back into obedient schoolboy mode. They wouldn't be challenging his authority tonight. Cole felt a little better. Then a voice, soft and quiet, blew air across the hair at the side of his face.

"Um…" it whispered.

"I said… back to your seats. That means you, too, Gracie."

"Look there." She pointed. "Isn't that a cabin?"

He shifted the vehicle into reverse, readjusted, and aimed the headlights. Damn if she wasn't right. It was small, probably the caretaker's residence during the season. It seemed sturdy enough; at least in the darkness it looked solid and undamaged. Should he wait until daylight to check it out? He inched the van closer and closer to the front of the structure, and he listened.

Mumbled conversations drifted forward from the back. "Quiet!" And he listened harder. Silence. They were in the tight tangle of ley lines and could possibly be safe from the enemy. He stepped to the door, pressed his ear against the glass and listened again. Gracie leaned close, too. He glared, hoping to intimidate her, but she shook her head.

"I don't hear them either. I think they're gone."

Cole drew in a ragged breath. How could she hear them? That wasn't possible. "What the hell are you talking about?" He watched her face closely, still listening for voices outside the van. It could be a trick, an ambush. They could be waiting out there to jump. They were like that.

Gracie shrugged. "I've been hearing them talking, talking, talking since before we left the Gate."

"What do you think you're hearing, little girl?" His eyes narrowed, sure she was trying to pull one over on him.

"I'm not a little girl and I have no reason to lie to you. I hear them calling, talking to each other in strange languages. They sometimes talk to me, and I hear them calling to you. I'm not afraid… at least I don't think I'm afraid. I just want to know what they are." Her eyes were sincere.

"That information is for your Acclimation." His heart ached, knowing her proclamation of fearlessness was just show. "Keep this to yourself, okay. We are in danger and you should be afraid, so do as I tell you and help me keep the others in line."

She nodded, turned to join her friends in the back of the van, but first swiveled to face him. "Why are they begging you to join them?"

"Promise me you'll help me protect all of you. Please, Gracie."

"You're not going to answer me, are you?"

He shook his head.

"Fine, but you promised me answers at my Acclimation."

"I guarantee it." He watched her return to her seat, the bulky dog on her lap and her expression serene and blank. "Okay, listen up." All eyes rose in attention. "Every one of you stays inside this van. Don't leave, no matter what. Gracie spotted this cabin and I'm going to check it out."

"Cool! Nice going, Gracie." Ben patted her shoulder and the others smiled.

"Hurry up, Mr. Masters. I really want a shower," Jenny whined and slouched in her seat.

Ignoring her, he scanned the kids. "You… Ben. Come guard the door. No one leaves and you don't open it until I come back." Ben seemed reluctant but stepped forward.

"Are we expecting a bear attack?"

"Maybe." Cole sat at the wheel and maneuvered the vehicle as close as possible to the small screened-in porch. So close in fact, that when the van door swung open, it pushed the screen door in. The screen ripped and the wooden frame jammed. Cole gripped it and pulled hard, freeing it from its hinges. "I'll fix that later," he said then turned to Ben. "Close this van door tight."

The kid handed him a flashlight and nodded like Captain America. They'd stay inside. No one challenges Captain America.

Now for his next task, how to get inside? Breaking and entering wasn't a new concept for Cole, he was just a little out of practice. Realizing that the cabin was in the middle of nowhere and not as important as the inn itself. He assumed that a key was hidden simply, in the mailbox or under the welcome mat, something easy like that. He finally reached up and slid his fingers along the window frame. Voila. Key in hand he heard a cheer from inside the van, turned a glare, and put a finger to his lips. No need to attract attention. Just because the enemy was quiet didn't mean they weren't there.

He turned the key and stepped inside. Jenny was about to be very disappointed but he was thrilled. The place had only been shut tight for a few weeks but already smelled musty. A flick of the light switch. Nada. The electricity was out. It could be the storm, but more likely it had been turned off until the inn reopened in the spring. He glanced out of the window at the ruins and felt for the owners. Too bad, but he had bigger things to be concerned with.

The cabin was cold, but there was a fireplace in the main living area, and a small bathroom and acceptable kitchen with running, very cold, water. The stove burners informed him that the gas was also off, but exploration just outside the back door confirmed the presence of a propane tank, ready to be stoked along with a water heater. Tomorrow he'd get on that. Under the back overhang, leaning like a massive mountain, stood a large stack of firewood, bone dry under tarps and ready for the fireplace. Lightning flashed and illuminated an outbuilding through a curtain of pouring rain, a nice sized structure probably loaded with extra supplies needed for the inn. At the side of the structure, leaning and shut tight, was the entrance to a basement. Could he get that lucky? He trudged through the downpour, soaked in seconds but desperate to check it out. Aiming his flashlight, he reached down and fingered the padlock. That would be easy to break in the daylight. If the space proved adequate, they were set. For now, he had teenagers and tons of stuff to move safely into the cabin.

Another sweep of the place gave him a good sense of the layout. After that night, the girls would sleep in one room, two of the boys in the other, one in the loft, and he'd camp out on the sofa. With the storm raging, they'd all be rolled in sleeping bags near the fireplace soon. Cole needed to feel the success of the moment. His heart gave a thud. They'd be safe tonight and maybe for the duration. With luck, he'd even located a private space to acclimate each kid. He could stop worrying about failing the most important challenge of his life.

"S'go!" he shouted into the van.

The first to enter the cabin was the dog who quickly evicted two tit mice and a squirrel, then stood at the door awaiting a congratulatory pat on the head.

"Seriously?" Cole said. "Takes more than that to get a purple heart, buddy. Go on, get out of the way or someone will trample you."

~*~

Waking was really hard. The voices had gone silent, there was no rain pounding on the metal roof of the van, and no one was grunting or talking in their sleep. The quiet weighed heavy and at first, was really scary. I sat up and looked around. We were five lumps buried in puffy sleeping bags. The big living room was decorated like a catch-all for old furniture. Everything seemed to come from a different time. The sofa had wooden curlicues at the arms and looked Victorian, the big reclining chair was vintage 1970s, the coffee table, something from the hippy era complete with cigarette burns. The carpet, only God knew where that came from. It was so faded the pattern was hardly distinguishable. But the fireplace was blazing and the room felt warm and comfortable. There were books on the shelves, along with boxes of board games and playing cards. No television. Dust had accumulated on every flat surface, but that could be wiped away. This could be a nice place to stay for a while. Outside the window the rain continued, plopping like a drippy faucet. It was fall, after all, and it rains in the fall. I wondered where we were. We left West Virginia long ago and drove in circles for a while. Virginia? Maybe Maryland?

Masters was nowhere in sight. I stood, stretched, and explored the kitchen. All the coolers, boxes of food and supplies were empty, the contents already tucked into cabinets and set on counters. A coffee pot was hot and full. Dare I check if there was milk? Opening the refrigerator, a waft of cold air drifted out to me and I smiled. Milk, cheese, eggs, practically everything we'd ever need was lined up like soldiers on the shelves. Housemother really hooked us up when she packed the food. I twirled in a joyful circle.

"Don't get too happy. I'm not sure how long the electrical connection I rigged up will hold." Masters stood at the kitchen door, set a wrench and screwdriver on the counter, and rolled up the sleeves of his rain-soaked shirt. "Gas is on, so we have hot water."

"Rigged? You rigged electricity? Is that even safe?" I had to know.

He shrugged and washed his hands in the sink.

"Do you think an electrical fire burned the inn?"

He gave me a look that made me shiver. His expression warned me not to go there. Those questions were for later. I hated it, but he was in charge. I had no choice but to wait. "So, where've you been, besides stealing electricity and playing with gas tanks?"

"Not your business, girly. Anyone else up?"

"Nope." I poured myself a mug of coffee and sat at the table. It was cleaned and there was even a bowl of sugar packets sitting in the center. Cole Masters must have a sense of home, or at least an idea of what homey is. He was like us, after all. From the Gate. I looked at his tired face. Poor guy mustn't have slept a wink all night. Could I like him? Maybe. Trust him? That was still up for debate.

Sipping coffee, I closed my eyes and wondered what it will be like to live a normal life. Normal was such an abstract concept. Most of my memories revolved around living in a boarding school orphanage, following a bazillion rules, and getting away for an occasional football game. We never even got to go to town to catch a movie. Even my weird, vivid memory of before Ariel's Gate didn't reveal normalcy. I was starved for normal, whatever normal was. It certainly wasn't spending a month in a cabin with stolen electricity. I had to admit that the five of us, under the General's guidance, had become a sort of family. It felt a little like being in the military, but my guess is that's only because we're kids and not the best judges of any given situation, especially not situations where we might get dead. I felt pretty sure I could count on my fellow travelers to have my back, and they could count on me for the same. Oh well, it's normal for now. I chose to go with it. Even though the General was more like a big brother than a knowledgeable uncle.

Over the next few days we fell into a routine. Masters would start each day off with strict reminders that we couldn't leave the cabin for any reason, especially if he wasn't there.

The van was parked ridiculously close to the front porch, ready for a quick escape, I assumed. Everyone else thought all the drama and rules were stupid and plotted ways of skipping out, everyone except me and Wally. I never talked about the voices I heard, or asked Wally what happened to him outside the courtyard. We just accepted that the other had good reasons to stick close.

When Masters left, he never really went far or for long. He always went across the back yard and down into the basement of the metal storage building. Sometimes he took boxes of stuff, other times we heard hammering noises coming from the depths. No one had a clue what he was doing down there, but it was a great topic of discussion.

"He's gonna torture us down there… it's something the General would do," stated Wally with a distasteful snort.

"Nah, he's probably building a new screen door to replace the one he broke." Jenny was so innocent. I never realized that before.

"I think he's building a radio, like old-school World War II stuff… something he can use to contact more troops, just in case one of us goes berserk and tries to kill him… or there's a bear attack… or a zombie attack." Ryan laughed and cuddled Jenny close. The only time he could touch her was when Masters was gone, and he took full advantage of it. I hoped they brought birth control.

"It doesn't matter what he's doing," Ben said with a grin. "We're getting closer and closer to getting this Acclimation thing over with. Are you ready? Ready to be free of all these stupid rules?"

Ryan shook his blond hair back from his face. "I'm not free of anything until my sweetie here is free, too."

Ben snorted. "Wally, you're the first. You sticking around after?"

"Not me, no way." Wally stood and paced the big room. "I'm outta here the minute he tells me all the stuff I need to know. No looking back, no ties, no nothing."

"Why thank you, my dear friend. It's good to know we can count on you if the shit hits the fan… bear and zombie attacks and all."

Ben sounded angry and that baffled me. Wally was the only one wounded by whatever's out there to get us. I could see how he'd be anxious to get away, maybe try his hand at protecting himself. Why was Ben so mad about it? I was about to say something, but Jenny opened her mouth and changed all our perspectives.

"All right, everyone." She reached for a notebook and pen on the coffee table. "I plan to bake a birthday cake for everyone. Wally, what's your favorite cake?"

"Uh…" Embarrassment painted his face. The poor guy must have expected everyone to hate him or something. Wally never had friends who stood by him before. He cleared his throat and looked out a window. "Yellow with chocolate icing."

"Perfect. Ryan likes German chocolate. Ben's next. What's your favorite?"

"Red velvet," he said, his eyes sparkling.

"I want banana cake, and what kind do you want, Gracie?"

Tears welled in my eyes. It was such a kind thing to do, especially for Jenny, especially since everyone had the perfect right to be long gone before I even reached my Acclimation. Did this mean she and Ryan would stay and wait for me? I wasn't brave enough to ask that question. "Chocolate, please."

Those cakes would be the real farewell and commencement. We were going to all leave and go in different directions. Ben reached over and squeezed my hand. Did that mean he'd go wherever I went? That he wanted me to go where he went? My heart skipped a beat. I sure hoped so.

Ryan kissed Jenny then held her at arm's length. "And how are you going to bake all those?"

"Housemother packed all kinds of cake mixes and ingredients, even recipes. It'll be fun. Gracie, want to help me?"

Yep, we had become a kind of family.

During those days before Acclimations started, I discovered that I had four wishes. These wishes seemed to define me at the moment, an important thing, since I never even came close to defining me before. With sadness, I realized that my wishes might mean nothing at all after Acclimation. Still, four silly wishes chanted in my heart like a mantra.

My first wish was to get my fingers into Jenny's hair. It was thick, shiny black, long, and curly. Every morning since we were little, I'd watched her slowly and meticulously, twist small wisps of it around and around her finger, then move on to the next batch until her entire head was an elegant bush of perfect curls that would swing when she walked and dance in the breeze. The morning ritual felt like an honoring of herself, her heritage, her present, and her future. I wanted to touch her hair, maybe I wanted to touch her commitment to being who she was. I promised myself that I'd ask to help her fuss with it one morning before her Acclimation. Maybe she'd let me.

My second wish was to find a way to know Wally a little better. I didn't have much time to make this wish come true, since he'd be the first to acclimate and the first to leave us all behind. He was skittish, confrontational, terrified, and angry. Always had been. Still, I'd love to understand what made him that way, and how the attack had intensified his rebellious nature. I liked the Wally in my mind. I hoped to find a way to like the real Wally before it was too late.

My third wish was the hardest to imagine coming true. I wished with all my heart that I could figure out that book we stole. Why had it been in a secret room? Why did the orphanage have a secret room in the first place? Half of me wanted nothing to do with it, to hand it over to Masters and be finished with all the espionage and intrigue. There was enough on our plates without stolen secrets to solve, right? The other part of me knew, without doubt, that book meant something important to our future. I shivered just thinking about it. Stealing it didn't sit well with me, but having the book had done one important thing—it bound us together, at least until Acclimation. Until Wally leaves. Maybe the bond was strong enough to hold the rest of us strong against whatever was out there talking, threatening, whispering. It had been quiet since we arrived at the cabin, but my soul knew they'd be back. That the danger wouldn't be over after Acclimation. That it might even be worse. Boy, I had a lot of questions for Masters. He promised to answer them. He better.

The book was our touchstone. Every day, as soon as Masters left for his covert operation in the basement across the yard, we began our own. Whoever was holding the book safe for the night brought it out and we all circled the coffee table in the big living room to lean over it and try to decipher the writing. Even Wally, a kid not known for his deductive reasoning, had ideas that we all considered. Everything was a possibility. The book could be from outer space. It could be from the USSR, created during the cold war and just a cool relic someone was keeping. It could be ancient. It could be code.

I never spoke of the voices and Wally never talked about what he'd seen the day he was hurt, but often we would catch each other's eye for a moment, knowing there was way more to this than the others imagined. Then the day before Wally's Acclimation, I noticed something strange. The first eight pages of the book had gone blank. Holding the sheets up to the sunlit window didn't reveal even a hint of the previous writing. Wally ran to the bathroom and threw up. Ben took the book and tucked it under his bed in the loft. Jenny checked her nails, and Ryan huffed in frustration.

"Who fucked with the book?" he demanded, and Jenny's attention rejoined the conversation.

"Not me," Wally called between gags. "Maybe Masters did it."

"No way," Ben rebutted. "There's no way he even knows it's here, much less where it is. We hide it somewhere different every day."

I shook my head. "It doesn't matter, it really doesn't matter. I remember exactly what was on those pages. I can recreate it if I have to. It may just be, I don't know… hiding from us. Maybe it's an illusion. No one did anything to the book. Let's check tomorrow. Maybe we're just missing something."

"Yeah, eight pages of symbols we can't read anyway," Ben groaned. "This was stupid. I should have just left it where we found it."

"No. You did the right thing. We need that book. No matter, we have it, so let's continue with the plan and try to figure out what it says."

"Gracie." Ryan stood and reached for Jenny's hand. "If you say so, I'm in. If anyone can figure it out, it's you. We're game."

He gave me a thumbs up, then led her to the boy's bedroom and left me and Ben alone. I could feel the book above my head in the loft, laughing at me, or shouting, or maybe it was my imagination. I sighed and leaned back against the sofa, stretching my legs out under the coffee table. Ben rubbed his eyes and shrugged. "Just you and me, kid… again."

I liked it when it was just Ben and me, which leads to my last wish. It was a wish I realized I'd wanted for a long time but was afraid to admit. With all my heart, I wanted Ben. I wanted him to kiss me the way Ryan kissed Jenny. Kiss me and take me to a bedroom and love me. I loved Ben. That truth vibrated under my breastbone like a symphony crescendo. At the Gate, I felt it was wrong to wish for that kind of intimacy but now, with Ryan and Jenny's obvious romance, it was all I wanted. We could become a couple, care for each other. We wouldn't be alone after Acclimation. We'd be together. Maybe Ben would do the same thing Ryan promised—wait for his sweetie. Me. My whole body grew warm and tingly with the future we'd have, the life, the careers, the kids. Normal. That would be normal. I wanted Ben. What a time to discover that small fact. The mere acceptance of it made me feel like I'd explode.

Later that afternoon, I pulled Jenny aside and made a few requests. Sure, she'd let me help curl her hair the next morning. And of course, she'd be happy to get a condom from Ryan for me. My heart went wild. I was on my way to having two of my wishes come true. All I needed now was to find the courage to ask Ben. How does one ask for such a thing?

~*~

I did everything I could think of to get a little closer to Wally. I even got up in the middle of the night to pace with him when he was freaked out, which was most of the time. He wouldn't really talk to me, but he did say something I'll never forget. It was the evening after we discovered the missing writing.

"Gracie, I got no clue why you'd waste so much time on me. I'm nothing. The only something you should be worried about is outside this cabin. I'm gearing up to face it because I think the General's wrong. I think it still wants to hurt or kill us after Acclimation. Whatever. I'm an idiot. I could be dead wrong, but I'd really hate to see you get killed because you trusted that guy." He pointed toward the kitchen door.

Masters was still out there, frantically doing whatever he was doing in the basement to be ready for Wally's Acclimation the next night.

"Do not trust that bastard, Gracie. I don't care about the others. Just be strong. You know that something's out there. And we both know it isn't a good thing."

I nodded.

"Go to bed."

"No. Please stick with us after."

"I can't. I can't tell you why, I don't know why, but I just can't. Go to bed."

"No."

And I sat up with him all night. Then it was D-Day for Wally.

It was a somber happy birthday, but after dinner we lit candles and sang to Wally, cut the cake and passed the plates around the kitchen table. Even Masters was a little on edge. I started to wonder if he knew we had the book. I wasn't willing to imagine he was afraid to acclimate Wally. Masters was our capable and all-knowing guide. He wasn't that much older than us but he had been acclimated. That made him an expert, right? He couldn't be nervous about doing his job, could he? No, it had to be the book. Maybe it would be best to hide that book so well no one would ever find it again, even if I had to escape the cabin to do it. Maybe not. We were in too deep with that stupid book. We stole it. Soon we'd need to face the music.

Wally never even took a bite of cake. "When?" he demanded.

Master's licked icing from his fork and sliced himself another piece. "Later, buddy. We'll start around eleven-thirty. Eat your birthday cake."

"No. Now."

The General's eyes rose to meet Wally's, and I realized it was the first time since arriving at the cabin that he'd looked directly at any of us. "Later. That's how it works."

Wally stood so fast his chair slammed back against the floor. "Don't give a fuck how it works. Let's do this right now so I can get the hell away from here!" Sweat dripped down his face and his eyes were red with exhaustion. I was prepared to defend him but Masters took an unexpected approach.

"Wally, man… sit down, enjoy your cake. I swear, there's nothing to be so freaked out about."

Wally glared.

Masters didn't glare back. "Listen," he said. "I know what happened back at the Gate scared the shit out of you. Trust me, I understand. But what's ahead… your Acclimation… it's like an empowerment… against stuff like that. It's a lot of knowledge that's going to help you for the rest of your—"

"I said now! Get this over with now!"

We all sat stupefied, afraid to move an inch. Wally had crossed into a place of terror so intense, I was convinced he might attack us.

"No can do," Masters said calmly. "You might want to get some rest. We start in a few hours."

"Now!" It was a child's cry. Wally was breaking. I looked to Ben but he seemed scared enough to make a run for it.

"Sorry." Masters carried his plate to the sink. "Get some rest."

Wally stomped to the boys' bedroom and we all looked to Masters for guidance.

"He's got reason to be scared. What happened to him was rough. If he had followed the rules he'd be fine, as it is…" Masters shrugged. "Ryan, keep an eye on him, make sure he doesn't leave the cabin. I'll come for him at eleven-thirty. The rest of you…" he looked at each of us and grinned, "…chill. Read a good book, play cards, whatever. Nothing bad's going to happen tonight. Wally's fighting his own personal demons."

With those words, a sudden cloud drifted across Masters' expression, his eyes trailed away and he cleared his throat. "I'm off, got some things to finish. No one leaves this cabin. No one. Especially Wally. Hear me?" We all nodded but he wouldn't have known. He'd already exited the back door on his way to the ominous basement across the yard.

"Fuck," Ryan said with a groan.

"Worried about Wally… or Acclimation?"

Ryan eyed Ben with a scowl. "Whatever. Don't act like the whole thing doesn't give you the creeps, too."

Ben shook his head. "I don't know what to think. Wally's always wanted to get as far away as possible after Acclimation. Something spooked him. He's just making it bigger than it has to be."

"The same way he overreacted to Tony's death?" Jenny sniped.

No one had anything to say to that. We didn't have a single clue what was going to happen in that basement. It wasn't going to be so bad. It couldn't be, right? I was still giving everyone, including Masters, the benefit of the doubt.

"Wally is going to leave, you know. He's said it a thousand times." I went to the sink to wash dishes.

"Good riddance," Ryan said with a grunt, passing me plates and cups.

"No, we shouldn't feel that way. There are only five of us. We should be nice, see him off when Masters comes for him. It might be the last time we ever see him."

"He's never been nice to me," Jenny whined and I turned to face her.

"Be the bigger person." Then I realized I wanted to play with her hair and get that condom she promised, so I grinned and winked. "It's just one time then he'll be gone."

"I can do that."

"I'm gonna go talk to him." Ryan grabbed a few cans of soda from the refrigerator.

"He won't talk. I've already tried."

"Gracie, guys talk to guys… say things they don't tell women." Ryan was on the defense, he must have known he was on a doomed mission.

"Good luck."

He spent an hour in that bedroom with Wally. When he came out, he tilted his head and twisted his lips. "Okay, he ain't talking. Just keeps saying he's outta here." He thumped into the big chair and we all sat around the roaring fireplace in silence, waiting, wondering, unsure what to think or say.

At exactly eleven-thirty, Masters stood in the kitchen. "It's time," he called.

Scared and shaking, Wally came from the bedroom and looked at each of us. He walked up to me and did something I sure didn't expect. He pulled me close and kissed me, hard, soft, warm, desperate. It was a kiss far more intense than I'd been wishing for from Ben, and it left me breathless for a moment. No one moved or commented. He followed Masters out the back door and we never saw him again.

~*~

Well hell! Why was Cole so surprised? Of course, they'd be freaked. They had no idea what to expect and the situation made everything bigger and more terrifying than it had to be. How was he supposed to do this and keep them all calm? Acclimation was personal, between the kid and their guide, one-on-one, and never with an audience waiting in the next room for a report. The situation was impossible, and with each Acclimation it was only going to get worse, he was sure of it.

Wally was long gone, off like a bolt of lightning the moment he could get free. It wasn't even dawn. He didn't even take a moment to say goodbye to his friends. To Gracie. Cole hid his grin. That was a surprise. Not a bad kiss for someone with so little experience. Poor Wally didn't think he'd survive the night. He thought it was going to be his first and last kiss ever. He did good, but how well will he do now, alone out there without guidance? It worried Cole in ways that surprised him. He thought he didn't care about this shit, but choices had to be made. Would Wally make the right ones? Was it Cole's fault if he didn't? Hell yes. According to Allerton, extracting a vow and commitment, either way, is a huge part of acclimating effectively. Maybe he never could have succeeded with Wally. No vow, no choice, no commitment. This left the Acclimation unfinished and more dangerous than it should be. He warned Allerton, he knew he wasn't the right guy for the job. He'd spent his life running away from this stuff, not embracing it with the intention of passing it on. Wally was out there alone and screwed. Cole couldn't even go find him; there were others to protect. This could be really bad. He had to do better.

He had four more chances.

That is, if they let him. Breakfast was a series of rolling eyes and sneers, angry scowls and grunts from his fellow diners. Even the damn dog snorted and turned his back when Cole walked into the kitchen. No one would look at him or talk to him. He had to walk around the table to reach the milk for his cereal because they ignored his request, three times. Even Gracie. Fine by him.

When he had enough Cole stood, tossed his half-full bowl of Wheaties into the sink with a crash and left for the basement. Inconsiderate shits. He had a life before this, things to do and places to go. His plans didn't include babysitting. There were no words for how much he hated this.

At the bottom of the basement steps he turned on the light. The single bulb glared and swung, floating illumination in waves over the mess left behind from last night. Time to clean up. Foul words flowing like a mantra. He folded blankets, gathered bloodied bandages, kicked at broken glass, and collected up the contents of an overturned toolbox. Slowing his breath and pounding heart, he put the various sized screwdrivers and wrenches in place. How could they treat him that way? He was trying to save their damn lives. They didn't even think about his sacrifice. They didn't give a damn. He stood then dropped, sitting haphazardly on an old mattress. Shifting to cross his legs Indian-style, he brushed away the fluff from a dark feather then squeezed his eyes shut. The truth was that they didn't understand what was happening. How could they? He didn't totally understand either.

Remembering Wally's terror teased bile up Cole's throat. He'd tried so hard to help the kid through it. His face dropped into his hands and harsh sobs pushed from his aching chest, unbidden, uncontrolled, painful. Tears soaked his fingers and he leaned his head back against the stone wall. Why did Allerton think he could do this? He was no different than those kids—scared, confused, living in denial and fear. He couldn't leave them like that when this was over. He had to leave them better. Better than him. And his mind wandered. Was Wally's intense negative response Cole's fault? Or was Wally bound and determined to leave no matter what he was told?

For years Cole had blamed Allerton for his own horrifying Acclimation experience, but was it in truth his personal failing? Would Allerton have done better with Wally? A light brightened in his mind. Did Allerton purposely include Wally in this group to teach Cole a lesson about the Acclimation process? That you can't win them all? That you can only do the best you can? Was Allerton that calculated? Hell yes. So, what did Cole learn from last night?

He had to guide them better, he had to improve his approach, and he had to do it against all his natural reluctance. With that realization came a tsunami crash of memories. The last time he'd known he had to do better. The last time he put the full power of his intent into motion. Afghanistan, a year ago. His body trembled so hard he could hardly stand. He wanted to run, helter-skelter through the woods. Let the enemy have him, let them kill him, because he could only be safe from those memories if he was dead. To hell with vows, to hell with responsibilities. He was not interested in doing this job. He had a life to live and if choosing to die was the best option, he was game. Why not? Who was there to stop him? Allerton was MIA, the Gate was gone. There was no one to answer to but himself. It wasn't exactly suicide. It would be a simple stroll through the forest. Anything could kill a guy in the woods—bears, wildcats, mountain lions, snakes. Lots of things could do the job. As long as it erased his memories. It was all he asked.

He could hear the enemy through the open door above, whispering, talking, demanding. With slow steps, he climbed toward those words. An ominous figure darkened the morning sunlight and blocked his exit. Cole blinked and prepared for the coming pain. As his heart jumped in his chest his senses kicked in, and with enough terror to choke him, he recognized her.

"Gracie! What the hell! Why are you out here?" He gripped her arm and pulled her toward the cabin.

"I'm sorry. We're sorry. We know Wally intended to go, we just thought you might be able to talk him into staying with us, that's all."

They'd reached the back porch and Cole paused to look into her lovely eyes, golden crystals sparked in them, nearly hypnotizing him. He tightened his grip on her arm and she winced. "You can't leave this cabin! Gracie, they'll kill you," he said in a hush.

"I know," she whispered back. "I can hear them. They're back." A tear slid down her cheek. "Please don't give up on us. We'll behave. I promise."

He pointed to the door and she skittered inside. Obviously getting himself killed wasn't in the cards. Time for a choice. The right choice. The idea of leaving those kids unprotected made his stomach knot. The mere idea that Gracie could have been sliced to shreds, dead, gone, loomed bigger than his personal nightmares. Just because they weren't supposed to be his responsibility didn't mean they weren't. Allerton might have made a serious mistake by choosing him as guide, but Cole had to see it through. He was invested, whether he liked it or not. There could be no more wavering if they were going to survive what lay ahead. No more seeking escape. It was time for a little truth. Trust worked both ways and he needed to cultivate confidence for them all.

Inside, the others sat around the coffee table, heads leaned in like they were plotting a murder or something. "Listen up," Cole shouted and they all jumped. There was shuffling and shifting. Gracie gasped and he turned to her. "Why are you all so damn jumpy?"

"Uh… Wally… Wally's gone…" she said, looking so guilty Cole could almost see it oozing off of her.

"Yeah, and is this news? Didn't he say he intended to leave? What's the big surprise here? Did you seriously think he'd stick around?" Cole dropped into the big chair and the kids watched him, like he might explode at any moment. They could tell he'd been pissed off, frustrated, crying like a girl. Too late to hide it so he sighed and shrugged. "I tried, guys. I tried hard to keep him close. I thought it would be a good idea… since we have the van… to acclimate you all, then just shuttle each of you off to wherever you plan to go." Cole never had that thought, but it felt like it was always his intention. Knowing he'd be moving ahead clearly mapped out the facts. He couldn't acclimate and run. He couldn't have any more Wally regrets to carry. He intended to improve at this Acclimation thing and this felt a lot like the first step.

"What happened last night?" Ben eyed him with suspicion and Cole straightened up in his seat.

"What do you think happened? I gave Wally a ton of information, a little education about the world out there, then I invited him to stick around for a free ride." That was another lie. He'd begged Wally, pleaded with him to hear him out, to take a little time before running off. "He left. That's all. He just… left."

"What did you do to him?" Ben's eyes glowed with a passion Cole couldn't identify.

"I acclimated him. He left."

"Did you hurt him?"

"Are you serious?" Cole stood. "What the hell are you accusing me of? I'm your guide. I'm here to get you through a simple process, nothing more."

"Did… you… hurt… him?"

"I never touched him." Cole glared, the kids leaned back and Jenny actually gasped with fear. The look on their faces tugged at his already thumping heart. "Listen to me. There's nothing to be so damn afraid of. This is a personal thing for each of you."

"So, why do we need you?" Ryan's face was red, his voice a hiss.

How could Cole answer that? He couldn't tell them that he was there to guide them through a change, to stop the bleeding, to soothe them into a new life, to gain a commitment, a vow, a choice. He swallowed hard and stood to look down at them all. Did he want to go military on them? No. All he wanted to do was comfort them. "The truth," he began as he lowered onto the edge of his chair. "The truth is that your life at Ariel's Gate was ridiculously, dangerously limited."

His audience nodded, a *no kidding* expression clearly written on each face.

"Right, believe me, I know. See, real life and the real world are nothing like the Gate. Whether you stick around and let me drive you to your destination, or decide to head off on your own, you need to understand how the real world works. How you'll fit into it. I'm a guide through a… change. Acclimation is like commencement from normal schools. The difference is that normal kids in normal schools live and function in a normal world. You never have. Acclimation is important lessons and information you need to survive out there."

"Normal," Gracie whispered.

Cole sensed the intensity of her desire and he felt real sorrow for the fact that she'd never find normal. Ever.

"And what about the thing that hurt Wally back at the Gate? Is that thing still out there?" Ben's voice trembled.

"Yes." Damn, that was the hardest to say, the most difficult truth of all. "Yes, and it's still a danger. That's why you all need to stay inside the cabin."

"If it's a monster, can't it just break in?" Jenny's eyes were big as saucers and ready to burst into tears. "I mean, if it could cut Wally like that, why can't it just break through a stupid door?"

"It can, but it can't." Cole shook his head. "I can explain more about that in your Acclimation. Just trust me, I'm trying to protect you. These rules aren't for my own entertainment. But if you stick to them, you won't get hurt. I swear." Could he do that? Could he protect them from an enemy that had the power to cross into a knot of powerful ley lines? Was Wally's Acclimation a beacon, leading them to the doorstep? Something to think about later, without scared kids watching him so closely.

"Too vague," Ben stood and paced, keeping his glare on Cole.

"What do you want from me, man? I'm doing my job." Cole rubbed his eyes and pounded his fist on the arm of the chair with a thump. Nothing about the situation was comfortable. He returned Ben's glare. "Sit down and listen to me."

Ben dropped onto the sofa with defiance.

"Usually this is done one at a time, alone and far from others. We're all in uncharted territory here. You all," he pointed a finger, swinging it across the room, at each of them, "need to mind your own business. Your Acclimation isn't his business or her business. It's personal and I'm just here to guide you through it. That's all there is to it. Enough with the interrogation!" He turned to leave but Gracie caught his arm as hard as he'd caught hers earlier.

"We're just scared."

"I told you, there's nothing to be afraid of."

"You're lying." Her eyes were sincere, terrified.

Something cracked inside of him, something he didn't know was breakable. His arms wrapped around her and pulled her to his chest. "I was scared, too. Still am sometimes. Seeking normal takes all my energy and I still miss it by miles. You," he looked over her head at the others, "you're all going to be fine. Great, in fact. You're all starting out with way more capability than I ever had. Just… please… trust me."

Gracie nodded against his chest and he released her, rather abruptly. Holding her like that felt way too good. He cleared his throat, pushed a hand through his hair, and looked at the others.

"And… one of these days, maybe you can tell me what you're all plotting around that coffee table. If it's not offing me, I may have a few good ideas to add to the caper." He grinned. Did he look as awkward as he felt? It took a minute but the others smiled and things, at least on the surface, seemed like they just might smooth over.

8

September thirteenth, and hot as hell in the city of Pittsburgh. The day blazed at over ninety degrees and sparked bright as a bonfire about to rage out of control. They called it Indian Summer but to Michael Allerton, it was sheer hell. His trial had lasted eight days and the verdict was coming down like a reign of terror, whether he was ready or not. He walked from his hotel to Forbes Avenue and looked up at the old structure. Impressive. Built of rusticated granite blocks in 1888, the Allegheny County Courthouse was one of the city's historical gems. It's the second courthouse to stand on that spot, the perfect site for a place of judgment, geographically positioned in the center of an immaculate circle of mystical ley lines. For hundreds of years people had been instinctively drawn to the power of that spot. Allerton's kind had known of it since the beginning of earthly time. While the native peoples of the land gathered every seven years on that exact plot of soil for trade, reunions, and politics, Allerton's people were already there, deep inside the earth, judging fairly in that, the most neutral location on the planet. The America continent had been blessed and cursed. There was creative influence in Los Angeles with its pure vortex of powerful inspiration; there was transgression power in the southern territories; there was prayer and God focus in the Midwest; but right in the middle of downtown

Pittsburgh existed a place of pure neutrality. The planet had been attracting those in need of such influence since God rested on the seventh day.

Turning the bend, he stopped to gaze in at the beautiful courthouse courtyard and say a brief prayer. The sparkling fountain whispered to him. It was not going to be a good day. He walked on, his feet refusing to move quickly. His mind wondered if he had the courage to just run. But that wouldn't be courage, it would be cowardice. He forced his steps ahead then glanced upward as he passed beneath the arched *Bridge of Sighs,* named for a similar bridge in Venice and designed to connect the courthouse and the jail. History tells of a daring escape from the prison in 1892, when the warden's wife, Kate Soffel, aided the condemned brothers Jack and Ed Biddle to their freedom. Allerton almost smiled, that wasn't likely to happen today.

To hear his verdict, he would need to be shackled and led over that bridge before entering a specific elevator for descent into the depths of Pittsburgh. His trial took place a full seven stories beneath the ground floor and directly under the structure's four-story tower. The same room would witness his verdict.

Inside he was patted down, given an orange jumpsuit to change in to, cuffed then rather roughly led down a long hall. His mind wandered to Cole Masters and the challenges he faced, curious about the first Acclimation and how it went, and hopeful that the verdict, whatever it was, wouldn't stop or hinder Masters' important work. During interrogation, he'd kept critical information to himself. Michael Allerton was on trial to explore his failures, not stop Acclimations in motion. Of course, the tribunal had never been tied to specific timelines or traditions. This situation was far more complicated—and that, too, was Allerton's fault.

The deeper the elevator dropped, the warmer and stuffier the air became. He found it hard to breathe and gasped every few breaths, desperate to gain enough oxygen. The doors slid open and two severe guards gripped his arms and pulled hard.

"Enough!" shouted Allerton. "This isn't necessary. Let me walk with dignity, for Christ's sake!" They released their grip and walked beside him. Another prisoner might have been surprised, but Allerton knew his station and his rights. Until he was convicted, he was free, even wearing garish orange and handcuffs.

The dimness of the courtroom was oppressive, intended to deflate a defendant's hope and make them feel vulnerable. He stood, head high and shoulders squared, in the dead center of a circular space. The domed ceiling was high and covered with tiny black chips of sparkling flint. The only light in the room came from small brass lamps along the wall. Around the shadowed room sat witnesses, at least a hundred of them, all there to see which way the tribunal would push the world at this crucial time. Up on a platform sat the three high judges.

The number three is important to Allerton's people. Since the beginning of time there had always been three segments of the race—the dark, the light, and the rebellion. To complicate matters further, within each segment were fanatical and militant groups of rogue warriors, some out for justice, others for blood and self-interest.

There were three different philosophies for the Acclimation of the young. These age-old distinctions drew vicious arguments and controversy. One faction trusted the orphanage system which offered a gentle, well-educated childhood followed by safe acclimation with an accredited guide. Another group preferred to raise their young fully aware of what was to come. A third splinter group rejected all responsibility for acclimation, preferring to send their youth out into the world to discover the truth of their existence, alone and without guidance.

The most dangerous threat of all came from the three extreme ideologies for the continued survival of the race. Everything depended on maintaining balance, but it seemed their inbred diversity fought hard against such balance. Disease and hostilities had played havoc and balance—always precarious—had become more and more unstable over the past two decades. On that hot morning in September, imbalance was worse than it had ever been since the beginning of time.

At one time in Allerton's life, when he was young and curious and grateful for any excuse to get away from his job at Ariel's Gate, he enjoyed sitting witness at such trials. Back then he tended to think of the high tribunal judges as the three stooges. Age and experience had changed all point of views and painted the Tribunal a very different color that day. The high judges represented the extreme right, the extreme left, and the fair center. The white, the black, and the reasonable grey. What they really signified were three opinions destined to never meet in the middle. Thank heaven for the ley lines. All extremes were softened, all edges blurred, and in that space, compassion ruled. Usually. Just looking at the expression on each of the three faces made Allerton think he might piss his pants. *This was sooo not good,* as his students would say. Maybe he should have run.

A verdict of a tribunal trial was always spoken by the neutral center member, the grey, the balance—but all balance seemed gone. However this turned out, it was ordained to influence the future of Michael's race and the human race, perhaps even bring about the end of days. This was never predicted by Nostradamus, never explored in the book of Revelations. This was off script, Allerton could feel it. Oh, hell yes, he definitely should have run.

While the center high judge read the long list of Allerton's infractions, sins, and crimes, he heard something else, something more. It bubbled in his soul, made him cringe, but also opened an avenue he hadn't previously considered for his defense. It wasn't too late, not until the verdict was spoken. To be sure of his plan, he listened with painful intensity. He'd be asked to speak on his own behalf, and he needed to be prepared. The high judge on the right refused to look at him. She was the white judge. She was sure of her power and her convictions, as was any highborn of her kind. She was also harboring personal rage against Allerton. Anger and pain so deep he wasn't sure he could raise above it enough to make a clear case, but it would be his only chance.

Listening, he noticed that at the end of each crime, a snap of bright light flashed like an electrical short in the wiring. The energy cabling was damaged, just like the direction of the trial was off track. Why didn't anyone else see it?

"Michael Allerton is accused of the following crimes… Mishandling of power within the Ariel's Gate institution." *Snap!*

"Misappropriation of funds within the Ariel's Gate institution." *Snap!*

"Mismanagement of five youths preparing for Acclimation, one of them Gracious Caine, a young woman of great importance to our race." *Snap!*

"Dissolution of all Ariel's Gate assets without tribunal authorization." *Snap!*

"Withholding information on the whereabouts of specific youths: Wallace Dean, Ryan Sutcliff, Benjamin Wheeler, Jennifer Perkins, and Gracious Caine." *Snap!*

"Endangering all residents of Ariel's Gate by sending them from the facility without Tribunal authorization." *Snap!*

"Stealing, and having possession of the Book of Vision within Ariel's Gate walls… a level one high crime… and subsequently losing said book." *Snap.*

"Breaking his sacred soul vow to his race." *Snap!*

"Michael Allerton, this tribunal asks if you have any final words on your behalf before judgment is passed."

"I have plenty to say. With your permission, Tribunal Grey?" He awaited a nod then immediately turned his attention to the white judge. "I believe that this is an unfair and unbalanced trial and should be stricken from the books."

The hundred witnesses shuffled and whispered, and the woman wearing a white judge's robe glared with tilted head. "You can *not* be serious."

"I am most certainly serious. This trial, and subsequently the judgment of this tribunal court, is tainted with your personal issues, Rachel, and you know it."

The black and the grey judges looked to the white and she shrugged. "He's grasping at straws, my fellow judges. He has failed and he must be punished for it."

"I still have the floor, do I not, Tribunal Grey?"

The grey judge looked like a grey being. His hair was pure white, his fleshy face faded, his hands gnarled. His eyes, however, were brilliant blue and showed the compassion all defendants prayed for. "You do, sir. Am I to understand that you are calling for a mistrial?"

"I am, your honor."

"Please explain your reasoning, Mr. Allerton."

"Tribunal Grey, this is a waste of time," Tribunal Black grunted but Rachel was growing pale. Sweat formed in tiny droplets across her brow.

"Rachel," Michael said with gentleness. "Would you like to explain?"

She revived her glare and high color returned to her face.

"Very well." Michael reached up and scratched his nose, the chains of his handcuffs jangled in the silence. "Honored tribunal, first and foremost, I am guilty of none of the crimes listed. This is so because you have not taken the grave nature of the emergency into consideration. My contract clearly states that under such conditions of enemy aggression, I am commanded…" he looked to all the judges who looked to their folders of paperwork, "…*commanded*… as stated on page fifty-eight, paragraph four, addendum ninety-two… to do anything necessary to protect the staff and students of Ariel's Gate. The danger was real there… just as it is here." He raised his arms and pointed to the ceiling. "Outside the doors of this very courthouse, on the streets of Pittsburgh, smack in the center of these all-powerful ley lines… I saw them. More than fifty of them. The enemy. Right at your door. I had over a hundred students and staff to protect and the enemy was close enough to scale the walls of Ariel's Gate. One student was murdered. One was attacked mere feet from the courtyard. Ariel's Gate, with no capacity to defend itself, left me to do the only thing I could to protect the future of our race. Send them off to safer ground. Secretly. Quickly."

Witnesses whispered louder and all three judges listened with thoughtful expressions.

"I mishandled, misappropriated, mismanaged nothing. I was the only one able to protect those kids and I did what I had to do. I admit to withholding information on the whereabouts of the listed youths nearing Acclimation. With the enemy at your own door, how could I trust divulging such information? How could I continue to protect them if I lead the enemy right to them?

He drew in a deep breath. "I strongly deny breaking my sacred soul vow.

How I could be questioned for such a thing is unthinkable. My vow is intact. I have not failed. The balance is off and the enemy is seeking to expand control within the resulting disorder. Our race is tipping into full loss, Honored Tribunal. You cannot deny it."

He remained silent for a full thirty seconds, pleased to hear the witnesses whisper among themselves and watch the judges lean back in acknowledgment.

Finally, he spoke. "I will accept guilt of one, and only one, of the listed crimes. I did acquire and hide the Book of Vision on Ariel's Gate property. We all know the power of that book, its ability to guide our choices—"

"For the dark!" shouted the woman in white.

"Or, in the case of my sacred vow and responsibilities, that book has the ability to guide for the light, for the right, with balance and equilibrium. In the hands of the enemy, it could have been used to their benefit. In my hands, it warned of the coming threat and guided my choice to protect what I could."

"But you lost the book."

Michael grinned at the black judge. "Actually, I have not. I know exactly where it is. It's safe. It's doing what it can to help our cause."

The grey judge leaned forward. "And, where is it?"

"With the hidden youths. To tell you where the book is would compromise their location."

The room fell silent and Michael watched the three judges sit still as stone, the white, the black, and the grey.

Finally, the black judge spoke. "You give us much to consider."

"No, no he doesn't. Endangering those youths endangers our survival," Rachel's voice croaked with anger. "What's to say that his decision hasn't been more hazardous than helpful to those young people? What makes his decision more valuable than the Tribunal's resolution? He never once requested advice or authorization."

"Judges, there was no time," Michael shouted. "The danger developed within thirty short hours. I did what I believed to be best. I stand by my decisions."

Tribunal White hissed her words, "But we do not! You had no right—"

"In his contract—" the grey judge tried to interject.

"Yes, yes, his contract, but what makes his unapproved actions correct? Are we to wait for the confirmed death or survival of these young acclimates to prove Mr. Allerton's success or folly? Wait-and-see has never been this tribunal's policy." Her face glowed with rage.

Judge Black shifted in his chair, aggravation written on his face as he glared at Rachel. "Let's just say that this is probably more of our folly than his, Judge White. Look closely. That's your… and my… signature on his contract. It's a moot point, my dear. Let it go."

Allerton lowered his face and privately grinned. "And this brings me to my final defense… the mistrial." He watched Rachel's face, her lips tightened and lovely eyes closed. "Honored Tribunal, I propose that this trial has been judged unfairly due to the white judge's personal involvement with the case."

He waited. She didn't speak up. He hoped she would, but it was the grey judge who pushed things ahead.

"We are not interested in delays and distractions, Mr. Allerton. If you have grounds for a mistrial, speak them now."

"Benjamin Wheeler is my own son… mine and the white judge's son."

A gasp from the attendees circled Michael, swirling like a thick, choking cloud as he continued.

"She and I were lovers. She conceived, and realizing that her life left little room for raising and acclimating a child. I took Ben to Ariel's Gate." Once again, he looked to her but she held her tongue, allowing him the freedom to smear her good name further. "The white judge has never forgiven me for taking our son and raising him traditionally, within our worldwide protective institutional system." He cleared his throat, unsure if he really had to say the next words. "She… Rachel… white judge of this high tribunal court… has proven gross prejudice against the traditional system and holds strong discrimination against me and for my position… for caring for our son in the way I believe most safe and appropriate." A tear slipped from his eye. "She has a wish for revenge, and I feel that leads to a confirmed mistrial."

She stood, shouting rose all around and the snapping lights flickered, making Michael wince and cover his face against possible injury. Again he wondered, why no one else was responding to those lights. Were they even aware of them?

"How is Ben safe?" she shouted. "You've sent him off with that useless failure! A criminal! For all we know, Ben's already dead!"

"No… no…" Michael raised his chained hands to get everyone's attention. "Listen! He's alive, he's safe. Cole Masters is a warrior like none I've ever seen. His soul vow is intact. He'll die protecting those kids. Rachel, baby, Ben is safe… he's safe."

She looked to her fellow judges and spoke in low tones, but Michael heard every word. "I agree to a mistrial for all accused crimes but one. He must be convicted for possession of the Book of Vision. The dangers of that book are too great to estimate, and his contract allows no clause for the possession of such a treacherous item. I vote for immediate conviction, and beg, as a mother, for a quick resolution of the issues at hand. We must locate the youths, as soon as possible. There is nowhere safe for them as long as they are in the hands of an untrained, unlawful guide. May I please call for a vote? For the possession of the Book of Vision, I vote… guilty."

"Guilty," stated the black judge.

"Guilty," the grey judge said then stood, waving his colleague to sit and the witnesses to silence. "Michael Allerton, you are found guilty of the illegal possession of the Book of Vision. This is a high crime, do you understand, Mr. Allerton?"

Emptied of all reason, Michael couldn't find the strength to nod, but his eyes did blink acknowledgment.

"You are stripped of all access to funds. You will receive no further defense and are denied representation to reopen this case. Michael Allerton, you will be incarcerated for thirty years in this very penitentiary, after which time you will be evaluated and considered for parole."

Michael gulped. His heart thundered in his ears. He had failed. The penitentiary was several levels below the courtroom where he stood. Thirty years. He would be seventy-nine. Would the world still be here in thirty years? He made no motion to fight the rough treatment of the guards who took him away. All was lost. Sparks shot from the stone floor with every step he took, and flashed like a bolt of lightning when the steel cell door clanked shut.

Good God, what had he done? Were they right? Was his ego so big he saw nothing but glory? Had he been wrong to attain and consult the book? Was he mistaken to follow his own path for the protection of those in his care? No, no. Not at all. His heart ached for Cole Masters, now completely on his own. It ached for Gracie and Jenny and Ryan—for Wally, already acclimated and most likely more scared than he'd ever been in his life. He worried for Ben. His son. His heart. How could he have failed his own son?

One flickering fluorescent light relentlessly illuminated the small cell so he had little sense of time, day, night. Sometimes he could make a good guess based on the food served. Eggs meant morning. A sandwich meant midday, a hot meal meant evening. The endless hours between meatloaf and scrambled eggs were the worst. Michael Allerton was a powerful being of his race, but the depths at which they imprisoned him greatly weakened his strength, his ability to analyze thoughts, his will.

He'd had nine breakfasts when a visitor arrived. "Mrs. Soffel? Is that you?" he said with sadness as Rachel, the love of his life, entered the cell and sat beside him on the bunk. She wore a tan wool suit and a brightly colored silk blouse. Her skirt was tight and her legs, as beautiful as he remembered. She carried a briefcase and dark grey heavy coat. She smelled like fresh cold air and impending winter.

"Michael…" she set her things aside on the thin mattress.

"Shall I assume autumn has come to Pittsburgh?"

"Rain, cold. They're calling for an early snow this week."

"Time moves on." He glanced at the briefcase. "Are you here to give me the death sentence?"

Silence.

"Rachel… there's no way I'll survive this. You know that."

She nodded then took a deep breath and opened her briefcase. Inside, folded neatly, were his clothes. Not warm enough for snow, but real clothes all the same.

"Oh, sweet baby… you are here to break me out of this filthy joint," he teased.

"Stop being an idiot." She tossed the clothes onto his lap and retrieved papers from the bottom of the briefcase, silently read through them then cleared her throat. "I commanded that the kids be located…"

"Yes, I heard that."

"Yes, and the fact of the matter is that you seem to be the only one who might be able to do that."

"You love me," he said with a playful grin.

"No… yes… damn you, God help me, I do… I did… but this isn't about you, Michael. It's about Gracious Caine. She's important. She has to be found. She has to be safe. Without her all could be lost."

"I know." He stood and unsnapped his orange jumpsuit, dropping it to his ankles while he pulled on his shirt then sat and dragged on his pants. "Trust me, baby. I did the only thing I could to protect her." Pants on, zipped and buckled, he turned and gripped Rachel's shoulders in his hands. "This is about Ben, too. Time has been wasted here. He's about to be acclimated and all we can do is hope for the best. I planned to be there for him… and especially for Gracie. I don't know if I can make it now."

Freeing her, he reached into his pocket and checked his wallet. Empty. No cash, no charge cards, no nothing. "Seriously?"

She rolled her eyes, opened her purse, and pulled a wad of cash from her own wallet. "Here. It's all I can give you right now. Your resources are blocked. The tribunal will not financially support your efforts. They're hanging on to the misappropriations accusation—"

"The crime I was *not* guilty of?" He glared and shook his head.

"You'll need to be creative. Be quick. You're to do this alone to prove yourself, but contact me here," she handed him a business card, "and I'll do what I can to get you where you need to go."

"You're flirting with treason, Rachel. Are you ready for that? You can always say I stole the cash from you, but to support my efforts further…" He shrugged. "You could be tossed from the tribunal for such actions. Imprisoned."

Her expression didn't waver.

"Have you already been disrobed?"

"Do you want my help or not?"

He tucked the cash into his wallet then reached for the cell door and tentatively pushed. It squealed open and he grinned. "Now what?"

"Here are your papers. I'll get you to the street, but after that you're on your own. Be careful, the enemy is everywhere. They'll try to follow you."

He nodded.

"Here." She handed him the heavy grey coat. "It's my husband's. He'll never miss it."

"You do love me." His voice lilted but she walked on, eyes ahead. "So, how is the husband… the Dark Lord? Rachel, Rachel, Rachel, you just can't seem to stay away from the bad boys."

"Shut up."

He reached out, gripped her hand and pulled her into an embrace. "I'll find Ben," he whispered. "And I'll tell him everything. He needs to know the truth."

"No," she said. "Tell him his mother's dead. I can't bear for him to know the truth. I'd have been a terrible mother anyway. Best he thinks—"

Michael kissed her tenderly then whispered, "You could have been a great mother. I never gave you the chance. Take that chance now. He deserves the truth."

"Let's get you the hell out of here."

He followed her up, up, past the courtroom, to the ground level and into the long hallway.

"These are the conditions of your release, Michael. When you find Gracious Caine, you're to bring her here where we will protect her. And you… your incarceration will resume."

He stopped dead and looked into her eyes.

"You must complete your sentence, Michael. I can't change that."

"Yes, you can."

"I won't."

His head dropped back in frustration. "You cannot mean that. We both know the world will be a whole lot different before I get back to this city. War will have begun and we need soldiers. Fix this, Rachel. Fix it."

She led him further, said nothing.

One of the guards who took him to his cell stood near the door and for a moment Michael's heart rose to his throat. The man simply nodded.

"Mr. Allerton," he said. "Good luck."

Icy cold rain splattered in, chilling his face. He squeezed Rachel's hand. "Fix this."

"No. Michael Allerton, I am authorized to tell you that if you don't return, we will hunt you down. You will suffer far more than a few decades in prison. You will be executed."

"You'd have to find me first." Her eyes narrowed and his voice hardened. "Now, go back in there and fix this."

He turned and stepped into the street. Cold fresh air assaulted his lungs but revived his energy and wits. He walked with brisk steps, along the street, under the *Bridge of Sighs*, past the courtyard. The extreme weather shift made him feel like he'd been in prison for months, but only eight days had passed. Eight important days. Turning on Grant Street, he reached into the warm coat pocket, took out the card she'd given him and tore it into as many pieces as his fingers could manage. If he used it he'd be flirting with far more danger than if he didn't. He dropped the resulting confetti into a trash can.

Running a hand through rain soaked hair, Michael looked left then right and crossed the street. Time to determine the best way to get the hell out of town. His destination was southeast. He was already being followed by both the enemy and tribunal spies, so close he could smell them. A convoluted route involving twists and turns, hitchhiking and local bus rides would be safest. He had no allies in Pittsburgh, little money, and the need to reach those kids before Gracie's Acclimation. Every moment that passed burned in his chest. Too much time had already been wasted. He refused to accept that he might already be too late. What to do after he reached Masters and the kids—as many kids as he'd managed to keep close to him—was his biggest dilemma. Taking Gracie to Pittsburgh never figured into the equation. Where on earth was a place safe enough for Gracious Caine? The survival of his race depended on choosing carefully.

~*~

Cole chose to spend most of his time alone in the basement. If he stuck around the cabin, they'd keep demanding answers he couldn't give. Solitude made things easier. He needed time to plan and find ways of being more effective. Sitting at a makeshift table under the bare lightbulb, he shook his head in frustration. Why the hell wasn't there a guide book for this? Something easy to follow. First, do this. Second, say that. Third, explain the vow.

He blinked and straightened in his chair. Explain the vow. He definitely didn't do that with Wally. He shuffled through his growing pile of notes, scribbled the idea then checked the Saint Angela's Church Calendar he found on the workbench.

Ryan would acclimate in two days. He couldn't fail with this one. He needed that kid's strength and tenacity if they were all going to survive. Ryan had to stick close. He planned to start earlier this time, to take Ryan down to the basement at ten instead of later. That would give him a full two hours before midnight, when things got hairy. Time to explain everything, to give Ryan time to digest what lay ahead. That was another good idea and he jotted it down, too. All his good ideas would need to be implemented then evaluated after each Acclimation.

Each of the remaining acclimates were very different and that could play havoc with any system he devised. He wasn't comfortable flying by the seat of his pants. It sure didn't work with Wally, but he had to consider every possibility. Each kid saw the world differently. Ryan was a natural leader, but had far too much ego to succeed without a few stumbles and bruises first. Ben. Poor Ben, he'd most likely been alone and confused his whole life. Cole wondered if he'd ever come to grips with his sexual orientation yet, if he'd even acknowledged it. To face Acclimation and coming out of the closet at the same time could be devastating. Add the discovery that Allerton is the kid's dad, and it could be a disaster. Ben sure wouldn't hear it from Cole. Cole scribbled, *handle with care*. Then there was Jenny. All fluff and little content, but she had a good heart, he could see that much. Acclimation was going to drastically change that girl's life. He'd need a lot of kindness with her. And finally, Gracie. The unknown element. Cole was sure that even Allerton had no idea what Acclimation would reveal for Gracie, a girl saddled with a handicap, determined but limited. All Cole could wish for was something good. She sure deserved it.

Cole needed to make sure that each one of them got through Acclimation safely and with a commitment and vow. He prayed they'd end up well-adjusted and ready for life ahead, but what were the odds? With a lot of luck, four wins to one loss. Poor Wally. The best-case scenario required keeping the remaining four close after Acclimation. He was going to need all the help he could get—even untrained soldiers were better than no soldiers. If he improved with each, maybe by the time Gracie made it to the basement, he'd have this thing perfected.

His heart skipped a beat.

Maybe not.

Something thudded in his chest, so hard that at first, he looked to the ceiling, curious if someone or something was up there. No, the pounding came again, a desperate tug at his heart, a sincere cry from his soul, something deeper, that thing he'd been pushing out of his awareness. The experience grew, excruciating, painful, demanding. Lights flashed behind his eyelids and even the smallest sound—the chitter of a tiny mouse under the mattress, the thump of raindrops outside the closed door, the pulsing of his own blood—became so intense he covered his ears and gasped. He knew what was happening, what had to happen. He understood. If he was to acclimate them well, he had to deal with his own terror.

His whole life slithered like a snake in front of his mind's eye. Slow, slow, so that he could see every sin, every failure, every mistake. The snake rolled over onto its back and showed a pure white belly, scaly but pristine. Images blasted into form. Visions of the optimism and dreams he'd had before Acclimation, visions of a positive future and hopeful ideas, visions of happiness and normalcy there for the taking. Visions of all the things he was sure could never be. When the snake rolled again it was a man, shrouded in black and bleeding. All around him vibrated the sounds of gunshot and explosions, mortar flying, screams, cries. Blood. Blood. More Blood. Cole gasped and reached for something, anything to stabilize him. The vision altered again. Nothing but light. White light, yellow light, green light, lightning over a strange landscape. Light and the sound of his steadying heart. He wasn't always a failure. When necessary, he knew well how to succeed. He just couldn't do it alone.

And Cole did what he'd wanted and needed to do since the moment this all started. He dropped to his knees and he prayed as hard as he could. He begged for patience and tolerance, for wisdom and compassion. But most of all he prayed for courage, something he never really had, even in Afghanistan. Even at that most powerful moment of his existence.

Shouting? Cole looked up and blinked. Was that shouting? He raced up the steps and pushed open the door. Ryan and Jenny stood, waving their arms on the back porch. "Gracie's gone! She ran out into the woods!"

"Where's Ben?" he called as he ran past. Those two were inseparable.

Good God, Cole prayed. *Please don't let me find them both dead out there.*

"He's inside. Hurry! She went that way."

He turned, almost tripped over a log. "When?"

"Just now, she ran off just now. That way!"

And he raced, slipping on mud and shiny fallen leaves. At that moment, the sun burst through the ceaseless rain clouds. Cole blinked, his mind spinning. How far could she have gone? The girl was a gimp and couldn't run fast. He looked for signs and there they were, a dragging slide every few feet. He followed the trail.

Voices grew louder, became clearer. *Come pretty girl, come.*

"No! Gracie, Stop! Wait for me!" He had to reach her before they did.

A scream. He turned, slipped and tumbled, then regained his footing and ran in that new direction. "Stop! Leave her alone!"

And there she was, leaning against a tree, out of breath and blessedly unharmed. This time his embrace was like an angry parent. "Good God! What the hell are you doing?" She was crying hard, sobbing and unable to speak. Lifting her in his arms, he turned to carry her back but she struggled.

"No, don't take me back there. Please."

Tucking her face under his chin, his eyes scanned for the source of the voices. They were well hidden but also well aware of how exposed he was. "Whatever happened, we'll work it out." His feet sped, faster and faster, almost faster than possible. Everything around him, trees, sounds, even the ground seemed to smear into a mix of colors. At the cabin, he pushed into the door, set Gracie onto the sofa, and glared all around. "Okay," he said between raspy breaths. "What the hell happened?"

All eyes turned to Ben. Gracie made an exit, slipping Cole's grasp to hide in the bedroom. The slammed door sounded as final as a death sentence.

Cole turned with a scowl, focused on Ben and silently counted to ten for control. "Okay, dude. She's in there crying her eyes out and everyone thinks it's your fault. What the hell did you do?"

Ben gulped, his eyes shifted right then left, then he just walked to the ladder leading to the loft.

"Don't just walk away!"

Ben stood there but didn't turn from the ladder.

Cole rubbed his eyes. "What did you do, man?"

Jenny stepped forward, looking a little more than guilty. "Ah… it's my fault, not Ben's."

"What's your fault?"

"I… well… naturally… I thought she wanted the condom for Wally."

Ryan shrugged and Cole watched Ben climb up the ladder, a broken, exposed man.

No clue what to say next, Cole shouted at the top of his lungs, "Goddamnit! No one's using condoms! Hand them over. Now!"

Ryan emptied his wallet onto the coffee table. There were five rubbers left. Cole blinked in disbelief. The kid had thirty packets when his kit was inspected. Even Cole, who believed himself to be a damn virile guy, couldn't use twenty-five condoms in eight days. Maybe hiding in the basement wasn't such a good idea after all. In addition to dealing with planned parenthood, he had a crying girl in the bedroom, and a possible suicidal gay man in the loft.

"You," he pointed to Ryan, "take care of that one." His finger shifted to the loft. "I'll take care of Gracie. And you, missy," he offered a potent glare that made Jenny wilt even further. "Keep your legs shut!"

Reaching for the doorknob, he drew in a long, deep breath. He had to smooth everything over. Ryan would be acclimated the very next night and solidarity was the biggest cog in Cole's plan. He knocked then slipped inside the room.

Gracie was a small huddled mess of tears and tangled wet hair on the mattress. He sat on the bed but didn't touch her. "Hey, you okay?"

"No."

"Did they get to you? Are you hurt?"

"No!"

"Okay, okay. Listen Gracie, you gotta talk to me."

"Why?" She still hadn't turned to look at him so he slid a fingertip over her shoulder.

"Because. What happened?"

"You don't want to know and I don't want to talk about it."

"Well," he gave a dramatic groan and shifted to sit closer. "Maybe you're right and I don't want to, but I have to know. You can't be running out there and you know it. You could have been—"

"No," she whispered and finally faced him. Pushing a hand under her eyes, she sniffled and shuffled to sit up. "No. Honest. They could have killed me, at least twice. I fell and they got so close but… it was strange… they just stopped and stared at me, like I'm some kind of an alien or something. Watching. Not one of them even reached out to touch me so I got up and ran further. At the tree where you found me, they were so close for a minute I swear I could smell something burning."

Cole was holding his breath, hoping she was lying, terrified that she wasn't. "You *saw* them?"

"Yes, and kinda… no. I saw something, something moving like ink swirls in water. Something that felt ominous. They talked to me, trying to comfort me, draw me closer. But actually, see them? No, I guess I didn't. But they were there." Her eyes challenged him to call her a liar.

He couldn't. For weeks before his own Acclimation the inky black swirls came to him, too. Talked to him. Invited him. Just like they had every day of his life since. Only now they weren't just wisps of darkness floating on the air. They were the enemy. Solid. Dangerous. Deadly. Why didn't they attack her? They had the perfect opportunity right at their fingertips. The way she described their activity indicated something more like curiosity, or was it possibly awe?

"You don't believe me, do you?" Gracie pushed a finger under her nose and sniffled again.

"I… yes, I believe you. Let's get to the bigger issue. Why the hell did you leave this cabin? Why would—"

"I wanted to… I thought I wanted to… um… die."

His heart stumbled a moment. "Changed your mind, huh?"

She nodded and turned to look out the window. The voices had gone silent out there.

"Why did you want to, you know…" He shrugged, unwilling to say the word.

She looked up into his eyes and tilted her head slightly. He'd never seen a girl so lovely, so intense and vibrant, yet so damn sad. "Masters… um… Cole?"

Okay, they were on a first name basis. He'd deal, for the time being. "Yes?"

"Am I horrible?"

"What?"

"Am I ugly? Too damaged for normal people? Am I too hideous with my…" her hand waved to her twisted foot. "Am I too awful for…"

"For what?"

"For anyone to love?"

Cole sighed. What the hell should he tell this very young, very insecure seventeen-year-old woman?

"Am I?" she demanded.

Those strange eyes tugged at his soul. His hand stroked her mussed hair and he searched for something appropriate to say or do. It came like the cavalry. He could even hear the bugle in his head.

"Does this have anything to do with Ben?"

Her eyes lowered and he watched her cheeks turn so red he worried they'd peel and flake off.

She nodded. "He doesn't want me. All my life I thought… I guess I imagined… I just…"

"Sweetheart, that was never going to happen and it has nothing to do with you."

"Of course it does. It was like, like I repelled him, like he was about to throw up or something."

"Trust me, Gracie, it isn't you."

"It has to be me!" She sat up straight and squared her shoulders, ready for battle. Good God, he really liked this girl.

"Nope, it's not you. It's him."

Her arms crossed and she gave him a glare worthy of an angry librarian. "Yeah, right. I suggest we make love and he runs the other way. What's wrong with him? Running disease?"

"Gracie," Cole laid a hand on her arm and spoke in soft tones. "Ben's gay."

"No, he's… he can't be… no, you're wrong."

He gave her a few moments to digest the fact, her expressions shifting and changing like the tide. "Jenny and Ryan know. I can see it. You just missed it, that's all."

Gracie pushed past him and paced the bedroom. "How could I not know something like that? That's crazy. No, my whole life I've known Ben and…" she looked at her own hands, as though the answer was written in the lines on her palms. "How could I not know?"

"You were looking for something else, maybe?"

"Why the hell would he just walk away? Not just tell me?" Tears glittered in her eyes and Cole pointed to them.

"That's why. He didn't want to see you hurt. You two are really close friends, right?"

She nodded, embarrassment rising again on her cheeks.

"Maybe he's afraid of losing his best friend."

"He could have told me. He should have."

"I agree, but it's not that easy for him, you know. He's probably been—"

"Hiding it all this time." She thumped onto the bed. "How stupid. How totally lame. How cruel. I thought…" She sobbed into her hands and Cole pulled her close.

"I know. I know." But he didn't know. He wanted to comfort her but his chest ached with wanting something else.

"I thought I was hideous."

"You are beautiful. Gracie, you're full of something so wonderful there aren't words for it. You are special and unique. Even those things outside recognized it. They didn't attack today, but next time—"

"There won't be a next time."

She rubbed her heated, wet face across his shirt and Cole grinned. "Promise me," he asked.

"I promise." She looked up into his eyes.

That was all it took. His lips lowered to hers in a soft kiss that tugged at his very soul. It felt right and good, yet seemed wrong on so many levels. As his mind reeled from the sweetness of her lips. He remembered this was about doing his job well, and kissing wasn't in the job description. He wasn't too old for her and she wasn't too young for him, but under the circumstances, it just felt a little out of sync. He finally broke from her and stood several feet from the bed. She looked up, shaking fingertips on her reddened lips.

"Uh… maybe I shouldn't have done that. But listen to me. Never, ever, and I mean *ever*, think men won't want you. You are… more than you know. Way more." He turned and nearly slammed into the closed door. "No more running, right?" He didn't look over his shoulder, afraid to see her face.

"No more running."

"And you'll make it right with Ben?"

"Maybe."

"Do it, Gracie." He finally turned, head tilted. "He didn't do anything wrong. He is what he is, and he needs his friend right now."

"Maybe. Maybe later. Not now."

Cole nodded. "Fair enough."

Alone in the basement, he rubbed his eyes, remembered that kiss, and accepted that things just got a whole lot more complicated.

9

After eighteen years of waiting and hoping and looking forward to an independent, normal life, everything was messed up, big time. Things started to move too fast, stuff kept happening and almost everything I imagined to be solid turned to pudding. I abandoned my journal, figuring there was no point in pondering whether God was here for me or I was here for God. Something existed outside the cabin that made no sense… and worse yet, it wanted to kill us. What kind of logic was that? Nothing I ever learned in Ariel's Gate, and nothing I clearly remembered from before that, indicated that anything but freedom and a great future awaited me after Acclimation.

Minutes and hours sped past and I had to force myself to stay aware and be present. Everything was going to keep changing and no one—probably not even Masters—knew what lay ahead. Our fearless leader had that wonky, wobbly energy around him. Especially after Wally left. Especially after what happened in the bedroom—that really odd thing I decided I probably shouldn't think about, ever. Too complicated. Too outside the realm of the world unveiling in front of me. I felt like I was in the middle of a really creepy Neil Gaiman novel. And still, weird things moved on, faster and faster.

German chocolate cake and candles. Another birthday, another coming

Acclimation. This one felt so different from the last one. Ryan had promised not to leave Jenny behind. That put a whole different light on the evening. Except for the fact that I couldn't look Ben in the eye, now I couldn't look Masters in the eye, and I really couldn't bear to watch Jenny's happiness. She'd become Jenny Crocker, cook and baker extraordinaire, preparing a really good dinner from the dry goods and remaining perishable foods. The cake was yummy, made from a box mix, but the icing was really delicious. She'd prepared it from scratch. Ooey, gooey caramel and coconut. Perfection. Who knew? I wondered if she was nesting, preparing for her life at UCLA with Ryan when they'd be sharing an apartment together without adult supervision. Playing house until they got married. The pride on Ryan's face was almost comical. Could there be a more perfect couple? Ugh.

At ten o'clock Ben shook Ryan's hand and wished him luck. Jenny kissed him, and I hugged him tightly. When he followed Masters out of the cabin I felt something split in my heart. Would he disappear, too? Jenny smiled and hummed a happy tune while she cleaned the kitchen and Ben retreated to his hiding place in the loft. I had to be alone, too.

In the living room, I took the strange book from where I hid it, right there on the bookshelf with tons of other books. I leafed through. Nothing new had changed. The first eight pages were still blank, and the symbols on the remaining pages, still impossible to decipher. I didn't have the heart to even try. My mind trailed to the kiss Wally laid on me before he acclimated and vanished. It was so desperate, so terrified. His fear melted into my own and doubled the intensity of everything. Then there was the kiss I tried to give Ben. I closed my eyes against the memory of that fiasco. It was like kissing a frog. A dead frog. All proving I'm no princess. Just thinking about it, I hated him even more. Then I realized something. If I didn't love him so much, I wouldn't hate him so much. Maybe, instead of trying to hate him even more, I could try to love him less, or not at all. Was that possible?

My damn freak show memory took over and every moment I'd ever spent with Ben at Ariel's Gate blasted like a movie in front of me—times when we played together in the little day camp for preschoolers, second grade when he defied teacher's seating chart to sit beside me, third grade when he fought Angus Forester because he pulled my hair. Ben got trounced for that and spent the night in the infirmary. Forester got worse, library duty for a whole semester and for him, it was hell. I recalled Ben defending me in the gym when my messed-up foot became suddenly important. How he held my hand when Masters yelled at us all for trying to leave the van while he slept. Every memory I had of Ben involved his love for me. Loving Ben wasn't an option. It was fact. So, how to stop hating him was the real issue. How would I ever see through the disappointment and embarrassment at the end of that long emotional tunnel?

I knew we always had been and always would be friends. I just couldn't see how to negotiate the path to peace. Masters was right. Ben didn't do anything wrong. He didn't do anything to me. This was my problem. I couldn't just sit around and wait for him to come and make things right. Ben was the wounded party. Sort of. Well, at least I could admit that he was wounded more than me.

I tossed my hands in the air as if someone was there to see my frustration. Why couldn't he come and just apologize for not telling me? Masters already answered that one, too. Ben hurt me and he couldn't face me. It was up to me to make this right. I just couldn't do it yet.

"Gracie?" Ben's voice floated down from the loft above.

"What?" I snapped without looking up.

"Uh… the bookshelf…"

"What about it?"

"It's the best hiding place ever… that's all… good night, Gracie."

"Fine!" I huffed and poked my head into the kitchen. It smelled of dish soap, leftover cake, and happiness, and made me cringe. "Where's Raffie?"

Jenny turned and swiped a dark curl from her face, leaving a puffy cloud of soap suds in her sparkling black hair. "He went with Ryan. He'll be back. That dog knows where his kibble comes from."

"Great!" Another toss of my hands and I went to bed. Since the day I arrived at Ariel's Gate, that dog had always slept at the foot of my bed. Now even Raffie had deserted me. I wondered if Jenny would come to bed at all. Whatever. The only real comfort I had was that Ryan would never leave Jenny behind. Nothing bad was going to happen in that basement that night. Ryan would be back in the morning. He might even divulge a few of Masters' secrets about Acclimation.

But Ryan didn't come back.

I woke alone as dawn broke on the first rainless morning since we'd left the Gate. Jenny never came to bed, not even to lie on top of the blankets. She must have slept on the sofa. I dressed and headed to face the day. The inviting smell of pancakes drifted from the kitchen and Masters sat in the big living room chair. He looked strange, almost apologetic. Jenny passed, smiling wide, and tapped on Ryan's bedroom door. She tapped again.

"Ryan. Wake up. I made pancakes." She knocked harder. "Ryan?" She turned to face Masters, defying him to deny her some privacy with her guy, then pushed into the bedroom.

Masters stood and took a deep breath.

"What?" I whispered and he held up his hand.

"Ryan!" Jenny shouted then turned a glare from inside the dim room. "His stuff is gone! Where is he?"

"I'm sorry, Jenny," Masters spoke gently. "It's his right, his option, to… leave."

"He wouldn't leave me! He wouldn't!"

"What did you do to him?" Ben shouted from the loft.

Masters suddenly changed; it was as though a steel rod had slid up his spine. "You heard me last time. Ryan's Acclimation is not your business, Ben. His decisions are his own." He turned to follow Jenny to the kitchen but first glanced my way. "I'll talk to her, you stay here."

"What did you do to him?"

"Gracie, give me a break here. I'm doing my job. When you acclimate, you can leave if you want to. That's how it works."

"He would not leave her. We all know that!" I shouted. I think I wanted to scratch his eyes out, hurt him really bad. I didn't like Jenny and Ryan's happiness but I didn't want it over, either. "He wouldn't leave."

"*All* of you have the right to leave," he said with a hiss then pointed to the loft. "So, you better make peace, girly, because Ben's next." And he went into the kitchen and sat next to Jenny. I stood there, dumbfounded. I couldn't take my eyes from her. She just stared ahead, probably trying to figure out how she'd survive alone in the world.

Masters turned a nasty glare and I did go to the loft. Not because he wanted me to leave, but I just couldn't bear Jenny's sadness. At the top of the ladder, Ben sat on his bed, rubbing his eyes. He pushed hair from his brow and avoided looking at me, like I wasn't even there.

I plopped onto the mattress and groaned. "Do you think he's killing them in the basement?"

"You read way too much Stephen King."

"Well? Do you?"

"I don't think he's killing anyone. He's probably right. We have the right to just… walk away."

Finally, I turned to him. His face looked as bad as the mussed blankets and twisted sheets. Sleep wasn't coming easy for Ben. Was that my fault? Nope. I still wasn't ready to take responsibility for this mess. As much as I felt for his misery, I still needed to be mad. "Great!" I snapped and stood, ready to leave. "You just go ahead and desert me, too."

"No, not me. I can't. I'd never leave you."

"That's what Ryan said and those two were really in love." I couldn't face him. The developing conversation was getting too close to agony for me.

"Gracie." His hand slid down my arm. "Ryan and Jenny have sex. We have real love. Not the kind you wanted, I know, but it's—"

"Fine!" I couldn't let him finish. Stepping down the ladder I blinked back tears. Ben was my best chance at a normal life. Not anymore. What I wanted still meant too much for me to just dismiss as impossible. And there were too many impossible things developing all around me.

"I do love you, and I'll be here after." The words tumbled like feathers from above.

I decided to go back to bed. Ben's Acclimation was six days away. I had time to make things right but before I did that, it had to be right with me.

Jenny was broken, shattered from the heart out. She didn't care about anything, not her hair, not her makeup, not anything at all. She stared into space and just breathed in and out. At first, I thought Masters would take her to a hospital, maybe even have her committed. That scared me more than anything. I simply couldn't lose anyone else. Every morning I'd twist pieces of her hair around my finger and just talk, talk, talk. I told her that Ryan had most likely headed for Los Angeles to register for UCLA. That he was getting them an apartment, that he was making it nice for her. That all she'd need to do was find him after her own Acclimation. "He didn't leave you, Jen. He's just so excited to start your lives together, he headed out to get everything ready."

She said nothing, ate little, and slept almost all the time. Days and nights passed and Ben's Acclimation neared. I felt useless and almost as ruined as Jenny. Then, one morning as rain tapped on the window, she climbed into my bed and laid there beside me. We hugged and cried together until Ben knocked on the door.

"Ladies, whatever's happening is playing havoc with this crazy book. Hurry. Get out here and look!"

Hurry wasn't a speed Jenny could muster, but I ran out in my pajamas and joined Ben at the coffee table. He handed me a mug of coffee, and another to Jenny when she arrived. "Check this out," he said and slid the book closer.

The missing pages were back, all loaded with symbols, just like before.

"What the hell?" Ben reached over and flipped pages, displaying eight full sheets of symbols. "It's all back. What do you think that means?"

Jenny perked a bit and shifted the book to see the pages better. "We must have been wrong and the symbols were always there. We just got confused, or were looking at the book backwards or something." She sighed, slumped, then climbed up on the sofa and curled up there.

I looked more closely and my heart started beating out of my chest. "Oh God… no… these aren't the same symbols!"

"Of course, they are." Jenny groaned and rolled her back to us.

"No, they're not. These are totally different. I remember the other symbols, every single one of them, and these are different. Someone get me some paper and a pen."

Ben rushed away but Jenny just groaned.

"Jenny, this means something big," I whispered.

"It doesn't matter. Nothing matters."

"Snap out of it! I need your help!"

"I can't help you, Gracie. I just don't care."

I reached up and dragged her down to the floor with me, nose to nose, and growled, "I don't care if you care or not. Something big is happening. We need to figure this out."

She slowly stood, looking like a refugee who needed a shower and a hot meal. "None of this matters to me, Gracie." And she went back to bed.

I watched her drop like a rag doll onto the mattress. She didn't even close the door. Ben handed over the paper and pen but I just watched Jenny, melting away before my eyes. I had known her as long as Ben. Neither of them were what I thought. I imagined that Jenny was so much stronger, that all of us were stronger.

"She'll be okay," Ben whispered and shifted the book again, lifting a page to the light coming through a window and looking for something that wasn't there.

"How do you know? Maybe she'll hurt herself. She's really broken."

"She'll get through it." He placed the book on the coffee table and waited for me to look at him. When I did I hoped my face was blank. "She will," he repeated.

"What makes you think she'll get over it, like it's something stupid and unimportant? He's the love of her whole life," I hissed and dragged the book closer, knowing full well that I wasn't talking about Jenny and Ryan at all. "She might never get over it."

"She will. We all get over shit. Are you going to help me figure this book out or shall I do it myself?" Now Ben was showing his raw edges.

"You can't figure it out."

"Maybe you can't either!" His hiss grew louder.

"She can," Jenny called from the bedroom and Ben stood, reached over and pushed the bedroom door closed with a thump.

"So," he looked down at me. "Figure it out."

I poised the pen over the paper but paused. It wasn't that I couldn't remember the original markings on the pages before they disappeared. I knew them like the back of my hand. I just had to do something before I started. It felt like working with that book demanded I had a clear heart or something. How stupid is that? But I couldn't shake the thought. I finally looked into Ben's eyes.

"Okay, listen," I said as calmly as I could. "I know I have no right to be so mad at you but I am. Maybe if you'd have told me or something. I don't know. All I'm trying to say here is I need some time. I thought I fell in love." I held my breath.

"Maybe you did, maybe you didn't… but Gracie, you have love. My whole heart full of it. It's just not going to be the happily ever after, white picket fence, two-point-five kids, and a dog kind of love, but it is love. It's the only kind I can give you." He waited until I nodded. "So, can we get on with this book thing or what? The general could climb out of his dungeon any minute."

He was right. Love was love and his was the most valuable thing I had. I'd just have to get over the disappointment. "I really wanted those two-point-five kids and a dog," I joked, and he smiled for the first time in a long time. Everything in my soul lightened and it felt like a fresh breeze blew right through me. Okay, now I was ready. I tore a piece of paper the same size as the book page and started recreating the symbols exactly as I remembered them. When the first page was finished I pushed it aside and started the next.

Ben compared the paper and the new first page and shook his head. "Damn," he mumbled. "They're seriously different." Then he turned to the next and did the same as I completed each of the eight pages of original script. "What the hell does this mean?"

"No clue. But if this book changes for some reason, I'm glad I paid enough attention to the original pages so that we can keep track of… oh shit!" The new pages slowly faded, much faster than I could look through them closely. Lost forever.

"Well, so much for that idea." Ben leaned back and dropped his head onto the sofa cushion.

I started to cry. I'd gotten real good at crying lately.
He put his arm over my shoulders and pulled me close. "Gracie, don't worry. Maybe the only thing that matters is what's on the page at the moment, so whatever was there before is… I don't know… maybe the past… over… not important."

I slapped the book closed with the new sheets still inside and handed it over. Ben tucked it onto the bookshelf between *Moby Dick* and *The 1968 Farmers' Almanac.*

"We'll never figure it out," I groaned and climbed up onto the couch.
"We will, you'll see."

"What the hell are you so optimistic about, anyway?"

"Because I know, really know, that I will not leave like Wally and Ryan did."

"How can you know something like that? Remember, the minute you acclimate you have money and a future and everything you never even dreamed of having. Why the hell would anyone stick around when they could be off, living?" I flipped my hand in the air and Ben gripped it tight in his.

"You. I will not leave you."

"Yeah, right."

"I'm dead serious. No way I'm leaving you alone with him." He jerked his chin in the direction of the kitchen door and basement beyond. "Chances are Jenny will fly the coop and, well, there's no way in hell I trust him alone with you."

My face got so hot I could feel it burn.

Ben tightened like a drum. "Did he touch you?"

I gulped. "Don't be so stupid. Why would he even think about touching me?"

"Your turn not to be so stupid. Steer clear of the general. Only God knows what goes on in his head. You're the last one to acclimate. He'll have free reign if someone's not here to protect you."

"Free reign to do what?" Now I was getting mad. "I can protect myself, Ben Wheeler!"

"Be quiet," came a shout from the bedroom.

"I… do… not… trust… him!" Ben said with a whispered hiss. "Neither should you."

"You don't tell me what to do," I said but leaned closer to Ben, comforted by his intentions, yet not willing to be too confident that he'd stick around. That disappointment might kill me.

"Yeah, I do tell you what to do where that guy's concerned. And I'm going to be here after Acclimation, just to make sure you're safe from him."

But what if I didn't want to be? The thought made me shiver and Ben hugged me tight.

"You'll be safe."

Did I want to be safe? I never felt anything like the kiss from Masters. I didn't know a person could feel like that just by touching lips. Besides all that, I had to face facts. Was there even such a thing as safety? Neither of us knew, and that meant we couldn't predict anything.

The next morning, we discovered that six pages in the middle of the book had gone blank, but the first eight were rewritten with completely different symbols. I started to obsess about that book and its mysterious pages, making so many versions of the vanished text that we ran out of paper. It wasn't like we could run out to the store, so the next time it happened I thought about writing the missing symbols in my journal. I never got the chance.

Masters discovered the book the afternoon Ben would go into the basement. The general wasn't happy.

Neither was I.

Jenny was in no shape to make a cake and I discovered that baking would never be my forte. The cake was dry and crumbly and the icing, way too sweet, but Ben acted like it was the best thing he ever tasted.

At the table that evening I watched Masters closely. He was different, far calmer than he usually was before an Acclimation. Almost cocky. Concern tightened his brow when Jenny left to go back to bed. Then he turned to me and Ben and I knew the question was coming.

"Where did you find that book? Allerton's been looking for it, you know."

"We didn't steal it," I piped up. "We intended to put it back but—"

"Back where?" The general was pulling rank and we had no choice but to fess up.

Ben cleared his throat and pushed his plate away. "There's… or at least there was… a secret room in the back of Makha'el Lecture Hall… behind the wall."

"Uh-huh. You didn't just steal it out of Allerton's office or anything, you had to dig around for a secret room, Harry Potter?" He so didn't believe us.

"Raffie found the room," I snapped in defense. "And no one stole anything. We borrowed it."

"Why?" Now all of his attention was on me. It was hard to see him look at me like I was a criminal, but I guess it was better than him acting like I was his girlfriend or something.

"We were curious," Ben jumped in. "I found it and the symbols were so weird, I figured Gracie could figure them out."

"Why Gracie?" Masters shifted and leaned toward Ben who didn't back down an inch.

"Maybe you're too stupid to notice, but Gracie's like a genius or something. She's the smartest person I've ever met. Definitely the smartest person in this room." And Ben actually raised his chin, tempting Masters to meet it with one of his tightened fists.

"Okay, so you were curious. Why didn't you put the damn thing back when you realized it couldn't be deciphered?"

"We tried," I bounced in my seat. "Really, we did, but everything in that secret room was gone! Vanished!"

"Poof!" Ben said and spread out his fingers. "Like everything just disappeared."

"Like the writing on some of the book's pages," I added. What was I trying to do? Get Masters on our side or convince him we were certifiably nuts?

"Huh?"

"The pages, those symbols on all the pages, several times they just vanished then came back different." I watched his eyes cloud over then jumped right back in before he could say a word. "Yes, they changed. I have photographic memory and I know they're different. I even drew the old symbols on paper and kept them with the new text. That way when I figure it out, I can compare. I—"

Ben put his hand out to stop me. "I think the changes in the symbols are changes happening in the world. Of course, we don't really know yet, but that book is important. I swear, I feel it."

"You say you wrote down some of those symbols?"

I nodded. "I left them inside the book."

We watched from the back porch while Masters ran to the basement, returned with a wad of paper, set a fire, and burned all my hard work. So much for my plan to compare the messages. At least he didn't burn the whole book.

"Ben," he called from the little bonfire. "Let's go."

Ben stiffened beside me and a cold breeze slapped at us, whipping hair over my eyes.

"It's only nine o'clock." I squeezed his hand and looked into his eyes. "Why now?"

"No big deal. I want to get this over with." He was so scared his hand trembled in mine.

"Listen, whatever you decide to do afterward is your choice. Don't sacrifice starting a real life for me. Do what you want to do."

"I'll be staying." And he left for the basement.

I sat on the couch and cried myself to sleep.

10

ravel was far more difficult and treacherous than a man in his late forties with a desk job was prepared for. Aside from the near constant presence of a dangerous enemy determined to stop his progress, nasty weather, hunger, and people who prey on the poor nipped at his heels. Escaping his tails in Pittsburgh proved tricky—three days' worth of tricky—but once he shook free of the tenacious spies and rival warriors, he took a more direct route to his destination. As each day passed, he struggled to push ahead.

Having missed Wally's Acclimation while incarcerated, Michael Allerton battled growing fear of never reaching Masters before it was all over. Spending eight days too deep in the earth to maintain his power left him frail and shaky. Being so far from his soul sword gave him little hope of recovering the strength of his true being. His soul sword—another reason he had to reach Cole. He'd hidden it with the others in the van for safekeeping. Was it safe? He hardly dared to think otherwise. Walking on the planet's surface helped regain some of his energy, but weakness rattled his bones. Within a week he not only felt like a homeless man, he looked and smelled like one. He plowed ahead, hoping and praying that things were progressing well for Masters.

He'd known when the Sutcliff boy acclimated and sensed the urgency pressing against his heart. Ben was next. In fact, his son would acclimate in a mere thirty-six hours and he was far from being there to witness and support. An ache bloomed in his chest and he rubbed it. Watching Ben grow into a good young man was his only solace. He'd never find the relationship he wished with his son; that wasn't his original intention. All he'd cared about was taking a squirming, helpless infant to a safe place. He watched that baby grow and develop into an acclimate ready to step up and take the necessary vow and commitment for his race. In truth, his aching chest was nothing but sentimentality. He'd done what he set out to do. Ben would be a worthy warrior for his people. He was sure of it. Even though his son was different, he was a soldier, through and through. Pride pounded, making the pain more intense. How he wanted to be there to see it all.

It had been a rough road. In Morgantown, West Virginia, he was mugged, stripped of his remaining cash and Rachel's husband's warm coat. Unconscious and hospitalized for two days, a kind social worker brought him a coat, filled his prescription for antibiotics, and begged him to stop at a medical clinic to have the fresh stitches above his left eye removed in a week. No time for such frivolity, Michael picked at them himself, only to end up in a free clinic outside Elkins for another shot of antibiotics and another lecture.

"Are you trying to kill yourself, mister?" The doctor looked no older than Ben. "Get your act together, old man. Get yourself to a shelter. It's going to be winter soon. Hey, maybe you can get a job somewhere… live like a normal guy… pay rent… taxes… be a productive part of society."

Allerton eyed the kid and gave a snort. What the hell did Michael know of normal?

The kid dug at the wound, reopened it, and cleaned it out. That meant new stitches, but at least the fever had subsided and the throbbing sting backed off. With luck, he could have Masters snip out the stitches. He had to get back on the road.

Rain had pummeled his shoulders since leaving Pittsburgh. He looked up and blinked against drops plopping into his eyes. "Seriously? A little help here would be nice?" He grunted and held his coat over his head. Maybe it would keep the fresh bandage dry. Another night of sleeping on the wet mattress of mud and fallen leaves, listening to animals in the darkness, worrying about the enemy, praying that they hadn't flushed him out yet.

A trucker picked him up ten miles south, heading west on Rt. 250 and assuring Michael that he'd take him as far as the Charlottesville exit in Virginia. This lucky break might actually get Michael to the inn in time for Ben's Acclimation. "I'm sorry, I have nothing to give you… I can't even help pay for gas," he said as he grunted into the passenger seat.

"No biggie. Been there, buddy. Sleep if you need to. Got some granola bars in the glove compartment if you're hungry. I'll wake you when we reach the interstate and you can tell me where you want me to drop you off."

Sleeping wasn't in his plan. Praying for another kind ride for some of the final twenty miles of his journey was his new priority. Baby steps, one at a time until he reached Masters. The truck's cab was warm, the granola bars, crunchy and filling, and he found himself nodding off and dreaming of the baby he held, late at night in the nursery when no one knew. The tiny fingers and toes, the bright eyes, the perfect child of his and Rachel's making. When the driver nudged him awake, Michael was smiling. He'd make it. He'd see Ben safely through the biggest event of his life.

"I can't thank you enough."

The driver gave a casual shrug and pulled over. "Gonna be cold tonight. Hope you have someplace to sleep."

"I do." And he watched the vehicle leave, turn the bend, and merge onto the interstate.

He put one foot in front of the other, willing enough energy to reach his destination. He'd driven that backwoods road with an excited acclimate at his side many times. The inn was one of his favorite locations to guide fall and winter acclimates. The ride was always beautiful, lined with brilliant autumn leaves clinging to their skeletal tree limbs, some free of their bond and drifting past the windshield in the autumn sunlight. Usually the road was much busier, too. That day it was dreary and wet, there were no other cars, no pick-up trucks, no farmers crawling along in backhoes or flat beds loaded with hay or pumpkins. The walk was long and evening climbed from behind the trees. A few times he stopped, sure he heard voices. The enemy? Campers? Loggers? Police? But the moment he held his breath to listen, all went silent. Darkness settled in for the night, rain returned, the blacktop whispered under his shoes. Michael searched for signs. Union Fork couldn't be far, but each mile marker told him it was farther than he thought. He felt washed out, empty, feeble, and wobbly. Old. Nearly beaten.

At a curve in the road he sensed a surge of energy, like a current, racing past, pressing against him, pushing him back. He stood and blinked away rain and sweat, hoping to see clearer. There was nothing there in the dark, just woods and an empty open space. He reached out, stepped closer to the trees and held his breath. Voices? Human? Enemy? Then before his eyes he saw a ripple in every-thing, as though the world in front of him had endured a hard wind then fought to regain itself. "What the—"

A sharp pain gripped his thigh and before he could turn to run he dropped like a rock to the ground. His fingers explored his leg as darkness seeped into his vision. A tranquilizer dart? What the hell? A damn strong one, too. As he lost con-sciousness, the only thought in his mind was that this was not the enemy's doing.

~*~

"Well?" Tobias stood outside Garta's camper, shifting from one foot to the other, looking guilty and concerned.

She pushed past him and reached into a cooler. Retrieving a bottle of cold water, she glared. "Really, Tobias? You could sense what he is. What on earth made you use that dart? His heart rate is through the roof, I can't get him to stay awake, and the poor man's energy is fading at an alarming rate."

"We need all the soldiers we can get, Garta. Don't let him die."

She turned and stomped up into the camper, slamming the door behind her.

"I'm not going to die," whispered her fragile patient. "Am I?"

"Of course not. I told him the dosage was too high. You looked like a far more robust man than you are." She pressed a cool, wet cloth to his brow then examined the fresh stitches beneath a filthy bandage. "What happened to you?"

"Too much. Who are you? Where am I?"

And without warning the man dropped into a deep sleep again.

"You rest," Garta whispered as she removed his grubby clothes and prepared to wash him clean. "It'll do you good."

~*~

Waking was like climbing Everest, painful, airless, desperate. He was plagued with the need to sleep but floating atop his inability to gain full consciousness, Michael carried a heavy, confusing load of anxiety and urgency. There was something he was supposed to do. Someplace he was supposed to be. Ben's face formed in the slipping, sliding images haunting behind his eyelids. He rallied, struggled, and finally forced his eyes open. Daylight illuminated the window. He was cramped and nearly folded in half on a small camper bed. At least it was soft, warm, and dry. Before his body demanded more sleep, he grunted and pushed himself to sit up. He pressed fingers against his stitches then rubbed his eyes. Why was he naked? Where was he? Memories of a strange vision in the trees, a tranquillizer dart, pain, then nothingness wafted and anger bloomed, heating him from his center to his flesh. He banged on the wall. "Where the hell am I?" he bellowed then fought the need to drop back to the lumpy mattress.

The door opened. "Relax. Be calm. You're safe and recovering." It was an old woman, only she was older than old. The hair on his arms and at the back of his neck stood at attention. Michael had never met an ancient before. Now he was captive to one.

"Safe?" he hissed. "I'm recovering from a damn attack."

"Yes, yes," she said and reached out to steady him. "I agree, the dart was overkill, but it's not deadly."

"What day is it?"

She blinked, glanced to the ceiling. "September… thirtieth. You've been asleep off and on for about forty hours. You are terribly weak… uh… what's your name?"

September thirtieth? He missed it. So close. So damn close. He slammed his fist against the thin metal wall again then dropped his head and sobbed.

The ancient sat at his side and ran a hand over his hair. "Hush now. My name is Garta. Tell me your name. We'll help you, whatever you need. Don't worry."

Lowering onto the pillow, he gritted his teeth then answered. "My name is Michael. You can't do a damn thing for me. Just get my clothes. I need to get the hell out of here and back on the road."

"Oh… well, your clothes I can get. I washed them. Here." She placed them on the bed and turned to leave.

"Then I can leave, right?"

"You need to speak to Tobias."

"No, I don't need to speak to anyone. I need to get moving."

"Sometimes," she turned her wrinkled face to him.,"things aren't what you think. Sometimes things are meant to happen. Trust me. It's all about the bigger picture, Michael." She stepped outside and he clearly heard the sound of jangling keys lock the flimsy door.

And he wondered, was he strong enough to push his way out of a paper bag, much less a circa 1953 Streamline camper?

Dressed and waiting for whatever came next, he listened to the activity outside. People passed the window, some curious and glancing his way, others just chatting, all walking in the same direction. How many people were in that camp? A hundred? Two hundred? More? Why were they there? He felt them all, their energy humming through the marrow of his bones. More than that filtered through his muddled senses. The vibrations of hundreds of soul swords sang to him, whispered to him, and worried him. He was among his own people, but he had no way of knowing their intentions. Would they really help him? Would they turn him in? Then there was that old woman. The ancient.

Could he trust an ancient? He'd heard that they grew callous, inhuman, cruel. It was said that there were only a handful of them walking the planet, all cursed with eternal life, none by their own choice. How could he believe the stories? No one he ever met had crossed paths with an actual ancient. For all he knew, his own wits were off kilter, distorted by the strong tranquilizer.

Evening had fallen, painting the world outside his window gold and blue. The dying sun sparked across wet tree limbs and skimmed along muddy puddles. At least it wasn't raining. He calculated the date and how much time he had left to reach Masters, how many days before Gracie Caine acclimated. Just eighteen days. He could talk his way out of the camp in eighteen days, couldn't he? Then the door opened and two large men stood, looking in at him like curious kids at the zoo.

"S'go, buddy."

He sat still, holding his breath. One of the burly men squeezed into the camper and gripped his arm. "Let me help you," he said. "It's Michael, right?"

He nodded.

"Cool. Well, Michael, dinner's ready, we're all hungry, and Tobias wants to talk with you before we get to eat. Can you stand up?"

Michael stood, clunking his head on the ceiling.

The man chuckled. "Sorry, small camper."

He led him out and down two steps into the cool evening, never releasing his arm.

The other man smiled. "This way," he said and reached out, but never actually touched Michael's back. These guys weren't dragging him to another trial, they were helping him.

"I'm good. Thanks."

"Hope you're hungry. Cookie's been at it all day," said the first man as they walked along a wide pathway.

"What is this camp?"

"Tobias will answer all your questions. Careful." They skirted a high tree root in the path.

Michael suspiciously eyed the many tents, the huge canvas shelter ahead, and a large sign lying on its side. Tilting his head, he blinked and his heart lightened. The Emmaus Magic Show was a rogue warrior group—a damn effective one, too, if he recalled the reports correctly. Relief washed over him along with a bout of weakness. Both men gripped his arms and stopped for a moment. These guys were on his side. He might actually be able to count on them for assistance. He nodded and the men continued to guide him into the big tent.

The smell of pot roast and vegetables, beer and sweets, leather and sweat accosted him as they passed through the canvas flap. Good God, this could be really good. He was led to sit on a chair, alone and centered, in front of a raised table. Six people sat, all looking down at him like he was from Mars. Hell, this could be good or it could be really bad. The old woman was there, and beside her, another ancient, a large man wearing a simple linen shirt and an expression of mixed curiosity and determination. What the hell had he stumbled into?

One of his entourage pressed a thick slice of warm bread into his hand. "You look hungry."

Michael unconsciously bit into the bread. It was slathered with creamy butter and bar none, the most delicious thing he'd ever tasted. The folks at the high table watched and waited. Who knew such a small kindness, a simple slice of bread, could give him so much comfort. He brushed crumbs from his hands and smiled. "How can I help you?"

The ancients glanced at each other and the big man drew in a breath. "I need to know who you are and why you're traveling alone."

That must be Tobias. His leader-like quality was pure dominance tempered with compassion. Comforting, but to Michael, not so much.

"Oh my God!" A young woman seated to the leader's left stood, grinned wide, then sat again. She leaned against Tobias's shoulder and whispered. He nodded and she stood and spoke for all to hear. "Mr. Allerton? Do you remember me?"

Did he? She was a pretty woman, gorgeous dark red hair and dangerous curves to match. But, yes, yes he did recall her face. He shifted in the chair. "You were one of my students. Dawn? Right?"

Her smile was radiant. "Everyone, Tobias, this is Michael Allerton, headmaster at Ariel's Gate." Looking at him again she shrugged. "The beard… I almost didn't recognize you."

He touched his face and his fingers threaded through a ragged mess he'd never even noticed. "Uh, well, weeks on the road without a razor will do that."

"Which brings us back to my question," Tobias spoke with authority. "Why are you traveling? Like a vagabond? Alone?"

Michael looked behind at all the waiting diners. "Ah… I'll tell you all about it when—"

"No," Tobias said firmly. "You need to tell me… all of us… now. Your presence brings the possibility of danger, and my troupe has a right to understand the risks we take by bringing you into our protection. Please answer. Are you running from something?"

"No," Michael straightened in his seat. "I had some… trouble… with the tribunal, but I'm not running from anything, except the enemy."

All heads nodded.

"Listen," Michael continued. "I appreciate all your help and you," he nodded toward the old woman, "have been so kind, but I can complete my journey alone if you just let me leave. I'm only about twenty miles from my destination."

"What destination?" The leader's eyes narrowed.

He gulped. "All right. Dawn," he looked to her with sincerity, "you can vouch for me on this." He cleared his throat to continue, hoping with all his heart that he wasn't about to make everything worse. "I have responsibilities to the young people about to acclimate. Huge responsibilities. You may or may not have heard, but I had to close Ariel's Gate."

Dawn's hand flew to her mouth in shock. "Oh no!"

"The enemy made it all the way to our walls, murdered one of our young boys... wounded another. I sent everyone, staff, babies, children, teens, all of them off to safer ground. I dismantled Ariel's Gate completely, leaving the enemy nothing of value."

The people at the table watched and listened. It appeared as though Tobias wasn't even breathing. Michael continued.

"A mere twenty miles from this spot, a few of my young people are awaiting, or have already experienced, their Acclimation. The final acclimate... she's very important... important in ways we can't even know yet. She is significant for our survival. I need to get there. I need to help the guide with that particular acclimation. Tobias," he stood and stepped closer to the table, "please, help me to get there. It's vital that—"

"When?" Tobias too stood, looking down at Michael with a strange glow in his eyes. "When does this acclimation take place?"

Michael's throat went dry as a desert rock. Nothing could be spoken and he wondered if he'd already said too much. Had he mistaken the intentions of the Emmaus warriors? Was everything about to be lost?

"Tell me." Tobias stepped around the table and stood face to face with Michael. "Will this young woman acclimate on the eighteenth of October?"

Michael weakened and dropped into the chair. "Yes."

On his knees, Tobias finally smiled. He gripped Michael's hand and shook hard. "We are here for her." He stood and scanned everyone assembled, his arms wide in triumph. "The vision was true. We will cross paths with a warrior of extraordinary power in eighteen days. We are exactly where we're meant to be."

Cheers rose all around.

"But I'm not!" Michael shouted. "I need to help the guide. I have to leave this camp."

"I'm very sorry but you can't," Tobias said with a sigh. "Bringing you inside has severely weakened our shield. The veil has been in place for weeks, but it's become fragile and your surprise arrival gave us no time to prepare for a breach. It will take days to regain the veil's energy. If you leave now, it will jeopardize everyone here."

"Why the hell didn't you just let me walk past?"

"They were almost on you. You were in their sights. You'd be dead if we didn't bring you in."

"Surely they know where you are now. They had to see you drag my unconscious ass in here."

Tobias grinned and bobbed his brows. "We're faster than the blink of an eye. They saw nothing. They're close but they can't locate us. And we need to remain protected, alive, and strong to fight alongside this new warrior."

Reality seeped into Michael's brain. The visual distortion he'd seen just before the dart was a ripple in the protective veil. Only a powerful ancient could create such a shield. The enemy was close, Tobias was correct. But under that veil, they were all safe and unseen. He glanced behind at the faces around him—young and old, educated and plain, men and women of all colors and races rallied together for the same cause. They, and groups like them, were the only hope for regaining balance, Michael was sure of it. Their resourcefulness and tenacity made the tribunal look like bumbling idiots. Those warriors cared about their people and chose to put their lives on the line to protect and preserve. Leaving was out of the question. He could not endanger them. He could not risk exposing them to so many of the enemy. But Ben? Gracie? Masters? What of them? How could he be so close yet so helpless?

Tobias led Michael to sit beside him at the table. He ate, he prayed, he hoped, and he wanted to sit in a corner and cry like a child. But something Tobias said poked and pushed him toward trust and faith. Was Tobias right? Would young Gracie become a powerful warrior? More amazing things had reared their curious heads over the past few weeks. Timing is everything and whether he wanted to or not, he was now part of a rogue fighting machine. It was easier for Michael to believe that Gracious Caine could lead them to balance, than that she should be hidden in the tribunal's prison for safe keeping.

The following days were challenging. The Emmaus camp was set up for battle training and he didn't even have his sword to practice with. He fumbled and flailed like a kid, swinging a wooden practice sword every day from breakfast 'til lunch. Then he sat with the troupe leaders and listened while they talked of the magic show performances, how they attracted and recruited more of their race to join the fight, how they battled, and how they traveled strategically. Following, always following the enemy until strangely, about the same time Ariel's Gate was closed, the enemy seemed to turn and chase them.

"Like they're trying to keep us away from something," Ballister Green explained. "Intelligence reveals that there are more of the enemy between here and the southern islands of the Carolina Outer Banks than anywhere else in America."

"Could be coming from Europe, south of the equator, even the Far East, too," Billio added, casually running a sharpening stone down his brilliant blade.

"Why?" Michael asked. "Why would they do that?"

Tobias sipped hot coffee. "There's something they want. I was guided to poise our troops to stand ready to defend. Until you showed up, we didn't know what we were to defend, just that we had to sit tight and wait."

Waiting was driving him crazy. Michael was a man of cerebral action. He was a manager, a planner, a strategist. His new environment demanded physical skills that had lain dormant for decades and he worried that no amount of training would help. Was he destined to be useless? He twirled the wooden weapon at his feet.

"Don't worry," Billio finally set the stone aside. "Your own weapon knows you… it'll do most of the work. You'll have it soon. It'll be like riding a bike." He looked up, his long face tattooed with snake scales, his eyes as dark as night and his expression one of camaraderie.

"You read minds?"

"Nah," he chuckled. "It's just easy to imagine what you're thinking. I'd be thinking the same thing."

Michael leaned back on his camp chair and looked around at the bustle. Everyone had a job, everyone knew their place, everyone understood what was needed from them. In a way, he knew too, he just wasn't sure he was up for the task. As Gracie's acclimation date neared, his feet twitched, desperate to run, to be there, to make sure it would all be done correctly. Of course, he knew Masters would do the best he could. The young man was certainly capable. Like he told the tribunal, Cole would give his life for those kids. It worried Michael that it could actually come to that. His heart raced for a moment, feeling the need to sprint from the protective veil and run to the inn.

"Don't even think about it," Tobias said, sipping coffee, his eyes intense. "I do read minds… and you can't risk us all. You need to trust your chosen acclimation guide, and you need to trust me."

Busted, face red, Michael lowered his eyes with embarrassment. Tobias was right, but his whole life had been about trusting himself, getting things directed, and corrected alone.

"Not anymore," Tobias added, his eyes twinkling.

"Stop that." Michael lifted his wooden toy sword and laid it over his shoulder. "Tell me, how the hell did all this start?"

Green chuckled. "When God created the heavens and the earth…"

"Actually, he's right." The leader waved to a woman who took his empty cup away.

The way she smiled made Michael wonder. Did ancients maintain their virility? Of course, they did. Dawn was totally taken by the man, all goo-goo eyes when she sat with him for meals. All smiling and glowing when she left or entered the camper they shared. Was Tobias a real ladies man? Curious. Then he realized that the guy could read his thoughts. He glared. "Get out of my head."

Tobias laughed. "So, how this all started… in the beginning. It's always been here. Balance is the goal and the struggle. But something happened about twenty years ago… an illness that drastically cut the numbers at the source… a catastrophe. You had to notice an influx of orphans showing up at your door."

Michael nodded.

"So, like any good opponent, the enemy chose to capitalize on such a weakness, build upon their superior numbers. There you have it… escalation of the never-ending war."

Bullshit, it can't be that simple, Michael thought.

"No, really. It is," Tobias said with an irritating grin then walked away.

"Ignore him," Green advised. "He's just messing with you. But he's right about the disease. Killed hundreds of us, mostly women, babies, the young, and unprotected."

Michael shook his head and looked toward the boarders of the big camp. East. Where the enemy gathered. Between them and Gracie. "Damn," he whispered.

~*~

Days passed. Michael gained his fighting skills with slow deliberation. His senses sharpened and his mind cleared. He was finally recovered from the tribunal's prison, and living so close to the vibrant warriors of his race had bolstered and enlightened him. His urges to escape to Masters never left, but he managed to control the impulse. He slept in a small pup tent someone gave him and learned the names of his fellow soldiers. He was no longer a headmaster, no longer a man of means or a protector of children. Michael had become a guardian of his race, what was left of it. What his fellow warriors disclosed shook him to the bone. All the secrets the tribunal kept to itself. All the disastrous news of loss. Much of it personal.

Tobias took him aside and told of the bus loads of Ariel's Gate children found dead. The private plane crashes, all traced back to Michael's students heading for safety. No one he tried so hard to protect had survived, except those in Cole's care. No wonder the tribunal threw him in prison. If they'd told him those things, he'd have imprisoned himself. The pain in his chest intensified, but there was no time to mourn. Tobias was determined to protect what was left of their race. But how was that even possible?

"Tenacity. Skill. Being on the right side… and allies we never expect," the leader answered. "Allies like you and your acclimates."

Just what Michael needed. More pressure.

He lay dreaming of a moment from his childhood, a tiny memory of a mother who loved him and held him and sang lovely melodies to him. One day that mother disappeared and was replaced by the Ariel's Gate nurse whose hands were different and songs unfamiliar. It was a time of confusion and tears.

Thunk!

He woke with a start, the fully painted face of a dwarf clown laughing down at him. The joker's breath was laced with garlic and his compact body leapt with joy. Michael rubbed his brow where the man had flicked a finger. Hard.

"Not funny, Benny."

"It's kinda funny. Wake up. Tobias wants to talk to you."

Michael yawned and stretched. It was still dark outside the flapping canvas of his little tent. "Now?"

"Right… now." And he flicked Michael's brow again, turned and walked outside, his giggle floating in the darkness.

"Someday, Benny!" he called a threat he'd never carry out. Benny had been waking him with a flick of his finger for ten days. It gave the little guy joy. Why would he stop now?

He dressed and thought about the calendar. Four days and counting. Four days and he'd know if Gracie was okay, if Masters had succeeded, if the world could go on. Tobias seemed far more confident than Michael. But then again, Tobias was used to running on faith. In four days they'd pack up and move. Four days. He tried hard not to wonder what would happen if they didn't find Gracie.

There was no one in the huge communal tent but Tobias, sitting alone at a table illuminated by the yellow glow of a small gas lantern.

"Can't sleep?"

The leader shrugged. "I need to do many things before we break camp. Sorry to wake you but…" he leaned back and looked at Michael, standing in front of him like a good soldier, awaiting his orders.

"But what?"

"You have done well."

"Thanks." Why was he so nervous? It was just a compliment. Or was it?

"Michael, I'm giving you command of six specialists, soldiers specifically trained for reconnaissance. Men who are basically invisible to the enemy. Do you understand?"

His head shook. Of course, he didn't understand.

"My spies are the best on the planet."

"Ah… you want me to be a spy?"

"I want you to take command and lead a team of spies." Tobias watched him closely.

Michael blinked. "Tobias, I don't even have my soul sword. How can I lead anyone… spies or otherwise?"

"Your mission is to take your men, locate and retrieve your soul sword, gain intelligence about your young acclimate, and get your team back here safe and unscathed."

"I can bring my acclimates and their guide, too?" Hope sped through his veins.

"No. Just your sword and your men. Things must progress as they will. It's the directive. It must be followed. Do not make contact."

"Uh…" How could Tobias imagine that he could get that close and not make himself known? Was that even possible?

"You leave in twenty minutes. Coffee up. Your men will be here in fifteen, ready to follow you."

"What time is it?"

"Two forty-five. You have until dawn, not a minute longer." He stood and Michael reached out to grip his arm.

"Wait a minute… the veil. How the hell can we get out without compromising it?"

"We're prepared. Garta and the illusionists stand ready. The window is mere moments for you all to get out. We'll be prepared when you get back."

Michael felt like stone, unable to move or even breathe. What if they weren't prepared enough?

"I need intelligence, Michael. I need to know how many enemy troops are between here and where you're going."

It was nice of Tobias to leave Michael one little secret—the exact location of the inn. But then again, the man had been roaming around inside his thoughts for days. He already knew. If so, why send him out? Why not send the reconnaissance mission under a different, more experienced commander?

"Because you need to see for yourself that your guide and acclimate are okay. And," he patted Michael's hand, still tight on his arm, "you need your sword."

The night was cold and moonless. The enemy was everywhere but paying no attention to Michael and his men. As he led them, moving with swift, silent steps, weaving in and out of the trees, he pondered the six specialists under his command. He knew them all well, but only by name, not yet by battle qualifications. His troops seemed like random choices, but the moment they left the veil, they showed their colors. They were six warriors he was proud and confident to serve beside. Two were barely twenty years old but that didn't concern him. Masters was only nineteen when he'd saved those soldiers in Afghanistan.

There was an Asian who could wield a sword like no one's business. To his right, a man so silent and stealth, he could hardly be seen in the darkness. One spoke only German, another spoke like a college professor, yet another almost never spoke at all. Finally, there was Frank Pincer, the camp mechanic. Michael expected none of them to be willing to serve under such an untried commander, but they all patted his shoulder and watched his back.

The camp was much closer to the inn than Michael realized and it took little time to reach their destination. Nothing hindered their movement and not one of the bad guys even reacted to their presence. The enemy stood perfectly still, staring toward the inn, vibrating anticipation and a terrible energy all around.

But the inn was burned to the ground and for a moment panic shot through his heart. Mr. Silent elbowed Michael and nudged his chin to the cabin, standing like a ghost in the darkness. Lights were out, all was quiet, and the van was parked right up against the front porch. *Good job, Cole,* he thought then pointed for three of the men to stand guard while he and Pincer retrieved the soul sword and his Asian sword master skirted the cabin to take a headcount of the people inside.

Michael's soul sword was exactly where he hid it, strapped to the under-carriage of the van. As he worked to free the blade, Pincer silently opened the vehicle's hood and tinkered.

"What are you doing?" Michael hissed, sliding then rolling from under the vehicle.

"A little insurance," he replied with a big grin, his teeth brilliant white against the black grease paint they'd covered their faces with.

In mere minutes, all were accounted for. They slipped away, walked through trees and past no less than three hundred of the enemy along their trek back, astounded that not one of them reacted to their presence. They were still as stone, eyes glazed over, unmoving, silent. It was like they were all hypnotized.

Finally, they snuck safely inside the veil. Only two hours had passed according to Michael's watch. He turned to Sam Lee. "What did you see... inside the cabin?" He had to know.

"Two young women, each sound asleep in different bedrooms. A man asleep on the sofa. And another man asleep in a chair."

"The men, what did they look like?"

Lee shrugged. "Like men."

Michael sighed. With two women sleeping and breathing, he was assured that Gracie was still alive. And with confirmation of two men, he was confident that Cole had recruited assistance. If only he knew for sure that it was Ben.

The report to Tobias was quick, clean, and satisfactory, so Michael and his men left the communal tent to find their beds and sleeping bags. All he could think about was his son. Was he alive? Unharmed?

"We'll know soon enough." The voice came from behind him and Michael scowled.

"Get the hell out of my head, Tobias."

"Good work tonight."

He turned to face the ancient. "What's up with the enemy? Did you cast some kind of spell on them or something?"

"No."

"It was really odd. They were like statues, in some kind of trance."

"I've seen something like that once before."

"Yeah? When?" And Michael waited, but instead of an answer, Tobias simply turned and left for his camper.

"Thanks a lot," Michael grunted, wondering if he'd get any sleep at all before Cookie rang the breakfast bell.

~*~

The fact that Ben was sound asleep on the big living room chair the morning after his acclimation did several things. First, it stilled my freaking nerves. At least there was something I could count on in my weird life. The other thing Ben's presence did was help Jenny to move from her mourning phase to her hateful, break-everything-she-could-get-her-hands-on angry phase. I guess I should have been glad—at least it was progress—but all that anger was aimed at me.

She gathered her stuff and moved into the bedroom Ryan and Wally used before they left. Masters watched the drama as she tossed clothes and duffel, pillows and blankets into her new bedroom.

"Now I'll have to sleep all alone. I've been sleeping in the same room with that… lunatic… since I arrived at the Gate."

"You can sleep with me," Ben teased. "No condoms required."

"Don't even go there," Masters growled. "We have bigger problems… I kinda hoped she'd snap out of her crap and start cooking again."

"Me too." I plopped on the sofa. "I can't cook."

"We know. But I think I can. I'll take the first shift." Ben peeked into the kitchen like it was a strange foreign country.

Masters looked at me. "Can he cook?"

I shrugged. When would we learn to cook at Ariel's Gate?

"Okay, Ben. But if you screw up, that leaves me," the general said, scratching his head. "And trust me, if that happens we'll all starve."

It turned out that Ben wasn't a bad cook. Our supplies were dwindling but he still managed to make the meals hot and fairly tasty. Masters stuck around the cabin a lot more, playing cards with us, telling stories about his time at the Gate, even acting as referee when Jenny lost her marbles and tried to pull my hair out. That, for me, was the last straw. I locked myself in her bedroom with her, determined to get to the bottom of all her crazy.

"What the hell?" I started.

"I know. Pretty lame. Next time I'll use scissors." She glared then turned her back to me.

"This has to stop. I had nothing to do with Ryan leaving. I told you, he's probably gone ahead… waiting for you at UCLA. He—"

"You don't know anything! He's probably dead. Or sleeping with someone else. Or just trying to get away from me."

"That can't be true. Boy, are you going to be sorry soon when you see him."

"If he's not already dead, I might kill him. He did this to me!"

"So why," I shouted as loud as I could, "why are you punishing me?"

She dissolved into a puddle of tears, gasping so hard she couldn't even talk.

I hugged her and pushed her hair back, wanting to apologize for being so mean but I needed to know. "Why are you so mad at *me*?" I whispered.

"I am so… jealous."

"Of me?" That came so out of left field I could hardly grasp the concept. "That's just stupid."

"Ben loves you enough to stay… Ryan… he…" There'd be no more words that night, just tears, and shaking sobs, and sniffles. She still wanted to sleep alone so I left her, wondering how she could possibly compare my situation to hers. Wow. None of us were as tough as I thought. We were all alone, orphans, scared, deserted. We all must be a little jealous of other people's brains, or personality, cup size, or even their clothes. We're all trying to stand out, to fit in, to not feel like waifs and strays. I decided that she could pull my hair and hate me all she wanted, if it helped her feel better. Someday I might need to pull someone else's hair and I hope they'll be as understanding. With a little luck, it'll be payback and I'll get a wad of Jenny's gorgeous curls in my fist. Maybe not.

But that day there were other things to focus on. Jenny's Acclimation was the very next night, mine only two days later. Then this would all be over. Then what?

It turns out crazy is contagious. Ben and Cole were acting like best friends, Jenny started to sing Eddie Vedder songs, off key and really loud, and I swear someone looked into my bedroom window last night. Maybe it was a bear. Maybe it was cabin fever. I hadn't been outside since my attempted escape. I didn't even think about outside anymore. My entire existence had shrunk to fit in the small cabin. There was no television or radio, so only God knew what was happening in the world. The cell phones Headmaster gave us didn't work, but who was there to call anyway? Ben's computer should have booted up, but no go. Not much chance to get online so far back in the woods, I guess. So much technology, and Jenny's electric toothbrush was the only thing working.

Things were changing all around. Masters wanted us to call him Cole. I was especially uncomfortable with that. Ben started calling him 'the general' right to his face but they acted like it was an inside joke, making me feel even more out of the loop. Worst of all, Ben would tell me nothing about Acclimation and that just wasn't fair. I was tired of being mad at people and having people mad at me, so I dropped the subject. I'd know in a few days. At least I was sure nothing bad was going to happen. Ben was healthy and even a little happy. He acted like his back hurt a bit but shrugged off my concern.

"The bed in the loft is crap," he explained. I guess that's why he started sleeping in the big living room chair.

I didn't even try to bake a cake for Jenny's birthday and Ben never thought to do it. He did make some really good macaroni and cheese with other stuff in it. It was different but pretty yummy. With only three days of rationed food left, we were grateful for his heroic efforts.

Jenny followed Cole out of the back door and down into the basement without even looking back. No goodbyes, no hugs, no nothing. I felt my eyes sting with tears. We were never the best of friends, but we'd been experiencing this strange journey to acclimation together. I wish she'd have at least looked back. At least for a second.

"She's leaving," I predicted with a gulp. She looked so small and frail. Could she survive out there in the world alone? What would she do? Hitchhike? Walk? She'd need to get to the nearest town to activate her charge cards and buy a ticket somewhere by train or bus or plane. All alone. I was shaken by the fact that she was a girly girl, not calculated and determined like Wally. Not resourceful like Ryan. Not in the frame of mind to make the right choice and stick close like Ben. "She's going to get herself dead out there alone."

"Nope. She'll be fine." Ben handed me a dirty dish. "I cooked, you clean up."

"No fair. I'm sick of always washing dishes. I'll cook tomorrow and you can clean up after me," I called as he left the kitchen. I followed. "I can make a big mess, too."

He sat in his big cushy chair and sighed. "I'll clean up any mess you make. However," he held up a finger, "the meal has to be edible." Ben grinned but there was stress in his eyes.

"You don't think she'll be okay either, do you?"

"She'll be whatever she's supposed to be. Like Cole said… this stuff is personal. Jenny has to make her own decision."

I sat on the sofa with a bounce. "I wish we still had the book. At least we'd have something to help take our mind off of being stuck in here."

"I'm not stuck." His eyes sparkled. "I choose to hang out with you."

"Seriously, I wish we knew where he hid it."

"It's in the basement."

I sat straight. "Great! Go get it tomorrow morning, okay? I'll hide it better this time."

"Nope."

"Why?"

"Cole thinks it could be dangerous. He's keeping it safe until he can get in touch with Allerton and find out how to destroy it."

"He can't destroy it! Tell him he can't." I was on my feet, still holding a dirty dish in my hand.

"It's what Allerton wants him to do. Maybe it's for the best."

"You… are… a… traitor!"

"No, I'm not. I'm just trying to protect you and do what's right. Jeez, Gracie. What's this obsession with that book? Let it go, already."

"I can't." He was right. All I did was think about it, remember all the writing on the pages, and imagine how the symbols might be mystically changing at any moment. I was like an addict. But I was also right. I could feel it in my bones. "Listen, I don't know how to explain it, but that book can help us."

"Do what?" He had that suspicious look in his eyes, the same one Masters sported every now and then.

"I don't know but I can tell you this much… it isn't over after Acclimation. Whatever's out there still wants to kill us. I know, really and truly know, that book can help us. Just please, sneak into the basement and get it tomorrow. Please."

"No." And he walked away. Ben had never done that—turned his back, no explanation, just a solid refusal to help.

"Stealing it was *your* idea!" Yeah, that was the best I could come up with. Whatever. I planned to convince Masters to let me see it after Acclimation. At the moment, I had dishes to wash and Jenny to worry about.

I slept in Jenny's room that night, hoping beyond reason that she'd come back. I woke to soft shuffling noises and switched on the lamp. There she was, but Jenny wasn't back. In fact, I'm not sure Jenny was actually Jenny. She looked different, tougher, resolute, and rough around the edges. Her hair was tied back and tightly braided. Jenny never braided her hair. She'd cut the sleeves from her tee-shirt and snipped a ragged V at the neck. She wore jeans and the only pair of boots she had, yet they held none of the fashion-forward quality they had before, when I'd wanted them so badly. Her eyes were clear, her face devoid of makeup. Jenny was more beautiful than I'd ever seen her. She looked up at me, but kept stuffing things into her backpack.

"Go back to sleep."

"What are you doing?" My heart thumped so hard I could hardly hear her response.

She stood. She looked like a soldier, like one of Masters' Marines. It made no sense. This was such a drastic change, I wondered if she was still depressed, or maybe she'd snapped. I raced to block the door and keep her from leaving.

"Jenny, listen. If you won't stay, go to Los Angeles. Look for Ryan. He's waiting for you. You'll go to college and have a wonderful—"

She grinned and huffed a chuckle that made my blood curdle.

"Okay, okay. Just… Jenny… let me know where you end up. Let me know so that I can visit you."

Jenny blinked, shrugged, pulled on her jacket then pushed my arm. I stepped aside. Before turning the doorknob, she did look back. "We'll see each other again."

That was all she said. She was gone. I watched her walk out of the room, through the living room where Ben slept like a baby, then out of the back door. She seemed like a dream, a mystical renegade, a woman no one would ever mess with. Then she simply melted into the trees, capable and casual as can be.

Masters was still in the basement. The door was open and light glowed in an upward shaft, floating on the night mountain mist. I was tempted to take a stroll across to him and demand a few answers. Then I heard voices all around.

We're here for you, pretty lady. Come out. Come to us.

My knees started to shake but I stood my ground inside the kitchen door. "No thanks," I said just as Masters popped his head from the basement. He looked into the forest then at me.

"Sweetheart, you need to get inside."

My skin rippled at the tenderness of his words, and my heart jittered as the strange, gravelly voices continued to call to me. Inside was best. Forty-eight hours and I'd know everything I needed to know. I went to my own bedroom and opened my journal. I sat on the bed until dawn and listed a full hundred questions I intended to ask at my Acclimation. At least making lists took my mind off of Jenny.

11

very moment I spent in Ariel's Gate was supposed to prepare me for acclimation. I waited for it every single day, pined for it like a star-struck child. I believed the stories—that the world was waiting for us all to come and make it better. That I could become anything I wanted, go anywhere, see everything. All of it felt like lies, tainted by the bizarre experience shared with four other acclimates over the past month. I could understand how much better it would be if acclimations were done one-on-one, to face acclimation blessedly blind to another person's dread, or panic, or excitement. Being last, I'd seen it all, played my role, and suffered everyone's ideas, suspicions, and fears. This isn't a game, and it shouldn't be played the way it had been. I suppose it began with those things outside the cabin talking, talking, talking. It began with Tony Ibanescu's death, and Headmaster's decision to close Ariel's Gate. Maybe it started long before that. Something major must have caused all the disruption in my simple world.

Poor Masters. To have to come back and do this must have been really hard. I tried not to look closely at him, but when I did, he appeared more worried and scared than I felt. I'd bet my life that even he wasn't sure what lay ahead. I wished I could help him.

Strangely, I slept well the night before the big day, dreaming lovely memories that made me smile and feel safe, at least for a while. My supersonic memory went into overdrive, and the dreams were so intense they ached.

My first birthday and my diaper's wet. There are voices all around, happy, playful voices, and there's an entity at my side, a memory not of fact, but of emotion and my current sensation of aloneness. Who knew I'd miss Jenny so much it would influence the truth of my past?

My second birthday. I'm looking down at my bare toes, one foot normal, the other rolled to the side like a tight rosebud. I feel mushy, sandy mud between my toes and I like the coolness of it. I like that the texture tickles. Thunder rumbles overhead, but I'm too fascinated with my dirty, gritty feet to care. Women's voices ring all around, and plants, some taller than me, shiver in the coming storm breezes. Ripe red tomatoes dangle and bob near my head, and vines dotted with zucchini flowers and fattening squashes cross the pathway. Lettuce dances and sparkles in the fading sunlight, then rain tickles at the edges of the rich green leaves. Lightning crashes and Mamma sweeps me up into her arms. She runs for shelter and I watch the basket filled with colorful vegetables and berries bounce at her elbow.

The birthday cake has three candles but there's a second, identical birthday cake beside it. My three-year-old mind wants to know which cake is mine. Who is the other cake for? The dreaming me again imagines that I miss Jenny far more than I realized. She's in my thoughts as I taste the sticky, sugary icing.

My fourth birthday. So much fun! Colorful candy, and cookies, and the intense sweetness of joy is all around me. I'm cradled in large arms, a man's arms and I lay my head on his shoulder, take in the scent of him. He passes me into a woman's arms then I'm moved to another woman's arms, then another. Finally, free on the grass I grasp another small set of pudgy hands tight and twirl and twirl until suddenly, my hands slip free and I fly back, into the legs of a sturdy old woman, her skirt tie-dyed brilliant yellow, orange, and deep green, like a blooming flower. I turn and hug those legs. I feel loved. I suddenly mourn the loss of that all-encompassing love.

My fifth birthday. Nothing is good. All around women are crying and shouting, and their fear ripples through me. Mamma pushes back her dark brown hair. Her green eyes are circled red and so wet, they look like twin worlds floating in a terrible sea. Another mamma lay on a bed, gasping her last breath.

I'm in a car, riding further and further from my home. I'm standing in Headmaster

Allerton's office, looking up at him and wondering… why am I here? I grow taller, endure oper-ations on my foot, and discover that I love to read, and learn, and write in my journal.

IS GOD HERE FOR ME, OR AM I HERE FOR GOD?

It's the morning of my acclimation day, my eighteenth birthday, and I think I'm about to learn the answer to that question. The strangest part is that I'm not afraid. I'm not trembling like Wally, or pretending to be brave like Ryan. I can't say that I'm as clearly sure of what I'll do afterward, the way Ben was, but I know I'm not as empty or hurt as Jenny. I'm me. I have faith in Masters. I trust him. I even like him a little. Well, maybe more than a little. He made me feel strong and willing to trust anything.

Anything except the basement across the yard.

~*~

"What? No. Why?" Leave it to Gracie to throw a wrench into the works. Cole had everything down to a system. Everything he needed was in that base-ment. All his experience was down there. He knew how to control the space, the acclimate, even the outcome. What the hell made her think it was no big deal to just change venue? "Tell me why you refuse to go into the basement… and this better be good."

Cole had been struggling with his feelings about Gracie since the incident in her bedroom. Kissing her like that made him feel wrong, but the fact of the matter was simple. He couldn't help himself. He felt way more than he should for her, but she was in his care, his responsibility. Against all his instincts to reach out, hold her, kiss her, he had to get her through the toughest thing she'd ever face in her whole life. He had to do this well. Especially this one. She still hadn't looked at him or answered his question. He needed a damn good reason for changing something that worked. "Well?"

"I just don't want to go down there."

"There's nothing to be afraid—"

"I'm not afraid. Really. It's just that… actually…"

And those gold speckled eyes pierced his heart. "Why?" He leaned closer to her across the kitchen table. His hand touched hers and she didn't pull away. The heat of her skin raced through his veins. "Gracie, do you trust me?"

"I trust you."

"Well then, I need a damn good reason."

Gracie didn't pull back or run away. She leaned closer. "I'm not a kid, and I'm not scared of a basement. I trust you, really. It's just that I… well… I feel like I need to control something. Can't we just do the acclimation here in the cabin?"

Okay, he didn't expect reasonable. Fear, desperation, and terror, yes, but not reasonable. No acclimate had been proactive and asked for something. They all just followed him to the *dungeon*. What Gracie requested was sensible but Cole had to think this thing through. "Everything I need is in the basement."

"So, bring it here. We have time."

"Gracie, it's supposed to be a private—"

"So, send Ben to the basement for the night." She drew in a calm breath. "Give me this, Cole. Please." Her fingers touched his and her face blushed. "Just this, it's all I'm asking. I don't want to go into the basement."

Hearing his name floating on her voice rattled him, relaxed him, excited him. Time for a few well-chosen rationalizations, something he was pretty good at. He was considering her suggestions because all this shit was almost over. But it wasn't over. He'd grown a strong commitment to stay with them, protect and take them wherever they wanted to go. Was that an excuse to stick close to Gracie? Yes. No. Maybe. It was a good choice. It rang true, even though he wasn't sure how much protection he could offer out there, where the enemy seemed to gain power by the minute. Everything he needed could be moved to the cabin, but should Gracie be permitted to push him into a situation that could jeopardize her acclimation, maybe even her life? But there was a solution. It could be done, there'd be enough protection, and he could give her what she asked. He wanted to, but more than that, he felt he had to. Allerton had warned him that Gracie was special, that her acclimation would reveal the reasons.

"Okay."

"Okay?" she squealed. "Thank you!"

"Right, Gracie." He led her to the living room then pointed into her bedroom. "Can you drag that mattress in here?"

"Why?"

"We can just go across the yard and—"

"No, no. I can drag it." She pulled at the heavy mattress and Cole pushed the coffee table to the corner of the living room.

"Ben!" he called, and the kid slid down the loft ladder. Cole spoke softly, watching Gracie struggle in the bedroom. "Bring the others in. Have them collect these items from the basement first." He jotted a quick list and handed it over.

"What's going on?"

They glanced toward the door where Gracie grunted and yanked, pushed and grumbled, dragging at the mattress as it stuck in the doorway.

"We'll do this in here. We'll need to block every entrance portal with protection. Do you understand?"

"Uh-huh." Ben left the cabin and Cole pushed the sofa back against the wall.

"A little help here," Gracie called, now on the floor and completely covered by the mattress.

Cole gripped and dragged it into the living room with one hand. "Push it against the sofa, leave room here, between the door and window," he instructed, then left to collect things from Ben. Setting them aside, he gave her another task. "Grab all the pillows and blankets from the bedrooms, and put them on the mattress."

"Make the bed?"

"No, just pile them on the edge, there by the sofa."

"Fine." She groaned but went off on her mission.

Gracie had been wrong… there wasn't enough time. With all the preparation, he'd be starting much later than he liked. He checked to see if everything he needed was in the cabin, spreading items over the kitchen table and thinking so hard his head ached. Raffie skittered back and forth, nearly tripping anyone in his path, panting and excited. Gracie staggered into the living room, nearly buried under a mountain of blankets, pillows, and sheets. Cole took them from her arms then sent her to the bathroom for towels. When she returned all was in place.

She turned and yelped in delight. "Oh my God! You're here! Ryan! Jenny! You didn't leave!" The slobbery dog barked his own welcome and leapt at them while she hugged her friends. "Where did you go? Why did—"

"I'm sorry, sweetheart." Cole checked the mantle clock, took her arm and led her to the mattress. "You can socialize after. It's getting late. We have to get started. Come, sit here. Just make yourself comfortable."

She settled, cross-legged with her trusty, ugly canine curled at her side. She actually smiled and waved to the others and Cole marveled at how young she was, how much she was about to change. He scrutinized the room. Soul swords wrapped in blankets and carpets blocked every doorway and sat guard under each window. One window and three doorways sealed. Check. The fireplace crackled and warmed the space, offering just the right amount of illumination. The lights were switched off—electricity never remained stable during an acclimation anyway. A pan of water, first aid kit, clean cloths and towels waited in the kitchen. And hidden beneath the mattress, Gracie's soul sword awaited its own awakening. Ben, Ryan, and Jenny sat silently on the floor behind him, and the task Cole most feared was about to unfold. Everything was as ready as it would ever be.

~*~

There was much to impart, much to organize, and much to prepare. More critical news had arrived, the runner nearly dead from exhaustion and battle wounds. Tobias called a final gathering before he broke camp. All were assembled under the communal tent. All but Michael Allerton, who was detained elsewhere, purposely assigned guard duty at the west gate, far from the important meeting. Much of the information dispensed would be too confusing for him. Too complicated. Too terrifying. He'd learn the news in a different place and a gentler way.

Tobias groaned. Fatigue pulled at his body as he strolled to the center of the tent. All eyes were on him; he couldn't show weakness. The time had come and nothing could change their mission. He cleared his throat then smiled with sadness at his warriors. Over the past three years their numbers had substantially grown, but not enough for what lie ahead. The camp count stood at one hundred seventy-three, including him and Garta. Not enough. Not nearly enough.

"We have received word from the coalition, my brothers and sisters at arms." The information threatened to choke him, and his soldiers listened with the intensity of warriors facing the worst. Telling them everything he knew was not easy, but they listened, nodded, drew in a collective deep breath and swallowed it whole. Tobias was pleased, but he had yet to explain everything to his newest soldier. Observation and performance proved that Michael was familiar with tough choices, difficult challenges, and honorable decisions. But was he a man ready to face a reality that the pompous tribunal and his precious acclimation orphanage system had hidden from him all his life?

His briefing complete, Tobias dismissed his troops and assigned new guards, relieving Michael to meet him at the central camp bonfire that burned night and day. Tobias prayed at that fire, made offerings of food and wine, beer and cookies, even blood drawn from small cuts at his own flesh. The constant flames bonded him to his ancient beliefs and comforted the contemporary men and woman who followed him. Around the fire sat his hand-chosen assistants for the task ahead. They were assigned to help Michael understand the future of their race, if there would be a future at all. This would be painful for the man to digest all at once. Those around the fire were charged with helping him, and doing so quickly. Camp would break the very next day.

Michael sat at the fire, smiled at those around him then focused on Tobias. "This isn't a social event, is it?"

"No, Michael. This is your own Acclimation… an acclimation into the truth about the threats facing your race. Please, have some wine, and please listen carefully… and if possible, hold your questions until after I've finished. Can you do that?"

Michael's hands shook as he sipped wine from a tin cup, but he nodded and waited.

"These people, Garta, our healer… Billio, warrior extraordinaire." Tobias grinned at the red climbing up the man's tattooed face. "Beauty Low, our illusionist… recruiter, Ballister Green… and finally, Dawn, one of your own acclimates… are all here to help you understand what I'm about to tell you."

Michael eyed each face around the fire then nodded.

Tobias looked into the flames and gathered his energy. "First, of the ninety traditional acclimation orphanages around the world, only one was able to save a few acclimates during the recent siege on those facilities. You," he pointed, "you saved five acclimates from quick deaths."

Michael's face became pale and hands trembled. One hand rose.

"Yes," Tobias answered before the question could be voiced. "The deaths are confirmed. Over the past six days, fourteen runners have passed through this camp with intelligence."

Allerton's head dropped but Tobias continued.

"Before I tell you more, I need to explain other things. We will start with the past. Michael, nearly twenty years ago a disease raced through your breeding communities, and within a few short years, took all of the adult women and any children not heroically hidden or rushed to safety. There have been few children of the race born since, a mere fraction of the usual number. There has, however, been a massive recruiting effort, along with a brutal eradication movement, launched and continuing among the enemy. Michael? Do you wish to take a break?"

The man was covered with sweat and Garta reached out to support him.

"Go on," he said through a dry throat.

"Give him more wine."

"No," he pushed the offered bottle away. "I want to clearly hear this."

"Good, good." Tobias ran a hand through his hair then unfolded a crumpled paper. "The numbers." He eyed Michael closely then continued. "The Emmaus Magic Show is one of a hundred and fifty-eight rogue warrior factions around America. There are another four hundred such groups in Canada and South America. Six hundred in Europe, Asia, Africa. We're all part of a coalition. We share intelligence, weapons, resources. Right now, there are ten armies… some carneys, circuses, and traveling entertainment shows like ours… all journeying to join us on the island of Ocracoke. About two thousand warriors. Total with the others, nearly nine thousand warriors."

"Why Ocracoke?"

Everyone stiffened but Tobias calmly responded, understanding Michael's need to comprehend. "It is where I've been guided to lead us all. Michael, if you can, please hold your questions."

"Yeah, sorry. It's just that I recall something from the records, something about one of my acclimates and that specific island."

"Good, then we're on the right track." Tobias smiled. "May I continue?"

"Sorry. Go ahead. The numbers."

"Are not good. Your reconnaissance mission reported three hundred of the enemy along the road between this camp and your young acclimates. Nearly eight hundred surrounding the cabin, and runners from the east report another ten thousand between that cabin and our destination, Ocracoke."

"Whoa," Michael sat straight. "That's way more than we'll have."

"Yes, more than double our number. And more are coming. Our coalition troops from the west will take weeks to arrive."

"Why? What the hell's the hold up?" Michael was on his feet and Tobias realized that his questions should be addressed, even if it took all night.

Ballister Green answered. "Recruiting," he said and tossed a glowing red-tipped twig into the fire. "We must constantly recruit, Michael. Warrior numbers have to grow, and the best way to do that is to lure our race in with the shows, let them witness the power of our collective presence, then explain what we're doing and how they can help. It's an age-old technique, but the only one we have right now… the only method that's proven successful. We'll be doing it as we travel to the island, too… stopping at several small towns to perform and recruit."

Michael settled into his seat, taking in deep breaths, obviously struggling to comprehend a system he never knew existed. "Okay," he finally said and looked to Tobias for more.

"The overall numbers are staggering. Four million of the enemy. That's four *million*. They use extreme recruiting methods… their primary focus has been new acclimates and those about to acclimate… to draw blood vows. They camped around the acclimation orphanages and snapped up young people before they even knew what was happening. Your student who died most likely resisted. The wounded one might already be among those between here and the cabin… passing on information about those inside."

Again, all the color drained from Michael's face and this time he did accept wine.

"We have much to fight for… our own survival, the stability of the human race, the planet. I am an ancient, not one of you, but you have to know, your race has far more numbers than the enemy, numbering in the billions, but most of them are not even aware of the war going on all around us. Tribunal intervention, the acclamation orphanage system, even the careless ones who allowed their young to discover themselves without guidance… it's all created this mess. So, Green's correct. Recruiting is our only resource for leveling the battlefield. Recruiting and… whatever your remarkable acclimate can bring to the table."

And it happened. Michael Allerton suddenly turned from the fire and gagged, shouting obscenities every time he caught his breath.

Beauty Low wrapped her arms around him and rocked him like a child. Garta prepared a tea to calm his stomach. Tobias stood to seek a silent place to pray and prepare. "We break camp tomorrow."

"Wait," Michael shouted and Tobias turned to face him. "The enemy… what the hell is up with them? Why are they all like statues?"

"I believe it has something to do with your acclimate, my friend. I truly believe that they're waiting for her… just like we are."

"But why? What are they waiting for?"

"I don't know." Tobias shrugged. "For now, talk with these warriors. They'll help you." He was too exhausted to answer another question that night.

He watched Michael turn to Dawn and talk quietly. It was a good plan, placing his lover on the assistance team. After all, they both saw the world in the same, distorted way. Dawn continued to struggle with the truth, but she had come far. She and the others would guide Michael toward peace with his own shortcomings, and into strength and passion for the cause.

Tobias felt a surge of surprising certainty. Michael Allerton could prove to be extremely valuable. He could be more than another sword, another warrior, another battle mate. He could be a strong liaison, one with the unique ability to implement change among the tribunal and unaware graduates of the orphanage system. He could assist in creating the superior numbers needed for survival and to reestablish balance. If willing, he could begin such an undertaking soon. If he survived whatever battles loomed ahead.

Tobias marveled at his luck, that such a man would stumble onto his camp. Now he could rest a bit, perhaps even sleep.

~*~

"Gracie, you're probably wondering why your buddies are here. Ryan and Jenny have been protecting us all from outside the cabin, but now they're going to be witnesses. It's acceptable and actually, in this case, helpful. You're safe from what's outside. You're protected. Do you understand?"

I nodded but my heart was racing like a freight train, threatening to crash right out of my chest. Cole—it really felt good calling him Cole—watched me carefully while my mind spun in a thousand directions. My mouth was dry and my hands, sweaty. I was so excited to see Ryan and Jenny, but worried that Wally wasn't with us. Thankful that Ben, steady as ever, had stayed close. And then there was Cole. Everything seemed to glow and warm between us. His eyes, sincere, his expression, serious. His heart, right there on his sleeve for me to see. I shivered and cleared my throat, embarrassment heating my cheeks. Still he watched me. "Sorry," I whispered.

"It's okay. Just relax. We'll start when you're ready, sweetheart."

That word. How he said it. Not like a dad or mom. It was different. Confirming. Solid. Something clicked inside my mind, like a light switch that illuminated the tangle of confusion, and I became cool as could be. Like an unexpected gift, peace drifted over my whole being, a soft cloud, a robe for warmth and so much more. I knew I was safe. I was aware of the others sitting behind him, but saw only Cole. He would guide me well, I just knew it. I raised a finger. "One minute. I just need one minute."

Closing my eyes, I let my thoughts float. So many memories passed like a damp breeze,
leaving behind the impression of events but details were lost in the mist. Then I saw Wally's face, so scared, so tense, so brave. *Wally, wherever you are, be safe. Please know that we care about you. Be safe, my friend.* Thoughts dissipated and I breathed a soft breath, in and out, then opened my eyes. "I'm ready."

He began and I braced myself for whatever was about to come out of his mouth.

"When I was acclimated," Cole adjusted himself to sit more comfortably on the carpet, "my guide chose to wait and tell me the facts… after. I think he thought it would be easiest but it wasn't. I never forgave him. So, I've been doing this a little differently."

"Okay," I said with a shrug. How could orphans be acclimated into normal life *after* they left for normal life? Didn't we need all the information first? It didn't make sense, but I wanted to let him tell all before I started asking questions.

The mantel clock chimed eleven-thirty and, even though the sound was soft and pleasant, I jumped a little. So embarrassing. The fire made snap, crackle, pop noises and Raffie huffed and snorted at my side. Everything, even the air, seemed to have weight and importance.

"I'm going to tell you things you're not going to believe. Things that might make you want to laugh, or scream, or even run away, but just… please… let me say it all. Let it get into your head, let it sit there and wait for the moment when it all makes sense. Can you do that?"

"Sure." Wow, a lot of preamble for a few simple socialization lessons. Behind Cole, Ryan and Jenny looked down at their hands. Ben seemed to be staring off into space. Only Cole focused on me. That seemed odd. Were my friends bored? They'd heard all this before, I guess. "Shoot." I flipped my hand, refusing to let their behavior rattle me.

"Gracie, you… all of us here… are not fully human."

The guffaw just burst from my mouth. It sounded like a goose's squawk and I snorted before regaining control. No one else laughed. Tough crowd. I expected a reprimand, or at least a scowl. Cole had a really good scowl. I felt like I should apologize but then something happened. My damn memory. Sometimes I really hate it. Racing at me from the past, I recalled overhearing those exact words. I was so young, lying in a crib, looking up at a sweet mobile made from seashells and tiny starfish, but I heard it clear as day. Someone beyond my vision was talking to another person. I could sense the tension in the room all around me. *You… all of us here… are not fully human.* My stomach clenched and I gulped. I knew something big was about to happen. I braced and readied. Cole must have sensed the change and continued with slow, quiet, well-chosen words.

"In the beginning, when God created people, angels came to earth often. They came to observe, to guide, to protect, to lead and fight important battles… and often they came because they found human women extraordinarily beautiful."

I was holding my breath and had to force myself to take in air.

"Celestial beings began to breed with human women long ago… it still happens. Gracie… you are the product of that breeding."

"You mean… Nephilim?"

"Yes."

"That's just crazy, a fairy tale… a distorted bible story." Ridiculous. Nephilim were supposed to be ancient giant beings and I'm not even five-foot-six.

"There are crazier things. And… there's more. Just hear me out."

I wondered if this was a joke, if they all got together and created this whole Acclimation thing to make me look stupid, or tease me, or—but that made no sense. Everyone would have to be in on it. The Gate, Allerton, even that strange book. This was not a joke, but was it real? "Okay, go on." I had to know it all, then I'd decide what I wanted to believe. Then I'd figure it out.

"First, a few details." Cole, comically, altered his expression and looked like a science teacher, all determined and dignified. I fought off the urge to laugh, but something had already begun to alter in my brain—as though it was growing into a different brain with different thoughts and different ideas. I listened to his words, but felt them more than heard them. It was like being pelted with a dodgeball in gym class. Each word almost hurt.

"There are levels of our race. A pure Nephilim is born of an angel… a celestial being… and a human woman. Now when a pure Nephilim breeds with another pure Nephilim, their offspring is called Norema, or High Blood Nephilim. Norema breeding with like, are also Norema."

Cole took a moment and I was grateful. It was getting harder and harder to pay attention. Something bizarre, corporeal, disturbing, holy, maybe even mystic was happening inside my head. Something I couldn't control or stop. Should I tell him? What if I was sick? Having a stroke? What if I needed help? I dragged in a ragged breath and rolled my neck. My head felt heavier, like it was getting loaded with something, but what?

"When a Nephilim breeds with a human, their offspring is called Calanine, or Lesser Nephilim. Most of our race is Calanine. Now," Cole shifted on the floor and sat on his knees, demanding all my attention. He had it. "Gracie, you need to understand that these titles are not a segregation of the race—they only define the power and strength of the individual, nothing more. Understanding our powers and abilities makes life a whole lot better. Trust me. I know from experience."

I blinked acknowledgment, but endured the movement inside my head. It settled into a new gelatinous form, a colorful, vibrant, expanded brain. He continued but my ears heard him differently, my eyes saw him differently, my soul felt his energy slip and slide and reach out to me.

"When a Calanine breeds with a human, their children are almost completely human, but those kids are born with certain gifts. They have psychic abilities, telepathy, empathy, ESP… like that. Those children never have an Acclimation. They are outside of our race, even though one of their parents is deeply entwined in our reality."

I swallowed hard. My logic didn't believe a word he said. It was all fairy stories, but something in my gut knew it was all truth. My next desperate need was to get to the bottom of it and find out what it meant. "And the things outside? What are they?" My voice was so raw Cole had to lean forward to hear.

"The easiest way to explain them is… demons. We call them the children of Morning Star… Lucifer's spawn… the enemy. But in truth they are us, turned to the dark, mutated and transformed into something not human at all, not angelic by any stretch of the imagination. They are Nephilim, Norema and Calanine who have chosen to follow Lucifer."

"The devil?" An ache had begun in my chest but I swallowed hard to push it down.

"Yes. Since the beginning of time our existence here has been a constant combat between good and evil, between the light and the dark, God and Lucifer. Human beings, with their blessed gift of free will, have been the battlefield. All Nephilim, being part human, are in possession of that gift of free will. The enemy has been determined to entice more and more of us to their side. Lately it's been… a lot worse." His eyes trailed to the window where even I saw them, hundreds of them, their eyes glowing, staring in at me. "It's a war, Gracie. I don't have all the facts, I don't know why, but what I've known as a simple struggle all my life… has become more. We're at war. And most important… what happens between us and the enemy vastly affects the human race and the planet. Balance is vital. We're at war to protect that balance, the people, the earth. All of creation."

War. Even before he spoke the word I saw it clearly, at first only as painted on the Makha'el Lecture Hall ceiling. Then I witnessed it in live action, Technicolor, right there inside my new mind—a twisted mass of bloodied and desperate beings, screams of pain and conquest, shouts of terror, the flash of ancient armor, puddles of mud and crushed bone, and the pounding feet of a million warriors. Suddenly I knew where this was all going, what Cole was telling me. What Acclimation actually meant… and I sobbed, "I don't want this."

"It's okay, Gracie." He moved closer to the mattress but didn't touch me. "It'll be fine."

"No, it won't!" The pain in my chest now pushed hard against my back, thudding like an animal trying to escape. Raffie snorted to his feet, barked once then raced to Ben's side. "I don't want this!" I cried. I wanted to be normal, simple, to be just a person like everyone else.

"It's what you are, but you have a choice. Do you hear me, Gracie?" He came even closer, positioning his face right in front of mine, forcing me to pay attention. "You have a choice."

The pain intensified, making my ribs feel like they'd splinter and rip through my flesh.

"Think about the words I'm about to say… think real hard. Okay?"

I forced myself to nod, to listen. My body felt like it was burning with fever, frozen for a billion years, suddenly awake to a world that could not exist.

"Give me an answer to this question." Cole actually climbed onto the mattress but still didn't touch me. I wish he had but deep down, I knew he couldn't. "This is the most important question of your life, Gracie… Is God here for you, or are you here for God?"

I felt my skin pull painfully at my back but I stared into Cole's eyes. "What?"

"It's your choice and whichever you choose, it's okay. If you truly believe that God is here for you, you can walk out of here tomorrow and live the kind of life you want. God will go with you and love you. You can go to college and marry, have children, teach… live a normal life."

I sensed heated blood dripping down my back but all my energy was focused on Cole's words.

"But if you truly believe that you are here for God, that choice brings you a very different life. The vow you take will set a life that is anything but normal at your feet. You will serve, you will fight… you will be a warrior for your race."

I screamed. The pain had become too much.

"Gracie!"

The flesh at my back ripped and the sting of it tore through my entire being. Panting through the anguish, I looked into Cole's compassionate eyes. My heart thudded hard and I breathed until I felt I could speak. "But I'm no warrior. I'm flawed, a failure before I even start. I can't fight. Oh… oh…" The pain intensified, rippling along my whole body and I twisted in agony. "I don't want this but I… have… no… choice."

The world swirled and strange colors glittered all around. I sensed myself lifting above my body, light as air, and wondered if I was dead and having an out of body experience. But as I floated higher I looked down at them all. If I was experiencing death, why were they all reacting like that? Looking up at me, standing, stepping back? I looked down, fully expecting to see my bleeding body crumpled on the mattress, but I wasn't there. I saw my own bare feet dangling and dripping blood several feet above the mattress, and the most miraculous thing of all, they were both normal. My entire heart warmed at the idea of walking like everyone else. Then my head cracked, loud and hard, against the high living room ceiling.

Cole reached up, a smile on his face. "You can come down, sweetheart. You control it."

Down? How the hell did I get *up*? Glancing around I gazed down into the loft bedroom, messy with Ben's things scattered over the bed and floor. I saw something else. My own reflection in the windows. It wasn't possible. It couldn't be.

Slowly I willed myself back to the mattress and as I settled there, weakness washed over me and a flurry of activity swirled. Raffie sniffed at my feet which I noticed were back to the way they really are. Sadness gripped my chest. Ah well, it was too much to hope for anyway. I wobbled then dropped into Cole's arms. All around me, the mattress was splattered with my blood.

"Quick, the water, those clean cloths, and the first aid kit. Now!" Cole bellowed as he tugged at my shredded tee-shirt and blood-stained bra. He unclipped the back with a quick jerk of his fingers then tenderly laid me, face down, onto the mattress. All I had the strength to do was listen and allow whatever came next.

"Christ," Ryan said, handing over clean washcloths. "Those wounds…"

"Yeah, I'll need to suture them." Cole's hands were gentle but a groan escaped my lips. "I'm sorry, so sorry. I'll be quick."

"Do you even know what you're doing?" That was Ben's big-brother voice.

Cole didn't bother to answer, just kept working. The needle hurt like hell, but I knew it would be over soon. I knew I'd already endured the worst. When I could speak, I gripped Cole's knee and he leaned his ear close to my face.

"What do you need, Gracie?"

"The book."

"Um… I'm not sure…"

But I heard shuffling, the kitchen door open and crash against the counter, and I knew that Ben had already gone to fetch it. "It's important. Trust me."

Cole Masters actually lowered his brow and nodded his head. No arguments, no objections. I squeezed his knee again and asked for water. I was so thirsty.

The mantel clock chimed one and outside the cabin everything had gone silent. I glanced toward the window. Where did they all go?

"Before we talk about the book, there's something else we need to do, Gracie. Can you sit up?"

Cole and Ben reached out to help but I pushed their hands away and grunted up. The pain had subsided so much that I wondered if it actually happened, if the reflection in the windows was real. If maybe I'd just lost my mind. Cabin fever. I read once that it could be deadly. I shrugged a shoulder. "Ow." Yep, it happened.

Cole reached under the mattress and pulled out something I never imagined I'd see—a shiny sword, long and brilliant, reflecting the fading firelight from the hearth. I wanted to touch it but sensed I shouldn't. I wanted to say something glib, but my new brain held it back.

"Gracious Caine… this is your soul sword. It is the gift you may choose or refuse. Speak the words 'God is here for me,' and this sword will simply dissolve into nothing and disappear, freeing you for a normal life. Speak the words 'I am here for God,' and this sword will live to protect you. Make your vow."

I blinked and Cole shifted closer, spoke carefully. "If you take the soul sword vow of service, you must respond when called. It's how I came to be here with you all. I was called. The vow is your commitment to serve when and where needed. Do you understand? Can you declare your choice? Select normal life… or a life of service?"

My choice? I wondered what the others thought when asked that question, if they had swords or a great normal life ahead. But this was the personal part Cole had been talking about. What the others chose did not matter. Tears ran down my face. I'd wished so hard and for so long to live a life like everyone else, but I wasn't like anyone else. And having no choice about my vow didn't make it harder or easier. It made the vow simple.

"I am here for God."

The sword glowed blue, so bright that it distorted everything in the room for several seconds. Cole smiled and the others released a collective sigh of relief.

Raffie resumed his position at my side and I lowered to lie on the mattress. I was so weak and tired, but I reached out for the book, took it from Ben's hand, and cuddled it close to my heart. "What now?" I whispered and Cole settled a hand on mine. So comforting. Exciting. Welcome.

"I figured a few hours of sleep then we can pack up the van and get the hell out of this cabin. Maybe get some breakfast at Denny's? Sound good?"

"Yes." My voice was nearly gone, my mind drifting and swaying with everything that happened, what I now knew, what I saw reflected in the window. I glanced around, astounded at what was so obvious. Cole had wings, grey and slightly blue, massive. Ben's wings, too, were huge, dark and pale purple. Jenny's were speckled with yellow and gold. Ryan's, white as snow. None of them were like mine. Like what I saw in the window's reflection. Was it possible? Did I have six wings? Brilliant white and glowing hot blue? I must have been mistaken. I couldn't have seen correctly. Or were my wings as mutated as my foot?

Jenny crawled onto the mattress to lay behind me and her fingers stroked my hair. I guess I fell asleep. I know I didn't dream.

~*~

Michael woke with a start, feeling, yet not hearing, a massive clap of thunder that shook his entire being. A silent shift in the universe. An explosive altering of everything. He left his tent and followed everyone else, all heading toward the central fire. They all stood there, arms outstretched, eyes closed, faces raised to the heavens.

"Gracie," he whispered.

Solidarity bound everyone around him. They were of one heart, one thought, one prayer. Strength raced through their souls. Tobias turned and smiled. Michael nodded. All was as it should be.

As a shooting star streaked across the sky, shouts of joy rang through the dark night. Excited embraces were shared, and hands reached out and clapped

Michael's shoulder. He knew he'd done at least one thing right. He'd found a way to save Gracious Cane.

~*~

They were all asleep, rolled like puppies on the floor and mattress. Cole needed air. Stepping out into the back yard, his arms rose wide and he dropped his head back. The night sounds were soft, comforting. No voices tormented him, no demon called. No enemy, anywhere. His eyes scanned the trees. No movement. What did it mean? The enemy had always been near, at least one of them, whispering at his shoulder. Granted he'd never experienced so many of them as over the past month, twisted and mangled together into the battle-heat creatures they'd become. Something bad was ahead. Cole fully expected another call to honor his vow, one that could be lethal.

The night was weak, nearing morning yet far from daylight. He would get no sleep, so coffee would help him think. Ground coffee was long gone, so he boiled water and spooned the last of the instant into his mug. Sugar, gone, too. Powdered creamer, none since Ben's Acclimation. So, black instant coffee it would be.

He sat at the kitchen table and examined the intricate yellow patterns on the Formica surface. Head in hands he fought tears. Joy? Terror? Exhaustion? Most likely all of the above. He'd done it, done the impossible. Almost. He worried for Wally, out there somewhere. He heard the shuffling but didn't look up until the intruder settled into the chair next to him.

"Coffee's gone," he said.

"Fine." It was Gracie and he looked up.

"You should be resting."

"Did you know that I saw Jenny the night of her Acclimation? I saw her leave the cabin. It was four forty-four, the exact time it is right now. She didn't need more rest. She was ready for battle." She smiled and Cole couldn't help but return it.

"You've been through a lot. You need more rest. Everyone's different."

"I can see that now." Gracie leaned back carefully, putting little pressure on her back, and watched him closely. "You did good, Cole."

He nodded then shrugged.

"How many Acclimations have you guided?"

He held up five fingers.

She snorted a soft laugh. "So, you really were as scared as you looked."

"More." He sipped coffee. It was bitter and cloying, almost satisfying. His hand drifted to hers, a fingertip touching with gentle pressure. "You feel okay?"

"Sore. But somehow… more awake than I've ever been in my whole life."

Cole grinned. "You know, that's the correct word… awake. We call those who've been acclimated, awakened."

She nodded and sighed. "I see things. Is that supposed to happen?"

"What do you see?"

"You. You're Norema, right? High Blood Nephilim."

"I am."

"Ben, too. Your wings, his wings… are huge."

Cole sipped the cooling coffee then slid it away. Hot it was tolerable, cold, unbearable.

"Jenny and Ryan are Calanine."

"Yes, but it doesn't make them lesser warriors, Gracie."

"That answers my next question… so we're all in this together?"

Cole watched her face. He knew this girl's mind. It was conjuring a million questions he wasn't sure he could answer.

"Okay, now… what am I?"

He swallowed hard and drew in a deep breath. This one he could handle. "I've never seen anything like you."

"Is that good?" Worry painted her pretty face.

"It is. Gracie, you are pure Nephilim. There are few, if any, like you alive.

I've never seen one… and I've been all over the world, practically. America, England, Germany, all over the Middle East."

"What does it mean?"

"You're special. What it means will come to light. Your role to protect the race will come clear. This is the time for patience." His hand gripped hers fully and she returned the pressure.

"Another question."

"Shoot."

"Will I always see them? The wings?"

"You can see them when we're stimulated to react for protection or battle, but you won't always see them. You don't have to. You'll know. We can sense our own. We sense lots of things. I can't explain or tell you what you'll know or experience. It's—"

"Personal." Her voice was so soft. "Can I ask something personal?"

The crappy coffee gripped in his stomach.

She lifted their clasped hands. "What does this mean?"

He leaned closer and closer to her soft lips. "May I kiss you?" he whispered, his voice raw with need.

"Not today." But she didn't pull back. Instead, she leaned the final inch and tasted his lips, a tender press that made his heart race. "Today… I want to kiss you." She did it again and Cole sat still as stone, allowing her full control. "But," and finally she pulled back, holding tightly to his hand, her gold specked eyes demanding his full attention. "I don't really want more just yet. Is that okay?"

Okay? Okay? Keeping himself from panting like an animal in heat took all his mental capacity. Was it okay? Did he have a choice? *Say something!* "Yes," came out and his head slowly lowered to the tabletop. It was cool and soothing and maybe he could just close his eyes and fall asleep right there.

"I know how tired you are, Cole, but I need to ask a few more questions. Please. It's about this book." She drew it from her lap and placed it on the table between them. Both hands finally free, she flipped it open.

He sat straight as an arrow, damn scared. That book felt wrong. It felt right. But it also felt evil. Too strong, too strange.

"Gracie, there are others who know about that book, I'm not—"

"Just tell me," she pointed to a symbol. "Do you know what this symbol means?"

"Uh… that one." He squinted. "Yeah. And this one, that one, too. Trust me, I've been pouring over this book since I got it from you guys. The most I can figure out is six, maybe seven symbols per page. Useless. Then the damn text keeps changing. It's way above my pay grade, Gracie."

"Tell me what this one means." Her finger poked again at the symbol and he scowled but focused.

"*Battle*. Well more like… ah… violent or fierce battle."

"Can you tell me what this one means?" Her finger slid to the symbol just before it.

"No clue."

"I know… it means *certain*. So… *certain fierce battle* but… oh, shit!"

The symbols shifted right under her fingers and she pulled her hand away as if the page might burn her.

"Oh! Look!"

He did. The new symbols were garble to him. He shrugged. "You got anything?"

"Yes! The symbol for *certain* has changed. It now means… *possible*. And that… the one you said means *violent battle*, now means… *controlled battle*. Don't you see? Between us we can figure some of this out, Cole."

"Yeah? And what about the other hundred symbols on each page? We're only seeing a tiny slice of the message."

She closed the book with an intense expression that made him nervous. "Between all of us, we'll know more. Besides, we'll meet others like us. The more the merrier!"

"Merrier? Gracie. You do understand… our race is at war."

"Yes, and with a lot of warriors, we might also get a lot of different symbols defined. We might be able to use this book to help us win."

"I'm sure there are people who can read this thing better than a bunch of—"

"Then let's find those people."

He opened his mouth to respond, to explain that he had no freaking clue where they were all to go, who they were meant to serve under. This mess made the U.S. Marines look like child's play. "Listen," he started.

"Hey," Ryan's mussed golden locks and bleary eyes poked into the kitchen doorway. "Didn't someone say something about breakfast at Denny's?"

"Battle is the untying with the teeth a political knot
that would not yield to the tongue."

~ *Ambrose Bierce 1842–1914*

12

In the time it took Michael to figure out how to take down and roll up his little pup tent, most of the vehicles were already packed and lining up for the caravan. His mind was jittery, vibrating like an electrical surge. Brilliant flashes of the past, the present, and the future blasted and crashed against his skull. He looked around, forcing himself to breathe evenly, regain control, create some semblance of ease. Leaving the veil's protection not only exposed him to the enemy, but also tribunal spies searching for him. Going back to prison was not on his agenda, but teaming up with Tobias pretty much guaranteed it. The Emmaus Magic Show was on the tribunal's top ten most wanted list.

Over the past weeks he'd come to shape his body into the warrior it was meant to be. He enjoyed working with his soul sword for the first time ever. As a young acclimate taking his vow, he thought he'd get to be Rambo, but his call to service was a far cry from glorious battle. He had been chosen to protect children, guide them, hope and pray for them, and he did his best. An ache charged across his chest, so intense it caused him to curl over on himself. All those children, babies, toddlers, preteens, dead. Lost forever. Was it because of him? Should he have tried harder? Moved quicker? Done more? The opportunity to fight beside his fellow soldiers was a gift, a chance to at least attempt to redeem himself, and

Michael Allerton was grateful.

The true way of things as explained by Tobias left him feeling unstable and displaced. Any loyalties he had to the tribunal had been obliterated, thanks to their unjustified actions against him, but loyalty to the traditional acclimation orphanage system remained, holding on to the edge of an abyss by its fingernails. For a thousand years the system had cared for the children of his race—taken them in regardless of background or financial standing, given them the best possible childhood, education, protection from the enemy, and guidance through a safe acclimation.

Perhaps the system had gotten too big for itself, become a prideful beacon that drew the enemy to action. Perhaps they'd all stopped protecting effectively. Ninety orphanages just like Ariel's Gate, all gone, dismantled, or destroyed in the span of a few days. The youth of his race, nearly obliterated. Every record was unquestioningly sent to the tribunal for safekeeping. Safekeeping? How could they have been so foolish? Nothing of the carefully documented records would ever be seen again. The tribunal was big on bonfires—the kind that eliminated discriminating evidence. Generations of vital records and Nephilim lineage, up in smoke.

He closed his eyes and imagined walking the Gate's beautiful halls and elegant, graceful stairways. Millions of dollars annually were donated to keep the orphanage up to the highest standards. He'd been able to recruit and hire the best of their race as teachers, instructors, guides, and workers. He saw the massive kitchen and recalled the smells of soups and stews, roasted meats and burgers, spaghetti and tacos. He guided his memory into the dorms. Since his own childhood, those huge rooms lined with neat beds had been broken into smaller, two student rooms.

Everything changes and so did Ariel's Gate. All the power of illusion, all stronger than real stone and marble, brick and mortar, and all dissolved back into its original form—a diminutive West Virginia mansion built in the 1800s and rotting to death. All gone. Everything he'd believed and built his life on was gone, or a lie, or something else altogether.

"Michael!" Beacher called from across the open space. "Tobias wants you to ride with him in Beauty Low's big camper. Take your tent and stuff with you. It's third in line."

"Sounds good," he called back. "Need help with the communal tent?"

"Hell, yeah! Appreciate all the hands I can get."

Michael stood near the big yellow tent, dropped his stuff then rubbed his hands together. Physical activity had become his new favorite thing. It occupied his mind and tightened his muscles. He'd need the strength when the enemy attacked. Best to keep himself in strong.

Ten men grunted, yanked, shouted, then pulled until the poles and canvas were down and ready to be rolled together. Once, while attending a leadership conference in New York, Michael had gone to see the Yankees. The game started with a rain delay, but when the tarps protecting the infield conditions were removed, they were carefully folded then rolled onto a long wide roll that sat along the edge of the third base foul area. The process for packing the massive communal tent was the same, except it smelled of sweaty men and Cookie's great food. Together they lifted the roll onto their shoulders and walked it to a nearby eighteen-wheeler flatbed. More grunts and a cheer completed the task.

Dissolution of the mystical veil that had kept them safe for so long took mere moments and only a few words from Garta—words Michael had never heard before, the language likely as old as the woman herself. He climbed into the big Winnebago luxury camper, its broad sides brightly painted with the Emmaus Magic Show logo and featuring specific acts. Beauty Low herself sat, grinning ear to ear, in the driver's seat. All was ready and Michael should have been thrilled, but he wasn't quite that sure of himself, or Tobias's vision, or maybe he was just afraid to face what lay ahead. If all went well, they should come across Cole and his newly awakened soon, but what were the odds? What if Cole left earlier or went the other way? Or if they were so far ahead there'd be no way to catch up? What if the caravan had left too early? Or too late?

"Have a little faith." Tobias sat across from him at the camper table, shuffling cards and laying out a spread for another game of solitaire. Michael recalled that as a kid, they used to call the game *Beat the Devil*. How appropriate.

"Tobias… man… seriously… get out of my head," Michael said with a glare.

"I can't. You're too loud." And he chuckled.

Michael sat, struggled to be still, stay calm, have a little faith. His hands were sweaty and his heart pounded. He tried hard not to think, because every thought began with the same words—*If we don't find my kids I'll…* Best to let that thought die before it completed. He had no clue what he'd do.

Not fifteen miles down the road the walkie-talkie crackled.

"Beauty, Beauty, Beauty," it said in a gravelly voice.

"What'cha got, Pincer?"

"Pay dirt. A broken-down van, half mile ahead. I'll pull in front, you pull that behemoth behind."

"Will do."

"I'll get that vehicle running then catch up at the end of the caravan. Here they are, come get your awakened kiddos, Michael! Out." *Crackle, crackle.*

He thought his heart actually stopped. Michael forced himself to cough against the pain just to get the damn thing pumping again. He was at the door and leapt out before the camper came to a full stop.

What to say first? What to do first? He ran to the kids who took several steps back before recognizing him. Cole peeked out from under the hood where Frank Pincer was already replacing the faulty spark plug he'd put into the engine during their reconnaissance mission.

"Cole!" Michael gasped to catch his breath. "Gracie, you're okay? Yes? Good. Ben! Ryan!" He reached out and shook the young men's hands, pulled Jenny into a one-armed hug then turned to Cole, who swiftly and without warning, slammed a practiced fist into Michael's nose.

"Just where the hell have you been?" Cole shouted before he dove onto his victim, kicking and swinging. It took two men to pull him off.

Tobias chuckled and helped Michael to his feet. "This is going to be fun. Come, everyone, let's get into this comfortable camper. We'll answer all your questions."

~*~

It took a while for Cole to gain full control of himself. All his anger and fear over the past month had rushed into his fists to attack the cause of that misery—Allerton. Release felt like heaven. The bastard had a lot of nerve leaving him high and dry like that. He was supposed to come help, check in, be available by cell phone. Okay, okay, so he had been tossed into prison by the tribunal, whatever that was. All he knew was that the guy left him alone with hundreds of the enemy and five scared kids to protect and acclimate. Left him on his own to deal with, care for, and bring the awakening of a pure Nephilim. No forgiveness warmed Cole's heart. This rage against the man started long ago—the night three years earlier when Allerton witnessed his painful and terrifying Acclimation. Rage turned to hate and that, with his full-out desertion in Cole's deepest time of need, evolved neatly into fury. Maybe he shouldn't have gone at Allerton like that. It just happened. Gracie looked pissed. Odd, he didn't think she was that fond of the old man.

When he could finally see straight, could look at Allerton's bloodied yet grinning face, he gained the tentative ability to not just listen, but hear and comprehend what those around him were saying. It was slow and he was sure they'd already repeated the words several times.

Crammed with him in the moving Winnebago were his awakened kids and the guys who pulled him off Allerton, leering and looking like night club bouncers. There was Dawn, a really hot gal he remembered from the Gate, and an ancient named Tobias. That guy was a conundrum. Not only because he was an ancient, but he was an ancient Cole had met before. In the man's eyes was a clear warning not to say anything about that, so Cole held it back, but memories of sharing a Pine Bluff Arkansas jail cell with the guy eight months ago haunted him. Back then he was still raw, fresh from his tour of duty, and the ancient could read his thoughts like a gypsy witch.

"So." Cole gulped beer and aimed the bottle at Allerton. He wanted to make sure he was getting it all. "You reported to some tribunal committee… and they accused you of a mess of crimes… then tossed your ass into an underground prison?"

"Yes."

"Okay, so how'd you get out?"

"Long story, but an ally on the tribunal set me free."

"Why?"

Allerton took a gulp of his coffee before responding, his expression pained and somewhat angry. "They sent me to find you all… they ordered me to bring Gracie back to the tribunal prison. They want me to finish out a thirty-year sentence… and they believe that locking Gracie down there will be the best way to protect her."

Gracie gasped.

He turned to her. "But I have no intentions of taking you. No intentions of going back there at all."

"Yeah, they call that jumping parole," Cole snorted.

"Yes, and I'm sure they're looking for me." Fear clouded his eyes.

"So, you were free," Cole said with a scowl. "You knew exactly where we were but didn't come and help me. Nice… real nice."

"Cole," Allerton said with a groan.

Tobias took over. "Michael was dangerously weak… he'd already been through hell, mugged, wounded… about to be attacked and surely killed by the enemy, so we took him into our protection. But once inside the protective veil, he couldn't just leave. When he was strong enough he wanted to slip away without warning, but he had to sit tight. Otherwise he'd have put us all in danger."

"Right." Cole snorted again. "Magic. And you guys are carnies that fight the enemy."

"What's so unbelievable about that?" Dawn interjected, her eyes flashing.

Cole rubbed his aching head. "Nothing. Nothing." He shot a glare at Allerton. "Why the hell didn't you check on us? Come help? You have no idea—"

"He did." Tobias sipped coffee. "I sent him to lead a reconnaissance mission. You remember reconnaissance, don't you, Marine? In, out, no contact, silent as the wind."

Cole blinked.

"We knew you were safe, we knew how many of you were in that cabin, and one of my men tampered with your van to make sure we'd connect with you today. It all worked exactly as planned."

"And you were just a few miles from us?"

"Ready at the first sign of real trouble. Prepared to protect and assist." Tobias leaned back in his bench and waited for an apology.

He wasn't getting one. "I needed that bastard's help!" Cole aimed the bottle again, this time sloshing brew onto the table.

"No," Allerton said, once again grinning like a lunatic. "You didn't need me. You didn't need anyone. You did it. I knew you could. I knew it."

The camper fell silent and Gracie finally spoke up. "Tobias?"

"Yes, my dear? Oh… damn." He shuffled in his seat. "Someone get this dog away from me."

Ryan gripped Raffie's collar and led him toward Gracie where the animal sat with tilted head, indignity written all over his ugly face.

"The reason this is a traveling magic show and not a circus is because I can't stand animals." Tobias brushed his hands off and glanced at the surprised faces. "I know, I know… everyone loves dogs but… well… I lost one… long, long ago. Never warmed up to animals again."

"Tobias." Gracie reached down and rubbed Raffie's ear for a moment, but never actually looked at the ancient. "Why were you under a protective veil… here?"

"That's a good question. I was guided to wait here until a specific time then move on. We found Michael in danger outside the veil and took him into our care. It's all a happy coincidence."

Cole noticed the questioning glare Allerton aimed at Tobias. What was really going on with the Emmaus Magic Show?

"Where are we going now?" Gracie asked, doodling on the back of a show flyer. She still hadn't looked Tobias in the eyes.

"Well, we are scheduled for several shows between here and our destination. There are reasons for stopping and performing."

"Sure," Gracie said with a shrug and continued drawing on the paper. "You need to make money, right? A carnie lives on the take at the ticket booth."

"Correct." Tobias wasn't smiling.

"What's the final destination?"

Cole blinked. The girl was nothing, if not tenacious.

Tobias sighed and crossed his arms. "The North Carolina island of Ocracoke."

"Uh-huh. Tell me, Tobias… does the Ocracoke lighthouse look like this?" She turned her drawing and everyone leaned in to look.

"It does. Why?" Tobias followed the lines of the squat white lighthouse drawing with his fingertip.

"Because I'm supposed to go there." All eyes focused on Gracie who began to blush. Then she shrugged. "I don't know why but I need to go there, and soon. Before you and the magic show arrive."

"My dear," Tobias ran a hand down his face and looked to Allerton. "I haven't told you everything. I didn't want to frighten you, but now I need to explain."

Cole listened with all the intensity his aching head could muster, and like actual magic, everything started to make sense. If in fact Tobias was instructed to camp exactly where he did, if Allerton did in fact stumble onto that camp, and if it was true that the carnie army was sitting tight and waiting for Gracie to awaken, everything might actually be exactly as it should be. Existentialism wasn't Cole's area of expertise, but he'd come to accept it was a major part of his life. He turned to Gracie and awaited her response.

"I understand… I think. But what I know is that I'm supposed to go to Ocracoke now, or at least very soon. I'm supposed to go there and wait for you and the others."

"Others?" Cole reached out to touch her hand but thought better of it and instead, slid the drawing closer for examination. Not nearly as comforting, but at least he'd dodged a bullet. Best not to open that can of worms. The last thing he wanted was a lecture from Allerton.

Gracie's gold specked hazel eyes finally rose to watch Tobias who cleared his throat. "Many other warrior bands will be joining us on our way to the island. It's going to take a while before we all gather, a few weeks, possibly more. We all must recruit along the way, gather as many warriors as we can."

"War," Cole said and the word nearly choked him.

"Yes."

"Either way, I need to go on ahead." Her voice was soft but sure.

"Gracie," Allerton reached for the hand Cole wanted and held it tight. "I think it's best if you stick with us, travel with us. We're all going to the same place and we can—"

"No, she's right." Tobias stood and stretched his back, then leaned with his hands on the table. "Michael, we all want nothing more than to protect her. She may be the last pure Nephilim on the planet. But we're not here to protect her… we're here to follow her lead. However, my dear Gracie, I do ask that you wait at least a week. We're constantly receiving reports. Let's get a good gauge of how many of the enemy you'll be facing along the way. Then I'll send the appropriate number of soldiers to travel with you."

"I'll go with her," Cole said, a little louder than he meant to.

"No, no. I need you here to help train the newly awakened and fresh recruits for battle. You're too valuable."

Valuable? Cole had never been pegged as valuable before. However, he had no intention of letting Gracie out of his sight. He had some time to figure out this wrinkle.

"Gracie," Allerton said, still holding her hand. "A week, okay?"

Gracie nodded and Cole leaned back and blinked. He knew damn well that a nod from that girl did not an agreement make.

They grew silent, deep in their own thoughts and concerns as the Winnebago drove on for hours. The travel was slow in a monumental effort to keep the caravan, and all the powerful soul swords hidden within, close together and strong. The sun played in the rusting leaves lining the Virginia country road. It splashed color and light into the windows that danced like fairy glow along the quiet travelers. Cole had his own thoughts shouting manically at him, demanding more information and requiring much more trust before he intended to be valuable to the Emmaus warriors.

Geographically, they were not that far from Ocracoke—less than a day. Tobias planned to roam around Virginia for weeks, performing and recruiting. On one hand, it kind of made sense to stick just close enough to the battlefield to keep an eye on the gathering enemy. Still, it seemed foolish. To seriously recruit, shouldn't they follow the better weather? Move further south to more populated areas in the Carolinas, Georgia, and Florida, big cities like Charlotte, Atlanta, and Jacksonville? Cole had to admit he wasn't a strategist and he wasn't aware of the arrangements made between the other armies and the Emmaus leadership, but if Tobias was being honest, recruiting was not his reason for hovering so close yet so carefully distant from their destination. There was something else at play. Thinking about Tobias made Cole nervous, especially when the guy glanced his way and raised an eyebrow. Not cool, eavesdropping like that. Cole turned away, sighed and scanned the faces around him.

Ben sat in the back, talking quietly with a bald tattooed man who could have been wearing an Olympian weightlifter's body. Tobias and Allerton sat across the table not looking at each other, confirming that the full truth was yet to be revealed. Ryan sat close to Jenny. Apparently those two had kissed and made up, but not fully. Jenny kept a tentative distance from her man, something that would have never happened before. Maybe she was still working on forgiving him for following Cole's request to protect the cabin from outside. Maybe she'd just grown up. Maybe she understood. Maybe those two had progressed onto a more mature relationship. How would Cole know? He'd never had a real relationship. A wave of jealousy whipped through him, making him shiver like a wet dog. Time to move his thoughts along. He turned to focus elsewhere.

The second bouncer rode shotgun beside the driver, a big woman who looked like she'd deflated, her clothes baggy and unattractive but her face glowing and happy. And bearded. A nice full dark beard, too.

At the other end of the sofa, Gracie had curled around her backpack and fallen asleep. Her extraordinary experience just hours earlier had taken its toll. He wanted to sit closer, to check her stitches, to nudge her to lay her head on his knee. To touch her. Did she look feverish? Was she really sleeping, or just thinking with her eyes closed? Her finger twitched and he smiled. Sound asleep and more beautiful for it.

Walkie-talkie announcements broke the silence. The bearded lady relinquished the driver's seat and Tobias took control of the camper, passed the few vehicles ahead, and led them all onto a vast empty fairground. With vehicles parked haphazardly, the warrior-slash-carnie-performers circled Tobias and awaited orders—far more people than Cole imagined were riding along in the caravan. His awakened kids stood close at his shoulders. They were far from seasoned warriors, just rookies, and probably felt safer with him. It was humbling, and it fed his weakening ego nicely.

~*~

What followed was a flurry of activity. Faster than the Marines could have done it, the camp came to formation. Cole roamed the grounds and lent a hand where he could. A village of tents was built around the far configuration of campers. The midway was established and with a wave of his hand, everyone knew exactly what Tobias wanted and where he wanted it.

Within an hour, one side of the midway was lined with food trucks, game tents, and small performance stages. The other side sported a long colorful low fence which enclosed the carnie rides. Lights were strung and plugged into strategically placed outlet posts along the fairground pathways. At the beginning and the end of the midway stood two huge arched entry signs boasting, *The Emmaus Magic Show, Eighth Wonder of the World.* In the dead center of the midway, Cole watched the unique big top rise slowly and with great elegance, then flutter in the breeze. Standing beneath it, he gazed up through the brilliant colored fabric slats. Pale evening had crawled in all around and the evening's first star winked down at him.

Cole was impressed. A massive amount of work reduced to small team tasks had produced remarkable results. His awakened kids had found activities to occupy them and keep their minds from impending battle, doom, and gloom. Ryan assisted in the raising of a massive yellow tent behind the camping area. Ben helped build the Ferris wheel which looked like a giant toy erector set come to life. Jenny and several performers held ropes tight while others created the high wire platforms under the big top. Gracie had gravitated to the ancient they called Garta, helping her set up her medical camper in preparation for whatever mishap or combat loomed ahead. A twang of concern coursed through him. What was that old woman telling Gracie? Would she scare her? Misguide her? Cole walked with long strides toward them but before reaching the small camper, Gracie had waved farewell and turned to find him.

"These are nice people." She smiled.

"Yeah."

"Are you mad at me?"

"Nope, at everything else." He turned and she followed, shuffling to catch up.

"Well stop. Being mad isn't helping anything. Garta says dinner will be ready soon. We can eat then figure out what to do next."

She slid her arm into the crook of his. He wouldn't break free, but he had to make his point. Gracie had no idea what was coming. Maybe that was his fault. "Gracie, what we do next is whatever we're ordered to do. Do you see how everyone follows Tobias? He's the leader, the general of this army. Even Allerton does what he's told."

"And who's telling Tobias what to do?"

He wanted to say God, but thought better of it. "Someone higher. We're here, we follow."

"But we get to choose, too, right?"

"Remember that vow you took? Gracie… *this* is your call to service." He waved his arm to the camp and carnival all around then turned on his heel and walked away. This sure as hell wasn't what he hoped would happen, but it was happening. Why was he surprised?

Hundreds of the enemy had surrounded the cabin, all in battle heat, all ready to move in for the kill. He'd never know why they didn't attack or where they all went after Gracie's awakening, but he knew they were amassing for a reason. War was coming and he could do nothing to change it. His anger had turned him away but within the span of two breaths Cole realized he needed Gracie, to be near her, not apart. Yes, he'd been a chronic loner before… but with her, for the first time, he felt complete. He couldn't give her the life she deserved, but he had to fix the moment and be what she needed. When he turned, he crashed right into her and had to grip her shoulders to keep her on her feet.

"You stalking me?" he teased. Heart pounding, his fingers slid up her arms and his eyes spoke his apologies.

"Yes. No. Whatever. We need you, Cole. I need you. Don't go all pissy on us again, okay?"

"Sorry." Oh, to just lean down and kiss her, assure her of his feelings. To be alone somewhere with her. But Cole knew better than to do any of that. People were watching. Tobias was reading minds. She wasn't ready. Hell, he wasn't sure he was ready. The past month had altered him. With Gracie, he seemed to instinctively know how to be a good man. Who knew a gimpy girl from Ariel's Gate could do such a thing? It made him feel happy and he hugged her under one arm.

A loud clanging bell rang and they stepped apart. "What the hell?"

"Dinner!" Gracie chirped.

All work, completed or not, ceased. The slow exodus from carnie construction to fellowship in the big yellow communal tent looked like a river. Cole and Gracie stood aside until Ben and the maybe-maybe-not lovebirds joined them. Ben tossed an arm over Gracie's shoulder and leaned in to whisper. She laughed. Cole smiled. He'd been a soldier. These are the most important moments, the calm ones, the camaraderie, the trust. The love. Before the battle.

They found a table and sat together, a tiny army unto themselves. He noticed a look of sadness wash across Allerton's face, but the man hadn't been there, hadn't witnessed their pain, and fear, and tears. Cole was. They were his, not Allerton's. His soldiers, his friends, his… well, whatever Gracie was or would be, it was his relationship with them that mattered now.

The former headmaster sat at the raised table with the two ancients and camp dignitaries. Tobias had great influence on everyone under that tent, but far more on Allerton than Cole realized at first. It didn't matter. It wasn't like he expected Allerton would be an ally or anything. Cole had managed and would manage. He knew how to follow orders. He knew how to fight. But when Gracie was released to leave for Ocracoke, desertion wasn't beyond his capabilities, either. He sneered at the raised long table then turned his attention to his own little dysfunctional family and the platters of food in front of him. The meal was exceptional, especially after eating whatever could be created from their limited supplies.

"Oh… my… God! I think I've fallen madly in love with Cookie!" Jenny announced through a full mouth. Ryan smiled then kissed the top of her head, pulling her into a quick hug.

Just as Cole licked the last smear of luscious chocolate pie from his fork, the sound of talking and laughter came to an abrupt stop and all eyes turned to the head table. Tobias stood. His eyes sparkled and his wide smile showed crooked white teeth behind parched lips. He looked like a proud papa.

"My friends and fellow warriors… again we travel and perform."

Applause rattled the canvas walls. Cole and his kids gazed around with interest. All eyes were glued on their leader. It was obvious that nothing would drive a wedge between Tobias and his warriors. Each and every one of them would willingly die for the ancient. Cole almost wished he felt the same. That level of commitment held a comfortable familiarity. It defined his days in uniform, saved his sanity, his life, and the lives of a few others, too. He never admitted it, even to himself, but he missed that life. He longed for it. Being led by officers he trusted left him nothing to think about or worry about. All he was expected to do was follow orders and perform to the best of his ability. It was the perfect scenario for a lost soul like Cole. Until the unthinkable and unexplainable happened, it was pure heaven. But unlike back then, now he had four young warriors in training to care for and protect. His first loyalty had to be to them. He couldn't just react anymore. He had to take strategic action.

Tobias continued in a clear, loud voice. "It has been a rough few weeks of intense training and preparation. Please, all of you… take this night to rest and replenish. We'll finish construction in the morning."

A round of quiet cheers rose from the diners.

"There are six small towns within a few miles of this fairground, so we'll be here for at least four days. Our permit allows for five, and if recruiting and crowds are good, we'll stay that long. Dawn will organize flyer production and distribution. Those on her committee please meet at the bonfire after dinner." He shuffled a few sheets of paper. Everyone sat silent and waiting. No one even coughed.

"Starting Friday, we'll be using this tent every morning after breakfast for continued weapons training. Mandatory. Don't miss it. Billio has posted the schedule… be sure to check it for your training time.

"Other business… guards will be posted at the east, south, and west gates.

Garta and Beauty Low have created protection at the hillside and wooded area in the north. For those of you who don't understand how the protective veil works," he carefully eyed each person in Cole's party, "it's best to avoid the north borders at that hillside… for your own protection." And he winked.

"Let's see… yes, Frank Pincer needs some help with the rides. Anyone who knows how to tinker with a small engine, report to him before breakfast near the tilt-a-whirl and get your hands greasy. All help is appreciated. Anything else? Oh, yes, our newly awakened warriors and Mr. Masters."

A tentative round of applause followed and Cole's head shot up.

Tobias grinned. "Welcome… and my heartfelt apology for leaving you all without tents tonight. There has been no time to accommodate, but I'll send someone to town to pick up a few new tents for you all tomorrow. Tonight, perhaps you can sleep in your van?"

Cole nodded. "Sure."

"That's it for now. My friends, tonight we rest and we pray. Tomorrow night… we perform!"

The roar of a cheer rose to the yellow canvas ceiling, but Cole and Gracie sat silent as church mice, watching, listening, deep in their own thoughts. The crowd dissipated, a few stragglers sitting at tables or standing and talking. Cole and his awakened sat tight, silent, until the last person left.

Cole lowered the brightness of their table's lantern and leaned in. "We gotta talk," he said and all heads nodded. "First, a few things. Just so you know, this group, well it's kind of common but seriously underground. As I understand it, there are a lot of armies like this around, trying to keep balance so that the planet and the human race can do its thing."

Again, heads nodded.

"Listen, this is important. Be careful what you think about around Tobias. He can read your thoughts."

"Nah-uh," Ben said and snorted a laugh.

"Yes, he can. Trust me, I know. I met that guy before. Since he's the leader here, we want to seem totally compliant, so keep your thoughts controlled."

Ryan grunted. "We're not compliant? What choice do we have?"

"Not a lot," Cole said. "But it's always best to watch what you're thinking around a super telepath like Tobias." He drew in a deep breath then looked into each of their faces, soft in the low light. "I wish I could have prepared you more, but war is here and we're right in the middle of it. So, tell me, what have you all learned? What are you all thinking?"

They glanced to each other. Jenny spoke first. "I'm not sure being with these people is a bad thing, Cole. They're prepared and organized. These are seasoned warriors. It's way better than being alone, and surprised, and having to face… battle… you know. Guarding outside the cabin, only a few of the enemy attacked but even one at a time, they can be vicious. I feel safer with a whole army around me."

"But," Ryan interjected. "What the hell are the politics behind all this? That stuff Allerton said about a tribunal, and prisons, and rogue warrior factions?" He shook his head. "That's what this Emmaus show is, right? An outlaw rogue warrior faction, breaking laws and doing what they want? Who's more powerful here? The tribunal or Tobias? Are we all going to end up in prison for following him?" He reached down and offered Raffie a crust of bread left on his plate. "Shouldn't we know more before we just soldier up and fight for that guy?"

Cole and Gracie looked to each other. "Ah…" Cole cleared his throat. "Truth? I don't know. I know what you know. I acclimated out of the Gate just a few years ago. This is an education for us all. I never knew there was a governing body like that tribunal. But jail? I have some experience with that and it's not something to take lightly. However, if we're here and the enemy attacks, we have to fight. Just like at the cabin. We have to survive." He watched their eyes, all lowered. "Ben, what are your thoughts?"

"I think Allerton's a royal A-number-one prick. A bastard. A fucking—"

"Yeah, we all have issues with Allerton," Cole said with a grunt.

"You were right to deck him. He knew we needed him. He should have been with us, not running to some tribunal. He had to know what they'd do to him. He didn't have to do that. He just deserted us! If he'd come to help, we'd be far away from here. It's his fault we're in the middle of this mess!"

Time for a little diplomacy. Ben wasn't aware of his parentage, so slamming his secret dad might not be productive at the moment. "Okay, yes, I see how you might see it that way but sometimes, no matter how hard we want things to be one way, they just go the other."

"I don't need a kindergarten lecture, Cole." Ben crossed his arms and glared.

"It's not. This is the reality of Nephilim life, buddy. A lot of things are destined to happen. It's just how it is… for you, for me, for Allerton. Think about it," Cole started. "He was doing what he believed was right and honorable. That man lost everything he worked so hard to protect. Everything he valued. That orphanage was his whole life. He lost his job. All his friends were sent away. All the students he cared for had to leave. Hell, he even lost your respect… you… the ones he did the most to protect. Who talked to him at dinner? Not one of you. Not me. We all have reasons to be pissed, but maybe we need to have a little compassion."

"Yeah," Ben snorted. "You first."

"Fair enough, I will. But there's something you guys need to understand. At any moment we could be fighting for our lives. All these people around us are here to protect themselves, us… the whole freaking world. It doesn't pay to be pissed at anyone in this camp. We all need each other."

Ben finally shrugged agreement.

"Have any of you learned anything that can help us here?"

"Sort of." Ben reached down and fed the snuffling bulldog a scrap of left-over pork roast. "Koeffer—he's the show's muscle man—he told me something I thought was kinda odd. He's been with Tobias for almost twenty years, and the Emmaus Magic Show has never been this far east. He said that Tobias suddenly started getting strange, mystical," he rolled his eyes, "magical messages and drove the show closer and closer to where we are now. Apparently, that broke some kind of territorial rules among the warrior societies, but they forgave him and let him do what he wanted. The problem is," Ben leaned in closer and everyone did the same. "Koeffer said Tobias was wounded in the last battle and hasn't been quite the same since. That it was totally out of character for Tobias to stop moving like he did. He also told me that creating that complete magic protective veil thing hasn't been done for centuries. Here's the kicker… even with all that weirdness, Muscle Man is totally confident that Tobias is doing the right thing. He said they trust Tobias with their lives, that we're lucky to be here. But you know what I think? I think maybe Tobias has lost his mind."

"Or received his directive," Cole mumbled, his head swimming with possibilities. There had to be a damn good reason so many contemporary Nephilim followed Tobias without question. Even though the weirdness Ben mentioned seemed strange, such things weren't so odd among ancients and strong Nephilim. There were signs of commanding directives from above. There was a lot to consider. After all, if Gracie was truly the last pure Nephilim on the planet, and Tobias was given a directive to wait for and assist her, something big was at play. "Crazy or not, he's been guided to lead a lot of strong warriors."

"Whatever," Ben grunted. "He's creepy. Is he human or Nephilim?"

"Neither. Tobias and that healer Garta are ancients… alive for thousands of years."

"No shit?"

"No shit. He's been around, knows a few things."

"How do you know all this stuff?"

Cole blinked. "He told me. It doesn't matter. There are ancients walking around. Most of them are like Tobias, leading small armies or helping Nephilim."

"You'd think that tribunal would grab up a few of them. An ancient might make a good ruler, huh? Like a king or president."

"Ancients don't get grabbed up, Ben. They don't follow. They get directives and accomplish specific goals to assist the Nephilim race." Cole rubbed the begging dog's ear. There were no scraps left on his plate to offer. Raffie finally gave up and dropped with a thud at Cole's feet.

Jenny laid her head on the table and yawned, and not the beauty queen kind of yawn one might have expected only a few short days ago. "I'm kinda looking forward to weapons training."

"Me, too." Ryan added his own wide yawn.

Cole grinned. All heads had lowered to the table. This was a group of kids who had complained to high heaven when asked to sleep in a comfy van only weeks ago. They had come a long way. He lowered his head to the table, his face only inches from Gracie's. Her eyes were open and watching him. He waited until he could clearly define the sleep breaths of each kid at the table.

"You okay, sweetheart?" he whispered.

She nodded.

"What are your thoughts about all this?"

"Cole, Tobias can't read my thoughts. Isn't that cool?"

"Are you sure? How do you know?"

"In that camper before we stopped to set up, I actually felt him trying. No go. He has no idea what's going on in my head."

Cole grinned.

"My thoughts about all this?" She slid a tiny bit closer. Her lips touched his and she pulled away. "I think I'm tired. I know you're tired. And I believe that whatever we talk about tonight isn't going to change how this whole rogue warrior, tribunal, politics thing plays out."

"And when are you thinking we leave for Ocracoke?"

"I'm tired."

"Gracie?"

"Kiss me goodnight."

He did, then turned off the lantern. His mind drifted and sleep teased at the depth of his hidden thoughts. Then everything went south.

Cole Masters knew his personal darkness like the back of his hand. He recognized the sensation of it trickling into the quiet corners and tight crevasses of his being. It called, longingly, like a terrible lover he needed more than air. All day he'd struggled to find a way to fit in with the people around him, regain the footing he'd found long ago with other soldiers, and locate a source of peace in the middle of brutal war.

Over the past month he'd run the gamut of emotions and rallied to find a solid center for himself. It was created from sheer determination and shaped by the responsibilities at hand. He felt like he'd been through a fire, burned to a crisp and reborn, only to stumble right back into the pit. Allerton. All Allerton's fault. But was it?

Having acclimated five kids, he realized how terrifying the job actually was. He'd approached it with a measure of compassion, especially after Wally ran from the basement without making his vow. Cole's own Acclimation was horrific. What he recalled tore more than the flesh at his back. Like an idiot, he'd believed what his teachers told him. That he had skills, talent. He could go to any college he wanted. He could be a pro football player. He could excel at anything he chose. In hindsight, it was all bullshit. Not because they were lying to him, but because Cole was nothing more than average. Average, but saddled with a birthright destined to horrify him until the day he died.

He was always an outsider. Belligerent. Confrontational. Determined to break rules, and especially thrilled when he got away with it. He wanted to be a good kid, make the honor roll, to have the headmaster look at him with more than distaste. If he could have felt more confident, more in control of himself, been more prepared, he might have become a different man. A better man. A stronger warrior.

Running was the key to his personal survival, especially after what happened in the heat of an Afghanistan firefight. Maybe he'd never have to face the truth, but he was called to face it when Allerton placed those acclimates in his care. He'd actually succeeded. How the hell did that happen?

Sleep pulled him deeper and deeper. Allerton, complete with a bloody nose and blackening eyes became the dragon burning him. Gracie became his salvation, his cool, healing water, just out of reach. The ground dropped out from under him. The rattling sound of enemy fire blasted, the chilling cries of his wounded fellow Marines rose, the explosions, light, dark, blackness then more light, this time so brilliant he jerked himself awake.

13

The ache in Michael's chest had grown beyond tolerance. He considered visiting Garta but hated to wake her so late, knowing full well it wasn't her medicines he needed.

He left his tent and walked the midway, lit by a thousand white carnival lights. It seemed like a waste of money, but Tobias never seemed concerned about cash flow. Curious. Did Tobias have financial supporters like Ariel's Gate? Anonymous patrons who poured cash into the operation? Who would those patrons be? He stopped dead in his tracks. Was it possible that the same patrons who supported the traditional acclimation orphanage system also supported the Tobiases of the world? It was entirely possible.

He rubbed his chest, coughed, then walked on. Exploring at the edges of the camp wasn't smart. The enemy could be lurking, tribunal spies could be watching. He stuck to the neat temporary pathways defining the show and performers' village. Stepping quietly, he heard random snores along the way. A young soldier sat, armed and ready, at the bonfire. As Michael neared, the kid's head bobbed and he jerked, stood and jumped up and down for a moment, trying to wake himself.

"I can relieve you, son." Michael reached out for the rifle.

"No, no, sir. I'm fine. Just another hour or two before my relief comes. I can make it."

"That's just stupid, buddy. I'm here, I can't sleep, and I'm happy to give you an extra few hours shut eye."

The kid bit his lip, considering.

"You know tomorrow the show starts, the recruiting starts, and you never know when there could be a battle. I'd feel better if I knew you had enough rest, young man."

"You need enough rest, too, sir."

"I've had enough rest. Go." He took the weapon and sat with a smile. "Shoo."

Michael watched the fire, slipping and flowing, sparking and sputtering, whispering, always whispering. He desperately needed something to ease the agony building in his chest. Usually fifty pushups did the job, but that night, a million wouldn't have helped. His body thrummed with the buzz of well worked muscles after weeks of training. He knew a rifle, he knew his blade. He could confidently kill with either. He'd become agile and quick. It was his mind that demanded a workout, but his thoughts represented a perilous arena laden with truths he had to face.

He sighed and pushed a burning log deeper into the fire with the toe of his boot. The camp was so quiet. He looked to the high guard posts. The lookout at the west waved to him and he casually waved back. Then he nearly jumped out of his skin.

Cole stood, chuckling right at his side. "Tense?"

"Damn!" he pressed a hand hard at his chest and drew in several deep breaths.

"You okay?" Cole leaned in, gripped Michael's shoulder and looked into his eyes.

"No." He stretched his back and twisted on the lawn chair. The pummeling Cole had given him earlier still stung his face, and his ego.

"You need something? Coffee? Scotch? Valium?"

Michael snorted a laugh. "All of the above."

Cole sat and stretched out his long legs, feet propped on the rocks circling the fire pit.

"Can't sleep?"

Cole shrugged.

"I can't sleep."

"You've been through a lot, man."

He eyed the younger man. "So, you're talking to me now?"

"I promised your son I'd be the first to show you some compassion."

Michael cringed. "Cole, you didn't tell him, you—"

Cole shook his head. "You asked me not to, but you should tell him. Soon. Who the hell knows what's coming next?"

"Not yet, not now. Not after…"

"After what? Getting yourself tossed in the pokey?"

Michael didn't smile.

"We're at war. He should know."

They sat in silence for several moments before Michael spoke. "Did you find that book?"

Cole visibly tightened.

"Thank God you have it. I need that—"

"Why?"

His chest tightened so much it almost choked him. "I just need it."

"You can't even read it. No one can."

"I can."

"All of it?" Cole sat up and glared.

Michael nodded.

"Where'd you get that thing?"

"I… ah… borrowed it… from the Tribunal archives." He cleared his throat, hiding his embarrassment. "Years ago."

"And you didn't get busted earlier? You must have some damn good allies on that tribunal."

"One ally… sort of an ally. Ben's mother."

"Well this just gets juicier and juicier."

"It's getting deadlier and deadlier." He was on a roll. He didn't look at Cole, couldn't face him. Couldn't face anyone. It had to come out and Cole was the perfect confessor. He'd get the full impact, see the enormity of it. "I can read the book," he said. "I've had my quickening. I've been empowered and somehow, I can read every single symbol. I even receive telepathic warnings about shifting messages. What I read was actually coming to pass and I… I just reacted. I should have fucking waited for instructions." He choked a sob that shook his entire body.

Cole set a hand on his back in an attempt to soothe him, but nothing would ease this misery. He looked into Cole's face.

"Remember the day you arrived at the Gate? All those buses? All those kids?"

"Yeah."

"They're all dead, Cole. Every single one of them. And the others I sent on planes and trains, off to safe places with reliable Nephilim waiting and ready to care for them… they're all… dead."

Cole gasped. "You gotta be mistaken."

Michael shook his head, his face soaked with tears. "Every employee, every teacher, guide, gardener… all… dead. And I did that. I knew a war was coming, that the enemy was at our door, and I foolishly sent them all out into the fire." He rocked and cried like a child. "I killed them all."

"Damn," Cole whispered and Michael felt the younger man tremble.

"Worse. It wasn't just Ariel's Gate. I reported my suspicions and ninety other acclimation orphanages did the same thing. Thousands of children, all condemned to death… because of me."

Cole looked stricken, pale in the firelight. "Other headmasters made their own decision. You didn't twist their arms or anything."

"The future of our race is gone, Cole. I read that damn book and now…"

"So, what? We can still fight the enemy. Tobias is recruiting. The other warrior shows are recruiting and on their way."

"Doesn't matter. The enemy already outnumbers us three to one and that's a guesstimate. They're recruiting, too. Faster."

Cole blinked. Shuffled in his chair. "What about all the others who've been acclimated through the orphanage system? There have to be tens of thousands of them."

"More. But… they don't know. Don't have a clue. The tribunal presses propaganda that all's well, but this is bigger, far, far worse than even they know."

"Shit," Cole grunted. "Tell Tobias to head for the big cities. That's where he can seriously recruit… warn the awakened that war's coming."

"He can't do that. Tobias is a wanted criminal. The tribunal will capture him in a heartbeat if he moves into high profile areas. It's a sure death sentence if he does that."

"Shit, shit, shit." Cole slumped deeper into his chair. "What the hell? This is hopeless."

"God, I hope not." Michael rubbed his eyes, wiped tears away with his sleeve then tossed another log on the fire. "There's one good thing. You."

"Me?"

"Yes, you. You did what no one else could do. You protected and acclimated four newly awakened Nephilim, one of them, spectacular."

"She is." Cole turned his face away. "You should have seen it."

"I wanted to be there. For Ben. For Gracie. For you. I owe you, Cole."

"Yeah, you sure as hell do."

"Not for this. You were called to service and you succeeded. That alone is worthy of respect and honor. I owe you because of your Acclimation."

Cole became ridged. "Don't want to talk about that."

"I have to… and you need to know. Cole, I've guided and witnessed hundreds of Acclimations and never once did it happen the way it happened for you."

"Great."

"Hear me out." He clamped a hand on Cole's arm, determined to keep him from running. The terror in his eyes confirmed Michael's worst fear. Cole blamed him. Of course, he would. "Listen, please."

Finally, the younger man settled in his chair and focused one hell of a scowl on Michael.

"Your records stated that you were to turn eighteen on June fifteenth."

"Yeah, my birthday. So?"

"But… it isn't. The records were wrong. Your real date of birth is apparently June fourteenth, not the fifteenth." He waited. The scowl deepened for several moments then it altered.

Cole's face opened and he blinked several times. "Holy shit!" he gasped. "You weren't ready."

"No, I wasn't. I took you out to the lake resort on the fourteenth, planned on pizza that night, then maybe some hiking the next morning, a nice birthday dinner then… I intended to take you to the cave I used for summer acclimations hours, before it would even begin. I would have had more than enough time to prepare you, but…"

He watched Cole breathe hard, stare into the fire, fight his own tears.

"I never planned for you to awaken in that hotel room. I know it was horrifying for you, terrifying and painful. Hell, I had to run down to the car for my first aid kit. Cole, I'm so sorry. I wasn't ready. I wasn't prepared."

It took several moments, but Cole's breathing slowed and he faced Michael. "Has that ever happened before?"

"I researched it the minute I got back to the Gate. It happened once, over eighty years earlier. The acclimate hung herself in Makha'el Lecture Hall. It must have happened in there… it was the day before her noted birthdate in our records. I didn't know anything about it."

Cole nodded, but there was still the shadow of anger in his eyes. "You made sure it wouldn't happen again, right?"

"Yes. Guides the world over instituted a safety rule. All acclimates are taken two days before their recorded birthdate and kept in a safe, protected environment."

Cole picked up a stick and poked the fire. "A cave, huh?"

"Yeah, I used it when acclimating the boys. It had stalagmites and stalactites. Kinda cool. The kids enjoyed it."

"I sort of wish I could have made it to that cave."

"It would have been far less traumatic for you. Me, too."

Cole laughed aloud and Michael wondered if he'd ever actually heard him laugh before.

"I am sorry, Cole. If I could have done anything to make it easier, I would have."

"Fine. Forget it." Then Cole looked him square in the eyes.

The intensity of that moment made Michael sit straighter, prepared to make a run if a fist came at him without warning.

"It wasn't your fault." The words were quiet and sincere. "Knowing that helps… a lot."

Michael drew in a deep breath and relaxed.

"You know, it's the same with all those lost orphans. It wasn't your fault. You did what you believed was safest for them all. People fuck up without intention. None of this is on your shoulders. It's not your sin."

Tears gathered again and he gasped.

"I like to think that there's always redemption. Fight well, save other lives, do what we can. It'll all work out. It worked out for me. Well, almost."

"Don't sweat over poor Wally. I'm sure he was blood vowed to the demons before he even left the Gate. It was a lost cause. What you did with the others though… so damn good. And they respect and follow you. You're exactly what I always knew you could be."

"Not so much, but I'm trying. Tell me something, you said you had your *quickening*. What the hell is a quickening? What's… empowerment?"

Michael thought for a moment, his brow curled. "Some quicken and become empowered immediately, but I've never seen it. A quickening can happen at any time, usually when you least expect but most need it, at your lowest point, or most dangerous moment. You've had your quickening." He paused, watched Cole actually shiver. "You know what I'm talking about."

Cole nodded then rubbed the arm that had taken three bullets in the Middle East ambush.

"Empowerment immediately follows, but empowerment can be any number of things. It could be heightened senses. It could be extreme strength, or speed, or courage. It might be an awakening of the heart or the soul. Hearing messages. Seeing things others don't. It's whatever comes to you. It could be just one acquired skill, or abilities I'm not even aware of. It could be a continuous delivery of powers over the rest of your life."

"Huh." Cole scratched his ear and shook his head. "So, what happened in Afghanistan… that was a quickening?"

"It was your introduction to the expanse of your true abilities. Your empowerment. It never goes away. It's yours forever. It can happen as many times as it needs to happen."

"Okay, I think. But listen, you need to explain this stuff to those kids. I told them what I knew. But I had no clue about quickening or empowerment, so they're in the dark, too."

Michael nodded. "Let's do it together, okay? Maybe tomorrow afternoon? Before the show starts?"

"Good."

"Now, about the book… I really need it, Cole. It should be destroyed before someone else…"

Cole stood and grinned down at him then pushed his hair back and just walked away.

Michael didn't get the response he wanted, but he did notice that his chest ached a lot less.

~*~

Everyone was excited, even if they didn't want to admit it. None of us had ever been to a carnival, or circus, or even an amusement park before. Our lives had been limited to the grounds within Ariel's Gate, classrooms, sports that only competed with the closest school around, and what went on inside our own heads. Nothing normal. Well, I'll never be normal, anyway. That *never be normal* concept didn't sadden me for once. I was going to see people, performances, and activities I'd never seen before. It was going to be magical.

Jenny couldn't take her eyes off the big top all morning. While we ate, did whatever we could to help set up, or awaited instructions for later when the ticket booths opened, she just watched everything and, no doubt, wondered. I realized this was the last of the previous Jenny still in existence. Yes, she still loved Ryan, but differently than before. Everything about her had changed, except her love of the dramatic. I hoped the actual performances wouldn't disappoint. She smiled when talking about how high that high wire was strung, how tight it had to be, how many cables it took to stabilize it. Her smile made me smile.

All day, Ben seemed to be anywhere Allerton wasn't. Ryan focused his energy on final presentation, pinning up bunting, wiping down signage, sweeping the pathway along the midway, removing stones or rocks that might trip a patron. Who knew he had such attention for detail?

I admit I kept looking for Cole in the hustle and bustle, but he was nowhere to be found. I'd just finished helping the food trucks stock up with napkins, paper plates, and plastic utensils, cases of them dragged behind me in a red wagon. Once finished I planned to make sure all the trash cans were lined with plastic bags. What might have been described as work was an opportunity to see everything else going on around me. It was fun and exciting in a tingly way I'd never experienced.

There was more. I had secrets. I'd never had secrets before. There are a hundred things I'd kept to myself and never told anyone, but those weren't secrets. Those were insecurities seeking a hiding place. I was dying to tell someone my secrets but who could I tell? Cole was the only person I trusted. It was like he'd vanished in thin air and I sighed. Did Tobias send him out of camp for something? Sent him with that Dawn woman into town? Jealousy whipped through me like a snapping snake's tail. Dawn was the kind of girl to give Cole what he wanted. She wasn't afraid of sex. She was really, really pretty.

"There you are."

I swung around and threw myself into Cole's arms. "Where've you been?"

"On guard duty. You okay? You look all frazzled and stuff."

I wanted to reach up and kiss him but there were too many people around. "I'm not frazzled."

"Listen, I need you guys all together at the big yellow tent in one hour. Can you find Jenny and Ryan? I already told Ben."

"Sure. Why? Is something wrong?"

"No, no. Tobias has instructions, and Michael and I need to have a little chat with you all. Then," his brows bobbed, making me smile, "if there's time, we can go have a private chat at the van… if you want."

"Good!" A private chat at the van meant I could share my secrets. They were getting heavy and a little scary.

I grinned and he grinned. This guy made me so happy. Was that a good thing? Whatever it was, it was real, I knew that much. I might have lived a very protected life so far, might be Nephilim, might have ridiculous giant wings, and might even have a club foot, but I was still just a girl falling for a guy. It felt odd and it felt right. It was nothing like in the books I read. This was far deeper and more, I don't know, personal I guess. I was going with it. With that decision made and Cole off to his next assignment, I turned and walked the midway.

Searching for my friends gave me time to explore my new secrets. Big secrets. For example, I could read that book. Every single symbol now revealed itself to me and it had very clear instructions about what I was supposed to do. It was chilling and thrilling at once. I had another secret. I saw everyone's wings *all* the time. I asked Ben if he saw wings all the time and he gave me a goofy look and shook his head. Not only could I see them, I could see how different each set of wings were. This wing thing had to do with more than lineage and fighting strengths. Wings spoke of other qualities. I couldn't clearly define them all yet, but I felt them.

In addition to that I could see something I was sure no other Nephilim in camp could see. Something the book told me to look for. I saw a light, just over each person's heart and it glowed. Some shimmered a soft, comforting mellow yellow, some brighter, with purpose and intensity. Others seemed menacing, as though their principles followed an agenda all their own. I understood that whatever these lights were—the soul, or the heart, or the ability to fight—Tobias needed them all. Still, there were a few of our number I felt compelled to stay away from.

There was another secret, so big I could hardly believe it was happening. Someone was talking to me. Inside my head. Shouting joyously and speaking kindly. The only problem was that I couldn't understand a single word of it. Okay, maybe I was losing my mind or developing schizophrenic tendencies, but it was there and actually happening and it felt important. I did realize that this secret might be best kept to myself, at least until I could figure out the language and the message.

I turned a full circle and took in everything around me. The sun inched toward the horizon, giving the midway a magical golden sheen. The sights, the sounds, the shouts and calls danced and intertwined like a choreographed waltz. The cacophony of several different amusement ride melodies drifted on the air. All those lights of real electricity lining the walkways and small stages, and all those lights of mystical energy glowing from Nephilim chests called for my attention. The scent of deep fried foods tantalized and teased. My flesh tingled with the building excitement floating on the air. Performers with painted faces and brilliant colored costumes rushed here and there. I found Jenny and Ryan near the far entrance gate. Our walk to the big yellow tent felt like a stroll through Wonderland.

Gathered together at the table nearest the opened tent flap so we could watch the activity outside, we waited for twenty minutes before Tobias arrived. Raffie was glued to his side and I couldn't help but suspect our previously loyal pet had gone all Benedict Arnold on us. Maybe the guy gave him better table scraps. What a little turncoat. Tobias didn't even like dogs. Cole and Allerton were a no show, making me feel a little uncomfortable because we were alone with an ancient. Tobias started with a big, almost creepy smile.

"My children! Welcome." He bellowed like there were a hundred people there instead of just the four of us.

"Where are Cole and Allerton?" Ben asked. He'd been especially confrontational since we hooked up with the show.

Tobias didn't look directly at him. "Busy with one thing or another, I'm sure. This will only take a few moments. There's not much time before we open the ticket booths. Already cars are gathering in the parking lots.

"I have a special assignment for you all, something that will be eye-opening and educational for you... even fun." He slid a stack of index cards to each of us. "Your job, my young ones, is to hand these out to the Nephilim who attend the show. They will be easy to identify—they'll be tuned in to so many of their own race, especially after experiencing the performances. Now, do not hand these out during the show, and do not give an invitation to any Nephilim accompanied by children. Only able-bodied specimens and only just as the carnival is closing. Post yourselves at the two midway exits and offer your chosen Nephilim a card before they walk out to the parking lots. Do you understand?"

"Why?" Ben said with a snort.

"Read the card, my young one."

"I'm not your young anything."

"My apologies," Tobias actually bowed slightly. "I mean no disrespect. You are a new warrior and I am most happy to have you with us. The reason for the cards is to invite those chosen Nephilim to join us in this communal tent for... a discussion."

"What kind of discussion?"

I kicked Ben under the table but he didn't even respond.

"Recruitment. In addition to handing out these invitations, I cordially invite you all to bring your soul swords and join us to witness one of the best recruiters on the planet, Ballister Green."

"The acrobat?" Jenny perked up.

"Yes, my dear. We all do many things here with the Emmaus Magic Show. Exposing the empowered abilities of our warriors is the show itself; explaining why we are warriors is the recruitment phase."

"What if a person doesn't want to be recruited?"

I kicked Ben again. This time he shot me a pointed glare.

"Then that Nephilim is free to leave. At any time, anyone is free to leave, including you. Children." He sat across from us, a serious expression painted his face and brightened his eyes. "This is dangerous. This is deadly. War is near and we need as many soldiers as we can get. But you are not only angel, you are also human, and your free will should always prevail. Otherwise you will lose your ability to freely commit to the cause and will unfortunately become… like machines."

I suddenly understood the lights at each person's chest. It was more than their soul, it was the combination of angel and human energy. It was their freely chosen commitment. Some of those pledges burned brilliant, some were fearful, and others were all about the attraction to battle and blood.

"Any other questions?"

We shook our heads like puppets.

"Now, I must get moving. Learn what you can. Stay inside the boundaries of the carnival camp. Be safe." He turned and just walked out.

We sat still as stone, waiting for Tobias to disappear into the growing activity beyond the tent flap.

"Well hell." Ryan slid low in his chair. "That guy sure knows how to take the fun out of everything."

"Battle and war aren't meant to be fun." I flipped through the invitation cards. We'd each received twenty. Not a lot of recruiting, if you ask me. The card said:

SEEN THE LIGHT?

FEEL THE HEAT

MIDNIGHT IN THE BIG YELLOW TENT

WELCOME, BROTHERS AND SISTERS

Too strange. Between the four of us we'd be inviting eighty. How many would actually attend after reading such a cryptic invitation? Would Ballister Green have anyone to recruit?

"Hey." I set the cards aside and looked to Ryan. "How can they recruit warriors if the recruit's Acclimation vow choice dissolved their soul sword?"

He shrugged.

Ben gave a growl. "I want to know why we have to go to a recruiting session armed with a weapon."

"Good God, Ben! Enough! I don't know what you're so pissed off about." I rolled my eyes. Maybe I like the dramatic, too.

"Seriously. Where's Cole?" Ben stuffed his cards into his back jeans pocket. "He'd know the answer."

"I know the answer." What was I doing? How could I know the answer to anything? I was as new at this as them but somehow, I just knew the answer. "Our soul sword is not just a weapon," I said, but actually felt the words thrum deep in my chest. "It carries the vibration of our power. All of them together might help the process. Our soul sword is an extension of each of us, our commitment, our strength, even our hopes. It's a sign."

"Of what?" Ben spat.

"Cool down, man," Ryan whispered.

"Of our trust in the vow we took." I turned away. Tears welled in my eyes. I had no idea what I was talking about and I wasn't willing to continue with the interrogation.

"You heard what he said about free will, didn't you, Gracie?" Ben's voice

242

was way louder than it needed to be. "I can walk right out of here. I can refuse to pass out his stupid invitations. I can pass on the big recruitment performance!"

"Free will isn't about being a jackass," Ryan spoke softly, forcing Ben to calm down and listen. "Free will isn't knee jerk reactions… free will is making intelligent decisions. Listen, I know you don't like Tobias."

"I don't trust him."

Jenny leaned over the table, her nose almost touching Ben's. "Yes, and you didn't trust Cole at first, either. Face it. We know nothing about all this stuff. Isn't it smarter to learn everything we can before making a decision to just walk away? Isn't it a little too late for that anyway? We took a vow." The word *vow* was loud and clear.

"An uninformed choice we were forced into," Ben rebutted.

"I wasn't forced." I glared.

"Me neither," Jenny and Ryan spoke in unison.

"A vow is a vow, Ben." I tried to sound sensitive but he was really ticking me off.

"And free will is free will." Ben crossed his arms, staring past us like a terrorizing toddler.

"Will you really just walk away? Leave us behind? Leave me behind?" I wasn't crying this time. I was just plain mad.

He said nothing.

"Fine. Leave."

He didn't leave. After a few tense minutes he actually shrugged and apologized. I think he was scared. Ben was always like that. I kept hoping Cole and Allerton would come and explain more but they never showed.

The sound of a brass band hit the start button and we all had things to see and learn and, well, invitations to hand out. Cole finally caught up with me at a food truck as night fully enrobed the fairgrounds. I'd just purchased a deep-fried peanut butter and banana sandwich and he reached out and took half, gasping when he burned his fingers.

"We were there… where were you?" I licked my lips. The filling was hot and gooey but really yummy.

"Tobias sent me to town on a wild goose chase. Turns out there's not one damn Starbucks in all of Millport. No freaking coffee shops at all. Hell, the town only has thirty-some streets and something like fifteen farms. How much recruiting does he expect from this place? Five towns, all the same size. This is a waste of time." He looked pretty pissed. "Did Michael talk to you guys?"

"He never showed up either. Tobias gave us an assignment, though. To hand these out after the performances."

Cole eyed the card in my hand, licked his fingers, and leaned up to order another deep-fried sandwich. "Let's hope a few get recruited. Want half?"

"You owe me half."

"I'm off to sit the west guard post. Listen, sweetheart, be real careful. Hand those out to the strongest, most level-headed Nephilim you can find. I'll be back to witness the recruiting with you. Oh," he said just before he turned to walk away. "And if you see Michael, tell him he owes you all an explanation."

And he was gone, melted into the crowd. I marveled. So many people had come to see the Emmaus Magic Show. Hundreds. It seemed like a lot of people for a few small towns. Maybe they all came opening night? Maybe people were visiting or passing through and decided to see a carnival, swelling the numbers. Or, maybe Tobias knew more about those little towns than anyone else. One out of every twenty or so attendees was miraculously winged—some with huge wings like Cole's, others with smaller wings. Nobody with wings like my monstrosities.

How would I ever know if those weaker-looking wings meant that they were weak warriors? Then I checked the light at their centers. The lights were there, but most of them were a nice cool blue. Standing aside, I could feel my own people pass me, their energy pulling and pushing at the same time. Some looked right into my eyes. I'd smile but usually they stepped away, as though they were making space between us. How will I ever make friends if people did that? I could understand it if they were repelled by my twisted foot, but their eyes never left my face. Was I ugly? Was I scary? Did some of them see my overly big, overkill six wings? That would sure scare anyone away.

Then there were the fully human people. The normal, wonderful, smeared up mix of good and bad, old and young, dull and exciting people. My heart swelled to be near them all, to watch them enjoy the rides and food, the little performances along the midway. The carnie was a break from their everyday life, a spark of fun and entertainment. Everyone was having a great time, especially for the pickpocket I caught running behind a tent. He was about ten years old with the expression of a ninja warrior. And… he had the smallest spark of Nephilim light at his chest.

"You should give that wallet back." I crossed my arms and gave my best housemother impression. "The old man you took it from might need it."

"You're not my mother!"

I gripped the back of his collar before he could run. "No, but I will find your mother and tell her."

He stopped struggling then handed over his take. Before I could lead him to the elderly man searching desperately for a wallet that wasn't there, a woman stepped up.

"Mom, I didn't mean to!"

I handed the kid and the wallet over and watched her make her child return it and apologize. And I wondered. Will I make a good mother? Someday? Then I sighed and realized that I just might not live long enough to find out.

I could feel them, too, you know. The enemy, lurking at the perimeters of the show. Not a lot of them, but enough to be concerned. I understood Cole's warning to be careful. I'd stick deep inside the fairgrounds and surrounded by seasoned warriors. Hell, I hadn't even had weapons training yet. I wasn't about to take a stroll down the road anytime soon, but that big top called to me. One more stop for caramel popcorn and in I went to find a seat high on the bleachers. Let the paying customers have the best seats, right? Oddly enough, the woman and her little pickpocket climbed up and sat right beside me.

She leaned close and whispered, "Is Tobias still with the show?"

I must have looked like a deer caught in a headlight.

She smiled. "I used to be with this show. Sixteen years… then this happened." She pulled her kid, his face covered with chocolate, into a warm hug. His eyes were pinned to the center circle. He looked determined not to miss a single minute of the performances that hadn't even started yet.

"Yes. Tobias is here."

"Good. Good. I have important information for him." And she said nothing else.

I sat there hoping I didn't do the wrong thing. I never noticed her and her son leave. I assumed they wanted better seats. Maybe she spotted Tobias.

Ben scaled the bleachers to sit beside me. "Uh, sorry. I don't know what's wrong with me."

"You're scared. We're all scared. Being a jackass is how you're dealing with it."

"Yeah. Sorry."

"Just stop. There's no room for a jackass in my life. I want my best friend back."

I understood that he was having issues with life. I leaned over and bumped him with my shoulder. He bumped back. No more fighting, we had a show to watch.

When the big top was filled with easily four hundred people, maybe more, all the lights went dark and everyone gasped. Quiet music played, then the mystical brilliance of a million twinkle lights grew and a blazing spotlight aimed onto the middle of the performance circle brought a strange new world to life.

Beauty Low stood front and center wearing a brilliant red and white striped long skirt and a hot yellow vest over a black ruffled blouse. A black top hat and black high heeled boots completed her ring mistress persona. Her face was beautiful, lit from within and sparkled with glitter at her cheeks and bright blue eye shadow. Even her dark, well-trimmed beard didn't distract—it sort of added to her tantalizing strangeness. She snapped a sinister looking whip, and the crack of it made the audience quiet and alert. Unlike her everyday attire, this costume fit to a T, making her too colorfully brilliant to take one's eyes from. My mind marveled. I knew this woman as a kind, friendly lady in baggy clothes. Beauty Low turned out to be an extraordinary show woman. A master attention getter. The perfect ring mistress.

"Ladies and gentlemen! Welcome to the Emmaus Magic Show, the eighth wonder of the world." Her voice was strong and clear, and it growled a little, reaching like tentacles out to the audience. "Nowhere on this planet will you witness more amazing feats of magic!" She turned a full circle, her finger pointing to the audience, her eyes sparkling. "My friends… magic is intangible. Magic is playful. Magic is… powerful!" she shouted and all eyes shot where the spotlights guided us. To the high wire. "See the wonders of the Emmaus Magic Show. Presenting, acrobat and magician extraordinaire… Ballister Green!"

Cheers rose as Mr. Green stepped onto the high wire, his foot carefully sliding along the cable, his hands out wide at his side. And I could see his wings, fully extended. People gasped and called out for him to be careful. The spotlight followed his every move then stopped, like Mr. Green, right in the center of the wire.

"Witness the miracle of magic!" shouted the now invisible Beauty Low from the darkness. Everyone gasped as the acrobat slowly, stiff as a board, leaned to one side, inch by inch. Screams and cries rose from the crowd. There was no net below, but the full humans among them couldn't see what I could see. As Mr. Green moved, nothing but his feet touching the high wire, his wings continued to be spread wide and fluttering. At one point he hung, completely upside down, in the exact same position he held when vertical.

"It's a trick!" someone shouted.

"It's fixed. That's not a man! It's a dummy! It has to be!" another bellowed.

At that point, the acrobat turned his head, looked down on the disbelievers, smiled and gave a wiggle of his fingers. The audience broke into loud applause and Mr. Green continued his slow journey back to the top of the wire where he quickly swung a precarious turn and proceeded to the platform.

Amidst shouts and screams of joy the spotlight darkened and relocated our focus to the center of the performance circle. Beauty Low smiled then raised an arm and waved it with the pointed movement of a dancer toward an average looking young woman standing on a small platform.

"And now, magic from the sublime to the ridiculous!" Beauty Low walked from the circle and the spotlight grew to illuminate the entire area. What followed made me catch my breath.

The young woman walked all around the circle, stretched her arms and legs long and smiled pleasantly. At the little platform, she planted her hands, then with very slow movement, raised her body to balance on her palms. Cool enough, and she received mild applause. Then, with the same deliberate movement, she lowered her legs so her toes touched her brow, then rose them again… only this time there were three legs! Her multiple knees bent and three sets of toes touched her blonde head. The audience screeched and gasped then laughed and clapped. With all those toes sitting on the top of her head, she waited a few moments then rose and lowered her legs and did it again. Four legs appeared. The crowd went wild.

Suddenly the lights went dark and a single spotlight called our attention to the far side of the circle where Benny Beans stood, looking appropriately clownish and sad. He looked left then right. The brass band played melancholy music then suddenly shifted to a lively beat and the dwarf clown stood straight. He turned a complete circle then suddenly, without warning or reason, sprouted more clowns. Two. Three. Five. Ten Bennys, all moving independently, all rolling and hopping, running and spinning. The music intensified then stopped with a nerve-wracking abruptness. Before our eyes every clown leapt right back into Benny.

"How the hell did he do that?" Ben gasped and shook his head.

I pointed and shouted. "This is crazy!" The entire clown staff of the Emmaus Magic Show trailed into the spotlight, brightly dressed and painted, one and all, proving that each and every one of them were different heights, shapes, and sizes. Then they all performed the same act Benny had performed until the circle was filled, edge to edge, with clowns. The audience was on their feet. I noticed that only the real dwarfs had wings, the illusions did not.

"Enough!" shouted Beauty Low from the darkness and each and every clown dropped his head and left the circle. "Clowns." She stepped into the light and shook her head. "Can't have a show without them but… really?" She shrugged and held up her hands, one still grasping the whip. The audience laughed and settled.

The brass band began again, a slow, pulsing melody that was both haunting and somehow familiar. It took several moments to recognize it as a dissonant version of "Somewhere Over the Rainbow". The twinkle lights mystically reformed into a colorful rainbow. The lighted strings waved in the breeze that drifted through the colorful big top canvas slats. Beauty Low looked up and stepped backward out of the performance circle and into the darkness. The music became more recognizable, the lights dimmed, and the audience collectively held their breath. Performers wearing pale blue tights circled the performance area then drifted, literally a foot above the ground, into a formation. What followed had the elegance and perfection of a water ballet. They twirled, bowed and reached, moved with perfection, their formation rising and rising all the way up to the twinkle light rainbow, then without warning they vanished, and a cloud of soft blue powder rained down on to the performance circle below.

Everyone was silent, locked in disbelief. Beauty Low returned and brought with her Billio, his scale tattoos looking especially scary in the harsh spotlight. He stood, shy, head lowered, until Beauty Low introduced him as the human python. He stripped off his shirt, revealing more tattooed scales running down his chest and back. I swear those scales even covered his ethereal wings. His body seemed to elongate, his legs appeared to become one, lengthen, then twist unnaturally as he lowered to the ground and slithered all the way to the first row. People squealed and pushed back. His tongue flashed out, long and split, hissing a menacing sound that came from deep in his throat.

The spotlight followed him, and all around, people cried out in fear and excitement. All was darkness but the slow trek of the human python until the spotlight stilled over a large cage and Billio slithered and coiled himself inside. The dwarf clowns carried the cage away, playfully making a show of it while his forked tongue dodged in and out of the bars at them.

The show continued for two full hours, never stopping, never disappointing. Ballister Green performed again on the high wire with a female acrobat. Once they leapt into the air, several feet above the wire, and spun for a full half minute before lowering again safely, the high wire straining under their regained weight. There were trapeze performers who defied gravity, and floor performers who defied reason. I saw all their wings and I wondered if any of the other Nephilim around me saw them, too. If perhaps they'd realized the power of this troupe of actors enough to hear the war-time message they'd be invited to attend. As the show came to an end, I become more and more nervous. Would I fail? Would anyone show up to hear Ballister Green's recruiting speech?

Ben and I rushed to man the east exit gate and Jenny dragged Ryan to the west. We handed out invitations as subtly as we could, saying nothing, hoping for results. Everyone left for their cars and by eleven-thirty, the parking lot was empty.

"Epic fail," Ben said just before several cars returned and parked.

"Where's this big yellow tent?" an especially large winged Nephilim I'd chosen to invite asked. We both just pointed like dummies.

~*~

Cole was on edge and fighting growing alarm by the time he joined Gracie in the communal tent. She'd sat deep in the center of the audience, so like her to try to hide in the crowd. Thank heaven for it that night, though. The enemy had been gathering all around the perimeters of the camp and carnival. Watching, listening, silent. If he didn't know better, he might suspect they were there to join the cause, but they were all twisted into battle heat, mangled, fevered, ready for one hell of a fight.

He wasn't the only one who knew they were there. Michael had just stood guard, too. Several times guards had turned to each other in silent warning and acknowledgment. As the night deepened, the enemy had surrounded the entire camp, pressing precariously against the protective veil and hovering near the entrance gates. They were disturbingly still and soundless. Would Gracie's presence save them all again? Or was it Gracie the demons had come to take?

He pushed past people, stepping on a few feet, never even thinking to apologize. Dropping into the empty chair beside her, he leaned close and whispered, "You and the others, stick real close to me tonight."

She turned and nodded, concern on her face. She must have sensed the enemy, too. Michael slid his way through to join them and Ben promptly slipped away to stand near the opened tent flap.

"I'll get him," Cole said, pushing Michael back into his chair. He gripped Ben's arm and pulled. "Quit being such an idiot. It's too dangerous to be alone tonight. Get your ass back to your seat."

Ben struggled to free himself and glared. "Is that bastard my father?"

"What?" Cole blinked. How the hell could he know?

"I feel it. It's true, isn't it? That prick let me think I was a damn orphan all my life! Treated me like a—"

Cole's grip tightened like a vice, causing Ben to cringe. He looked directly into the kid's eyes and hissed his words. "That prick saved your life. I'm trying to save it right now. Get your ass inside. Learn something. Nothing about this is personal. It's all about survival."

"He's ashamed of me!" Ben hissed back and pulled to free his arm.

"He's still protecting you! Put yourself in his shoes… what would you have done?"

Ben blinked and Cole waited. One minute. Two. Finally a contrite expression grew. "Fine." Ben pulled his arm free. "But I'm not talking to him."

"Sounds like a pretty normal father/son relationship to me." Cole led him back to the center chairs, turning back once to listen for the enemy's calls. Still silent.

Looking around, Cole noticed Jenny, totally focused on the front of the room, waiting to see what would happen next. Ryan, usually calm as a cucumber, sat with his sword between his bouncing knees and eyes flitting around the room, frequently turning to the tent openings. Ben ignored Michael and Michael tried to keep his eyes from Ben. At some point he'd have to tell the father that the son knew his secret. If things went as badly as Cole expected that night, those two might have to figure it out themselves.

Tobias, the ancient healer, and a few other camp dignitaries entered the tent. Forty-two recruits sat along the front row of chairs and Tobias shook hands with each one. He scanned the crowd and locating Michael, waved for him to join them at the raised stage. Michael subtly declined. Cole grinned. Tobias didn't.

The tent hushed and Tobias spoke loud and clear. "Welcome, welcome one and all. Without a moment's delay, I introduce… Ballister Green." He bowed and sat.

Green wasted no time with frivolity or carnie silliness, although many of the armed performers were still in costume and makeup. There was nothing entertaining about the reason they were in that tent. All his attention was on the recruits, but occasionally his eyes trailed to Cole and his newly awakened.

"You know why we're here," Green said. "You know what is needed. Outside this camp the enemy gathers, just as they have been after most performances all over the country. The balance is critically off and warriors are needed to secure the survival of our race. We do the only thing we can do. We recruit." He eyed each of the brave people in front of him, receiving grunts and nods in response.

"Each and every one of you chose your vow carefully, with attention to your capabilities and interests. Your choice is a bold and honorable one, and my intention is not to imply otherwise. But you see it, don't you? The danger? The horrors ahead? The thing we must fight?"

Heads bobbed.

"You sense them. Hear them. Know what they want."

More nodding as a few fidgeted uncomfortably.

"I know, I really know what you're thinking. What can you offer? Your life has been all about serving your God in other ways. You," Green pointed, "you're a preacher. You," he pointed to another, "your life is in service to the homeless and mentally challenged. You are ex-military, and you are a community leader. You are all valuable and important right where you are. But you have chosen to come and hear what I have to say. Are you ready to hear? Is your soul prepared for the reality of our failing race?"

Cole, along with everyone else, held his breath.

"My friends," Green dragged a chair to sit front and center, his attention only for those in front of him. "We aren't failing because we are weak or incapable. We are failing because of a strange, inexplicable disease that tore through our race years ago, taking hundreds of our breeding females and nearly three thousand infants and children. Entire colonies were wiped out all over the planet. The disease lasted only a few years, but the repercussions stand, roiling in battle heat, everywhere. In cities and towns, forests and mountains, villages, tribes, everywhere our race had lived and procreated, anywhere on earth. The enemy has taken advantage of this imbalance to create more imbalance. My friends…" His voice became very quiet. "…We could feasibly be facing extinction."

Gasps and groans rose from the recruits. Two stood and left the tent, the others slid closer together, filling the empty seats, listening with intensity to every word Green spoke.

"The enemy has continued to attack and murder our future by killing off thousands of our young, presumably safe and secure within the traditional orphanage system. As managers and headmasters scrambled to ship off the young to safer places, demons moved in and eliminated them all… or… tragically… drew unwilling blood vows for their own armies."

People gasped. Gracie shuddered, and Cole took her under his arm.

"Of the nearly fifteen thousand global acclimates ready to awaken over the past thirty days, my friends, only five have survived. We have four of them here tonight. Please, young ones, please stand," Green spoke directly to Cole's kids.

No one wanted to stand up but Michael encouraged them. They stood then immediately sat. Cole retrieved Gracie's hand. He needed her warmth as much as she needed his strength.

Green's voice was soft but clear. "We are in dire straits. What has until recently been minor rashes of irritating battles for almost a decade, has rapidly evolved into full war—the war that will determine the survival or extermination of the Nephilim race." Green stood and paced, allowing his words to sink in.

"When this all began, when the first celestial being reached out and loved a human woman, God was greatly displeased but His compassion reigned supreme. Our race received a command. We were to maintain the precarious balance of good and evil on this planet. This was our responsibility, our sole reason for continued existence. As long as we kept the balance intact, the Nephilim race could continue to breed and live and prosper. That balance is gone, my friends. Global warming, paralyzing disease, human war and terrorism… it all reveals the inability to keep our end of the bargain our fathers', fathers', fathers made with our true Father. We've reached the end of the line and war is our only chance for redemption. That war is very close and we need warriors."

A recruit spoke up. "Did the demons create the disease?"

"Does it matter?" Green shrugged. "There's no proof of it, lots of suspicion. As a point of fact, the Tribunal system denies the disease ever happened. Among our own race there is only confusion and misinformation. Was there a disease? No disease?" He gave a dramatic snort and shook his head. "Although the breeding of the Norema and Calanine continues outside the defunct breeding communities, our drastically diminished numbers prove that the disease—and the recent mass murders of our young—have had an enormous impact. It happened. We're in this position. We must respond."

The confrontational recruit gave a huff. "So, we're not punishing the demon nation for killing our breeders? Are we punishing them for killing off our children? Our future?"

"We're not punishing them for anything. We're fighting for balance. For our survival. We're at war. Tonight, I ask if you will join our empowered warriors in the fight for our lives."

Green showed no irritation, which impressed Cole.

Gracie leaned close and whispered, "Does it have to be kill or be killed? Isn't there another way?"

"Not that I know of," Cole sighed.

"There has to be another way. Maybe we should be fighting to regain the balance, instead of—"

Green bellowed a battle cry and everyone stiffened in their seats. One recruit leapt, prepared to run for safety.

"Now is the time!" Green shouted. "We are mere months from the biggest battle since pre-biblical times! Will you join us?"

"And if we don't?" The man was still standing, unsure whether to run or take a pledge to die. "What happens if we don't?"

"If we don't fight and we don't win, the end of us will come, my friend. It… will… come, no matter where you are or which vow you live. Perhaps the human race and this beautiful planet would be better off without us?"

"So, either I die in battle or… how?"

Green just shrugged. "If we do not fight and prevail, all Nephilim will die. We will have failed our primary vow to our Father and left the human race to the mercy of the enemy. Death will come. How is not a question worth exploring."

Another recruit stood and paced in front of Green who stood patiently, watching and waiting. "How can we do this? We have no soul swords."

Cole blinked. This was what he wanted to know. Would the recruits without swords be relegated to the support teams? Die horrible deaths without a weapon for defense? How the hell was this going to work?

"Do you agree to fight?" Green asked.

"I do," answered the recruit. He knelt in front of Green and everyone stood to see better. Green crouched down and spoke quietly to the recruit who nodded several times then shouted at the top of his lungs, "I am here for God! I vow a life of service!" Every electrical light strung from the canvas ceiling flickered as the energy flowed and swirled around the tent, pushing and heating the air, hissing like fire, flashing like lightning. Then, there in front of the recruit, glowed a soul sword.

"Tell me," Green asked. "Is that your personal soul sword?"

"It is!" cried the recruit and Green patted his shoulder.

"Welcome, my brother. Weapons training starts tomorrow."

Green sat and leaned back in his chair, appearing exhausted. He didn't ask the other recruits to follow suit, he just closed his eyes. Within moments every one of the remaining recruits knelt in a long line. When Green opened his eyes, they glowed with tears and he smiled then repeated the miracle again, bringing about the regeneration of thirty-nine powerful soul swords.

Their numbers had grown and Cole felt a tiny twinge of ease. Before the logistics of absorbing forty new people into the camp and show dawned on him, a massive explosion shook the ground and horns blew from the guard posts.

Gracie. All Cole could think of was Gracie.

14

t wasn't anything like I expected. The Revolutionary War, Civil War, World War I and II, Vietnam, Baghdad. I watched those films and read my history books. Those wars, all those battles, had leaders, officers who strategized and prepared, plowed into battle with confidence and determination. This was nothing like that. This was something else entirely. Total mayhem.

I leapt to my feet like everyone else, looked around then pushed to get out of the tent. Cole held onto my arm and Ben struggled to get through the crowd ahead of me. I watched Ryan's broad shoulders beside me, often turning full circle to see everything he could. Jenny gripped the hem of my shirt and shouted, "Stick close!"

Leading the way was Allerton. Before we exited the tent, he bellowed, "Protect Gracie!"

I was angry that the enemy decided to attack. I was ticked off that I never got a chance at weapons training. I was irritated that everything was so damn confusing. But most of all I was pissed off that everyone thought they had to protect me. My foot would hold me up enough to fight. If I had the strength to swing my sword I'd be just as effective as anyone else. Dealing with panic and anger was one thing, but something bigger was happening and it happened in the blink of an eye.

With my friends tightly wrapped around me, I felt the twinge at my back. Stitches didn't tear, but the tightly sewn flesh pulled as muscles swelled to accommodate unfolding, powerful, terrifying (to me) wings. I gasped as they fiercely pushed everyone away then lifted me several feet above the ground. My eyes scanned the fairgrounds from nearly the height of the Ferris wheel. A lightning strike in the hills outside camp had created the startling ground rumble we felt. The accompanying downpour kept a fledgling fire from spreading. Pounding rain was a heavy wet curtain causing even more confusion for both us and the bad guys. The enemy was everywhere, swarming into the carnival and camp, attacking with crazed abandon. It looked like demons in battle heat didn't need weapons. So much evil oozed from them that a mere touch of their blackened slimy flesh burned a victim at the third degree. Worse than that, right in front of my eyes I watched a warrior's burns spread along his skin, eating away, deeper and deeper until bone and muscle, possibly even the soul, became exposed. The man screamed and thrashed in agony. My heart slammed inside my chest. Cole was right. It was kill or be killed.

"Gracie! Gracie!" I looked down at Allerton, his hand reaching up to me. "Come. Fight. Trust your weapon. Your soul sword knows you. It will protect you." He swung a turn so elegant he looked like Spartacus then slammed his own blade down, splitting a battle-heat demon in half and jumping aside just in time to protect himself from flesh burning contact.

Okay, lower, come on, lower. Lower. I can do this. Finally, I reached the ground, planted there on two perfect feet. *This is the warrior I am, a whole fighter.* I glanced around, swung once but missed a demon that squirmed away on four human looking legs and several arms, all in the wrong places. Shouts and cries, bellows and the screeching sound of demons crashed through the rain and air around me. I gripped the hilt of my sword tighter and focused. Drawing in a long, deep breath everything seemed to slow down, like a ballet flowing at half speed. Battle-heat demons were not just one demon, but the melding of two, three, and sometimes four demons tangled together for strength and flexibility. They were no longer human in any way, creepy as hell, and constantly in motion. Blackness oozed, dangled down from the points of each creature, elbows, noses, knees, fingers, dripping, poisonous. Warriors still in carnie makeup twirled and stabbed, sliced and pummeled. I smelled a burning stench behind me and wrapped all my terror tight in my fist between palm and the grip of my weapon. *"Trust my sword,"* that's what Allerton said, so I did. I spun a full circle, holding my blade level. I heard the screams of multiple demons then watched as not one, but two, battle heat creatures dropped to the ground, black blood sliming the midway.

Something had altered in me and in the battle raging all around me. Power and white energy flowed from the Nephilim warriors, pressing them into unnatural acts of courage and strength. Pushing, pulsing, we all drove ahead, forcing the enemy back. Demons climbed the Ferris wheel and leapt to tree tops several yards away. They raced along the roofs of campers and trucks, and scuttled away like cockroaches, many disappearing into the rainy darkness. Cole's shoulder slammed into mine as he slashed an enemy at the knees then drove his sword deep into its middle. Ryan bellowed a battle cry from somewhere in the chaos, then there was a split second of silence before a cheer rose all around. The enemy had run.

Breathing was hard but oh so satisfying, considering the alternative of not breathing anymore. I scanned the midway, locating Jenny sitting near a low stage and holding her bloodied arm. I dropped to my knees and ran my hands over her. No burns. No burns.

"Some of those bastards have blades," she gasped.

"Yes, and some have guns. Can you walk?" Allerton asked and she nodded. "I'll take you to Garta."

"I can help."

He smiled. "Gracie, she'll be fine."

"But you're—" His fingers of one hand were twisted and gnarled, surely broken.

"I'll be fine. Check on the others. Get everyone together and wait for me."

He turned, stood and reached out with alarm. "Cole? Cole!"

And beside me, my rock, my strength, my… okay, my love, just dropped like a sack of flour. Allerton handed Jenny over to Ryan and knelt to check Cole's wounds. Nothing was visible until he pushed up Cole's tee-shirt and revealed a massive purple and blood-red bruise just below his chest.

Allerton looked around. "Ryan, find Ben… please." His voice shook. "Gracie, I will need your help after all." He grunted and groaned but lifted Cole over his shoulder.

Jenny leaned heavily against me as we walked, my heart wild with worry. I wanted to scream, to cry, to yell at God or anyone who'd listen. The midway, the campsite, the entire carnie was a mess, strewn with grunting Nephilim and oozing dead demons. It had all taken less than ten minutes.

There weren't as many wounded as I expected at Garta's camper. In fact, except for one of the new recruits, sitting, bleeding, and grinning like a lunatic, we were her entire patient load. She patched Jenny's cut and set Allerton's fingers. Hearing his screams coming from inside the camper almost made me sick. I'd be doing my best to protect my fingers in the future. When he came out, bandaged and splinted, he sat and explained Cole's condition.

"Garta says it's just a broken rib, but Cole needs to rest. Frank Pincer's going to help him to the van where he can stretch out and sleep."

Relief raced through me but that left another tiny issue. What would be the best way to explain that I'd be sitting with Cole all night? A way that wouldn't give away what we'd become to each other? Allerton reached over and squeezed my hand. My face heated. Why did I feel so guilty?

"He'll be fine. You can check on him later. For now, we need to locate Ben."

Ryan had headed off in one direction earlier, so we went the other, calling Ben's name over and over. Panic slipped and slid around in my belly. Was Ben strong enough to get through okay? It was our first battle and Ben and I were totally in the dark. It was the first time we'd ever seen the enemy fight. Was he hurt?

Burned? Or worse?

Allerton and I walked to the perimeter of the camp then moved outside, into the trees and near the hillside. So many of the enemy had died. They littered the ground like lumps of wet coal and mud, deteriorating before our eyes. The rain had slowed but everything was soaked, especially us. I couldn't stop shivering. It was cold, but mostly I was terrified of what we'd find. Further into the woods we heard Ryan calling for Ben.

"Ryan!" we shouted and he crashed through the trees.

"Anything?"

He just shrugged. Allerton looked like he'd lose it, spinning around, shouting Ben's name again and again, sounding more desperate each time. I tried to reach out and calm him but he'd already raced off into the darkness. Shuffling behind as fast as I could, I heard a thump and a thud. Headmaster had tripped over a downed log. "Ben," he cried out. "Oh God, Ben!"

"What the hell do you want?" Ben walked out of the darkness.

I ran up and slapped his shoulder hard. "You had to hear us calling! Why didn't you answer?"

"I was following the enemy. Green ordered me to stand watch at the hillside. I got a headcount and their retreat direction." He grinned, all proud of himself.

"And you couldn't answer?" Allerton glared, but he also looked kinda hurt.

Ben turned away and headed for camp.

"Hey, Mr. Allerton," I whispered, sliding my arm under his as he got to his feet. "Ben's had some… things happen. He's just, I don't know, being weird. It's nothing personal."

Allerton's eyes lowered to me and he sighed. "Call me Michael. I'm just a soldier like everyone else here." He followed Ben and the rain dripped to a stop while I watched him melt into the black mist.

"Gracie!"

Did I hear that? Did someone call my name? I looked to Ryan and he nodded. He'd heard it, too.

"Gracie!"

It was a cry, so raspy and damaged I was terrified enough to run away, but I stepped ahead to investigate.

"Ben! Michael! Over here!" Ryan shouted, gripping my wrist to keep me from going anywhere.

"Gracie, please! Gracie!"

The voice was so weak and it was a voice I recognized. I broke free and ran my hobbling gate, nearly slipping on the mud and fallen leaves. I stopped, listened, waited.

"Gracie!"

By then the others had caught up. Panic raced through me so hard I could hardly speak.

"Gracie! Oh please, Gracie!"

"It's Wally!" I knew it. I ran, everyone yelling for me to hold up, wait, shouting that it could be a trap.

"Gracie!"

There he was, part of a three-demon creature. His flesh was black as burned coal but at that moment, the clouds opened and I could see clearly. It was Wally, ghostly, ghastly, illuminated by the pure white moonlight. His blackened body struggled, twisted, and he cried out as he painfully ripped himself from the dead demons attached to him. He reached out and gripped at the slippery ground, sobbing and sounding more and more human with each split of his skin. He pulled harder and harder, crying out my name.

"I'm here, Wally!"

"Don't touch him!" bellowed Allerton. "Gracie, don't touch him!"

"He needs help!"

Wally cried like a child, grabbing at anything he could to pull and rip himself apart. When the final tear at his hip released him, he was catapulted a few feet.

"Gracie," he cried out. "Help me!"

I reached for him but Ryan wrapped his arms around me, determined to hold me back.

"Ben, run back to camp," Allerton's voice was calm and direct. "Grab a few blankets, anything we can wrap around him."

For the first time in a long time, Ben did exactly what he was asked. Tight in Ryan's grasp I watched in horror while Wally thrashed in agony. In mere moments Ben returned, soaked blankets in hand. They wrapped Wally's burned and blackened body.

Ben lifted our friend into his arms like a child. "Now what?"

"Garta. She'll know what to do for him." Allerton tucked the fabric tighter around poor Wally who continued to sob hopelessly. We turned toward camp but before I could take another step I had to throw up. What Wally had to do to break himself free was so disturbing, I knew I'd have nightmares for the rest of my life.

"What if she won't help him? I mean, he is the enemy, right?" Ryan ignored my puking fit. He was cool that way.

"She'll help. She's a good woman and an amazing healer."

"Too bad she can't fix your foot, Gracie." Ryan kicked at the mushy ground. "That would be great, wouldn't it?"

I shrugged. For the first time ever, I realized that my deformed foot was a gift, something that made others think I'm weak. Besides, it would be weird not to hobble and slide along. I wasn't lame when it mattered, so what's the big deal? I turned to Ryan, ran a hand across my mouth then grinned. "Nah," I said. "My foot is my brand. It's what makes me… me."

We reached the healer's camper just as she sent off the patched-up new recruit. Inside, Ben laid Wally on the bed then turned to Allerton. "You tell her."

"Michael?" Garta watched the sobbing patient. "Is this a wounded and burned Nephilim?"

"No, this is a heroic demon. This is one of our kids, one who was forcibly blood vowed by the enemy before he even left Ariel's Gate."

She stepped back and placed a gnarled fist over her heart.

"Garta, he literally tore himself apart, calling for Gracie."

Tears filled her eyes and her hands hovered over the sobbing patient.

"Can you save him?"

She moved with purpose, shifting around us all as though we weren't clogging up her tiny hospital. She unwrapped Wally with tenderness, whispering soothing words to him, careful not to cause him more pain.

"Don't touch him," Allerton warned and she shook her head.

"Only the battle-heat demons can burn us. This boy has done the impossible and split his own soul free from the demon nation with full intention of rejoining his own race. He is burned so severely though... I'm not sure... I just don't think..." She turned sad tearful eyes to us.

"Please," I begged. "Please try."

"Of course, yes, of course. Now all of you, please, give me space to work."

We left Wally still crying and calling my name. Everything inside of me was shaking. I'd never seen anyone in so much pain. I worried for Cole, sure his injury was worse than they'd told me. A person doesn't lose consciousness from a cracked rib... unless that rib did something really bad to something else really important. I glanced toward the campers where our van was parked. He was there, all alone. But so was Wally. Allerton left to talk with Tobias. An agitated crowd of warriors had begun to gather around Garta's camper. It seemed that having someone who was once the enemy in camp was a crime.

"Kill that bastard!" someone shouted.

"Why waste healing on such a creature?"

"Come out, Garta! Protect yourself!"

Tobias pushed his way through the mob. I leaned against the camper door, determined to protect Wally from anything he might command.

He ran toward me, bellowing and shouting, Allerton at his side trying to get a word in edgewise. I stood, my hands fisted and my back ready to spew big ass wings that could protect my wounded friend.

But Garta opened the door and stepped out, her eyes sunken and wet. All the energy had drained from her. She had tried everything she could and I started to cry before she even said the words.

"I am so sorry."

"Well, thank our lucky stars," Tobias spat, his nostrils flaring like a mad bull. "Someone get Jack Beacher to clean this mess up and get rid of the garbage."

I stood straight, ready to swing my sword, or shout my piece, or just slap him hard across the face. "That is Wallace Dean. He is one of us! He is not garbage!"

"Step aside, little girl. And you?" He glared down at Garta who was weak and sitting on her camper step. "You know better. Move aside."

Allerton tugged my arm, maybe hoping to keep me from killing the ancient leader, but I pushed him away and took a step closer. I wasn't sure what I intended to do, but whatever it was, Raffie interrupted.

At first the old bulldog just barked, and barked, and barked. Maybe we'd upset him and he didn't want us all arguing. Then the dog went, well… kinda crazy. He twisted and ran in a small circle, yelping like he was in pain, snapping at anyone who came near. We all stepped back and I wondered if the demons had gotten to him, burned him or worse, drew a blood vow. But a vow from a dog? What good would that do? Then Raffie leapt and spun like a top, flipped and gyrated. Every movement was unreal and hard to watch. It had to hurt, twisting his compact, arthritic, seventy-pound body like that. Suddenly the dog screamed and the sound was almost human.

"Raffie!" I yelled.

Before our eyes the lovely brindle fur split wide at Raffie's belly and the brightest light I have ever seen blasted from the wound up to the heavens. Many ran, most just stepped further away. I, like a crazy person, stepped closer. "Raffie!" I reached out but out of the brilliant light a massive human-shaped hand appeared and brushed against mine.

People gasped, warriors who had no fear in battle wet their pants, Tobias dropped to his knees.

A giant man-shaped form made of light and energy, stood butt naked right in front of us. He must have been twelve feet tall. He rolled his neck, stretched his arms high then shifted his shoulders. His humungous wings flapped and knocked over all of Garta's well organized boxes and coolers, and damaging her canvas porch roof. She managed to escape from underneath just in time.

"I am sorry, Garta." The monster smiled and as we watched, he slowly shrunk to normal human size.

"Holy moly!" Jenny gasped and as much as I didn't want to, my eyes, like hers, were glued to the new arrival's exposed, um, parts.

His hand made a swift move to cover himself. I think every woman in the crowd sighed disappointment. Holy moly was right.

"Well, I seem to be once again among the modestly clothed. Will someone please give me a blanket?"

Garta tossed one to him. "Welcome," she whispered.

He turned to me and it was terrifying. He looked like a living marble sculptured David. His eyes glowed golden, his hair was long and wavy, shiny and soft, yellow with threads of sparkling silver. His chest was well defined, his thigh muscles, hard and rounded. He bowed. "Gracious Cane. Good to finally talk with you." His voice was like liquid honey.

"Who are you? And what…" I pointed to poor Raffie's shredded fur. "…What have you done to our dog?"

He laughed and his face actually brightened, if that was possible. I stood my ground, determined not to be afraid.

"My dear Gracie… I *was* your dog. I have lived in the body of that animal for a hundred years, watching over Ariel's Gate, protecting you all… waiting for you."

"Me?"

"Oh… oh!" Tobias seemed to have come to life. He climbed to his feet and stepped closer, reaching out to touch the angel's face. Tears filled his eyes. "Rafael!"

The naked angel bowed again, careful to hold his blanket in place. "Tobias, I am once again guided to travel at your side. I have missed you, my old friend." He patted Tobias's shoulder then his golden eyes hardened. "But we have an issue here, don't we?"

"Yes, yes. I know. There's a demon, thankfully dead, among us and I will have it disposed of immediately. Beacher! Jack Beacher is our cleaner, he'll—"

"Tobias, you have lived too long among the demons and warriors… been too long at war, my friend," Rafael said softly. "You forget. All are God's creatures, but in the case of that boy," he pointed and elegant long hand toward the small camper, "he is a blessed, courageous, hero. He should be honored with a hero's passing-on ceremony."

"But—" a voice called from the crowd.

"But? But what?" Rafael walked the circle around him, eyeing everyone as he moved. They all stepped back. "Emmaus warriors!" he shouted and the very air trembled. "This could happen to any of you. Any Nephilim… pure, Norema, or Calanine… could be forced into a demon blood vow. And if that happened, would you be strong enough, brave enough, willing to endure the unbelievable pain of tearing yourself free to claw your way back to the light?" All eyes lowered and Raphael shook his head. "That boy has taught us much. He should be sent off in a good way."

Tobias looked at his followers' faces. Beauty Low shrugged. Garta glared back at him and crossed her arms. Beacher and Green shook their heads, eyes laced with fury. They were seasoned warriors and so many years of fighting had made them hard.

Tobias looked into Rafael's eyes and I started to understand. He and the archangel had a past, a history, but they also had a future. Tobias had been sole leader of the Emmaus warriors for centuries, but he now had help and guidance.

I sensed that he'd willingly step aside if it was best for the cause, but Raphael had not asked him to do that. All he asked was for Tobias and his warriors to apply a little compassion and grace in a difficult situation. Raphael actually took a step back and watched Tobias like the others, an action that reaffirmed the ancient's leadership. It seemed Raphael knew more than a little about human politics.

Silence, accented with the occasional plop of rain from remaining autumn leaves onto canvas and camper roofs, continued for several moments. Tobias turned full circle, focusing on each warrior, each wrapped wound, each expression. His face exposed his deepest fears and hopes. Finally, Tobias squared his shoulders and announced, "Raphael has caught me and my pompous ego. He's caught me at my fearful worst. He reminds me of the reason for everything. I humbly apologize to you all… most especially to you and your friends, Gracie. So long at battle… it has darkened my heart and blinded me to the possibilities. We will take care of Wallace Dean in the way most fitting his sacrifice." He looked to Raphael who nodded approval.

The angry discrimination of Tobias's warriors altered and softened with his decree. I knew Wally would be given a good send off. I just wasn't sure how many of the warriors would attend. I stepped closer to the beautiful naked archangel. "Thank you," I whispered.

"It is my duty and my pleasure. But," he leaned very close and spoke softly into my ear. There was a crackle of electricity as his hair touched mine and the scent of him was clean and crisp. "Gracie," he said in a hush. "Is there not somewhere else you're to be?"

I pulled back and looked into his eyes, swallowed hard, then nodded. Damn, he was one scary guy.

15

wanted to be there for Wally, to say goodbye and see him off with everyone else but I couldn't. An actual archangel told me to get moving. I ran to my new little pup tent and stuffed everything into my backpack, everything but that book. I had to flip through it first. The very first page confirmed. It was time to blow this Popsicle stand and do what I'm supposed to do. It didn't occur to me to consult Raphael or the mysterious book on exactly what I was supposed to do or how. All I knew was that I didn't want to do it alone.

As I suspected, few left camp to attend Wally's passing-on ceremony on the hill. Head down and walking fast, I skirted the people still milling around. They were busy dragging dead demons out into the woods or cleaning up and repairing the carnival. They'd do another performance in twelve short hours. How did they do it? Change from warriors to entertainers in the blink of an eye? I didn't have to like them, but I had to admire their tenacity.

Skulking in the remaining darkness I felt myself getting more and more nervous. Not about whether I could survive without the others around to protect me. I was nervous about what I had to do first. It was crunch time. I was about to learn if Cole felt the same way about me as I felt about him. Did other eighteen year olds deal with this crap? Probably not. They did all this mushy, confusing stuff at fourteen or fifteen. I am so out of step with the rest of the world.

It was after five in the morning. Pale pink teased at the eastern sky. There wasn't much time. Funny, all that sneaking around and not one person I passed seemed to care. They'd look through me or past me, their eyes blank and unfocused. Were they still really mad at me for bringing Wally to Garta? Well, none of that mattered anymore. I was striking out on my own. I didn't feel much like Jenny looked right after she got her wings, all tough and gritty and ready to fight the world. I wish I did. There was a job to be done and I was not going to drop the ball. The survival of our race was at stake.

I stopped dead in my tracks, turned and puked again. That's twice in one night. Well, best get through all the tough stuff right away. A warrior can't be carrying a barf bag around. Was the entire Nephilim race really relying on me? Should it? I wanted to whimper like a scared kitten but huffed, readjusted my backpack making sure my soul sword was securely attached, then stomped my way to the van.

Garta told me that the enemy could inflict more than burn or weapon wounds, and there were various levels of magical wounds. Cole had been affected by one of those, a spell designed to weaken him so they could easily go in for the kill. The magic needed a few minutes to take full effect but luckily the battle was brief. She countered the magic and Cole should be fine, all he needed was rest. The cracked rib would ache for a while, and possibly every time it rained for the rest of his life. Poor guy.

I slipped into the van and moved to the back bank of seats where he lay sound asleep. As quietly as possible, I set my backpack aside. He looked peaceful. Sleep was never easy for Cole. We'd all heard him cry out at night during our stay at the cabin. Something haunted and hurt him all the time, but at that moment, he seemed so calm. It felt wrong to wake him. Maybe I could let him sleep a few more hours, but then we'd have to deal with people asking questions, wanting to know where we were going. That wasn't going to work. Besides, there was a good chance he wouldn't go with me. Then he could just go back to sleep. I'd cry myself down the road on foot, but at least he'd get the rest he needed.

I whispered, "Cole, wake up."

"Gracie? Everything okay?" He reached for his sword before he even opened his eyes.

"Yes. I'm leaving. Will you come with me?"

He blinked, rubbed sleep from his tired eyes and shook his head hard, groaning with the motion. "What do you mean, leaving?"

"I have to go there… Ocracoke. It's important."

Eyes clear, he shuffled an aching grunt to sit up. "Sweetheart, Tobias is waiting for intel. Too many of the enemy could be between here and there. Just give it a few days. We'll all be moving on. Maybe wait until we get closer?"

"I can't. I have to leave. Now."

"This is about Wally." He ran a warm palm down my arm. "Garta came by, told me about it before she left for the ceremony. I'm so sorry. You're just upset."

"No, yes, but that has nothing to do with this. I have to leave and I have to leave right now."

His eyes grew narrow. "You don't just desert. This is an army. You have to follow orders."

Was he mad at me or just testing me? "Sometimes you can't. I can't."

"Listen to me, it doesn't work like that. There's a reason for a chain of command—"

"What if the command is wrong? Allerton knew the tribunal was wrong. He did what he had to do. I'm not saying Tobias is wrong, just that I need to go. Now."

Cole chewed his lip, shifted on the seat, and scowled.

"Listen, you don't have to go with me. I know you're hurt. I can take care of myself. I know I can. You saw me."

"You did fine tonight, real good… this time. What about next time?"

"I'll be ready. Really. Cole, I shouldn't have come to you. You've had such a hard time with all of this."

"We're talking about you."

"But I'm talking about *you*. You have been bleeding all alone for so long, fighting all the crap Allerton made you do to awaken us. Maybe you can't do this with me. Maybe you need this army." I was so proud that I didn't start crying, but my voice was crackling, threatening to break any minute. I had to get out of there, fast. "I understand."

I turned and Cole reached out and pulled me back into his arms. I wriggled then turned to argue but his lips captured mine. His touch took my breath away. Lost in the warmth and sensations I didn't even have words for, I wanted to just melt there, stay in his embrace forever but I had to be stronger than that. "I have to go." I spoke with all the determination I could muster. "Goodbye, Cole." I tried to break free. No go.

He kissed me again this time hard, his hands in my hair, his breath heavy, his voice, a growl. "Give me two minutes to get my shit together." He finally released me then rubbed his eyes again. "Let me think. We need a plan."

"You're going with me?"

He gave a tilted glare that made me stupid happy. "You go nowhere without me."

Don't smile too big, don't smile too big. "Shall I meet you at the edge of camp?"

"No." He swung around to reach for his clothes. "The guards will report to Tobias. There's another way out of here."

He moved fast and fluid with only an occasional gasp or groan. I hurried to turn my back as he struggled into his jeans and tee-shirt. "Cole?"

"Yeah?"

"What did you do before you came to acclimate us?"

"Why?"

"This is such a bad boy move for you. I thought you were all… *follow the rules and do the right thing.*"

He snorted. "Funny, I thought the same about you. Let's go. I need to push this van about fifteen feet then it'll drift down that hill." He pointed. "Can you steer?"

"Your rib!"

He shrugged. "It'll heal after we get out of here. Get behind the wheel. This is the brake… take your foot off of it when I say I'm ready to push then press on it to slow down. Steer if you're heading for a tree or something. I'll be right behind you. The hill's not too steep, the van should just roll then come to a nice quiet stop. Ready?"

Did I have a choice? I settled behind the wheel, gripped it with white knuckles and twisted to look behind, hoping with all my heart he wouldn't hurt himself worse. He waved for me to release the brake. In the side mirror, I watched his face twist into a painful grimace as he pressed a shoulder against the back of the van, anchored his feet, and pushed. The van started moving and my first instinct was to hit the brake but I didn't. It wasn't pretty but the vehicle slipped through the trees without incident, then rolled silently down, down, down. I worked the brakes and steered like he told me, just missing a tree trunk and a rock the size of an armchair. Finally, it came to a stop and I let myself breathe again. Cole climbed in, covered with sweat and obviously in pain. He started the engine and drove, one-handed, bumping over the rough terrain, all the way to the empty paved road. His other arm pressed tight against his side.

"You okay?"

He drew in a long breath and nodded. "Get the maps out of the pocket there in the door. We're about fifty miles from Interstate 64. Find our location then plot out the quickest route to Ocracoke."

I did the best I could. Of course, I understood the basics of a map, but never had to actually use one before, much less several at once.

"So, how far are we?"

"Um… about… eleven inches." Cole laughed and I couldn't help but smile. "Give me a minute to figure out the mile gauge." I did the math in my head, twice. "It's a little over three hundred miles."

"Six, maybe seven hours." He reached over and patted my knee. "A lot closer than I thought."

Then my stomach clutched. Ahead was Ocracoke. What would I find there? What was I supposed to do there? My ridiculous memory sparked. I was positive I was born there, but I was about to learn a lot about myself I didn't know. Would I be warrior enough to accomplish the goal? Smart enough to understand the mission? My backpack sat at my feet and I could feel vibrations from that book. It was changing, doing so a lot quicker than before. Someone or something had urgent messages and guidance for us. At least I hope it was guidance. Good guidance. I just couldn't bear to face those symbols at the moment. Cole was still weak and sweating but looking more and more focused and in control every minute.

I turned and looked back, realizing everything I'd left behind. Wow, where was my head? Maybe we all should have left together. I might need their help. Already I missed Ben… well at least the old Ben, my best friend on earth. I was sure going to miss Ryan and Jenny. If nothing else, they were a kind of how-to guideline for my foray into this romantic stuff. I knew I'd miss Headmaster Allerton. *Michael.* He asked me to call him Michael. I hoped I'd get the chance to see him again. He was such a huge part of my life, always there, leading, reprimanding, guiding. Protecting. And I'd definitely miss Raffie.

"Oh, Cole. Did you hear about Raffie?"

~*~

Michael drew in a deep breath, coping with the returned ache in his heart. Another death. He had so hoped and prayed that Wally was somewhere, in a city, finding his way, smoking a joint, listening to loud music, or shooting hoops with other kids his age. Alive. But instead, another tragic, fruitless, death.

In the center of a small opening on the hill overlooking the Emmaus Magic Show, Jack Beacher prayed over Wally's body. The corpse was wrapped ceremonially in a pale blue sheet. Beside Michael stood Jenny and Ryan. Ben waited at Beacher's side, having been asked to assist.

Nearly fifty years a Nephilim and Michael had never witnessed such a ceremony, but something deep inside his senses knew it well. It was ancient, spoken in the old language, musical and guttural at once. The words were foreign but passed along the feeling of comfort and moving on to a better place. At Wally's head knelt the newest arrival, the remarkable archangel Raphael, looking like everyone else there, tired, overworked, scruffy. Sad. Such a being had to know the best way to blend in, the best way to serve and support. Whether as a dog living an impossibly long life in an orphanage, or as Tobias's long ago traveling mate, Raphael glowed with his commitment. It comforted Michael in ways he couldn't define.

Beacher's voice rose with a shout everyone was compelled to repeat, the power of it rising above the dripping wet trees toward the coming dawn. Fewer than ten people attended. Tobias, quiet and contrite, stood in the back. Beauty Low and Garta, tearful and holding hands. A few of the soldiers who'd done the reconnaissance mission with him stood with eyes lowered. He worried for Gracie, obviously too upset to attend. He'd need to talk with her, find a way to comfort and strengthen her for what lay ahead. More of the same. More death. More passing-on ceremonies. More loss. And Michael wondered who would comfort him?

Jenny sniffled when the pale blue canvas was gently removed from Wally's still body. It was Wally as he used to be, young and strong, no burns, no black slime, no tightened and pained expression. Raphael stood with an air of satisfaction and Michael wondered how much of this was an illusion, how much was real? How much came from prayer? How much from magic? Then, as Beacher sang a low chant, softly then louder and louder, all eyes watched Wally dissolve, and the sparkling particles of his being lifted to dissipate in the crisp morning air. Wallace Dean, the belligerent kid who made him laugh and cringe, worry and shake his head, was gone. Really and truly gone, and Michael permitted a sob.

The crowd turned and walked back toward camp. "Jack," Michael reached out to Beacher. He too looked drained and exhausted. "Listen, I know how hard it was for you to do this. Please understand how grateful we are."

Beacher raised his brows. "I'm a soldier, Michael. I do what I'm told."

"For what it's worth, Wally was a good kid. He'd have made a good soldier, too."

"Sorry for your loss." Beacher nodded and left for his sleeping bag.

Michael prepared to lead his sad awakened back to their tents. He'd sleep close and watch over them carefully while Cole recovered. Ben stepped closer and pushed tears from his eyes. Seeing his son hurting ached in Michael's already ravaged heart. "Let's get some sleep, kids."

"Michael." Tobias stepped up, Raphael at his side. "A moment, please. I must speak with you."

He sent the kids ahead, assuring he'd be there soon. Michael didn't know exactly what to do or say. He cleared his throat, looked around, at the trees, at his feet. Waited. Standing so near an archangel felt massive, biblical, surreal.

But Tobias appeared far more nervous. "Oh… ah… Raphael, I have something I… was planning… maybe I should discuss this with you before I speak to—"

Raphael laughed and the sound lightened Michael's agony.

"Tobias, I have been the dog at your heel since the moment I arrived in this camp. I know what you've been thinking and I know what you have planned. It's a very good plan. I suggest you get on with it." He bowed a nod to Michael, smiled, and walked away.

"Raphael?" Tobias called.

The archangel in baggy jeans and a torn sweater waved without turning. "Do what you need to do. I'm hungry and I can smell Cookie preparing breakfast." Then he turned with a playful grin. "I'm sick of dog food!"

"Amazing." Michael didn't even realize he'd said it aloud.

"Yes, amazing indeed." Together they stood in a moment of awe, then the ancient shook himself and spoke, "Come with me."

Tobias led him over the hill and to a small clearing. A stream flowed, making a musical gurgle that soothed and calmed, maybe a little too much. Michael's eyes began to droop. "Can we do this later, Tobias?"

"No. Before I begin, you should know that Cole and Gracious Caine have left camp."

"What?" His heart jumped and his feet wanted to run.

"It's as it should be. Raphael assures me that she is to be in Ocracoke. It's good that Cole will travel along and protect her."

As his thudding chest regained a rhythm more fitting a tired man, Michael wondered what else Cole would be doing with Gracie. He'd seen them together. Was this a good thing? Did it matter? It was too late to change it. "Great, just great."

Tobias smiled. "I shouldn't have stopped her. For now, there is a far more pressing matter."

"What matter?"

Tobias merely waved a hand toward the trees then turned and walked away. Before he could follow, the sound of movement caught his attention and a man walked out of the trees. Not just a man… the Dark Lord. Rachel's husband. Gregory Parkland, Grand Regent of the Americas and head of the Nephilim Worldwide Intelligence Bureau. The damn head of the NWIB for God's sake! Michael swung around. "You bastard!"

Tobias turned, walked a few steps backward wearing a contrite expression with his hands wide. Then he trotted after Raphael.

"Let him be, Michael. Tobias and I have been working together for a long time now."

"Together?" Michael gulped. "I'm not going back to that fucking prison, Greg."

"I know." He grinned his handsome grin, blue eyes sparkling. "You'll kill me with your bare hands before you let me force you to serve out your rightful sentence for your horrific crime." He chuckled. Parkland was as different from

Michael as two men could possibly be. He stood in the damp woods wearing a two-thousand-dollar suit and polished Italian shoes. His hair was in place, his nails were clean, and his expression was way too playful. "Chill. I'm not sending you back. The whole thing was a fiasco and we both know it. My wife can be one hell of a scorned lover, can't she?"

Michael blinked. Best to let that statement pass. "What did you mean… working together? How are you working with Tobias? Helping with cash and weapons?"

"And many, many other things. You did well in the battle last night. I was impressed. I'm not sure I can even lift my soul sword."

Michael thumped down onto a fallen log and rubbed his chest. "What the hell do you want?"

Parkland actually unfolded a crisp clean handkerchief, laid it on the log, and sat beside him. Michael rolled his eyes.

"I understand Gracie has left."

Michael nodded.

"Good, good, that's very good. She could just turn the tide for us."

Michael wondered how a handicapped girl with no weapons training, pure Nephilim or not, could turn any tide. "How the hell do you know she left?"

Parkland grinned again and bobbed his brows. "I know everything, remember. I run the damn NWIB. Every runner Tobias receives intelligence from… is sent by me. Every penny Ariel's Gate and every other orphanage in the Americas received… came through me. I'm aware of every battle, every death, every passing-on ceremony. It's my job to know, Michael."

Every penny? Every death? A new light illuminated everything. That much weight would kill Michael. That much knowledge, that much power, that much influence among all sectors of the Nephilim race could be a horrific burden. It could also lead to unimaginable corruption. Everything tightened inside him, snapping like electricity along his spine.

"I'm sure you've guessed that a lot of what I do is, well, secret… unknown by most of our different governmental sectors."

"So, who do you really work for? The Coalition? The tribunal? The government? The NWIB?"

"I work for the balance. We must survive. This shit can't be swept under the carpet and ignored by any of us any longer. Too many are wearing blinders, imagining that their way is the only way. The time for pompous attitudes is long gone."

"Ah, so Rachel doesn't even know."

"Hell, no." He shifted to face Michael, his eyes sincere. "It's time for the next step. We both know it's foolish to imagine that Tobias and the other rogue armies can raise an adequate force. Someone has to move outside the carnie circuit and into the mainstream. Someone who can speak to a Nephilim's sense of honor and survival. Someone to make them understand that the balance has severely shifted *against* us. That we must regain that balance or die trying. I've been watching you for years and you," he poked a finger into Michael's chest, "are the one."

"The one what?"

That irritating grin was back and Michael shot to his feet.

"Are you mad? I'm just… I can't… I'm not—"

"Ah, but you are. Highly educated. Well spoken. Remarkably charismatic. I can't even get a dog to roll over." He gave an undignified snort. "People automatically, instinctively follow you. You clearly understand the various strata and systems within the Nephilim race. And you're battle tested and well aware of our critical situation. Seriously, Michael? Who else could I send off to recruit big numbers in the big cities? There are mere months before this war will begin. Who else? I beg you. Tell me who else I can send and I'll send them, too!"

Michael blinked. Parkland had shouted. He'd never heard Gregory Parkland shout.

"Any suggestions?"

"No, I don't know. Why me? Holy shit, Greg!" He paced in front of the dandy sitting on a square of linen. "I can't leave here. We just lost our best warrior trainer when Cole left with the Caine girl. I have young awakened to prepare and train and—"

"Tobias is far more qualified to manage that than you are."

"I don't see why—"

"Listen, Michael. I am aware that Raphael has returned. I'm as sure as you are that Metatron is up there writing and rewriting his guide for balance *as we speak*. I know the book left with your pure Nephilim. There's a reason for it all. Shit is happening and what we want to do, or think might be the best thing to do, is irrelevant. This is what we have to do."

Michael dropped back down onto the log. The Dark Lord was making sense.

"This is our Hail Mary. The key is to stop this before it gets too ugly to hide from the human race. Michael, I need your help to make this work."

"Exactly what am I supposed to do?"

"Recruit like crazy and… negotiate."

"What?"

"We need warriors… *and* we need a negotiator to bring rational solutions to the table… all the tables. This is the only way to regain balance. It can't be all killing. If that was the case, we've already lost."

"Negotiate?" Michael laughed with a snort. "With who? Battle-heat demons aren't big talkers, Greg."

"There is one to negotiate with."

Michael's heart skipped several beats in a row and for a moment, he thought he'd pass out. "Him?"

"The Morning Star. Yes."

"The fucking devil? You want me to negotiate with Lucifer?" He was back on his feet but immediately returned to his seat. His voice was a croak. "I can't do that."

"You can. You're carrying the best of all our Nephilim people in that aching chest of yours. It's supposed to be you. If you accomplish the recruiting goal, we're saved. But trust me, if it comes to negotiating with Lucifer and all sectors of our race, you can do it. You know the core."

"Yeah, and the devil makes the rules."

"No, he doesn't. Our Father makes the rules. We dropped the ball, never forget that. This is our fault. It's time to regain balance or we're sure to disappear from the face of the planet."

"Why don't you do it?"

Parkland sighed. "Keeping my inside position is the only way I can continue to be effective. Support the cause. I have to stay where I am. Come on, Michael. Think about the cosmic symmetry of it all. It's perfect. You're already considered a criminal among the upper echelon. It won't be a big shock if you associate with Lucifer. Among the lower factions, you're a hero for going rogue. Among those acclimated out of the orphanage system, you're a freaking god. There's no one better to do this."

Parkland stopped talking and gave Michael time to digest. Lots of time. The sun rose higher and heated the damp air, prickling sweat at his brow. He paced and thought, wondered and worried. Gracie was in Cole's protection. Tobias would train the acclimated well. The only real concern was his own ability to accomplish such lofty goals. He'd need to recruit several thousand warriors and possibly have a heart-to-heart with the devil.

"I'm a wanted man. They'll catch me and—"

"Your sentence has been expunged."

Of course it has. "The recruits… their soul swords are dissolved."

"And you are given the power to return them to each warrior."

Damn. "How could I possibly talk to that many—"

"I have already booked and promoted ten major conferences throughout the U.S. and Canada. More than a hundred-thousand interested Nephilim from all walks of life will hear your message. These are your plane tickets, hotel reservations, charge cards. In Charlotte you'll pick up a cell phone, computer, everything you'll need to keep in touch and report your progress."

He shuffled through the documents.

Parkland stood and brushed off his sleeve. "You need to leave immediately. You can do this. Use your head, be tactical. Determine who will best serve as a military resource, and who might be better equipped to change things at a diplomatic level. Oh, and take your son with you." He reached into his jacket and pulled out another stack of documents.

"What?"

"Yes, I know about Ben. Not exactly covert intelligence… Rachel told me years ago. Take Ben with you. He can be valuable to you, and I can't imagine a better person to protect and train him."

Michael's eyes squeezed tight. He'd actually believed that Ben would never need to know. That Rachel would never tell. The hardest thing he'd ever done was speak that truth to the Tribunal. He groaned, confused and angry, terrified but excited. "I don't know whether to thank you or kill you."

He opened his eyes and Gregory Parkland was nowhere in sight.

16

et's dispense with the Darth Vader, Luke Skywalker crap. Before you open your mouth, I already know you're my father and guess what? I don't give a flying fuck."

Okay, Michael probably deserved that. At least the kid waited until they were alone in a private jet before dropping that bomb. Ben sipped from a soda can and glared out the window.

"How do you know?"

The kid shrugged. "Just know."

Michael smiled. "You've had your quickening."

"My what?" He turned, offering a full view of his face. It was a strong face, an honest one. A face coping with massive confusion and misery. Ben hadn't taken Gracie's leaving well, but having been ordered, by the archangel Raphael of all people, to travel with Michael had shot the kid into an adolescent rage. Adequately ignored, he finally climbed onto the craft and buckled in, shooting a substantial glare to assure Michael wouldn't sit beside him.

He sat across, looking at his son in an all new light. "Your quickening is the point when you're given powers… gifts. Yours seems to be a heightened sense of perception. What else do you know, Ben?"

"I know I don't care to have this conversation."

Michael sipped fine whiskey and tugged on the crisply pressed cuff of the new white shirt provided. At a Charlotte hotel, they were given wardrobes in loaded suitcases, clothing appropriate for their assignment and position, as well as their ages. Ben had no gripes, wearing soft new jeans with a ragged tear at the knees, biker boots, and a grey silk tee-shirt. He'd showered and his hair, still wet and haphazardly spiked, glowed brown with golden streaks from the sun shooting through the small window. The boy was beautiful with many of his mother's features, some of Michael's ruggedness. Mostly Rachel's snarky attitude. "It's a long flight, young man. Best we use the time to cover essential information about your new responsibilities and strengths."

"You are not my headmaster anymore."

"Well, shall I talk to you as your boss? Your superior? Or… your father who loves you and has done everything possible to protect you? A father who is ridiculously proud to be traveling with you on this important mission? Who do you want to talk to, Ben? Because we will be talking."

"Don't try to be all fatherly, *Michael.*" The kid sneered. "It sure as hell doesn't suit you."

Michael rubbed his chest. "Fair enough. I haven't been a real father to you, but it's time to change that. Whether you like it or not, Ben, I am your father." He playfully did his best Darth Vader breath.

Ben turned to stare out the window. "So, what's this important mission, anyway? We off to kill California demons on surf boards? I don't like being your son, but I will admit I don't mind fighting at your side. You swing a mean sword. You are gonna teach me how to do that, right?" He finally looked into Michael's eyes.

"I will, but the biggest part of our mission is far more important. We're doing what Tobias can't. We're recruiting in ten major cities. We must bring thousands into the warrior society, and we have to do it quickly and efficiently."

The kid gulped cola, trying hard not to look impressed. "What's the hurry?"

"There's a deadline. The Nephilim race was given a primary responsibility to maintain and protect the balance between good and evil. The human race counts on us for this, even though they don't know it. Without balance, everything falls apart. Our existence is a ticking clock and our Father was very clear. When imbalance reaches its maximum limit, the final endeavor can only be played out on the battlefield."

"War, like what happened at the camp?"

"Much, much bigger… hundreds of thousands of the enemy against us. This is our last-ditch effort. If we can't level the battlefield, we'll have no chance of survival."

"And if the bad guys win, the world will be run by demons?"

"No. Without regaining balance, we *all* die. Demons are us, Ben. Nephilim. They're like Wally, they have either involuntarily or voluntarily taken blood vows to fight for the dark."

Ben released his seatbelt and shifted to lean forward, elbows on knees, his face twisted in concern and confusion. "How the hell did it get this bad? Who's in charge?"

"Too many with different ideas about how to handle or not handle the issue. Maybe it's my fault. The orphanage system prided itself on giving each acclimate free choice. Maybe we should have shielded you all less and just told you the truth. That our world is in a shitload of trouble."

Ben sat quietly and bit his lip. "So, we're out to gather orphanage-system-awakened to fight at our side. The ones who didn't choose their soul sword."

Michael was pleased, Ben got the point. They would focus only on those acclimated out of the orphanage system. Unlike the Nephilim who had no guidance, often called *free winged*, orphanage-awakened orphans were given information and a fair understanding of the race, its factions, and flaws. Around the world there were millions of them living quietly. "Yes, we're going to reach out to the orphan acclimated, like you… like me."

Ben paused but didn't look up. "But those people didn't choose the vow of service. Why would people with nice, cushy, safe lives give that all up to come and fight?"

"You heard Ballister Green. Even if they don't fight with us, they'll die anyway. It will be a purge. Our Father will correct the mistake celestial beings committed long ago by creating the Nephilim race."

The kid shook his head. "So, we're like… an abomination."

"No, Ben. We're also part human and our Father so loves the human race, he gave us every chance to carry our weight, use our awakened powers for the good of the planet and all its inhabitants. We're not an abomination, but we're definitely not in favor at the moment. Time's almost up. And since the Nephilim race is responsible for allowing such imbalance, we must all go to a place apart from the earth and be counted on the battlefield."

"Are you saying that we need to kill exactly the right number of demons to create balance? Or," Ben raised his terror filled eyes to meet Michael's. "Are you saying we need to just go there and fight to the death… of all of us… demons and Nephilim… until we're all eliminated?"

Michael didn't answer.

"And are you saying that if more Nephilim don't come and fight they're going to just… poof… be dead and gone anyway?"

Still Michael remained quiet. He wanted to give Ben's new ability a chance to work, a chance to see the answer.

"Tell me!" Ben stood, fists tight and shaking.

"Use the force, buddy," Michael teased.

Instead of lashing out, which he fully expected, the kid slowly sat and closed his eyes. It took a while, until Michael finished his whiskey and poured himself another, but finally Ben straightened and spoke.

"Damn. It's almost the deadline. All we have to do is prove that we can balance the battlefield. If we do that, if we actually bring as many Nephilim as there will be demons to that place… that battlefield… then it's over. There will be no battle, no war. Balance! Balance will be achieved. Right? Am I right?"

"Almost. That's quite a powerful gift you have there, Ben. You're close to exactly correct. There's one other element at play, though. It's—"

"Free will."

Michael sighed and rubbed his eyes. "Nephilim have free will, but demons do not. It's been taken from them. They can't, at least never until Wally, change their loyalty. What that boy did has never been done before. It's not likely to ever happen again. We must assure a balanced number of warriors for the good guys."

"Damn. We got a lot of work to do."

"So, you'll help me?"

Ben stared out the window, rubbed his hands together, visibly struggled to choose an answer. When he finally spoke, Michael had been holding his breath for what seemed like an eternity.

"Yeah." Ben looked his father directly in the eyes. "I'll help."

And for the first time in a long time, the pain in Michael's chest completely disappeared.

~*~

We were driving way slower than I expected, stressing me out, making me worry that someone from Tobias's camp would catch us any moment. Watching Cole like I was, out of the corner of my eye, determined not to let him know how happy I was that we were together, I could see what I didn't want to see. He wasn't just tired and aching from a damaged rib, the magic curse slapped on him during the battle must have been stronger than Garta realized. He struggled to keep his eyes open, yawned often, and shook his head making himself grunt with pain. Not only were we crawling along a major interstate way below the speed limit, we might just drive across the median into oncoming traffic. Not the way I planned to die. Just as I was about to say something, he slowed to a crawl and pulled the van to the side of the highway.

"Sweetheart, I need just a few minutes to sleep."

I wanted to say *of course, whatever you want.* I wanted to pull his head onto my shoulder, feel his weight and listen to his sleep breath, smooth, calm, warm against my neck. I wanted a whole mess of things, but stuff had been altering inside my brain since my wings showed up. I opened the map and followed the interstate we were traveling with my finger. Two miles. "Can you drive two more miles?"

Cole yawned so wide his jaw cracked and I laughed. "Yeah, yeah. Two miles. To the next exit. Good idea. We'll find a parking lot and I can crash for about a half hour."

Folding the map, my mind raced. Cole needed a bed. He needed rest. I needed him to be strong and clear because I had no idea what we'd be facing in Ocracoke. With that thought forming solid as marble in my head, I shoved the map into the glove compartment and an envelope fell out, right onto my foot. "What's this?" I opened it. "Holy crap! Did you rob a bank or something?"

"Not lately." Cole reached for the wad of cash, counted it then snorted a laugh. "Damn. Ten grand. Exactly what Allerton said he'd pay for my Harley. Just like the bastard to stick it in there and not even tell me."

I blinked. "You had a motorcycle?"

"Yep."

Oh, hot image, Cole astride a Harley. "And Allerton bought it?"

"Yeah."

I could not imagine Headmaster on a Harley, no matter how hard I tried. "So, let's get a motel room. That way you can sleep. We'll hit the road again when you're really awake." I never saw so much money in one place before, and when he pushed it into my hands and merged onto the highway, I couldn't help but fan it like playing cards. Good Lord, what we could do with all that money. We could not only get a motel room, but gas and an oil change, rent a cottage when we reached the island. We could buy a few new clean clothes. I really liked that idea. Well, no time for a shopping spree, but maybe we could find a laundromat.

A motel sign peeked over the trees along the side of the highway and I started to feel a lot of things, abrupt, prickly, bizarre things. So much was altering—how I thought, how I saw things, how I interpreted what I heard, what I expected, what I needed. It all meshed like chainmail, like protection, heavy and cumbersome. Nothing came out of my mouth without thinking first anymore. Maybe I was just adjusting to the world outside Ariel's Gate, or maybe I was actually changing, but changing into what? I found myself not asking Cole things, like if he'd like to sleep in a motel. Instead I just stated fact. He would sleep in a motel. Weirder than that, he actually did what I said. Okay, he was dead tired and probably couldn't get his act together enough to argue, money or not. But something more was happening inside me.

Sitting in the van, watching him go into the motel office, I felt this terrible ache inside, like I needed him close by. Like he was an important part of me, suddenly detached. The void actually ached. Oh, no, no, no. I did not want to be *that* girl. I glanced along the line of motel room doors and gulped. Would he expect me to, you know? My gut roiled with excitement and terror. Yes, I wanted it. No, I didn't. Not yet, not in that motel. Not when I felt so stupid in love I could smell regret right around the corner. No, no, no.

He climbed in, started the engine, and I felt relief that he was back at my side, a little freaked about what he'd expect.

"We've got a room right there." He pointed. "I'm going to park directly in front. Listen," he turned to me, worry all over his tired face. "This van is loaded with weapons… guns, pistols, ammo. Our soul swords are in here, too. We're going to have to keep an eye on the van. We can't lose any of our arsenal."

Arsenal? Oh, right. We were heading for war. Guns were important. How silly of me, worrying about stupid sex. I nodded. "I'll watch the van from the window while you sleep."

"Thanks. I just need a few hours." He leaned over and brushed his lips across mine then moved the van and parked. Duffels and backpacks in hand, we entered the neat room. I'd never been in a motel room but hey, it looked exactly like motel rooms on TV.

I pulled the heavy curtains open a little and settled on a chair at the small, wobbly table.

"Gracie, you want to shower first? I can sit watch for a little."

I didn't answer, just dragged the least stinky clothes I owned from my bag and went into the bathroom. It was the fastest shower of my life, but boy, was I grateful for it. Dressed, hair sloppy dripping, I rushed out to find him sound asleep in the chair. That wasn't going to work.

"Cole?"

"Yeah, yeah, I'm awake." He ran his arm across his mouth to catch a string of drool. The guy even looked good drooling. *Arrgh!*

"Get into bed. You can shower when you're awake. You need sleep."

No argument. He let me guide him to one of the two big beds and dropped like a rock. There was a groan but it quickly changed to a soft snuffling snore. Damn. He was even pretty snoring.

This was so not good. I'd gone all gaga over a guy. I can't be doing that crap. But even when I showered, I could feel a spark of him through the door, calling me close. Dragging me into him. What was that all about?

I pulled the strange book from my backpack and flipped it open, not exactly asking for answers about my burgeoning love life, but getting them all the same. The symbols seemed playful. They combined things like home and body, touch and air, protection and softness. Like when movie stars date and the tabloids invent a single name for them. Like Cole and I were becoming one thing. I rubbed my eyes. Maybe I was misinterpreting the symbols. But there in front of me was the proof. Two pieces melded together. Okay, let's just assume the ever-present mysterious author of the book approved of my inexplicable deep feelings for Cole Masters. Or maybe the author just had a mean sense of humor.

At that moment, the symbols shifted and redrew themselves. The combined symbol for the two of us was now leading armies, gathering strength, building something, but not without difficulties. Shattered symbols told the story of what really lay ahead, and even though I understood that war wasn't easy, this story featured complications of biblical proportions.

I glanced out the window then back to the book. More shifts, and I wondered why the book even had pages. The mystical author worked so quickly, an entire epic novel could be told without ever flipping to page two. That author also understood how long it would take me to digest and understand each message. The symbols never changed until I completely grasped the point. At least I hoped I was grasping the point, after point, after point. It seemed I was on the right track. I was supposed do this with Cole. And I was meant to endure the changes and tremors and shifts going on inside my mind. My brain was expanding, growing into an instrument able to comprehend what would be revealed in the book and in the world around me. Sometimes my head ached with the mounting pressure.

Another glance out the window. A couple passed, one with brilliant white ethereal wings, big ones… he was Norema. His companion was human, super pretty with a Barbie doll figure and long blonde hair. Without even seeing a bump, I knew, really knew, that she carried his child, a tiny Calanine, growing in her flat belly. Wow, TMI.

Across the street was a restaurant. That triggered my ever present and accounted for hunger. My empty tank gave a rumble so loud I checked to see if it might wake Cole. There was a candy machine just outside our hotel room. Dare I attempt a little shopping? It would hold me over so Cole could sleep longer. I thought I'd be fearful of being alone out there—after all, it was a whole world I had no experience with. My stomach set the challenge with another substantial growl and I snuck out the door, leaving it slightly open while I slipped coins into the machine. Funny, it wasn't fear that a surprise demon would attack, even though I could hear them whispering all around. It wasn't fear that a human mugger would reach for me that shook me to the bone. It was the fact that even though I could see Cole sleeping several yards away, I needed to be closer to him. I worked my new brain hard for an answer to that conundrum, postponing my choice between a Snickers bar or bag of chips. Was I being all ooey-gooey in love and acting like the world would end without his smile? No. This was something else. Yes, Cole was there to protect me, but I was there to protect him, too, and I could. I turned a sudden glare at a particularly slimy demon dripping battle heat and skulking in the nearby motel crossway shadows. Two sets of glowing red eyes glared and several twisted feet and arms backed away. I was so grateful humans couldn't see those ugly things, and I wondered if the Norema knew it was there. His girlfriend certainly had no clue. No matter, it was gone.

With that taken care of I was back to thinking about the Cole dilemma. I didn't think I was being a silly lovelorn girl. I wasn't even sure what that girl was like. This felt more like a command than infatuation. I was part of Cole. He was part of me. Yes, I was falling in love with him, but that wasn't the primary demand chiming inside my bones. I wanted him when it was the right time to have him, when it was the right time for him to have me. But we needed each other and something bigger needed us together. We had important work to do. Potato chips it would be.

Without a second thought, I crawled on the bed beside him, crunched potato chips, and watched the van outside the window. He woke three hours later. His hand slid over my hip and wrapped around me, tugging me close.

"You stink. You need that shower." I rolled over, grinned and let him kiss me. It was soft and lingering. "And I'm hungry. There's a diner across the street."

He pushed aside the empty chips bag making crinkling noises under his elbow. "We'll be on the island before morning," he called from the bathroom before the door closed with a thud.

Suddenly all my hunger turned to jitters. Opening the book, it was more of the same. Disjointed images, battle, wounds, pain, tears, and Cole and I in the middle of it all.

~*~

Cole paced the small bathroom, blasted the shower then sat on the edge of the tub. "What the hell *almost* just happened? Holy shit." He glanced toward the closed door. "Half asleep and I wanted her. Bad. She's not ready and hell, I'm so not right for her. She's pure Nephilim! I'm nothing. Nothing. I need to give her space. I can't be doing stupid shit like that again."

His whispered chants continued under the steaming spray and while rubbing himself dry with the flimsy towel. Gracie was not for him. She was significant. All he had to do was protect her. She had vital work to do and he was supposed to just help her. He squared his shoulders and left the bathroom. Gracie had already packed up the van and was waiting for him in the passenger seat. Her pretty face glowed. So pretty. He groaned.

They sat in a booth. Three in the afternoon so the diner was fairly quiet, just a middle-aged couple quietly bickering at the back-corner table, and a young businessman working on his laptop at the counter. The scarred tabletop was clean, fresh paper placemats in place, and the fake leather banquette seats squawked and groaned under their weight. The jukebox played Elvis Presley's *Jailhouse Rock*, and sunshine blasted through the window on them. Everything about the place irritated Cole.

"Oh yum, I want a cheeseburger and fries… or maybe those tacos… oh, grilled cheese!" Gracie read the menu like she'd never seen one before.

Hell, she never had seen a menu before. There were ten thousand things she'd never seen or experienced before. All that pressure was on his shoulders now. To make sure she understood the world, how it worked, and how to function in it. In a lot of ways, she was like him, minus the criminal record and a nasty case of PTSD, of course. They were the same because they were different from the human world. There were things about them, even within their own race, that set them apart. Gracie's twisted foot might have helped her deal with that sort of thing but still, a ton of responsibility had just been piled on her frail back, along with a set of substantial wings. Romance with the wrong guy was not going to be loaded on, too. Lord knew he didn't want to stop what had started—it was the only thing holding his soul together, the precious thing he feared he couldn't live without—but he just couldn't let it happen.

There were options. Nothing said he had to take this on. The care and feeding of a newly awakened pure Nephilim was way beyond his abilities. He could step back, return to camp and have Allerton or Tobias send someone else to protect Gracie. He could. But he couldn't. He just plain couldn't.

Across the table, unaware of the conflict raging inside his head, Gracie had become animated. Noticing the nerdy patron at the counter, she dug into her backpack, turned on her own brand-new laptop and squealed with excitement. "It works! It actually works."

"Why wouldn't it?" he grumbled, pushing around a puddle of coleslaw.

"Cheer up or I'm going to have to smack you. Oh, look! I found the Ocracoke ferry schedule. Let's see…"

His heart ached. He couldn't take anymore. He stood and left for the restroom. Maybe he should just cut out the back door? Through the kitchen and past the garbage dumpsters seemed an appropriate escape route for a coward. He had to run. If he couldn't help her the way she deserved, if he couldn't love her the way he already did, what was the point? She'd do what she was born to do with or without him. If he couldn't have her, if he couldn't have her; *if he couldn't have her*, he couldn't bear it.

"But you can love her, Cole." The voice was like thunder, vibrating in his chest, loud and painful.

The light in the three-stall restroom altered, became intense, dazzling, and seemed to shatter like shards of sharp glass, each crack radiating rainbow colors that felt like needles piercing his eyes. He jumped back, slammed into the wall next to the sink and slid to the floor, his hands desperate to protect his face. Surely that kind of light would burn the retinas right out of his eyes. He squirmed and leaned to the side, his hands up and feet slipping on the floor, trying to make himself as small as possible. His breath became ragged and he scrambled to regain control. He pushed himself to his feet and stood, his hands shielded his eyes, one a ready fist, the other opened like a fan. The exposed skin on his face and forearms felt burned and his knees trembled, but there were few things he felt worthy of true cowardice. Whatever supernatural light was currently torturing him wasn't among them. It might crisp his flesh, but it wouldn't break his heart the way leaving Gracie would. He squared his shoulders and moved his hand from his face. With his strengthening stance, the brilliance of the light softened and dulled until the restroom was only slightly brighter than normal. He took in one big gulp of air.

The most beautiful celestial being he ever saw, the *first* celestial being he ever saw, stood in the middle of the grimy tiled restroom looking down at him. Cole's heart sped until he wasn't sure if it was even beating anymore. A hum of rattling blood hissed in his ears. "What the—"

"Relax," said the angel. "I'm here to help you… and her." He nudged a perfectly formed chin toward the door and diner beyond. "Do you really think you can walk away from this?"

"I… I… she…"

The being smiled and reach out a hand. "Name's Raphael. Nice to finally talk with you. I remember when you smoked that cigarette in Allerton's office." He chuckled. "You put it out in—"

"In his jogging shoe… then I ran for my life."

Raphael snorted. "Just fourteen years old. After midnight. You were going to be in so much trouble if you got caught."

"I almost did." Cole felt his heart slow down and finally shook the outreached hand. "The dog…" *Raphael? Raffie.* "…ah man… *you*… you saved me!"

"Tripped the headmaster and gave you a chance to escape."

Cole smiled. It was a good memory, but a strange one to share with an archangel who was once your dog. "Why did you help me get away?"

Raphael sighed. "Because I knew today would come, and the time for helping you escape would end. You cannot walk away from this."

Cole glared. "Unlike you, I have free will."

"And even with that free will, can you really leave Gracie behind?"

A million things raced through his mind. Things he didn't want to think about. What he could and couldn't do. Things he could and couldn't deal with. Things he couldn't explain, even with Allerton's brief tutorial about the quickening. Gracie deserved so much better. It seemed Raphael and his old friend Tobias shared the same telepathic ability.

"Ah yes, your quickening. I'm here to tell you that you will receive another one."

His head shook in horror. "No. I don't want this. No."

"Which? Another power? Or Gracie?"

Cole's mouth went dry. Raphael tilted his head, his eyes compassionate and knowing. "You need to understand… your first quickening was immense because you are made to carry massive power."

"No. No thanks." Cole thought to slip around the being and out the door. Those smelly dumpsters were looking better and better to him. Raphael placed a large hand on his shoulder, both supportive and restrictive. Cole was going nowhere.

"You're built to carry massive power because your grandfather is Makha'el, the archangel warrior. You were born to do this, and to do it with Gracious Caine."

Cole's head shook, at first slowly as he let the information gel in his brain, then faster as it lit with comprehension. "You're wrong. I'm nothing. I'm not…"

Raphael leaned in, practically nose to nose with Cole. "You were born to do this and she cannot do it without you. She has a very specific goal. It will be revealed to her in her place of birth. She will need you to help her understand and fulfill that goal. It's the last cog in this survival machine. Cole, you must understand, I cannot fight at your side… none of us can. The promise was made by your race and you must regain the balance. I can only advise, and guide, and I am speaking truth. Your grandfather is Makha'el. He loves you and sends me to tell you so. To make sure you know your path."

Cole's mind spun like a top, the kind that flashes sparks of tiny lights. Could it be true? Memories covered his thoughts like heavy cream. Dreams. Visions. His calling to fulfill his vow. His remarkable, shocking quickening. He shivered in the heat of Raphael's nearness. Helping Gracie was the only path to survival. Could he possibly be the right person to assist with such a task? But swimming in the thick miasma of his past and present, he finally understood the gift his quickening brought, the horrible power of it, the terrible need for it.

But there was his human side, the side that helplessly loved the girl playing with a computer and munching French fries. The part that feared he could never give her what she deserved. That he'd never be enough. "I don't know if I'm... good... for Gracie."

"That kind of flawed thinking has served you all your life, Cole. It's given you freedom to do as you pleased. I'm here to tell you that's all over, my young friend. Your second quickening will reveal much. You are important. The human race and this planet need you to accept it. To strengthen your vow and help Gracie regain the balance."

Cole rubbed his eyes, did his best to hide coming tears.

"She loves you, too, you know. It's right. It's good. It is a blessing, Cole. To be loved and cherished. It's a bonus." Raphael smiled. "We didn't plan it, you know."

Watching the archangel's face, Cole's heart loosened and stopped aching. He loved Gracie. It was okay to love her. He could love her the best he could. He still didn't feel it was the right time to drag her under the sheets but when the time was right, he'd know and love her fully.

"Be prepared," Raphael said as he slowly faded into thin air. "Your next quickening will come soon after you cross the water to Ocracoke. It will help you both greatly with what lies ahead."

Without warning or reason, Cole opened his eyes. When had he closed them? His brow leaned against the cool mirror over the sink, and the sound of a flushing toilet roared in his ears. A man came out of a stall, leaned in and washed his hands, took a quick, suspicious glance across the grimy porcelain then left. Cole's skin tingled like sunburn. "Did that really happen?" He felt the cosmic shift inside his heart. He felt good. Really, really good.

"I want cherry pie," he said as he slid into the seat across from Gracie. "Then we need to hit the road."

"The last ferry leaves Hatteras at midnight."

"Piece o' cake… we'll make that one, easy." His eyes sparkled and she smiled.

The pie was delicious and Cole knew two things for sure—he wasn't going anywhere without Gracie, and he wasn't going to think about that second quickening until he had to.

17

knew the moment it happened. I knew Jenny was dead. I felt her strong, crazy, beautiful existence drift out of the world like a wisp of cotton on the breeze and my heart broke. "Please pull over."

I know Cole didn't want to stop but his face told another story. He felt it, too. "Good God, Gracie." His voice was a rasp.

We sat on the side of the highway, silent, hurting, sad. It was the second crushing blow of war in two short days. Wally, and now Jenny. "Is this what it's like? All the time?" I turned tearful eyes.

Cole reached for me and held me close. "I'm sorry." His voice broke. "This is what it's like, sweetheart. This is the reality of war. Poor Jenny."

"Was it battle? It's not even dark. The performances haven't even ended. Oh God, was she on guard duty? How did they get her?" I remembered her determination, her intention to protect me during the battle at the carnival. My God, why wasn't someone protecting Jenny?

His hand rubbed my back, and I wondered how we both knew at the exact same moment. Could we be that much in sync? Are we all connected? All Nephilim? Even the ones who chose the dark? Was that why Cole and I could hear them hissing, whispering, talking all the time? Even sitting at the side of the road I could see them, traveling in huddled groups, moving ahead, toward the same destination. My home, Ocracoke. Why?

Since the diner, Cole had been driving like we'd just broken out of jail, search lights and barking dogs on our tail. It felt like we were on the run, speeding from the prison of what we are, and what we had to do to keep breathing and being what we are. We were running toward our existence with desperate hopes of protecting it. It was all moving too fast.

The sun had set and we weren't far from crossing onto the Outer Banks. There was still an hour or more to drive before we reached the ferry and another hour on the water. Could this really be happening? My friends were dying in the fight for all our lives. How was this right? Oh, how I wished I'd brought them all with us. At least Jenny would still be alive.

"Cole?"

"Uh-huh?" I felt his mumble through his chest, vibrating in my ear.

"Do you pray?"

"What?"

At Ariel's Gate, we had one chapel. It held services for five different religions—Christian, Muslim, Judaism, Hindu, and Buddhism. No student was required to attend any service, but many did. Religion's so confusing to me but what the hell, I'm the freaking spawn of an archangel. A pure Nephilim. War was all around me, killing people I knew and loved. It had to be time to start praying, right? "I asked if you pray?"

"Why?"

"I was sort of hoping you'd teach me how."

He raised his face from the top of my head and sighed. "You're afraid, aren't you?"

"Yes… but aside from that I just think I should pray. How do you pray?"

He shrugged and shifted in the driver's seat, leaned back against the door and watched me. "I just talk to, you know… God."

"Do you? Really?" It wasn't that I didn't believe him, it was that he seemed to not believe himself when he said it.

"When things are really, really bad… when I'm sure my lights are about to go out, when I'm shit-my-pants terrified… yeah, I pray."

I blinked and waited for more.

"I know it sounds like desperation and it is. I always figured real praying was what people do while they're living—picking up groceries, washing dishes, driving to work. Stuff like that. If we do that stuff with a good heart, then," he shrugged, "we're praying. What you're asking me about isn't what I think of as prayer. It's what I think of as… begging."

I smiled and pushed tears away.

"Begging happens when I know I haven't been doing the other stuff, praying while I work or play or whatever. Doing it well and being aware." Another shrug.

"You're a good guy. You must pray all the time."

"No." His head shook and his eyes lowered. "No more. It's a fairy tale. Gracie, I wasn't a good guy, I wasn't even an okay guy. Since Afghanistan I've done a hell of a lot of not-so-good things."

I guess everyone did that. I argued with people, stuck to my guns when it wasn't kind or considerate, been demanding and selfish. "You know what? I like your idea of prayer a lot. I'm going to do that from now on."

"Truth?" He held up a finger. "It's not so damn easy after bad shit comes down on you. It gets harder and harder."

"So, we'll help each other." There. Problem solved, but Cole had left a big door open and I just had to crawl in. "I need you to tell me what happened in Afghanistan."

There, I said it. I didn't even ask, just told him to tell me. I was sure that his nightmares had to do with that experience. I expected him to shut down, start the car and completely ignore me, but his face tightened then relaxed, tightened and relaxed again. I curled my leg under and readied to hear Cole's truth. He did the same, only his body looked far from comfortable. He watched me while I watched him, and in that moment, I knew that what I'd asked would not only be hard for him to tell, but hard for me to hear.

"Two weeks and my tour of duty was done. I was thinking of re-upping. I mean, why not? I felt useful, had friends, a job. Training, too, a little bit of medical training, weapons, some communications, tons of recon. Mostly they trained me to follow orders, no matter how stupid or ridiculous or dangerous they sounded. I wasn't bad at being a Marine. With my range of skills, everyone from a private to an officer needed me for something, had to talk to me, got to know me." He gulped, rolled his neck, and continued. "I was a Devil Dog with wings but no one knew. No one in my platoon, at least.

"Over there, it's what I imagine hell must be like. Two years melting under layers and layers of camo, head to toe. Hot as a furnace all the time, sandstorms, sunburn so bad my face turned blood red, my hair, almost blond.

"All that time, not a scratch, just a mess of lost sleep and heat rash. No Haji ever hurt me. Men fell around me, some seriously wounded, but I always came through unscathed. They called me Superman. For a while, I thought maybe I actually was a superhero. Invincible.

"Promotion was never in the cards for me but that last mission, I was assigned team leader… way above my rank but they knew I was leaving, at least for a while. Maybe it was a test, maybe they figured I could handle something so basic. I knew it was just a token position, but I played it to the hilt."

He actually grunted a dark chuckle that made me shiver.

"It was a simple mercy mission. No kill zone, just a tiny village no one thought important enough to put on a map. Friendly fire destroyed their well… they needed food and water. We carried supplies and tools to clean up the mess and get the well working again. Not a bad way to spend my last few days in uniform. No major assault weapons, just four armed humvees, two supply trucks, eighteen men—one of them, Sergeant Patterson, an engineer. The plan was to get there, fix the well and get back. Two days tops. Quick and easy."

Cole became so silent I reached out and set a hand on his knee.

"You okay?"

He nodded.

"You don't have to do this."

"Yes, I do." A nervous roll of his shoulders and he continued. "Sixty, maybe sixty-five people, mostly kids, women, old men. I would have given anything to have more candy with us. Anything to make those kids smile. Anything. We handed out bottled water and food, worked on the well, almost got it functioning, then… something… I can't explain it but… *something*… told me to look up. A glint of sunlight flashed off a metal surface and I shouted a call for weapons and cleared hot. Too late… too fucking late… we scrambled for cover. It was a fucking firestorm from the rooftops. I tried to reach overwatch, request protective fire but no go, radio was out, blown to smithereens. It was a relentless damn shower of high-powered fire raining down on us. We could barely get our personal weapons active. I led the men to the building ahead, the building where six, maybe seven Hajis blasted bullets down at us. Inside… they actually looked to me… *me*… for orders. I had three men down… then four… twisting in pain and bleeding or motionless in the street. I ordered three men up the steps, and two to slither out the back to climb the two-story structure.

"With the shooters' focus shifted to Marines blasting through windows and doors at them, me and Freddy ran to gather the wounded. One supply truck was shielded by another and our goal was to get the casualties onto the protected vehicle. God, Gracie… kids, women, wounded, dead, littered everywhere. I reached for a toddler but he was already gone, his belly opened and pouring out. We dragged and lifted Marines, did it again and again. I pulled Patterson, my arms under his… he was shot up so bad his left arm actually fell right off. The damn bloody thing just laid there, middle finger shooting the bird at the building. The weirdest thing I ever saw. In the truck he laughed, crazy laughing, hysterical, and pushed himself back to make room for others. 'Sir, you need a tourniquet!' I shouted but he just laughed and waved me off. One of the other wounded was already on it, pulling his belt free to do the job.

"Gracie, I don't fucking know exactly what happened next. It's all a blur. A muddled mess. At one point, I had two dead and fifteen wounded and able Marines inside that truck. I jumped out to get to the wheel and three armed Hajis—one holding one of our own AT4s—came right at us. God, oh damn… God." Tears rolled from his eyes and he gasped several times before he could breathe well enough to continue.

"I took three bullets in my shoulder but I don't remember it. All I remember was opening my arms and spreading my wings so wide it hurt. I was so fucking mad, so pissed, so scared. I begged, I prayed, I hoped for something, anything that could save my team. *Anything.*

"And something happened. Before that bastard could even shoulder the grenade launcher, heat gathered to a ridiculous intensity inside my body, so much heat, so blazing, so painful that for a moment I thought it would consume me. Instead it built and built until it blasted right out of my body… my eyes, my mouth, my fingers, I have no idea how it did that but… but…"

Cole was silent for nearly five full minutes, his eyes closed, his breathing heavy, then slower, and then normal. I sat and watched cars speed past us and I prayed I hadn't done him more damage by making him talk about it than the experience had already caused.

"When I came to myself I'd fallen back onto the truck among the wounded. They were looking at me like I was some kind of monster. Outside, the surviving village people called out and shouted with joy. On the ground lay five Hajis, their flesh, stupid pajamas, and weapons all burned to ash. Ash, Gracie. *Ash.*"

"My God, Cole. What happened? How did you do that?"

He shifted, looked out the window, toward the back of the van, anywhere but at me. "I didn't do it. It was a quickening. It's when we receive gifts… powers. I prayed and help showed up, just not the kind of help I can explain too easily."

"Those Marines must be so glad you were there."

"Ya think? Hell no! Gracie, the private who told the truth about what he saw is still in a mental institution. Maybe they're glad to be alive, but those men can't ever tell a soul how they escaped a killer attack. Someone started passing around the story that I used a weapon, a flamethrower we didn't even have with us, to burn the shooters… but we all know different." He pushed a hand through his hair, finally eyed me and gave a nervous laugh. "They gave me a medal and an honorable discharge with a side note that I wasn't exactly welcome back."

"I'm sorry, Cole. You deserved some kind of thanks. You saved all those lives." I gripped his hand and he squeezed back, still steadying his breathing, still sweating like the mere memory had brought back all that powerful heat.

"Don't need thanks. Peace, I could have used some of that. I've been hiding from this for so long, and now… now… peace is way out of the equation."

My mind slid from his war in the Middle East to our war. "But, okay, so you can really do that? Shoot fire out of your eyes and stuff?" I was amazed. How useful could something like that be against battle-heat demons?

He scratched his head and shrugged. "I don't know. I never tried. Not even the time it happened."

"Maybe you should try. Practice. It's a strong weapon. A really good one."

"It could be, if it keeps itself hidden from the human race. If… and this is a big *if*… I can control it."

I leaned in and kissed his lips. "Cole," I whispered. "You're a hero. I know I'm safe with you."

"Yeah, sure. Now that you know my superpower."

"I always knew I was safe with you."

He kissed me long and soft and I wanted to stay right like that forever, but there was someplace else we had to be.

~*~

I couldn't recall the last time I slept. A little at the table in the dining tent the night we arrived with the Emmaus show? Odd, I wasn't tired at all. I felt alive and strong, ready to face the world, if not the war.

Looking around I shook my head, perplexed by the number of battle-heat demons riding the ferry with us. Not one turned our way, not one seemed to give a crap that we were even there. They seemed obsessively determined to get where they were going. I counted a hundred and three, and each melded being represented two or more single demons. They settled on top of vehicles, under them, perched on the railings, and slithered along the passengers strolling the deck. They were ugly, but more than that, alarmingly close. We could smell the burned odor of their flesh through our closed windows. Every one of them dripped hideous black slime the humans on the ferry couldn't see. Each one of them looked toward the island. My poor Ocracoke. The place was only a nine-and-a-half-mile land mass. Where were they all going? How could so many of them converge there? We'd seen thousands of them since leaving camp. It was like a demon convention. At times, the road was black with them. Now the ferry was covered with them. I felt antsy and irritated at once. Why now? Why me? Why war?

"We really need a lot of recruits." I marveled. There were so many of the enemy. Was that the reason I needed to go home? Were Cole and I supposed to fight all those demons? Hold them off until Tobias arrived with more warriors? Of course, how could we fight them when they didn't even acknowledge we were there? I tried so hard not to be horrified, to not make anger my shield against it. "What are we supposed to do here?"

"No clue. We'll figure it out. We'll get some kind of guidance. All I know is I'm supposed to help you and here I am, your personal superhero."

I watched the ferrymen tie the craft in place while demons leapt and scrambled off, brushing past them, completely unseen. We drove along the road, seeking a room for rent. It was past eleven and most lights were out in the B&Bs we passed. "Maybe we can just crash in the van tonight," he suggested.

"Oh!" I pointed. "Turn here and follow that road." So much had changed. New buildings, new roads, tourism development. Around the bend were several pubs and bars, outside seating full and noisy with night life I didn't expect for such a sleepy island so late in October. A lot was different but enough was the same and my photographic memory pinged. We drove to a split in the road. "Left." Then another. "Right."

At the clearing Cole stopped and leaned on the wheel. "This is where you wanted to go?"

The moon was full, the sky clear, and everything was visible. Well, at least everything that wasn't there anymore. "This used to be a beautiful, happy, vibrant little community," I whispered. "Lots of women, lots of kids. Tiny houses all around this area." I waved a hand to the right then climbed out of the van. Cole came to my side, already playing the protector, but there wasn't one demon anywhere in sight. Where did they all go?

I looked around. "Back there is a weeping willow tree. Super old. Massive. I remember we used to gather there… sit in the shade. The women would talk, and laugh, and we kids would play. It was so safe here. No one from town bothered us. They never even came around."

"Gracie, do you know what this was?" He did a slow spin on his heel, taking it all in.

"Home."

"More than that. Sweetheart, this was one of our breeding colonies. You felt safe… no one bothered you… because this place was celestially protected."

"Not anymore," I sighed, spying the overgrown weedy gardens and shabby ruins, broken down fences that once held a milk cow, baby goats, chickens. My memory played the sounds of them, the music of them, the thrum of their lives. All gone. I also recalled the lovely faces of the women, one of them my mother. Also, all gone.

There was one house still standing, a soft light glowed from a window. Rather than drive up and possibly frighten whoever lived there, we decided to walk. I recited the names of the herbs from the healer's now defunct garden, recalled the game we played near the pond, how I was afraid of the big white geese. How beautiful my life once was.

Just as I reached for the gate, we turned, startled. A vehicle rushed toward us, horn blasting as it slid to an abrupt stop dangerously close to the wobbly fence. We jumped back and Cole pulled me close.

It was a grimy army-green Jeep with a sign painted on the driver's door. *Hell to Pay Pub*, it said in artfully dripping blood-red paint arched above the classic skull and crossbones. The door flew open and a young woman, her hair short, spiky, fuchsia and bright blue, shouted at the top of her lungs. "Who the hell are you and what are you doing here?"

"Uh…" I started but Cole stepped in front of me.

"You first," he growled like a bear. "Who the hell are you?"

The woman, around my age, was tattooed and pinned everywhere. I lost count of how many rings pierced her ears. One looped through her nose, another spiked her lip and when she spoke, I could swear a glint reflected from something silver stuck through her tongue. She gave a snort and actually stepped up, nose to nose with Cole.

"My name's Esther and I fucking belong here. You don't. Get that damn van off my property." Her eye slipped a critical glower at me. "And take Molly Sweetbreads with you."

I felt Cole tighten. Felt him shiver. Felt him actually melt.

"What?" I stepped out from behind my hero and looked into his eyes. They were locked on Esther.

"What the—" He looked at me, then her, then back again. "Gracie, don't you see?"

I shook my head, but Esther gasped, glared at me harder then opened her mouth. For a full minute she said nothing, her eyes scanning every inch of me… and I retreated behind the wall that is Cole.

"Oh hell." She shook her head and walked a full circle around us, staring at me the whole time. My heart raced, sensing something sinister. Her next words changed my whole world.

"Well… welcome home, sis. I guess you want to come in. Cia probably has some dinner left over. I suppose you two want a bed." She turned and opened the gate.

"Wait!" I felt breathless, like I'd just run a marathon. "What do you mean? I remember everything, I mean *everything*! I don't have a sister."

She turned with a huff, crossed her arms and gave me a look that could melt steel. "Yeah, yeah, I know… you're the twin with the photographic memory, but I'm the twin with the power to wipe whatever I want from that memory. God, I should have recognized you from that foot. Whatever. Come on in."

Cole stood like a stone pillar, his hand still holding mine, eyes still shifting back and forth from her to me. I kicked his shin, hard. "Uh, yeah, okay."

Esther turned a luring glance his way. "We haven't had a strapping Norema around here in years and years. Cia will be thrilled for the company." She walked across the small overgrown yard and into the house, leaving the front door wide open.

"I… I… I don't understand? She's lying. I don't have a sister… a twin."

"Good God, Gracie. Just look at her face. Except for her hair, the shitty personality, those demonic tattoos and piercings… you two are identical. Absolutely identical!"

I didn't see it. What I did see at the doorway was beautiful Cia, a well remembered woman I now knew to be an ancient. She was old in my memories and even older now. She'd lived with us all in this strange place, perpetually wearing a brightly colored tie-dyed skirt just like the one she wore now. I recalled her making those skirts for our mothers. The playful image of brilliant dyed fabric floating and dancing from fences, clotheslines, trees and bushes made me smile. Her expression was joyful, welcoming, and combined with the aroma of pot roast, like a magnet drawing me into her outstretched arms.

Behind her stood Esther, checking the chips in her black nail polish. My gut knotted. Something felt so right yet so very, *very* wrong… like I'd fallen into a parallel universe. I had a twin sister? Growing up at the Gate and believing I was an orphan, all alone in the whole world, was a lie. I had a sister. A twisted, rather odd sister, but a sister all the same. I should have been jumping for joy but I wasn't. I was so pissed off I wanted to scratch out her eyes, maybe take a brutal tug on some of her earrings. Of course, none of that was going to happen anytime soon, at least not until I was less afraid of her. Esther was one scary gal. She smelled like whiskey, dressed like… well, a hooker, and looked like she hadn't washed off her eyeliner for three days. Jenny would be appalled. I was appalled. Cole… well he was curious, eyeing her every minute she wasn't eyeing him. Thank heaven for Cia.

"Sit, sit, oh my dear, my dear sweet Gracie! Look at you!" She took my hands in hers and stood back. I remembered those warm golden-brown eyes, the way she made me feel. Special. Important. Loved. She shook her head, wiped tears away on a dish towel then turned to the stove. "Gracie, you are lovely. You look so much like your mother!"

I glanced at Esther, slouched at the kitchen table and flipping through screens on her cell phone. My guess was that she wasn't checking the weather. Leaning close to Cole, I whispered, "Who does *she* look like?"

"Beelzebub?"

Score. He still preferred me. Thank heaven. For a moment there, I was terrified he'd choose Esther over me. Of course, I'd had the same thought about Dawn back at camp. I really needed to keep this girlfriend jealousy stuff under control. Cole chose me then. He still chooses me. I grinned.

Loaded plates of comfort food far better than I remembered were set in front of us. "You're not eating, Cia?"

"No, no, Gracie. Enjoy. I ate much earlier." She sat across from us, her hands gnarled and calm, settled on the table.

Her smile was radiant and I hated to ask but I had to know. "What happened here?"

Esther snorted, took her plate into the living room and turned on the TV. Fine by me, she gave me the creeps.

Cia patted my hand and looked to a faraway place beyond the old house. Her eyes became glassy and she sniffled softly.

"The decision to send you away was so difficult. None of us wanted to separate you girls. It broke your Father's heart to see it happen but… he tipped the scales when he told us you would have important work to do. The decision had to be made. Poor Natalia was the least sick. She chose to take you to the orphanage. She died coming home. I never saw her again.

"Oh, my dear, it was so awful. All the mothers died first. One after the other in quick succession. The pain, the cough, the terrible fever. I could do nothing to help. Nothing. A week after you left, the children started to fall ill. I watched them die. Buried most of them myself. To protect Esther, I took her someplace safe and checked on her every hour. Every single hour… and she survived."

"Someplace safe?" Where could it be safe from a deadly disease? Where could she hide a child and still check on her every hour?

Cia nodded. "It was a risk but I had no other choice. Esther lived for six months on the other side of the portal." The last few words were whispered.

Cole and I straightened, setting aside our dinner.

"Portal? There's a portal? To where?" Cole ran a hand across his mouth, his eyes intense.

"Yes," Cia said with a sigh. "I know what's going on. So many of them, all going through. Once, it was the safest place short of Ariel's Gate for a child destined to be pure Nephilim. Now, it is a place crammed full of demons. War is coming."

"Oh jeez, enough with that crap!" shouted Esther and she turned the volume louder.

I turned to Cole and he blinked. Good God, of course. A war couldn't be waged on tiny Ocracoke. It couldn't be raged with humans around. There had to be another place. A portal to the battlefield. "Show me," I demanded but Cia shook her head.

"It's far too dangerous to go anywhere near there."

"Cia, we came across on the ferry with over a hundred battle-heat demons. They didn't even look at us."

Her eyes narrowed. "I see. Well, that's a focused determination I've never seen in the enemy before. They're all thinking the exact same thing. Following one order."

I stood. "Please, show us the portal."

"Not tonight. You're so tired." Her eyes shot to the noisy living room. "Best to do that tomorrow, when it's more… quiet."

Cole nodded agreement then shoveled a forkful of mashed potatoes into his mouth. Maybe it was a guy thing. Maybe it was a Marine thing. Eat while you can. Me? I'd lost my appetite.

We were shown to two bedrooms, Cia carefully wording her offer. We could choose one. And I wondered, one for us both? Or one room each? Living with Esther might have given her the impression all girls were like that. I picked the yellow room. Cole chose the blue one right next door. It was so late and the exhaustion I thought I was immune from, finally caught up. Maybe the shock of having an evil twin was just too much. I slipped between the blankets and fell asleep almost immediately.

~*~

Cole considered skipping out and exploring, maybe locating the portal himself, but the ancient insisted on waiting until Esther wasn't around. They might learn a lot more from Cia without Beelzebub hovering. Sleep played at the corners of his thoughts and he relaxed into the soft mattress. He wondered if Esther was abusing the old lady. He wondered if the portal was where he'd have his second quickening. He wondered if there was garlic in the pot roast. He wondered if Gracie was still afraid of geese. He wondered himself into a deep, silent, and dreamless sleep.

Until a sensation triggered a dream he couldn't quite define. A touch. Not soft, not loving, not even compassionate. A shove, a push. Then erotic pleasure washed over him, leaving him to shiver with sweat. He pushed back, he rolled, he grunted.

"Come on, big boy. I'm not prissy like my sister. You can be rough. I like it rough."

Cole's eyes shot open. This time his push was violent, thrusting Esther from his body as he leapt to stand several feet away. It was one swift, desperate movement that left him coiled and ready to strike. "What the fuck?"

"Cole!" Gracie's voice? Gracie's voice!

Good God, he prayed. *Please let this be a nightmare.* It wasn't. Gracie stood at the open door, her face red with so much shock and disgust he could hardly breathe. It felt like a slam to the chest.

"Gracie, sweetheart. Listen—"

Esther laughed hard and rough, stood naked as a jay bird and strolled out of the room, pushing Gracie into the wall as she passed.

"Gracie, listen. Please!"

She left too, feet thumping on the wooden floor. Grabbing jeans and doing the *holy-shit-what-the-hell-did-I-do* dance to get into them, he raced to follow her. Out onto the porch and into the coming dawn. The moon lay low in the western sky, shedding little light. He couldn't make out Gracie's expression, but her body language told the whole story. She stood at the edge of the garden, fists tight, shoulders squared, physically hating him, sending fevered vibrations through the air. He was almost afraid to approach but his feet had another plan and charged ahead. "Gracie," he yelled, afraid she'd melt into the trees, alone, unprotected. She didn't move.

"How? How could you do that?" she whispered with her back to him, but he heard every word. Birds began to chirp their morning greetings until she shouted louder, "How could you?"

"Gracie, I didn't… I mean… good God, Gracie, you know I wouldn't…"

"What? Betray me? Screw someone else? I don't know why not. I didn't offer so what the hell, sell your soul to the she-devil down the hall. Obviously, *she* offered. Whatever. See if I care!" She turned to leave but he gripped her wrist.

"Don't touch me!"

He snapped his hand back but moved closer. "Please, sweetheart. I did not do this."

She blinked. "Then who was in your body… *inside hers?*"

Cole swallowed hard and pushed his hair back. The morning chill raced through his bare chest and shoulders. He needed her warmth. He needed Gracie.

Tears soaked her face but she had enough anger to hurt him if she wanted to. It felt like the coming dawn, the waking birds, the entire universe, had stilled to see what would come next.

"Gracie, please. Just let me explain—"

"There's nothing to explain. She thought she'd take something from me but the joke's on her. It was never mine to take. Now she can have it."

The words stung worse than a slap, worse than death. "Gracie, please…" He'd begun to ache, imagining she'd never understand, never know the truth, never forgive him.

"I want you to leave. I don't want you anywhere near me. I can do whatever I have to do myself."

"No."

"Go away!"

"No!"

Then it came, the quickening he feared. Pain blasted like a slow rolling thunder and crawled from his core to his flesh. It tingled along his skin then moved deeper again, into his muscles, weakening him until he cried out and collapsed.

"Stop that," Gracie crouched down and hissed. "Stop! I'm not interested in your dramatics, Cole. Just get up and go away!" But she didn't stand, didn't leave. She remained close, so close he could almost feel her heat.

Almost. So much was happening inside his body. What was real and what wasn't smeared into distortion. He couldn't speak or move, except to writhe with agony. Limbs trembled and curled unnaturally. His heart prepared to explode. In a flash, sensations altered. All the pain, all the intensity, all the uncontrolled motion tightened into a knot… then, with agonizing slowness, dissolved into a pinpoint and moved to his eyes. He breathed, lay in a fetal position, eyes squeezed tight.

"Stop this. You're scaring me, Cole."

He heard that. His heart rate smoothed, his body relaxed. She still cared. There was still hope. "It's okay. I'm okay." He didn't recognize his own voice so he cleared his throat and said it again. Still his ears seemed to deceive him. With great effort, his hands pushed himself up. He sat, his jeans wet from the morning dew, his heart trembling but strong.

"Good, now leave."

He opened his eyes and looked into hers, unbearably close, concerned, hurt. "No."

Gracie backed away. "What happened to your eyes?"

His eyes? It all went to his eyes. He stood and wobbled a moment, then looked around. Nothing was as it should be. It was all there, the trees, the house, beautiful Gracie, but it was more. So much more. Every living thing glowed, enrobed in light and color. He blinked, blinked again, and looked to Gracie.

"Your eyes look… different."

"How?" He needed to know.

"Darker. Deeper. Not right."

He blinked, looked around again. The sunrise was brilliant and he could have marveled at it forever. Gracie's voice had light, her energy sparked like electricity. Her anger. Her concern. Her confusion. All of it had brilliance.

"Hey, lovebirds!" Esther called from her Jeep. "Off to work. Now you two have a good day."

She drove off, spewing small rocks and sandy soil at them as she passed. Cole swung to Gracie. "Did you see that?"

She stepped back, waved a hand and refreshed her anger. "Just leave."

"Did… you… see… that?" His voice was forceful and still not fully his own but it caught her attention.

"See what?"

"At Esther's chest. Did you see it?"

Gracie blinked confusion.

He gazed at her chest, a glow as bright as the sun. He looked down at his own, a golden orange radiating from his flesh. He pointed. "Look here. What do you see?" He knew she could see the lights newly revealed to him. He'd watched her search for them at camp. Wondered what she was seeing.

"So?" she said, hissing poison at him. "We all have a light there."

"Did you see Esther's light?"

Gracie blinked, glancing in the direction of the long-gone Jeep.

"Did you see it last night? At all?"

"She must have a light. We all have…"

He let her think for a moment. "She doesn't have one, Gracie."

"She's pure Nephilim. I saw her wings. How could she not have a light? What does that mean?"

He reached for her hand and she pulled away.

Looking into his face she sharply turned away. "Your eyes are so strange."

"Sorry. Gracie, I see things I never saw before. Yes, the lights… but so much more. Don't you realize what Esther is?"

She tilted her head, scowled.

"She's demon."

A laugh burst from her. "Wow, I guess a guy will say anything when he gets busted but… a demon? Enough! Just get away from me!" She walked further from the house and he followed.

"Gracie!"

"Leave!"

Like a pulsing thud, he was called to a dark blue glow in the woods to their right. He could convince her of his new quickening power. If she'd only listen, he could show her. "The portal is over there."

She turned and grimaced, having once again looked into his eyes. "How do you know? Pillow talk?"

What else could he do? How could he persuade her? "I can see it, calling to us. It has a blue light."

She rolled her eyes and he realized it was time to give up. He could try again later, when she was more willing to listen. If that time ever came. "Or… I see the portal." He felt defeated and was sure he sounded it, too.

"Children!" Cia called, walking toward them. "Would you like breakfast?" She came closer, noticed their stance, their energy, then Cole's eyes which caused her to step back. Oddly enough, she then bowed. "Honor to your quickening, Cole."

"Don't encourage him." Gracie turned away, swiping tears away.

"Don't be like Esther, my dear. Now, would you two like breakfast before we leave for the portal?"

Gracie smirked. "And just where is that portal?"

"Well," Cia handed Cole a tee-shirt and his boots. "There are two that I know of. One to the south, just past town and offshore."

Gracie snorted.

"But the one I used to keep Esther safe is right over there. Can't you see the blue light, dear?"

Gracie huffed and Cia winked at Cole.

"Fine, let's go. Cole's leaving."

"No dear, he's not. You need each other. It's time to grow up, Gracious Caine. Follow me." Cia lifted her bright colored skirt a little, exposing brown hiking boots, and led the way. Gracie followed and Cole took up the rear, still a little wobbly, still getting used to his altered vision, still curious as to what it was for, and still guarding Gracie.

It was very close, a slice in time and space right in the middle of a tiny grove of peach trees. Gracie reached out with her hand but Cia tugged it away.

"There's much you need to know about this portal before you can breach it… if it's even wise to attempt to do so. Come!" She whispered the last word and they all slipped back into the shadows. Fifteen tangled battle-heat demons trudged right through the brilliant dark blue light and disappeared.

"Where are they going?" Gracie again moved closer to explore, this time not reaching to penetrate it. "What are they doing in there?"

Cia lead them away. "It's a massive field."

"A battlefield."

"Yes. *The* battlefield. I have been watching demons enter for almost three years. There must be millions of them."

"Millions?"

"I can't be sure, but I do know there are many such portals all over the world. It's possible the enemy has been using them all… if they know about them."

"Many portals? How do you know?" Cole chimed in and Gracie shot him a wicked glare.

"Well children, that's a long story I'll be happy to tell you over a nice hot breakfast."

18

Now I understand how deserted and betrayed Jenny felt when Ryan disappeared on her. How did she forgive him? My heart hurt so bad I could hardly function. I totally understand why they call it a *broken* heart when this kind of thing happens. It was more than just seeing Cole with Esther. Like that. Doing that. It was the loss of my heart, my protector, all my trust. Sitting across the table from him even hurt.

His eyes had drastically changed. They were disturbing and different and just too hard to look at. Cole's eyes used to be so beautiful, a nice light grey, sometimes blue, sparkly. Now they were deep blue and circled with a strange ring of silver that seemed to glow. It made his whole face different. He looked at things the way a bird might—focusing, waiting, analyzing, then moving on or reacting. It was almost robotic. Would it change as he got used to seeing the things he saw? I hoped so, but it really didn't matter. I didn't want him around me anymore. I couldn't hurt like this and fight a war. I just plain couldn't.

I scooped scrambled eggs and listened to Cia hum a melody while she pulled hot biscuits from the oven. Butter melted, the scent of bacon everywhere, homemade strawberry jam. Half of me was thrilled to be home, but the other half trembled with terror at what lay ahead. I'd really be doing this alone now, whatever it was. If Cole could get his damn quickening, why the hell couldn't I get information about my mission? What on earth was I supposed to do?

Cia sat and ate with us, babbling about how the peach trees used to bear the best fruit before the demons started passing through the grove, how the village had changed, how Esther grew up.

Cole wiped his mouth with a napkin and kept watching me. I couldn't look back. His eyes creeped me out and I just didn't want to acknowledge him. All I wanted was revenge. To hurt him as badly as he'd hurt me. How could he do that? I prepared to stand and leave but his next words stopped me cold.

"Cia," he said so softly. "About Esther. She's demon. How did that happen?"

Cia's hands were soft, the flesh wrinkled like crepe paper. They trembled like frightened birds as she twisted them together. Her sweet eyes poured tears and I hated Cole even more for asking the question.

"I don't know where I went wrong," she whispered. "Esther was such a good girl. I've raised hundreds of children and she was perfectly normal. The terrible twos don't bother me, I'm aware of adolescent antics, and understand that the teen years are difficult for everyone involved. But… Esther… my dear Esther… she has been voluntarily blood vowed to the dark since her thirteenth year. I talked, I argued, I rationalized, I begged… I did everything I could think of to help her pull from that hateful vow but…" Cia sobbed and I rubbed her trembling shoulder. "This is her choice."

She drew in a long, deep breath, letting it out as though she'd just relieved herself of a massive burden. "This is worse than just one child's misguided choice. Those demons are following a command."

"Whose command?" Cole beat me to the punch.

Man, scowling was starting to make my face ache but everything about him pissed me off. I wanted to ask that question. I guess we were still on the same page. We'd just never be in the same bed. An invisible fist tightened around my heart. We'd never be lovers, never be together. Never be anything to each other now. I felt myself go pale and sipped water. Cia took a while before responding, like she was waiting for my undivided attention. Holy crap, I had to focus. Another reason Cole had to leave.

"There is only one who can command demons. Only… one."

I blinked, looked to Cole who was holding his breath.

"L-Lucifer." His voice was a choke.

Great. Just great. Another new dilemma. There was a devil? Really? I wish I'd have stepped into that chapel once in a while. The archangels we were taught about at the Gate—the ones that guarded us in stone and marble form—all seemed more like comic book monsters than reality. The whole world had taken on a different shape. There were angels, there were demons, and now there was a Lucifer. What else could get piled on?

Cia nodded and leaned back in her chair. "The imbalance is reaching its limit. Nephilim and demons are to gather and be counted. Battle if need be. End… if they all fail. The battle-heat enemy has been called to fight a war.

"But… the portals, you wanted to know about the portals." She cleared dishes from the table and sat again, watching us both with intensity. "What I know is valuable information. Vital. It can greatly help the Nephilim cause. But…" and her glare was more substantial than mine by a mile. "You two must hear and digest it together so that you can use it together. I do not fully understand your joint role in this, but I clearly understand that it must be managed as one. Do you understand?"

Cole nodded but I shook my head. "No, I don't understand. He can do what he did and I'm supposed to—"

"Rise above," Cia said with the voice of a disciplinarian.

I felt insulted. I'm a grown woman and I can choose who I want to hang out with and who I don't, right? Wrong. I wasn't actually that grown up or I wouldn't need to be spoken to like that. I wasn't a grown woman or a grown pure Nephilim… not yet, not until I understood everything I needed to understand. I could get way ahead of the curve if I could just get past this aching heart. The problem was that I didn't want to get past it. The pain was all consuming and forced me to see what I almost had, what I'd lost in the blink of an eye. Rise above? How could I do that? I wanted him to leave, but inside my soul, in the deepest part of my being, I knew that I couldn't be far from him. This was a major dilemma for my shattered heart.

I looked into Cia's beautiful eyes. "How does a person rise above?"

"A person rises above by putting her critical responsibilities ahead of her heart."

How? It really didn't matter, I had to do it. "Fine. Done. But you," I pointed at Cole, refusing to make eye contact, "stay away from me."

"I can do that."

I could feel the pain in his voice and felt bad about it. Then I remembered him and Esther, naked and… "Good," I spat. "Now, about those portals, Cia?"

Her head shifted from Cole to me and back like she was watching a tennis match. Finally, she acknowledged the truce and moved on.

"Children, an ancient is perpetually drawn to the Nephilim race. We offer much… historic reference, knowledge of the world beyond the Nephilim's experience, even talents and powers outside of the celestial range."

I relaxed in my chair, still feeling the dragging pull from Cole across the table. Ignoring it, and him, I listened to what promised to be a fascinating story.

"A long time ago, in the 1700s, I lived a rather different life. I was here on Ocracoke, a survivor from an English ship, wrecked in a terrible storm a half-century earlier. There were twenty-two of us. I watched every other survivor age and die, age and die, and feared I would forever live alone on this tiny island. Then came a man. A large man. A dangerous man who was also a substantially empowered Norema. His name was Edward Teach and he was a pirate. They called him Blackbeard."

I perked up. Was this going to be another fairy tale? "Cia, you sailed with a pirate?"

"Yes."

"I'm supposed to believe that?"

"Yes."

"But—"

Cole huffed a sigh. "Gracie, just let her talk."

I wanted to jump out of my skin. "You can sit here, but don't think you can tell me what to do."

Cole gave as good as he got. "I can and I will tell you what to do when it's important. Dammit, Gracie. You've been winged less than a week. Use your head. I'm trying to help you. Cia's trying to teach you. She's trying to help *us*."

I felt everything collapse into my middle. All I wanted to do was hide somewhere and cry for a few days but there wasn't time. Lucifer's minions were gathering for war and we were way behind the headcount. We'd be annihilated if we couldn't level the battlefield. I wanted time to cry and be hurt but that wasn't in the cards. No time for a broken heart or dealing with loss. No time. No time. "I'm sorry. Please go on, Cia."

"I sailed with a pirate. I was his lover for a while. I gave birth to a girl child, but it was wrong, twisted, too ill to survive her first week. He loved me well, but mostly I was his helper, his guide, his healer."

I marveled. What must it be like to be an ancient and witness so much, live so long, so fully?

"He stole and he killed but what many do not know about Edward was that he worked hard to maintain the balance. He built a pirate community here on Ocracoke, all Nephilim, although he purposely chose lower Nephilim, knowing they were less likely to oppose him or mutiny. His life was rough and harsh but much of it focused on the balance and the Nephilim's duty to the human race and the planet.

"Edward did one thing all of the Nephilim race will thank him for one day, but only if… only if…" Cia glanced out the window, seeing her handsome pirate off in the distance, no doubt.

"It's said that Blackbeard buried his treasure on Ocracoke and he did. It was not gold doubloons, pieced of eight, and gems. It's something else, something far more valuable." She looked around suspiciously then leaned in and spoke softly. "Edward located the two portals here on Ocracoke and a hundred more on the other side. He explored them and discovered that through those gates, he could travel vast distances in a very short time. So many places, so much of the world was revealed to him… Africa, Australia, Europe, Siberia, the Arctic and Antarctic circles. For years he learned from Nephilim wherever he traveled and meticulously recorded it all… portal locations, where they led, what one might find there, everything… in several handwritten books and meticulously drawn maps. His primary concern was helping one navigate the massive field just past the portal notch. There are vast dangers with venturing too deep into the openness, as Lucifer had already commandeered most of the space as his own. Safe passages to the next portal, and the next, and more are all outlined to assist the Nephilim lucky enough to find those books and maps. That, my children, is the treasure.

"Maintaining his pirate persona was fun for him… he had a deliciously wicked side… and it hid his true intentions from the demons his crew often fought. He orchestrated the rumor of buried treasure and let it loose on the world as he prepared to die. It was a bloody battle, November, not far off shore… exactly the kind of thing he loved most. Edward was most alive when he was closest to death."

Cia fell silent and Cole sipped coffee. I tried hard to digest what I just heard. A pirate? Hidden buried treasure? "Seriously?" The word escaped my mouth completely unchecked.

Cia tilted her head, eyes narrow and angry. "You have a question, Gracious Caine?"

Oh-oh. My full name. Now I was in trouble. "It's just… is there really a buried treasure? I mean, it's a small island, every inch of it must have been dug up looking for Blackbeard's famous buried treasure, right? Did he really bury it here? Where?"

"You tell me, girly." Cole almost growled his words. Called me 'girly,' too.

I really must be in trouble. "I'm just asking."

Cole set down his mug with a thud. "Think about it. If you lived here, if you were a pirate and knew about those portals… where the hell would you bury a treasure?"

Good God, how could I be so stupid? "On the other side!" I stood. "I need to get it. I need those books and maps!" I headed for the door, barely escaping Cole's grip and moving as fast as my signature hobble could carry me.

"Stop! Where the hell do you plan to look?"

I swung around long enough for he and Cia to catch up. I was suddenly winged and my feet were toe wigglingly perfect. I could outrun Cia and out-fly Cole. "I know exactly where to look! It has to be where you kept Esther safe. Right?"

"And where is that, young lady?" Cia was really, really mad at me. She stepped closer.

"I don't know but it can't be far. It has to be a protected area so I'll be just fine." And without warning my wings withered and I stood on twisted foot. My false confidence was unable to keep me celestial. No matter, I turned and ran as best I could.

"Stop!" Cole shouted but I sprinted, a hop-drag, hop-drag toward the peach grove.

Suddenly I felt a hard, vice-like grip on my upper arm and was swung around. It wasn't Cole facing me, it was a fire-eyed ancient, bound and determined to keep me from going through that portal. Damn, she was strong for an old woman. "Let me go! I'll find it! I will!"

"No, you won't. I have not, nor will I, tell you where it is until I know you've received your directive." She bellowed in a voice I remembered her using only once before, while chasing a few boys who'd knocked over her clothesline and ruined her wash.

"A directive?" I spoke quietly, hoping to soothe her anger so that she'd loosen her grip. I could already feel bruises blooming on my arm.

"Yes. There is something you… and him," she jerked her chin toward Cole who looked ready to leap to my rescue if she got any more violent, "are supposed to do. It's time for you to receive that directive!" And she literally, I mean *literally*, dragged me, my feet and knees sliding along the dirt, into the distance.

Cole moved to her shoulder. "Cia… Cia, I know she can be frustrating but she'll cooperate. Come on, no need for this."

She shot him a glare that made him shrink back, but only for a second.

"Cia, let her walk."

"She needs to get her directive and she needs to do so before she does something terribly dangerous… dangerous to your entire race, not just her selfish self."

I scrambled to get my footing, worried that she'd break my arm, sure that I wasn't going to like wherever she was dragging me. When she suddenly came to a stop, Cole again attempted to intervene for me.

"Cia, please."

She pointed ahead. "To ease your mind, Cole, you go in and make sure it's safe. See that this is a good place for our little Gracie to sit and think for a while. Maybe even pray."

Pray. Yes, I needed to pray, or maybe it was actually some begging I needed to do. I climbed to my feet and saw where she'd sent Cole. It was the tree. The big, wonderful weeping willow tree. I pulled at Cia's fingers with my other hand and she freed me. Gazing at the place I'd known since childhood as comfort and safety, I rubbed my reddened skin and waited for Cole to return.

He walked a slow pace around the tree several times, examined the ground, the drooping branches above, the raised roots around the base. At one point his entire body, wings and all, were hidden behind the girth of that ancient trunk. He stepped up to Cia and nodded solemnly.

Ah, so they were in this together? Heat rose into my face but then it subsided. What was I thinking? Nothing meant more to me than learning what was expected of me. Not even Cole meant more than saving the Nephilim race.

Whatever I could figure out under that tree—even if it was nothing more than the fact that I'm a silly lovesick idiot—would be valuable. A little downtime would actually be nice.

"Okay, okay." I looked up into Cia's eyes and tried to smile. "I'm sorry. I'm just so scared, so confused… so hurt." From the corner of my vision I could see Cole's body roll in on itself. He was hurting, too. "I guess I do need a time out."

"More than that, you need a time in." Cia held out her hand and I moved toward the tree.

Just beneath the first outreached limb I sensed something happening. It was like walking through a wall of warm water. Past that was comfort and light. As though the leaves were made of cut crystal, slivers of color caught and dispersed brilliance everywhere. And I remembered that, too. The magic tree. The place of real and pure safety. If the long-ago community was once celestially protected, then that tree was still protected. But the magic of it wasn't there when Cole circled it. The magic had just happened.

Outside my bright little environment, I heard Cole cry out. "Is she safe? Damn it Cia, is she safe?"

"I'm safe," I whispered and walked all the way around the magic tree. My fingertips trailed along rough bark as the sunshine created a million colors to dance and flash all around. Calm and happy for the first time all day, the first time in a long, long time. I settled, cross legged at base of the mammoth trunk. "Hello," I said softly, patting the beloved trunk. "I have missed you."

"And I have missed you," came an answer that shot me to my feet with an unladylike yelp.

19

t was a man's disembodied voice, deep and rich and heated on the breeze around me. I was so scared I think I peed my pants. Just a little bit. I was more concerned about panic taking over and making me do something really stupid, like scream for help. Wings unfurled for the second time and the hair on top of my head tangled in the leaves before I realized I was aloft. Deep breaths. Deep breaths. Finally, I lowered to the ground, regretting that my foot would return to its tight twisted state and I wouldn't be able to run fast if I needed to.

I gulped air. Breathed again and again. "Who are you?" That's when I got my second jolt of weirdness. The man spoke in that strange language I didn't know, the one droning on and on inside my head since my awakening. The odd, musical language had become a background sound, playing constantly under everything. He spoke it softly all the time.

Now, I understood him.

I felt my heart race and spun a full circle, looking up and wondering why this Nephilim thing had to be so damn scary. "Who are you?" I asked again, this time careful to speak plain old English.

"Don't be afraid."

"Too late."

"I am sorry."

"Listen buddy, if you can speak English, why have you been babbling that other language all this time?" Yeah, anger gave me courage. Go figure. "Answer me! Who are you?"

"My name is Metatron. I am the scribe writing the book you have been studying. I am impressed with your ability to comprehend."

"Uh… thanks." I was still too shaken to sit so I stood, twirling, looking up into the billion leaves, flashing colors down at me.

"The language is the old words. I'm sentimental. I like it, and now you can understand and speak it with me."

"Okay… Metatron, why the book? Why keep changing the message? And why can I read it?"

There was a moment of silence and I felt a wash of gentle calm come over me. I sat and leaned back against the tree, waited, determined to be a little less demanding and a lot less angry. I wished I could see this archangel the way I got to see Raphael. His voice was pleasant, patient, it danced with all the colors glowing around me.

"You can read the book because I wish you to know my advice and instructions. So far, it's been nothing but simple symbols, some even Masters and Allerton can decipher, but soon only you will understand the messages."

"Why? What's the book for?"

"Assistance for the children of my brothers… assistance to you, my beautiful, brilliant daughter."

I felt his words swell in my heart. A scent came to me, a clean crisp scent close to my nose as I, a mere infant, had laid my head on his shoulder. "Daddy," I whispered.

"I am here Gracie. I am always here."

Holy crap, all I wanted to do was revel in the news. I wasn't an orphan. My mother may have died but my father, Metatron, has always been with me. "You have two daughters." I cringed, thinking of Esther's tattoos, especially the one on her rounded rear.

"I have two living daughters, but I have had a hundred Nephilim children over the centuries. All are gone, except for you and Esther."

"Yeah, what happened to her? Why's she so… so…" I needed a nice way to say evil. He saved me from finding one.

"Esther has chosen her path. She's chosen the dark."

"You don't sound too upset about it."

"How can I be? You and Esther are half human. You have been given free will."

I sat and twisted a strand of grass around my finger. "But why did she go that way? How could she do… the things she does?"

"Gracie my dear… use that miraculous brain of yours. Balance. The Nephilim existence is all about balance. When twins were born to Aisha and me, it was always understood that one would choose the dark."

"My mother's name was Aisha?"

"It was. And I loved her well. When the disease came and readied to take her I chose to send you away for protection in a place surrounded by the light. I knew that my beloved Esther would be cared for in the portal, and Cia diligently did so. All is as it was meant to be."

"And was Esther supposed to seduce… never mind. *Never mind.*" My head filled with images of Cole, eating with us all in the cabin kitchen, guiding me through my acclimation, into my awakening. Protecting me, supporting me, touching me, lips to lips. Touching Esther. I gasped a sudden sob and covered my face.

"Esther sits at the side of my brother, The Morning Star. Her actions are at his bidding."

"Or… maybe she just hates me because you sent me someplace safe?"

"Esther never hated you. She loves you still. I know you do not remember, but you cried bitterly as we prepared you to leave her, struggling to grip her hands and never be parted. Esther used her power and did the only thing her five-year-old mind could think of to comfort you. She wiped all memory of her from your mind. It was the first and last time she used that power. Lucifer has commanded that she wipe all memory of the gateway portals from Cia's memory but Esther has feigned an inability. To protect her, I have taken that power from her and put it in a safe place. She may need it one day, should the balance be regained."

I huffed, picked a few more blades of grass and chewed on my lip.

"You must forgive him, Gracie. He has suffered greatly in his life, all to be brought to your side."

"That's not my fault."

"It is the fault of us all, my daughter. The grandson of Makha'el will suffer even more to protect you and regain the balance."

"Please, I don't want him to suffer." *Even if his granddad is the archangel of battle. Even if he did screw my sister.*

"Then perhaps you might consider forgiveness? Esther was ordered to create this schism and weaken the joint power you and Cole hold over the dark. Apart you are strong, but together you are a formidable weapon against the enemy. Do not punish him so. He was not at fault. He was not even awake."

"You watched it?" I was kinda icked by that.

"I watch everything."

"Ew."

My dad chuckled and I felt myself wanting to chuckle with him. I suppose the trivialities of those of us down here would be kinda funny to him. If I could only forget what I saw, it would make things a lot easier. Too bad Esther was one of the bad guys. Too bad Dad took her power. I couldn't exactly ask her to delete a few minutes of my memory, just a tiny favor, just between sisters. I'd have to do this forgiving thing the hard way, while trudging through my misery on the road to war.

"I will try. I… love him."

"As is right."

I settled my heart and continued to sense a calmness dropping down on me from the colored lights all around. "This is a lovely place."

"It is. But I have much to impart to you, my dear child."

My eyelids became heavy. "I'm so sorry, I'm so tired. So very tired."

"This will be easier if you are asleep and open to receiving the information."

My shoulder slid down the tree trunk and I rested my head on my arm.

"What I will teach you began in the very beginning of the Nephilim race."

I yawned then drifted into the softest, most tender place I'd ever known.

~*~

I don't know how I knew it, but I was under Metatron's spell for two whole days. It was just past dawn when I stood, refreshed and confident, filled with information, and courage, and the undying commitment to protect my race. Oh, and I was really hungry, too.

Just a few yards from the dripping willow branches slept Cole, rolled to his side, his face beautiful, his massive wing rolled over him like a blanket. So much had altered inside of me. So much about my race now made sense. So much was revealed about how to protect us all. But still I struggled with the challenge to forgive him. It was my first love, my first hurt, my first forgiving. I'd work at it, but it was not going to come easily. Dad was right, though, there was no need to punish Cole any more than necessary. After all, if he didn't love me, if he didn't love his people, he wouldn't have been here with me in the first place.

I walked to Cia's house, stretching my back and arms high. I located the mysterious book, which I now knew was correctly entitled *Metatron's Guide to Balance*, and not *The Book of Vision* as the tribunal had called it. A severely inaccurate translation, Dad explained. Very few still spoke the old language. Fewer grasped the nuances of it.

Collecting my journal and flipping through to make sure there were enough blank pages to work with, I then grabbed a loaf of bread, a jar of peanut butter, and returned to the tree. I sat at Cole's side to work. He slept long and deep and I felt joy that his nightmares didn't disturb his rest. When a curious bee buzzed too close to his nose, I fanned a sheet of paper to blow it away, waking sleeping beauty and his bizarre, yet beautiful, eyes.

"Are you okay? God, Gracie, you were in there for so long!" He sat up. Sniffed. "Peanut butter?"

I pushed breakfast his way and focused on the book, feverishly making notes—in the old language the way Dad taught me. Best to be cautious. Lucifer's minions were near.

"Gracie?"

"Yeah?" I didn't stop writing.

"Look at me, please."

I did. It still hurt but I squashed down my nastiness.

"I… am… sorry."

"Why? You didn't do anything."

He blinked, leaned back on stiffened arms and eyed me with his strange peepers. "What happened in there?"

With a sigh, I set the guide book and all my notes between us and leaned in. "I met my dad, Metatron. He's the author of this book. He told me I need to forgive you but I just can't, not right now, okay? I don't want to hurt you or make you want to leave, but I just can't be all… you know… until I feel better about this. I know it wasn't your fault. It just… still hurts. That's all."

"Fair enough. You don't want me to leave, that's all I care about." He looked like he might cry.

"Don't go all soft on me. I got my mission and it's a doozy. I kinda need you tough and mean for this."

"I can do tough and mean."

I didn't doubt that he could, even though I'd never really seen it. Still his eyes darted around, making sure I was safe and protected. Still his lips called me close. And still, damn it, my heart ached. I wished Garta was around to give me something to feel better, but chances are, only I could heal this.

I opened the book and turned it for him to read. As my father said, he couldn't.

"What the hell? I could at least make out a few of the symbols before. Is it my eyes?"

"No. I'm the only one to read it from now on. I didn't want that responsibility, but there's no way around it. I've also learned to speak the old language. I'll teach you a few key words we might need in a tight spot. Whatever plans we make and perfect, I'll record. If anyone steals them, they won't be able to understand them."

"Anyone… like Beelzebub?"

"Esther sits at Lucifer's side, Cole. Her job is to do his bidding. Metatron has cast a spell to assure that my version of the language will be too abstract for even his brother, Lucifer, to decipher."

Cole munched peanut butter bread and watched Cia's house. "The evil twin… is she in there?"

"I didn't see her."

"Cia said she hasn't been back since you went into that… that… place." He pointed to the tree, a squeamish expression on his face.

"You went in to check it for safety," I teased.

"Yeah, well, what I scanned for safety wasn't where you went. You were… gone. I was terrified for you."

A twinge made me wince. He cared so much, I so wanted to care right back. "It was fine."

"So, what's the mission, Sergeant Caine?" He smiled. I didn't.

"It seems impossible but sometimes, in a flash, it seems very possible. I am… *we are*… to gather and recruit the free winged."

Cole blinked. "No way. Gracie, that's practically impossible. There are no records of them. We don't even know how many there are. They awakened with no guide, helter-skelter, anywhere, anytime… totally fucked-up by the whole thing. How the hell are we supposed to do this?"

I wanted to slap him, no doubt that *not forgiven* stuff still pushing my reactions. Instead I pushed sheets of notes around.

He scrutinized them carefully for several moments. "Translation?"

"Well, this is my third idea… I'm inspired by language and levels of communications. I suggest we devise a kind of language or dialect only the free-winged can relate to. Then build a website, use all the social networks. We'll reach out and invite them to be recruited. Sort of like Ballister Green did with his invitation card. Then we'll use the portal gateways to travel and recruit." I felt so damn smug.

His head shook, slow and with purpose. "Won't work. Finding them is the whole issue. These people aren't online, Gracie. They're traumatized, terrified, hiding. Most are homeless, on the street, under bridges, or living on a mountainside somewhere. They're in mental institutions or prison. They've fallen through the cracks. They join the military hoping to get dead. They join cults or try to start cults. These are not people who want to be found, much less the kind of folks who have smartphones and twitter accounts."

I blinked back a tear. So, this mission was not going to fall under the easy category. "Are you saying we can't do this?"

"No, no, sweetheart. I'm saying that I know these people." Cole rolled his neck and drew in a deep breath. "After Afghanistan… I was one of them. I think we can find them but at least at first, creating a language… social media… it might all be a waste of time. And time is what we don't have a whole lot of."

"So, does any of my plan have promise?" It took me hours to develop plan three.

"Using the portals will help. Our first challenge is to get where the free winged are and dig them out of the alleys and sewers."

"That sounds pleasant."

"It's not… it's their life."

My heart started to ache for an all new reason. My free winged sisters and brothers, lost, living in hovels, scared, thinking they're alone.

"Gracie." Cole's eyes scanned the distance between us and the peach grove. "Do you think we can do this?"

"Does it matter?" I stood and brushed off my jeans. "We have to. First step…"

"Dig up the treasure." Cole grunted to his feet and we headed toward the house.

Cia waited, seated on the porch step, two shovels and a coil of rope at her side. Her smile was brighter than the sunshine.

"S'go, Cia. We've got a lot of work to do."

And I wondered, what lay beyond the portal? How hard will it all be? At least I had Cole at my side. He took my shovel, carrying it over his shoulder and whistling a happy tune.

I gave a half-hearted glare. "Not forgiven."

"I'm a patient man. Stick close, ladies."

And we stepped into the unknown.

To be continued…

ACKNOWLEDGEMENTS

Why did I write about angels? Why the battle between good and evil? Throughout my life there has been spiritual guidance, and not-so-spiritual guidance. I have always been drawn to holy men and women with insight and compassion, knowledge and instinct, power and gentleness beyond description.

I'm not a bible-thumping kinda gal, but religion has played a massive part in my life journey. It started with being raised Roman Catholic, and long talks over a beer with young priests seeking friendships and acceptance within the parameters of their strict limitations of mind and body. These men were brilliant, funny, committed, and honest. They brushed away the illusion of Catholic priests being more than human, an image I held strong until my twenties. After all, how could a human man refuse the love of a woman? How did they survive that lack of intimacy? And what did God hold over these men that made them choose such a sacrifice? I learned a lot from those two young priests. God and faith, spirit and inner joy ARE intimacy. It's all in how one looks at sacrifice. Thanks Michael and Joe. You started the opening of my eyes.

Then began a journey through every church I could find. Temple, Mosque (thank you and bless you Gabrielle Al Kahtani,) every protestant church, the Unitarian church, even the personal church of what's-inside-my-own-head. I've prayed with Jews, Muslims, Baptists, Presbyterians, Lutherans, Episcopalians, Methodists, and even the Assembly of God (thanks to my dearest friend Natalie Preston.) You name it, I was there searching for... something.

It wasn't until I met and followed a Native American Chief and Medicine Man that I discovered what I was searching so desperately for. I wanted a depth of prayer that would connect me with the Creator. Make me know, really know I was His and He was mine. I'm still searching for that, but Chief Luciano Perez, who carried a Sacred Lakota Medicine Bundle, took me closer to that place than anyone. His compassion and strength, mystical power and kindness carried me into Sundance, Vision Quest, Peace Dance, and the stunning Inipi sweat lodge and Yuipi healing ceremonies. He laughed and told stories of glory and magic. But beyond the Medicine Man, was the glorious Medicine Man's wife, Cheryl Perez, my friend, my guide, my fellow Brad Pitt fan, and the strongest woman I know. These two people pushed me into deeper mysteries of love and God.

When Chief Perez, my beloved uncle and teacher, left this world for the next, my journey continued. At this time in my life I'm more curious than ever, seeing similarities in spiritualities that are both baffling and surprising. Even in a political time of discord between conservative Christianity and more liberal religions, these similarities blaze bright. As my personal journey pulls me deeper, I find myself wondering more and more about what if? How could? And wouldn't it be amazing should something remarkable happen? Something that fictionally connects human beings more obviously with the God World. Something like Angels and Nephilim, the half angel/half human beings mentioned in most religious tomes. Could they exist? Could they still be running around the planet, doing whatever it is they're meant to do? Does the existence of such beings explain a few conundrums we're always chewing over? And, what would happen if a child Nephilim had no clue what he or she really was until the stroke of midnight on their eighteenth birthday. Now, THAT would be something, wouldn't it?

But writing The Orphans, book one of The Lost Race Trilogy wasn't easy. It didn't just flow like water onto the page, it called for research and logic in the midst of totally illogical situations. It called for a super suspension of reality that could draw a reader into the lives of these young people driven to save the world, a world crumbling by no fault of their own. How much crazy could I add? How much strange would be acceptable? How many historic, playful, and dark elements could gather within the pages to bring a reader so deep they couldn't wait for the next book?

Pieces of this book live in eliminated scene files, fallen onto the cutting room floor in sacrifice to more powerful or intense approaches. Two years of imagining, a year of research, and finally a year of writing went into building book one alone. Still Gracie, Cole, the Emmaus Magic Show Carnie folks, and the remarkable Ancients that work with the Nephilim are already plowing ahead for the remainder of the trilogy. There are times when I wonder, who is really writing this story? Who's telling it? And who will love it?

I'm not sure if you know this, but writers flip out. We intentionally, and unintentionally, delete entire documents and we lose important research. Unlike my characters I'm only human, but the passion to see this trilogy through outweighs many, many things. Things like the intense, sudden, and inexplicable inspiration to write a bizarre dragon story, the call of a stand-alone book that demands at least a few hours a week of my attention, and the demands of everyday life, like food or sleep. Yep, I flip out. I have an occasional literary nervous breakdown and spend a few mindful, silent days just meditating or reading wonderful books by other authors. I learned to cook Middle Eastern food. I drop myself into my business of helping authors find marketing success. I even tried to bake once. Um. Never again.

But after the breakdowns, after the flip outs and consumption of a billion calories, Gracie calls and I return to The Lost Race. These are the moments when I wonder what I'll do after it's completed. I just may need to learn to fly a plane or hang glide before I can slip comfortably into the next project, the next trilogy, or series. There's no shortage of ideas or developing characters in this fertile imagination. But there is something about wings. Feathers. Flying. Soaring. Seeing the world from an eagle's point of view that will always call to me. That and the exploration of how this world works within the constant battle between good and evil.

At this point I want to acknowledge Natalie Preston, the artist who created the beautiful cover for The Orphans. She's also my fearless roommate, tolerant of my unique style of crazy, and patient when it's my turn to have a nervous breakdown and not hers. I'd like to thank Demi Stevens, talented editor and wonderful friend to me and so many other authors. And finally, to my wonderful readers—my mom Genevieve Funaro, Cynthia Streicher-Maraugha, Sarah Broz, and Michelle Onofrey. These sharp readers caught incongruities, inconsistencies, questioned theories and explanations, and generally helped me hone this into a strangely believable story. There are angels everywhere and they are among us.

metatron's daughters

Book Two: the Lost Race Trilogy

Deborah Riley-Magnus

YESTERDAY

As I pushed my reluctant self through what felt like a wall of warm water and took my first step into the unknown, I stole a moment to explore what I knew to be real and true. A week ago, I was just a girl getting her freedom from an orphanage. I'm no Little Orphan Annie and there's no Daddy Warbucks on my horizon. It turns out I'm Nephilim, pure Nephilim, in fact. That means I have six ridiculous, massive wings that tend to sprout when I get ticked off or really scared, and a war I never knew was coming. Turning eighteen was way more complicated than I imagined but, hey, those rainbows looked so cool.

Raising my eyes, I gasped in the thick, fragrant air of the strange place Cole, Cia, and I had entered through the portal in my dying peach grove. We were not on Ocracoke anymore, that was certain. The colorful ribbons of light twisted and interlocked, crisscrossing the sky from every angle, and created a glow so odd and brilliant I had to squint.

"Gracie!"

I turned to Cole's voice. Such a good, strong voice. My ears told me he was right beside me but I could see he was easily twenty feet away. Then the voice turned garbled, bubbled, and came as an irritated shout.

"Gracie! Damn it! Stay close!"

I thought I *was* staying close. The rainbows weren't the only distraction. A vibration buzzed at the tip of my head like a constant whispered warning. I swear I saw angels, just like the ones carved and painted all over Ariel's Gate Orphanage, floating above me and pointing in a hundred different directions. Then I blinked and *poof!* they disappeared. What was real and what wasn't? What would, and easily could, vanish in the blink of an eye? Everything that ached in my heart, every loss, every death, every painful discovery over the past few weeks expanded and pressed against the walls of my chest.

"Gracie! Don't stray!"

Okay, Cole couldn't be yelling at me like that. We're not a couple, or whatever we almost became, anymore. I snorted and took another glance at the sky. Tiny lightning bolts crackled from the arcs of each rainbow. A million streaks of color flashed and shot up from all the other light surrounding me, closing in on me, prickling and poking at me. Something was not right about this place.

A boney hand gripped mine. I focused on it, the cool touch, the tight clasp. It had to be Cia, but she was nowhere in sight. The woman was ancient and comforting, the best memory I had. She brought us into this place to find… something. What were we looking for? I forgot. I swung around and the hand held me tight, pulling, pulling, pulling, until my face slammed into her chest. Arms tightened around me then a set of wings wrapped us both. Cole protected, Cia's breath was heavy and anxious, and me? I just let the panic run its course, shiver through my body, then still. I swear I could hear the surf, but all around me was nothingness. How would we ever find our way back?

"Listen to me!" Cia shouted into my ear, making me wince. "This place is designed to confuse and deceive. Stay close!"

"I'm trying."

"I got her," Cole bellowed and his voice caused ripples in the thick air.

"No, you don't!" I broke free of his grip, focused as hard as I could on his and Cia's strangely distorted faces, then pointed ahead. "Lead the way."

"We can't lose you, baby. I can't lose you." Cole whispered but it was so loud Neptune, deep underwater on another planet, could have heard.

"No one's going to get lost. Cia, take us to the treasure." Yep, that's right, we were seeking buried treasure. I remember now. Heart pounding, I stomped ahead, Cia at my right and Cole at my left. The ground felt wonky, like it wasn't quite solid, and I found myself walking with my knees loose and bent for balance, my curled foot compensating far better than expected. I wanted to look to Cole for comfort, but I was still mad at him. It had been made clear that he and I were to stand together for the challenges ahead, but I wanted more. At least once I wanted more. Now, gasping in the heavy atmosphere of a dangerous and confusing alternate plane, I knew I'd have whatever fate saw fit to give me.

"Why is it so hard to breathe?" I choked and gasped again.

Cia's hand tightened on mine. "We're traveling under a protective veil. It's temporary, and if we don't move quickly, it will dissolve before we can get what we came for."

I nodded, then suddenly, as though I'd awakened from a dream, everything stilled. The sky was normal, the ground under my feet was firm, and Cole was sweating bullets digging in the sandy dirt. Had time slipped ahead? Were we still inside the portal? I held tight to Cia's fingers and glanced around. Empty. Open. A desert of nothingness. The Sahara? Mars? "Where are we?"

"This is the safe place where I protected Esther. Close your eyes, Gracie, just for a second then open them again. The illusion will clear and you'll see."

Okay, that was better, but really, was it? If this was a safe place in the middle of all that crazy, how could my twin sister have ever grown up normal? I grew up in an orphanage thinking I was all alone in the world. So, Esther had her challenges, too. That could explain *a lot*. I'd need to explore that concept further, but after seeing her naked with Cole, I had no interest in thinking about her at all. Well, maybe later. Much later, in fact.

My head swiveled slowly, wanting to take in everything around me. If this wasn't the illusion, what was it? The alternate plane might be a hundred parallel worlds at the same time, or it could be only one diabolical place, floating and twisting over and through itself inside the real world. Who made it? God or the devil? The answer would give me something to grasp onto, and a better idea of how to trust such a place. The surroundings were so like the place I grew up, I could hardly believe it. The gardens flourished, the air was sweet, the little houses were neat and well taken care of. The only differences were that the old weeping willow was nowhere in sight, and neither were people, human, Nephilim, demon, or otherwise. For all its familiar beauty, it was achingly desolate.

Cole grunted and stepped on the shovel, driving it deeper for another load. He ran an arm across his brow and continued. It looked like he had some experience at digging up buried treasure.

"We're nowhere near Ocracoke," Cia explained. "This is the portal near Nassau."

I handed Cole my bandana to wipe away his sweat. Commandeering it without even a nod of thanks, he tied it over his soaked hair and kept burrowing.

"So, these portals are how your pirate seemed to appear out of nowhere, not a ship in sight. Tricky guy." I marveled. I have to admit, it was still a stretch to believe that Edward Teach, the famous pirate known as Blackbeard, was Nephilim, once Cia's lover, and astute enough to create a treasure that could help us through the coming war.

"He was one of a kind. On this plane, there are about three thousand portals." Cia knelt and looked into the hole. Cole was waist deep. She shook her head and reached for the other shovel. "Not even halfway, we need to reach it faster." But before she could slide into the hole that had started to look like a grave, I snatched the shovel from her hands. Sitting on the edge I gripped Cole's shoulder and slid in. I might have a messed-up foot but I'm not helpless. With a grin, he moved to one side while I began working on the other.

Cia, down on her knees, talked in a hush. "Every portal on the planet leads here. This is the place of the counting."

"What's the counting?"

We looked up at her and she blinked then nodded. "I see. You don't know.

This isn't the first time the Nephilim have dropped the ball, children. It is the fifth. No Nephilim is still alive from back then, and there are no records of the countings." She gave a shrug. "The Tribunal is big on bonfires. But we ancients know. Many of us have seen, even assisted with, the countings of the past. When the balance is off, all Nephilim are commanded to this place to be counted and face judgment if necessary."

I looked to Cole. "So," he said. "No battle? No war?"

"That depends on the counting," she stated. "It depends on how much each side wants balance, or imbalance. It depends on a lot of things. I will tell you this much." Her wrinkled face puckered as though she might cry. "In all my knowledge, all that's been passed down to me from other ancients, and all that I know from the 1802 counting, it has never been this perilous, this dangerous... this far from the center. And Lucifer has created his race of battle-heat demons to push the imbalance even further."

"There weren't battle-heat demons before?" My gut knotted. I had to know.

"Later. We'll get all that information later. For now, dig." Cole pushed his shovel and so did I, again and again until we heard a thump. It sounded exactly like it did in the old black and white pirate movies, too. We dropped to our knees and pushed the last of the sandy dirt aside. A flurry of activity followed, us scrambling out of the hole, slipping ropes under the trunk, then raising the thing to the surface with grunts, groans, and a few well-chosen obscenities. It was heavy enough to be loaded with gold doubloons and pieces of eight, but I knew it wasn't.

With a turn of a key that had hung around Cia's neck for as long as I'd known her, the lid was lifted. Scrolls and heavy books were set inside in neat piles. We gathered them and followed her through the rainbowed world. Her protective covering had dissolved, making it easier to breathe and focus on our escape but as we walked, the vast emptiness became heavily speckled with black battle-heat demons heading one way or another, paying no attention to us at all.

"So very odd," Cia whispered as we stepped near the portal to our world.

As we passed through I heard a grunt, a small gasp, then the usual sounds of the island. Bees droned, birds chirped, a distant seagull called, normal. The grass felt soft and comforting and I dropped onto it. Ah, the sensation of gravity as it's meant to be.

A battle-heat demon rushed past me through the peach grove then disappeared. Two heads, two sets of arms and legs, all mixed up and moving like a demented spider. One set of eyes looked into mine as the air sizzled with its passage. "Wow."

"Maybe they're too focused on their assignments to give a damn about us." Cole grunted under the weight of his heavy booty. He reached down to help me to my feet. I turned and tripped over the big book Cia had carried. It was safe on our side of the portal.

But where was she?

"Cia!" I yelled as loud as I could, aiming my voice into the invisible portal, ready to run back inside.

Cole dropped everything. "No! Stop!" He turned, his eyes ablaze with concern and determination. "Gracie, they have her!"

"And… oh, Cole… we don't know how to find her." I was so cool and in control, rational, logical, except for the tears soaking my face. "We can't get her until we understand all this stuff we dug up. Otherwise, they'll have us, too."

We stood, staring at each other while despicable, slimy demons walked right past us and into the portal. I sniffled and fought the need to fall against his chest and sob. How could we have lost Cia? She was our ace in the hole, the only person with the answers to all my questions.

Cole added the heavy book to his load and led the way, his shoulders and ethereal wings drooped in despair. Looking back, I half expected to see Lucifer himself laughing at me.

1

Sickness twisted Cole's gut. He'd received his second quickening just days earlier, an awakening of yet another inexplicable and terrifying power, and still he couldn't see how to fix this. Why on earth should there be an entire race of part-human part-angels if they can't fix this shit? Cia was gone and with every passing moment, he knew the chances of getting her back melted further out of reach.

The old house creaked against a raging storm. Outside the window, the occasional slither of battle-heat demons whipped past, heading toward the peach grove. To the place of the counting. The place he couldn't figure out if his life depended on it. Thunder rattled the door then a gust of wet blasted into the room. He turned to see Gracie dripping rain in the dim light, watching, waiting for him to do something. Already he was failing her.

"I have an idea." She didn't lash out or show her disappointment. Gracie stepped forward, like she was afraid but brave as ever. "I'm pretty sure we can do this together," she whispered and held out her hand. "We can."

For eighteen hours straight he'd been agonizing, sweating, and crying over the maps and books, unable to comprehend anything at all. Time was running out.

They could try to rescue Cia, or they could try to rescue their entire race. How the hell was he going to explain it to Gracie?

"Where've you been?" He grabbed a ratty blanket from the sofa and wrapped it around her.

"I went to the tree… tried to talk with my father. He was a no-show. Maybe the great Metatron doesn't like thunderstorms." She shrugged and sat, looking over the maps, scrolls, and opened books spread haphazardly on the floor, a few still fluttering from the wind's fury seeping under the door.

"It could be worse than that." He shrugged. "Maybe it's too late to get any help from him. From any of them. Raphael said we're going to be on our own when this all comes down. It was our race that made the promise to protect the balance, not the archangels."

She tossed up her hands, spraying rainwater across the room. "Right, they didn't make any promise, they just made babies. Us. Damn, damn, *damn.*"

They sat in silence for several moments, listening to the squall roll away as the dawn whispered in. Somewhere a boat horn groaned on the heavy air. The day would go on like any other on Ocracoke. Ferries would race across the water, coffee shops and businesses would open, humans would go about their lives oblivious to the fact that Nephilim exist and have forgotten to keep a vow. That the earth was struggling under the horrific weight of it all. That they, too, would suffer for a failure that could, and should, have been corrected.

For the second time since Cia's disappearance, Cole lost his temper, but this time it was bigger, more powerful, more dangerous. It would destroy far more than the tea kettle he'd tossed against a wall. Desperate to save the house, he charged outside and blew the gasket he couldn't hold back any longer. "Stay back, Gracie!" he shouted. She shrieked and turned her back, huddled for safety and protection just as flames blasted from his eyes and mouth, from his fingertips, from his feet, from his very heart. For the first time since Afghanistan he felt the full weight of his specific responsibility. He had to do what was needed. He could not fail.

Cole struggled to let off steam in a safe direction. They needed Cia's house. It was the only structure standing on the three acres that were Gracie's property. It was sturdy enough and kept the rain out. But just outside the front door, the rickety fence was ashes and the overgrown garden, burned to the soaked ground. Nothing sparked or flamed, it simply fizzled into the soaked dirt. If he had to do it, at least he felt he'd controlled it. Angel Fire, he called it. The first of his two awakened powers. Angel Fire had only come to him twice, both times in desperation. His second power was always present and ached in his eyes and his chest. Thinking about that extraordinary vision kicked something into gear and brightened his mind.

"Holy shit!" He charged back inside and knelt at the maps, pushing books and scrolls aside, focusing as hard as he could. "Damn it, Gracie, I wish I had your memory."

"Why?" It was a small, shaky voice but she was there, right at his side.

"Remember how I recognized the portal at the peach grove?"

She nodded.

"I saw lights like that inside, too. Across all that space, I saw portals all over the place. The problem is…" He shuffled maps and turned them, held them up to the light then smiled and drew in a deep breath. "Holy shit! That damn pirate is a godsend!"

She drew closer, looking at the same parchment. "Um… what are you talking about?"

Laughter bubbled, freshening and cooling the heat in his throat. "Our portal is blue, like a dark, rich, royal blue."

"Uh-huh, and?"

"The portal near Nassau was green. Hot, lime green."

"Okay."

He gripped her shoulders, grinned, and planted a kiss on her lips. His heart fluttered and his body reacted but he had to keep everything in perspective. Cole wanted to lean in for another, but before she could protest or remind him that he was still in the doghouse, he pointed to the map. "Look real closely. Gracie, they're all marked by color and location. Blackbeard had the same awakening power I have… at least something like it. He saw the same colors, was able to identify the portals, then he mapped them out for us. Do you know what this means?"

"I have no clue. Cole, you're so tired. Maybe you need some sleep? Maybe some water? Your voice is raw and—"

"I need you to listen to me and trust me, baby. I can navigate these portals. I can travel like Teach did, go anywhere, recruit like crazy. I know how to find the Free Winged. I can gain their trust, their vow, bring them here."

"What about their soul swords? They'll need their weapons if we have to fight."

"I'll deal with that when I have to. Maybe I can regenerate them. Who knows?"

Her brow was curled but her breath came fast and hard.

"Think about this. Those portals can bring Nephilim from all over the planet to the counting plane, Gracie! They just need to know how to get in. I can do that. Now I can recruit all over the place and I can guide our army through as many portals as we need." He stood and paced a wild circle around the maps. "Tobias needs to know about this. Someone needs to get out to the other segments of our race and tell them. We can do this, I—"

"And what about Cia?" Her eyes glistened with sadness and he wanted to hold her close but that wouldn't make a leader of her. That would only make her more dependent, or more rebellious. Neither was the best version of Gracie Caine.

"There isn't time. If we take the time to search for Cia… baby… we all die, the human race suffers, and eventually the planet implodes. You know I'm right."

She said nothing, just watched his face, her eyes locked on his.

"You know I'm right. And you know Cia would agree. I'm sorry, Gracie, I wish—"

"No. No more." She gasped back a sob then pulled the largest map up to the kitchen table. "How long will it take you to figure out a plan? Where will you start?"

~*~

Watch for Metatron's Daughters
Book 2 of The Lost Race Trilogy, coming soon!

OTHER BOOKS BY DEBORAH RILEY-MAGNUS

FICTION

Cold in California, Book 1 of the Twice Baked Vampire Series
Monkey Jump, Book 2 of The Twice Baked Vampire Series

NONFICTION

Write Brain / Left Brain: Bridging the Gap Between Creative Writer & Marketing Author
Cross Marketing Magic for Authors: New Avenues for Advanced Book Marketing
Author Marketing Playbook #1
Author Marketing Playbook #2

AUTHOR INFORMATION

FICTION

Fiction Website – drmagnusfantasy.com/
Angel Moments Blog – angelmomentsweb.wordpress.com/
Pinterest – www.pinterest.com/deborahrileymag/
Twitter – @MyAngelMoments

NONFICTION

Writaholic Blog – rileymagnus.wordpress.com/
Teaching Website – theauthorsuccesscoach.com/
Twitter – @rileymagnus
Facebook – www.facebook.com/deborah.rileymagnus
Facebook Coach Page – www.facebook.com/authorsuccesscoach/
LinkedIn – www.linkedin.com/in/deborah-riley-magnus-4ba15a1a/

www.ingramcontent.com/pod-product-compliance
Lightning Source LLC
Chambersburg PA
CBHW060932120726
47910CB00002B/299